Forbidden

Fruit

The Curious Post Volume 1:

Forbidden Fruit

By Various Authors

Title Page Verso

NEWTON

PRESS

Imprimatur: Ex mandato Ordinis Caeli Subterraneī
Copied faithfully from the fragmentary Codex Ichorii, discovered in the Trench

Visit online at newtonpress.carrd.co

Cover Illustration by Nicoletta Ceccoli
Book and Cover design by Nico Harlakenden
Interior Illustration by Nico Harlakenden
Book Formatting by Newton Press
Editing by Nico Harlakenden
Text set in Baskerville

ISBN 978-1-969590-00-9 (Paperback)
ISBN 978-1-969590-01-6 (eBook)
ISBN 978-1-969590-02-3 (Audiobook)
10 9 8 7 6 5 4 3 2 1

To the snake, the apple,
& the fool who thought we'd regret it.

Exordium

Remember: You were not meant to read this.

Even now, as your eyes settle here, I know what you're thinking. That it can't hurt. That it's just ink. **But ink remembers.**

An archive like this was never supposed to cohere. It was meant to decay quietly—scattered across matchbooks, voicemail tapes, half-waking visions.

Do not try to reconstruct it. Do not go looking for patterns. And whatever you saw just now—*in the mirror*—forget it. It's safer that way.

Make no mistake: I warned ████ what would crawl through once the seal was broken. What would wake up.

Enjoy it, then. Call it a story, call it nothing.

So read, sinner. Read and say you found nothing.

— The Editor

Contents

Pickaxes & Poor Choices 9
  by Mara Lynn Johnstone

Let the Pruning Hooks Remain Themselves 15
  by Emily R. Prehn

The Father of Vermin 27
  by Sinclair Adams

After all, what can kill a king? 43
  by Maia Brown-Jackson

Fowl 47
  by Konstantin Asimonov

Alice Underground 63
  by K. D. Paige

Old Bones 69
  by Benjamin Bagenski

Pine Blight 83
  by Nico Harlakenden

Sawdust to Sawdust 117
  by Ryan O'Leary

Bound 121
  by Chelle G. Lowe

Too Far From the Sun 127
  by Evan Satinsky

Deities in the Dark Matter 143
by Sophie Mutiara Nova

The Forgotten Before 179
by Jimmy Mack

To Be Frank 187
by J. R. Phillips

P3nt3kost 203
by A. P. Murphy

A Punishment Worth Taking 233
by Landon K. Mar

What Lies Buried Below 239
by Amy Leanne Johnston

Hope and Prophecy 273
by Cera Tansy Reid

The Starlight Lounge 301
by Lena Starlight

Pickaxes & Poor Choices

by Mara Lynn Johnstone

Them hills outside of town were a place nobody went, at least nobody on two legs—at least nobody human, except for visiting idiots like Ricky Whistle ...Let me start over.

Crown City was a fine place. Humble compared to the big cities back east, but a respectably sized bit of civilization out here among the scrubland. In the old days, it was just crops and livestock to go with the homes cut into the cliffside, then after pale folks started drifting in with wagons and dreams, a hodgepodge of buildings gathered there as well. That river flowing past the cliffs and into the canyon held fish enough for everyone, and people mostly got along.

That's more than I can say for some other areas those wagons rolled up on. Almost like there was magic at work here, keeping things peaceful. But I'm sure that's a coincidence.

Anywho, Ricky was the sort who thought the sound of his own brain rattling in his skull was opportunity knocking, and he ignored a lot of advice. When it was hinted strongly that he should leave a certain area be, that just made him all-fired curious to see it for himself.

And that's how ol' Ricky Whistle found a lump of god in the hills outside town.

It'd been caught in a crevice, glinting between the leaves of some spiky flower he'd never seen before, and he might not have noticed if not for a mouse scurrying away from a hawk's shadow. The motion caught his eye, then the shine, then he was over there ripping up the plant and snatching the gleaming nugget into his greedy little paws. It shone like a sunrise, with more colors rippling across it than human eyes were meant to see.

I've heard there are frogs somewhere with bright colors kinda like that, and it's meant to be a warning on account of their poison skin. Don't think Ricky'd ever heard of those frogs.

Ricky's little bean-brain was caught on two thoughts: this was worth a lot of money, and other people would want to know where he got it. So he stashed it in his shirt and hot-footed his way back to town, where he bought passage on the next coach to the nearest big city. He raised a lot of eyebrows, since his idea of playing it cool looked like a feller itching for a chance at the outhouse. But he kept his secret.

At least until he got to the city, and he went straight to the biggest high-roller he knew of.

Now Jasper White, he had brains. Heart and soul and compassionate nature, not so much. But he did have boatloads of cash and his own casino, and that's what Ricky was concerned with. He managed to get himself a private audience by whispering a few very attention-getting words in the right ears. Then he showed off the shining nugget in Jasper White's private office, and offered to sell it along with the directions to the location. For the right price.

Those of you familiar with men like Jasper the Asp might already be guessing how this conversation ended. I won't go into lurid details about Ricky's unfortunate fate, but I will say that he at least thought he was getting a good deal while he was describing the place he'd found the nugget. He died happy, thinking he was a wealthy man.

Jasper put the magical little lump of god into his own private safe, then threatened his lackeys so they'd keep their traps shut. And he began gathering people and supplies.

When he arrived at Crown City with two wagons and a dozen men, the locals were surprised. When he only stayed long enough to water the horses and sneer at the best the saloon had to offer, people were concerned. Then when he aimed those wagons off-road toward the hills, several oldsters set out on their porches to wait. But Jasper didn't see none of that. He was in the lead wagon, fixated on the hills with a pickaxe on the seat beside him.

Jasper and his cronies were more eagle-eyed than Ricky. They spotted the thistles colored like stained glass, and the snake that burrowed through solid rock. When the wagons couldn't go no further, they carried those pickaxes out on foot, sniffing for any taste of magic. The wind carried snatches of song, nearly too quiet to hear. In any other patch of wilderness, that melody might have come from sweet-throated songbirds, but the only birds in sight were distant vultures whose shadows rippled over the ground.

The men knew they were getting close when they happened upon a **passel** of mice trying to take down a jackalope. The hare with horns would have been memorable enough, but all those itty bitty mice wore itty bitty hats, and they flung lassos made of braided grass. Their tiny voices squeaked with cusswords.

Jasper scattered the rodeo with a few stomps of his boots, sending dust and critters in all directions. The jackalope bounded off into the scrubland, trailing ropes. The tiny cowpokes raced to hide in a gap between rocks, holding their hats in place while they ran.

If anyone had been paying attention to the wind, they might have noticed when the singing stopped. But who could bother with that when Jasper was peering into that gap, swearing he saw something glinting in the depths? His lackeys all readied their pickaxes, but he told them not to waste time and just get out the TNT.

Mice and lizards fled during the setup, legging it into the distance or diving for the safety of other crevices. Quiet scraping sounds marked snakes burrowing deeper. Jewel-bright beetles scuttled past Jasper's shoes.

He paid them no mind. He was about to get his hands on more riches and raw god-magic than any mortal could dream of. Probably.

They lit the fuse from a fair distance, but not far enough. Rocks blasted into the sky and seemed to twist as they flew, curving to smash both wagons with perfect aim. The horses whinnied and bolted in the same direction the jackalope had gone. Broken boards and wagon wheels scattered far across the landscape. Men swore into the rising wind.

Before Jasper the Asp could rally them to inspect the hole they'd just blown in the hillside, something crawled out of it.

Something that glowed like a sunset, with more colors than their startled eyes could take in. Something that seemed made up of many small things—animals, weeds, the rocks themselves—with a shifting form that looked like all of them at once.

Hawk wings spread wide, lizard claws flashed, and beady mouse eyes pinned them in place. More than enough arms to grab every single one of them lashed out.

Now I don't want to give too many gory details and put you off your feed, so I'll just say that the noises made by Jasper and his lackeys carried easily on the wind toward town, where all those old folks were lined up waiting to hear it. Much nodding and cackling was done. Bets were won and lost about how long it had taken. Somebody in need of new horses caught the strays.

And things settled down in those hills outside of Crown City, with mice scurrying around on business of their own, and plants growing in a variety of lovely colors. The river flowed by as it always had, spilling past the cliffside shaped like a crown and into the vast canyon below. If a body were to look at that canyon from high up—higher than the birds dare to go, above the clouds—then you might fancy it looks a bit like a person.

A fallen person, asleep or otherwise, spread out on the ground—one hand up in the hills. Wearing a city for a crown.

But surely nobody could ever get that high up in the heavens, so I really couldn't say.

Let the Pruning Hooks
Remain Themselves
by Emily R. Prehn

The azalea is enormous. Taller than you, though that is no great feat at your age. It is far taller than the old woman, even if she were not always bent over like a willow these days. It would even surpass the height of one of the boy-cousins, full-grown men, if they were here.

"It has been left too long on its own," the old woman explains in her creaking-wood voice. "It barely flowers now, and the limbs are stretched and twisted, bare of leaves or buds." She leans on her walking stick and points down, down, to the very heart of the azalea, where its body converges into a single trunk, burying its feet in the loam. "All the way back, child," she says. "So that it grows back right, thick and flowering."

You take pruning hook in hand and kneel in obeisance, a worshiper of sorts, to reach under the branches to one of the great limbs, nearly as thick as your skinny arm, that, further out, branches again and again, *ad infinitum*. Dust, pollen, and other exhalations of the earth soon cloak you, dirtying your skin and white robe alike. Sweat drips onto your bare arms, its trickling streams revealing golden veining of your skin intermingling with the gray dust, making a painted statue of you, and when you wipe your face with your forearm, your face is made stone, as well.

Finally there is a snap, and a portion of the bush, bigger than you in all directions, comes crashing to the ground. You take a moment to gaze at it, relishing the triumph, then bow back to your task.

At the end, when there is nothing left of the behemoth but six inches of trunk coiling back on itself, its knuckles standing out like the old woman's, and a pile of branches so large the hired man will have to drag it away tomorrow, you look down at your arms, stained with nature's ephemera, blotchy like a fungus from the spots of sweat, olive underneath from the sun and crimson from scratches and scrapes, and your peplos that started the day white but is now just as soiled as you, and under the exhaustion burns the fierce pride of victory over your foe. You start to grasp, for the first time, why the Lady is goddess of both household industry and the battlefield.

The old woman hands you a cool drink and runs her tree-twist hands down your honeyed curls, now tangled into locks with twigs and leaves. Well done, child, she says.

* * *

You stay on her farm, near one of the small towns that grows just past the edges of the city like the feelers of an overgrown shrub, until you are marrying age and beyond. There are many in the small town that would take you to wife: The neighboring farm's sons, the blacksmith's son, the young man they say was sent away in shame from one of the great temples.

You are pretty, beautiful, they tell you, clearly favored by the gods. But you have never had an interest in any of them, in any of the village's sons or men. You stay on the farm with the old woman, listening to her wisdom, even as it begins to wrinkle up and wither away, a willow tree on the bank of a river run dry.

After she dies, the farm is given over to the boy-cousins. If you want a home of your own, they tell you, you must marry and make children. But you have never wanted that, and you think your Lady understands.

So you gather your belongings, your tools, your clothes and sandals, and the little money the old woman gave you before she passed, and you walk to the city. The temples always need gardeners, and you want to see your Lady up close.

The temple built for Athena Parthenos, the Virgin Athena, cannot compare to the beauty of a shy blossom half-opened, gilded with dew in the pre-dawn light, but it is as awe-striking as a man-made thing can be. The columns are towering and endless, a forest of barren white marble. In the back of the temple, in the pride of place, stands the statue of the Lady, straight and sharp as a cypress, dangerous as a bared blade. She is stern, armed and armored, shield and spear and serpent at hand.

But you know your Lady, and the cypress, impressive but ornamental, good only to look at or to build off after its death, is not her tree. The olive tree is hers, stunted and gnarled, unlovely and fruitful beyond measure.

You look hard at her statue, past the image the men who built her held, and finally see her there in the knowing upturn of her mouth, in the veins standing out on the hand gripping her shield, in the muscled thigh barely showing past her peplos. Only then do you make your obeisance and present your offering.

The women of the temple take you on as a tender of the gardens, more impressed by the calluses on your hands than by your beauty, and you are content. You spend your days much as you always have, nurturing and pruning by turns, the old woman's wisdom whispering to you like a breeze through fluttering fronds.

The plants here are more exotic than the old woman's, brought in from around the empire to please the goddess, but they want the same things as the plants you were raised alongside. You are happy here, feeling the burn of your muscles as you battle disorder and decay, every sense awash in the beauty of your charges, and the fiery sun, burning so close to the acropolis, slowly turns your skin to deep bronze, your hair to rivers of gold over streaking the dark soil of the countryside.

Then he comes.

You know him by the ocean-wildness in his eyes, the storm-salt wind he carries that makes your plants shrink away, folding their leaves in escape, and you wish yourself small enough to hide within them. He does not see your calluses or your work or your earth-stained peplos; he does not see your heart.

All he sees is the reflection of the sun off your hair and the curve of your body beneath your clothes, and he wants. And so he takes.

* * *

They say your Lady punishes you for his theft. You believe it yourself, at first, before you understand that your curse is a blessing, her favor doubled.

* * *

You are banished to a rocky island, away from the mainland and the temple and the old woman's farm. There is a long period of twilight, your dark days, when your spirit withdraws deep within you, living sap running sluggishly through a winter-dead tree.

But there is life even on stony strands, and you cannot deny the work in your hands, even while your soul sleeps.

There are yellow azaleas and pale pink rhododendrons, and if the old woman's azalea from your childhood was long abandoned, these have never been tended at all, left overstretched and naked, shivering in the sea spray. So, like a sleepwalker, you fetch your tools, tuck up your skirt, and bend to your work. In time, these plants will spread their flowers and their fruit, growing back thicker and stronger for each cut made.

Like your hair.

Not really hair anymore, not since your Lady turned your soft curls into writhing golden serpents. During the first dark days, you tore them from your head, hands bloody and heart frozen in horror, but they only grew back thicker, more numerous. Like in the far regions of the empire where women shear their babes' heads after they are born, so their hair will come back in thick and curly.

After exhausting yourself with grief and revulsion, you sleep, waking again with blood sticky on your fingers and under your nails. You turn to the olive tree near the center of the island, beside the rough cave house that has become your home. The tree, as stunted and twisted as any you have seen, drips dark with its fruit. You pick the olives almost blindly and press them into oil for a salve, with a spirit too bruised and numb to understand why you should, or why the Lady would leave a gift of her tree to one she has cursed.

The only other vegetation on your stone-scattered island that seems to be content and thriving is a fig tree, growing opposite the olive tree on the other side of the cave house entrance. Its wide branches and dense leaves shelter the mouth of your home, protecting it from the elements, and you can see from its budding that in time it will be covered in its sticky, succulent fruit.

You wonder if you will still be there to see it.

* * *

Your muffled, sleepwalking daze is shattered one evening by the splash of oars in water, a wooden keel scraping across pebbled beach. You freeze like a prey animal, peering wide-eyed between branches as a man steps out of his boat, a local fisherman, perhaps, swaying like a river birch as he walks. But all you can see, can feel, are sea-wild eyes and rough, bruising hands, and the salt-sea wind carries with it the scent of tears and blood.

You remain frozen aside from the ever-writhing, ever-hissing serpents on your head, as he turns toward you, catching just a glimpse of you between the snaking branches of the rhododendron. But instead of approaching, of claiming, of making you bleed, he blanches, face going bloodless in horror. As you watch, his white face stiffens, is run through with gray veining that sweeps across his body in a wave, turning hair and flesh and clothing to stone. As you stare, he topples slowly backward into the ocean, and with only a ripple to mark his passing, he is gone.

It is then you realize that your Lady has given you a blessing, not a curse, and your twilight clears to crystalline darkness. Your spirit stirs.

* * *

You find the clutch in the heart of the farthest azalea, closest to the sea, huddled against a jagged cliff face. The eggs are grayish and leathery, too large and round to be snake eggs, but not round enough to belong to sea turtles. You do not recognize them as belonging to any creature the old woman taught you, helpful or harmful, so you decide to leave them be.

A week later, they hatch, and you see hydra for the first time.

They have only two heads when they emerge, slick and membranous, from their eggs. You sit patiently nearby, and eventually they totter towards you, perhaps sensing kinship. When no mother returns for them, you catch fish to feed them.

When they are a few days old, a bit bigger and stronger, you catch one and carefully pinch the base of one of its necks. Neck and head come free like a lizard's tail, and by the next day, that hydra has three long wavering necks, three curious heads looking around it. You continue your treatment, pruning the hydra more carefully than rose bushes, until they have enough heads to defend themselves. They are destined to die, monsters in this world of men and gods, fodder for a hero's glory, but they will not go easily.

You are not certain if it is something about the island, or if it is your presence, but the hydra are only the first monstrous interlopers you find nestled among the roots of your wild garden. You find a three-headed pup, abandoned by its dam, and nurse it until it is old enough to wean. Then you gift it to the Lady of the Under, who misses sweet above-ground things, but takes her responsibilities below-ground seriously. In return, she gives you a pomegranate sapling grown from the seeds she did not eat, and you add it to your garden.

She comes and talks to you often; you suspect an entrance to her realm is near your island, which may be why you find such strange creatures. You know of her husband, but do not know if he is like his brothers. You do not know if she was taken, or if she chose, and you will not ask. If she was taken, it was not as it was with the rest of you, sown with child and then cast aside. All you know is that she is a ruler of the dead as truly as he is, and that is a comfort.

You can feel his children inside of you, sometimes. No, your children—he has no claim. You can feel that they are monsters, like you, and you know there is no way for them to leave you by natural means. When the time is right, when you are ready, you will ask your Lady to send someone to take you apart, so that they can live. But for now you will keep them inside of you, where they will be safe.

You think you are not quite mortal anymore. It must have been your Lady's work, because you have heard of plenty of girls taken by him and others like him that died as mortals, disgraced and forgotten by their families. You thank your Lady that she has kept her favor on you. Perhaps someday you can return it, protect her with the gift she has given.

You know that one day a hero will come to slay you, as all monsters must be slain. You think about the men from the village, and how you never wanted them, and you wonder how long you have been a monster. You think you should be more worried, but you are not.

* * *

The first woman comes to your shores when the fig tree is bearing fruit, after you have spent three seasons alone. You are standing beneath it in a break from your labor, savoring the fruit's heavy sweetness and letting your serpents lick the juice from your fingers, when her boat scrapes home on the rocks. She is the first person you have seen since the fisherman, and you watch her warily.

Her stomach is round and tight like the fig in your fingers, and bruises like crushed cherries creep across her olive-gold arms and face, one large, dark eye swollen shut. Her peplos, however, is as clean as a gift to the gods, marred only by a few drops of blood from her split lip, and her thick, dark hair is neatly combed, braided and wrapped.

Head down, one arm cradling her belly, she carefully picks her way toward you across the rocky shore. As you stand, hoe in hand, dirt and fruit juice streaking down your robe, she kneels stiffly before you, outstretched hands offering an earthen vessel planted with blood-red poppies bobbing their heads in the ocean breeze. "For the Lady of the Serpents," she says.

Wordlessly you take it from her, and her shoulders drop, tension falling away like a bow unstrung. But she does not say another word, and you do not know how to answer. Finally she makes a small noise of pain and sways on her knees, and you set aside the poppies to help her to her feet.

She puts a hand to her back, and you gently touch her stomach as you guide her to sit on a low stone. "Soon now?"

She nods, her gaze darting to meet yours for a heartbeat, two, before looking down again. "A month, perhaps." She kneads the muscles in her lower back, then her hand drifts slowly up toward one of your golden serpents, as if drawn by a lodestone. Rather than hissing at the intrusion, the snake strokes its head along her fingers, before coiling itself loosely around her wrist.

She laughs in disbelief and delight, looking directly at you for the first time, and you stop breathing. But there is no horror in her face, no bloodless paling, no encroaching stone. You tentatively smile, the expression feeling out of place on your face, like your skin is the one turning to marble and the smile will crack it, but she does not seem to mind.

The next day, after planting the poppies, you notice a beehive in the olive tree that was not there before. You carefully divide it, leaving most of the hive in the tree, but creating a small one near the azaleas and rhododendrons. The old woman's wisdom extends so much further than plants, and her willow-words whisper instructions to you as your hands obey. The honey from that hive is kept separate, for special purposes, and you are already making plans for harvesting from the poppies.

* * *

Euryale gives birth to her daughter with a cry that can be heard across the island. Both are healthy, and you leave a jar of sacred honey and a bottle of opium at the foot of the olive tree as thanks. In the morning, the gifts are gone, and a nanny goat has her horns caught in the tree's low-hanging branches. She has a third horn protruding from her forehead, and her pupils are slits where they should be square, but she gives good milk.

* * *

Euryale's daughter is not yet weaned when Stheno arrives.

A fierce gale is sweeping the island, forcing your garden to sway and bend. But you know that your charges are sturdy, flexible, and will not break. They are stubborn, and they will outlast any storm.

You are sitting in the cave house, rocking the sleeping babe and watching Euryale spin goat hair into yarn by the light of a flickering oil lamp, when there is a knock on the door, nearly lost in a clap of thunder. You have barely risen to your feet when the door swings open and a woman as straight and dark as an evergreen strides through. She is drenched, her tunic rent and bloodstained beneath the water soaking it, and she drops to her knees in front of you, her head unbowed. Her dark, coiling hair, plastered to her head with water, is cut short.

She extends her hands, a foot-tall sapling cradled on each palm. "For the Lady of the Serpents," she says, meeting your eyes, "I bring almond trees, both bitter and sweet."

Euryale reclaims her child as you take the offerings from the newcomer's hands. "Thank you," you say, setting them gently aside. Then you kneel before her, your hands tracing over her blood-stained clothing. "Are you injured?"

She laughs, and there is blood on her teeth. She reaches to one of your serpents, which twines happily around her fingers. "The blood is not mine—most of it, anyway."

You sit back on your heels and look at her for a heartbeat, two, and she meets your gaze with nostrils flared, lip curled, fierceness in her eyes.

You smile. "Welcome."

* * *

You plant the almond trees side-by-side and add a bottle of cyanide to your regular tribute to your Lady. An owl appears often in the olive tree after that, and you greet her with a respectful nod.

* * *

Other women come and go in the following years, but Euryale and Stheno, your sisters, remain, even after Euryale's daughter has grown and returned to the mainland.

Euryale's long braids, always neatly wrapped, have become thick bronze serpents that hang freely to her waist. She laughs at the way they constantly twine around her wrists and hands, and sweetly coerces them into holding her spindle.

Stheno's serpents are smaller, no thicker than a pinky finger, and stay in tight coils close to her scalp. Their bright gold against her dark skin is breathtaking, and she likes to run her fingers through them when she is thinking.

Your serpents remain fond of licking fig juice from your fingers, and they reach for your sisters anytime they stray within arm's reach.

* * *

The time comes. You spend a long night sitting beneath the olive tree, dappled in starshine and moonshadow as you speak to the owl. She keeps watch on you with a single eye as sharp as her talons, before finally bobbing her head and taking wing.

You take to climbing the rocky peaks above the cave house while your sisters slumber below. When they ask you what is wrong, you tell them it is nothing, and they do not argue, but you see the knowledge in their eyes, regardless.

You know that when it happens, Euryale's screams will echo across the island, and Stheno will bare her teeth, seeking blood. But the hero has been told that you are the only mortal Gorgon, that the others cannot be killed; your final request of your Lady.

It is as you sit in the gray pre-dawn light, eating a pomegranate from the tree bursting with them, that you spy a flash of light flickering across the ocean, coming ever nearer. You set aside the fruit and stand, and your skin is cool and pale, the last vestiges of night making a statue of you, even before your death.

He does not look at you, afraid and cowering behind the Lady's mirrored shield, but you do not mind. He is nothing to you, and you want it to remain that way. Instead, your attention is caught by the shield held up before his face. It is your first time seeing your reflection since before your banishment, before your blessing or curse, and you brace yourself to see a monster.

Instead, in the moment before his sword swings down and takes you apart, you see simply yourself, and you laugh.

The Father of Vermin

by Sinclair Adams

The era that transformed the "Forbidden Lands" into the "Great Frontiers" shook the natural order of things. Battalions of men left their quiet villages to bring the wild world to heel, armed with sharp new weapons the likes of which the world had never seen. These Frontier-Men built new settlements at the foot of thick forests and black mountains, seeking to claim every resource they could find.

When the veins of ore and coal ceased to bleed their riches, a new era began: an era of Great Monsters.

They crawled from unknown depths beneath the earth, dragged themselves from the depths of the seas, and manifested from all the spaces cleared out by the men and their blades. Spiders who wove webs as thick as a hangman's rope, gorgons who cast death-spells from mouths in their hands, goblins with teeth lining the back of their throats. Exterminating the horrors of a world much older and far below became the new mission that bound the Frontier-Men together. Except they fancied themselves going by a different name: the Hunter-Men.

One day in the era of Great Monsters, a lone man walked to an abandoned mine. His thin, birdlike legs tripped on almost every protruding tree root or stump that lined his path. On the road to the mine marked by his own footprints, the few trees left in the forest were studded with wanted papers posting bounties: gold coin for dead monsters, silver for dead warlocks—a new order of men who branded themselves monster-friends and learned wicked magics from the depths from which they came. The lone man also passed warning signs, reminding all adventurers to never leave home empty-handed.

But he carried nothing with him. The other men had cleared out this area of monsters decades ago. Besides, he was no fighter.

When he arrived at the hollow at the side of the bald white mountainside, the man lit his lantern and readied himself to explore the interior. Within moments of entering the cave's mouth, one foot in the light of the sun and the other still suspended mid-step, he sensed that he was not alone. Another being, much larger than him, shared the dark space. The man froze, prepared for his life's end at the jaws of a beast or acidic burn of a spellcaster. A shallow breath in and out, and he had accepted this unsurprising outcome.

The dim light only revealed so much, but the man could hear the scratching and skittering of thousands of legs deep within the mines.

An insect, a long body as black as oil, thick as a tree trunk. A being as ancient and unseen as mankind's creator. Its prodigious length went back deep into the tunnel's throat.

A Great Millipede. A reclusive and rare monster, a dangerous procurer of the earth's magic.

Its dark antenna shone like eyes in the lamplight. The top segment of its body lifted upward, casting a shadow of a great claw on the cave's wall. It leaned closer to him, curiously.

[Who are you?] she asked him.

Her voice came alive in his head, as if it were his own thoughts.

"You...you can speak?" the man whispered.

[I cannot speak in your tongue,] the millipede explained. [But many centuries ago, I cast a charm on myself, so that I may speak to any creature.]

The Millipede made a buzzing noise that expressed laughter. The rest of her body did not move with the sound, living in the perfect stillness that only insects could.

[I suppose your kind might call me a warlock.]

Not even three steps into the cave, and the man had stumbled upon one of the most dangerous monsters he could have found. He was only lucky he hadn't crossed a goblin, which might not have any interest or talent for conversation.

The man started to move his lantern up higher, but stopped himself. He didn't want to frighten her, and perhaps meet his end before he had the chance to leave and tell anyone about what he had found.

"Can you come closer to the light?" he asked. "I'd...I'd like to see you better."

Her smooth exoskeleton glittered like carved obsidian against the yellow flame. She lowered her long body down on one a set of forelegs closer to the base of her head. The two stood eye-to-eye.

The lone man wanted to get a good measure of her. To estimate just how many men it would take to subdue and butcher her body to pieces. To appraise his bounty of copper coins and drinks of mead from the other men of his village, and taste the brotherhood he was not offered before he had become so unlucky as to cross paths with a monster.

But when he saw the fullness of her size up close, the only thing he could think or speak was one word.

"Incredible..."

[Is that your name?] she asked.

"N-no. The men of the village call me Abash."

He did not explain that "Abash" was also a word commonly used as an insult.

She dipped her hooded head closer to him. He could see tiny hairs that festooned her small face and the tips of her antennae. As the distance between them closed, he could see them tingle with interest.

[But is "Abash" your name?]

"That is what they have always called me. So that is my name."

[You carry no weapons.]

"Never have. I'm no good with them."

[May I smell you?] she asked.

"B-be my guest," Abash said, wondering why she asked his permission. He understood when the Millipede's pinpoint antennae traced his face. Gentle scrapes of her appendages peppered his cheeks, his nose, his chin, causing goosebumps to spike all along his neck and arms. Her body shifted closer to him, but she touched him no more.

[You smell much like the inside of this cave,] she said.

"I'm a geologist. I study rocks. I'm with them all the time," he answered, regretting his terse choice of words. "Ummm...what's your name?"

The Millipede let out a noise.

"Naaaarrrrrrr...ey-yah?" Abash put the sound into his own comfortable syllables.

[I am afraid my name does not translate well,] she admitted. [It means "she who climbs" in my language.]

"Narre'ah," Abash suggested, placing her native sounds to his own tongue. "I had no clue there were still Millipedes left in these tunnels. Will you stay here for long...?"

[Oh, this is not my home. So I will not be here long enough for you to come back with a score of Hunter-Men to claim my hide.]

Abash felt his face burn. Had she read his mind and knew of his thoughts to trap her? Or had that become the only possible assumption when a monster and a man crossed paths?

Narre'ah's head swayed upwards, extending her reach to the very top of the cave. [I am a mere explorer, traveling from tunnel to tunnel. My true den is in a land the opposite side of this planet.]

"The planet?!" Abash imagined the distance in his mind. It was enough to almost make him topple backwards. Not all men accepted that their world was round and had opposite sides.

She made the chittering noise like laughter again. [It is all dirt and tunnels to me.]

Abash set his lantern down. He only had half an hour's supply worth of oil, and his bag hung empty on his back. He had already made the rarest discovery the caves could offer, but he could not take it back home with him. At the very least, he could take back knowledge.

"What are you exploring for?" he asked, taking a seat on the dirt.

Narre'ah crawled further inwards, resting herself in a circle around him. The gooseflesh rose on his skin again as he felt her rigid presence all around him, but he made no move to escape her serpentine windings.

[I search for more of my kind,] she answered.

Abash considered her honesty. If she truly was alone, then there would be no fear of retaliation if she were caught and killed by the men of the village. The many legs of this Great Millipede had carried her right into a perfect trap.

But she was not an unintelligent monster, and perhaps could evade any way that the men might ensnare her. The machinations in Abash's mind could prove to be fruitless against her unknown powers. An unsettling feeling in his stomach held a more potent sway over his next words.

"You won't find more of your own here," he said. "Many men of my kind have already killed all the monsters in this area. If you stay here for long, the same will happen to you."

Narre'ah's countless rippling legs lifted her body up again. [Climb on my back, human. I wish to show you something.]

Abash peered deep into the dark cave, then at his flickering lantern, remembering the thinning supply of oil.

[I promise you, where we go, you will need no light. Not when I have my spells.]

Abash's eyes went wide when he imagined the possibilities. Was this how men were corrupted into warlocks? Consorting with monsters, entering the underground as novice-and-master?

But perhaps this monster would take him to depths of his precious cave deeper than he could ever traverse alone.

Abash's love for understanding the world outweighed the love for the men in his village.

He dimmed the lantern. Crouching forward, he reached out for Narre'ah's smooth backside.

"Are you sure this does not upset you?" he asked, sliding his leg over her smooth carapace and hugging his body against her.

[Only if it does not upset you,] she answered. [Aren't you afraid I'm going to eat you?] The magic she spoke with carried a teasing tone.

"No," Abash said. "Your kind are herbivores."

[You know of my kind?]

"Only a little. I study the earth's riches that dwell underground. I've learned a few things about those who walked these paths before my time."

Without warning, the Millipede darted through the dark tunnels.

Abash hugged his arms and legs around her body as tight as he could, pressing his face against her exoskeleton. Her thousands of limbs seemed to increase her speed by a thousand factors. The whooshing of rocks and stalactites passed overhead. Narre'ah jerked right and left in a pattern Abash could never keep track of.

Then, Narre'ah began to slow down. A heavy burst of damp air broke across Abash's face, along with the smell of old and dank air. Though Abash could not see a thing, he assumed they had just plunged into a deeper cavern underground.

Abash heard clicking noises, the sound of her countless legs twitching in the dark. But this time, her feet moved slower. Her legs stepped one by one, drawing sparks of blue magic from the ground. Starting from her legs and ending across the walls, light poured into the darkness, glittering against each gemstone in the walls.

With the added light, Abash saw Narre'ah's movements and understood. She summoned the energy of the earth by tapping each of her millions of legs in a purposeful order. The earth was a harpsichord of magic, and she knew which keys to play to draw out its melody.

And then, he saw the mural.

Abash slid off of Narre'ah and took slow steps closer. Not too close —as if his breath would damage the ancient markings of this sacred place.

Petroglyphs of long bodied, many-limbed creatures crossed the walls, stretching up to twenty times Abash's height. At the very top of the mural were figures of two large Millipedes, with a hundred smaller ones pouring down beneath the peak of a mountain.

[It's a story,] Narre'ah said, all her legs trembling in excitement. [When a mated pair was formed, they traveled deeper into the earth, building new dens of their own.] She moved forward and stretched herself as tall as she could, so her front legs grazed the surface.

"It's incredible," Abash said. "I never knew how deep your tunnels could go." He had been whisked away into the heart of the tunnels. His chest surged with a feeling of finding everything he ever needed. The quiet solitude, the history etched in walls, the chance to sit and study undisturbed until his curiosity was satiated.

Narre'ah lowered herself down, hovering near him.

[Do you think me a monster?]

Abash smiled. "I've had no other word for what you are. You have taken me farther than I could have ever traveled alone. Thank you."

Narre'ah dipped her head to level with his, then moved lower, gently pressing into his chest. He knew she was a gentle creature, but the proximity of a stone-hard insect to the vital sections of his body tested him —his heart raced, his muscles tensed with action.

But she drew away, leaving not a scratch on him.

He sighed and placed his hand to her head.

"What do you think of me?" he asked.

[I believe that you are someone who should return to the surface.]

As she lowered herself for him to climb on, he felt sick with regret that he couldn't stay there for longer.

[Come back to me, human,] her voice filled the empty space in the dark.

Once again, she had either read his thoughts, or she knew him too well.

* * *

Abash and Narre'ah met nearly every day. The man would bring her plant clippings, corn cobs, spoiled fruit—the trimmings of plants and decaying matter that her kind loved to devour. He would bring himself a lunch of bread, cheese, and an apple, then toss her the core once he was finished.

Her greatest gift to him was her company. He stayed with her in the cold cave for hours, listening to her talk about the shape of the land on the opposite end of the planet until his fingers went numb and his lips turned blue. He would explain what little natural science he knew of how gemstones were formed. The elements of the earth and space, all aligned in an organized table.

[Why must your kind name and label things? Why draw charts instead of pictures and murals?] Narre'ah once asked, lifting her head towards the petroglyphs carved by her own kin.

"Some men do like to draw murals," Abash said. "But some of us like to understand the world around us with numbers, instead of pictures."

Narre'ah curled herself around her human. [The more I understand, the less I seem to like. I wish to keep some things a mystery.]

"What have you understood?" he asked.

[That being the last of your kind is a fate I would never wish on anyone,] she answered.

One of very few silences occurred between them. Her magic of her last words left a thin hum in the cold air of the cave. Or was that just the tension Abash felt?

Eventually Abash asked, "Have you had no mate before?"

[No. No spawn has passed through me.] Her antennae jutted in rapid movements, demanding an answer. [Have you had no mate, human?]

He could feel his clothes beginning to dampen, slowly soaking up the ancient moisture buried deep in the ground.

"No," Abash answered. "No spawn."

[A shame for your species,] Narre'ah said, her antennae flicking upwards. [Without matehood and spawning, your kind will cease.]

"Men will always come," Abash said, thinking of how his village was always replenished itself with ceaseless new arrivals of more burly men to the frontiers. No matter how many men were slaughtered and genealogies discontinued at the cost of killing monsters, more men came to pick up their felled battle axes and replace them.

[There are few men like you. Do you wish to die out?]

Abash did not answer. Without the use of math or magnifying glass, Abash had just come to understand something about a friend and her fears. He put his hand on her cold carapace, offering what little comfort he could think to give.

* * *

One day, Abash made haste through the forest, walking double the pace his scrawny legs usually managed. On his way past the spiked wooden gate that enclosed the human village, one of the hefty guards stopped him. With a smile, an expression rarely expensed on Abash, the guard reminded him of the payment for bringing down monsters. The legendary renown it could even bring to the smallest man among them.

Abash promised he would not let them down. He scurried as fast as he could through the forest, cutting the skin of his calves on sharp sticks and rocks. As his legs pumped forward, he reminded himself that the promise he made to the village guard was a lie and not worth keeping. Narre'ah did not have a face that could produce a smile like the humans of his village, but he could not betray her now.

When Abash arrived at their meeting spot, he felt the blood drain from his face. She was not there.

Blinking in the fading light, Abash stumbled through the cave, searching for her, calling out her name. Fearing the worst, his bones shook. He did not want to return to town and see his friend's long body being paraded on a row of spikes.

"Narre'ah! Narr!" he called out into the dark.

Not seeing where his foot landed, he slid down a rocky tunnel that snagged and cut at his clothes.

The tunnel spat him out in a cavern with no light. But he heard the faithful skittering of her countless legs and relaxed.

[You!] she said, her voice scratching inside his mind like a branch of dry brambles. [What are you doing here?]

He felt her cool, hard face nudge against his chest.

"Currently, I am bleeding," he answered, "because you weren't at the cave when I came."

[You...you!] He heard her speak in her native dialect, a series of hisses and moans he did not understand. Then, her voice returned to his mind. [You need to leave!]

Without warning, her long body rushed him up and through the tunnels, back to the very opening where they would always meet.

"Why?" Abash said. "I thought you knew I wouldn't bring you any harm!"

[It's not me I'm worried about.]

"Then what? I suppose I was wrong to assume we were friends."

He ran after her as she slinked back to the dark tunnel.

[Don't you understand? You should be friends with other men, not me.]

He knew he couldn't catch up with her so he shouted, "You don't understand!"

She stopped running away but her head was deep in the tunnels.

[As I've said, I have never found joy in understanding.]

"Then I'll tell you. I'm lonely, too."

Narre'ah backed out from where she stood. It took a while for her long body and segments to crawl out to face him again, but when she did, Abash saw her dark, unblinking eyes shimmering in a new kind of light.

[How can such a kind man be alone?] she asked.

"I...I wouldn't say I'm kind," Abash answered, looking down. "I'm just different than the men of my village. I like to be alone in the ground. And I kept going back to the cave, because I thought I would find something special. And I did."

Her antennae stood erect at his words. Slowly, she swerved her head over towards him, pressing against his chest like she did many times before. Except this time, she did not draw away. She only pressed against him further, as if trying to force herself into him, into one being.

"I don't want you to be alone," he said, placing his head into the top of her carapace. "Neither of us should be."

A pause, as the Millipede considered his words. He felt her long body crawl up him, her needle legs digging into the soft flesh of his chest. He winced at the slight initial discomfort, but as she pressed the top half of herself flush against his chest, he only felt a deep satisfaction at the limitless touch of her legs. Heat flooded all throughout his torso. He clung his arms around her smooth exoskeleton, fingers running up and down the ridged segments. They were just two beings, holding each other up in the darkness. He hoped she could feel his warmth, too.

[Dear friend...I would not ask this of you if we were not as close as we are.]

"You can ask me."

[There is a new spell I want to try. It is not one of the earth.] There was a pause, then she added, [It is very dangerous.]

Dangerous for him, or for her? Either way, if it was what she wanted, he would hear it.

"What is the spell?" he asked.

[My wish is for neither of us to be lonely or divided by differences.]

His body became soft with comfort, yet tight with purpose. Abash gave into the weight of the Millipede, allowing her to wrought her magic upon him as she would.

* * *

Months later, the men of the village stormed through the forest and towards the abandoned mine. They carried blades and poles to kill a monster, and ropes and chains to catch a traitor-warlock. The shifty-eyed skulker they called "Abash" was never part of their kind, and was perhaps always suited for sharing life with hell spawn deep under the earth's crust.

Not too far from the cave mouth, the hunters found their monster.

The husk of a Giant Millipede lay on the dirt, curled and bone-white, already dead. If someone tried to uncurl it in this state, its pale and dry corpse would crack into pieces.

They still had to find Abash.

The men of the village would wander the dark tunnels for miles, blindly, no magic to guide them. No light to shine on the murals that told the stories of a civilization as old as the earth itself.

No one would notice the three figures roughly scraped at the bottom of the cave wall: a Millipede, a man, and a smaller creature between them.

* * *

Abash stepped lightly through the woods, trying to not break a single twig or crush a single bug beneath his sandaled feet. A cloak coated his whole body. He clutched a bundle fast against his chest.

He tilted his head up to the sky, the sun beamed a blinding light through bare branches of autumn. Brittle brown leaves crunched beneath his feet. The air of the forest was dry and thick with pollen, making his nose itch and drip. His heart ached when he remembered the cool cave.

He hoped he had not strayed from his path to the east. Away from the Great Frontiers of violent men searching for things they could call monsters. Closer to some people who might take pity on him. Curious warlocks of nature who understood the need to understand.

Or so he begged he would arrive there, with every gentle step.

The bundle he carried began to squirm. Abash felt the sharp scrapes of chitin against his chest and stopped. He sat on a log half-sunken in a heap of leaves.

With one hand securing the bundle to his chest, he used the other to sling his rucksack down, then fished out an apple he couldn't finish earlier.

Next, he settled the bundle down on his lap.

"At some point, I'm going to have to tell you this story. I'm going to have to get it right," Abash whispered.

Out sprawled a human baby, his soft arms stretching, and his face scrunching in the sunlight. The bottom half of him—a segmented torso of a Millipede—rolled out. Countless tiny legs squirmed in the open air. Two different species of being, split down the middle, pressed together to make something new.

Abash licked his dried lips as he tried to think of a place to begin the story he would tell his son.

"Your mother and I were friends. She created you with her magic, so she wouldn't have to be the last of her kind. She needed the substance of someone else to make the spell to work. I let her use me." He didn't like how he phrased that. He remembered how he felt in the dark, with the Millipede-monster curling up against him, evoking a magic between them both that neither felt before. She never used him. They were one in that moment. As they always were.

Abash took a bite from the apple in his teeth, then, pinching it in his fingers, he held it in front of the infant's face. A foam filled his tiny flesh mouth, dissolving the fruit and allowing him to slurp it up. Still technically a newborn, unable to grasp his own food, Abash held the apple for him. It would be surprising just to see in what ways the child was a human and what was he was not. It would be a lifetime of understanding for them both.

"The magic spell was unlike anything else she had ever tried. It cost her life, and now she's gone." Abash flinched at his own words. Narr'eah wasn't "gone." Her withered body was left behind in the cave. She died. He couldn't save her.

He had rid the world of a monster, just as the men of his village wanted.

But he hadn't wanted this. The ancient magic she knew, he could never understand how it unfurled.

Did she want this? Was this her parting gift to the world?

Abash's eyes snapped open when he heard the infant cough. The apple bite was gone.

Abash took a finger and swapped the inside of his son's mouth so that he wouldn't choke on any leftover chunks. He wasn't entirely certain if the infant could even choke on his own acid, but he did not want to test the theory out. Abash wiped the foam on his shirt. The acidity burned a few holes in the fabric.

If only he were a weaving-man, not a geologist. Then his shirt wouldn't have any holes.

If he were a weaving-man, not a geologist, so much would be different.

Abash placed the baby against his shoulder. He clenched his teeth when he felt the child's insect-half and one-hundred legs pierce through his chest. But he let his son fasten himself, so he wouldn't slip away.

"One day, I'm going to have to tell you this story," Abash repeated. For the first time since the strange child was delivered into his arms, Abash's heart felt warm again. There was so much he could share with a little one that was half of him. So much knowledge about rocks and stones, the legacies of the Great Millipedes that tunneled under the ground for generations. A legacy that the little one now shared, fulfilling the long-awaited wish of his mother.

Abash didn't know how to tell his son that despite being everything his parents wanted, the nature of his existence was an abomination. Even to his own parents, he was less of an offspring, and more of an invention. A compromise. Abash felt a noxious churning in his stomach whenever he looked at the child for a few seconds too long—and he couldn't tell yet if it came from grief or disgust.

Men hated monsters, hated warlocks, hated bugs. Killing these things made the world safer for them. Abash knew he could not be a normal man. A normal man would not have chosen a Millipede as his only friend, or had allowed such a horrific hybrid creature to enter the world. When he and Narre'ah were alone and together, it all made sense in their own dead-end way. Now that she was gone and he could never go back to the home they made, he could see perfectly just how every decision he made was wrong to the world.

Despite all the appropriations of culture and nature they caused, there was no person more affected by Abash's and Narre'ah's decisions than the little creature they made.

After all, what can kill a king?

by Maia Brown-Jackson

Am I making myself a martyr
because I still believe in the potential of humanity,
or because I'm so tired of it trying to prove me wrong?

My tongue is a weapon
and the crooked twist of my smile
is a harbinger of justice,
because when they learned what I had done
that already doomed me to the fifth circle of hell
they let themselves forget I was human:
my skeleton as fragile as theirs;
my blood as easy to spill;
they think of me as more weapon than girl—
yet if we're all just mortal, surviving on borrowed time,
then why not risk the girl spurned by everyone but her own shadow?

I protested that I was just another Lucifer escaping an uncaring tyrant,
another Lilith refusing to be made small,
but I am merely judged as harshly as them, my motive unheard.

And now, it's all demands:

Why should I not stand between them and danger?
Why should I not promise a few miracles on the way to my inevitable end?

Wherever I go, the people plead,
they implore,
they *pray* to me as
the lone champion who can
teach them how to kill a king.
(Not so worried about my sins now, are they?)

I know when I die
it will be painful and public
and
I don't care anymore,
because I'm already burning, *burning*,
for the gods who did not deign to come,
and in death I might finally escape
the endless
(endless)
(endless)
inhuman
duty.

Until then, I just bare bloody teeth and
let the drum beating more and more rapidly against my ribs urge me
forward
as again and again I surrender to my fate;
because for what is a girl born if not
sacrifice?

Fowl

by Konstantin Asimonov

Dumbfounded by this blooming spring
I will take flight into the evening sky.
And sweeper Stepanov will stare mid-swing,
And hide his broom and also fly.
—Aleksei Iwashchenko

"Sisteen ruble," said the somewhat apologetic vendor.

Alferov handed him two crumpled ten-ruble bills, picked up a plastic, cold-to-the touch glass of kvass from the makeshift stand, and patiently waited until the swarthy Kyrgyz man found a few wet coins in the pocket of his blue apron.

Ah, you churka, you, thought Alferov in a peaceful, even affectionate manner, as he counted the five grimy coins in his hand—three one-ruble coins and two fifty-kopecks. Then, quickly, in four mighty gulps, he finished the cool, frothy drink, carefully placed the glass on top of the overflowing garbage bin and flew up.

It was chilly and crowded in the air, even though rush hour had long since ended and the main hustle and bustle had subsided. Alferov quickly oriented himself towards the northwest by the barely visible sun peeking out from behind low autumn clouds. He flew not too fast, leisurely spreading his arms to the sides, dodging the ever-hurrying teenagers and bankers resembling giant, shapeless sparrows.

Next to him, a policeman streaked past like a big blue bird.

Alferov, however, was in no hurry. The smooth, slightly intoxicating kvass pleasantly weighed down on his satisfied stomach. He lazily glided, almost resting on the buoyant airstream, blissfully surveying the surroundings.

The Ring was jam-packed. Hundreds, if not thousands, of toy-like cars resembling colorful matchboxes stood and were contemptuously honking. Along with the noxious fumes blowing into Alferov's face, a strong wave of anger and irritation hit him. His eyes immediately welled up with tears, and he had to veer slightly to the side, assume a vertical position, and, rummaging in his voluminous briefcase, retrieve the eye drops. Awkwardly clutching the puffy briefcase under his arm, Alferov painstakingly squeezed beads of fragrant, viscous liquid into his already moist eyes. The moment the drops touched his eyes, they stung, and his eyes teared up even stronger.

Flying directly over the monstrous, yet alluring in its mighty beauty, building of the Ministry of Foreign Affairs, Alferov carefully circled its towering spire and was just about to fly above the lively and broad Arbat Street when three misfortunes struck him all at once.

Firstly, some adolescent with a foolish-looking face and bulging eyes came out of nowhere and crashed into his left side, causing Alferov to instantly lose both physical and spiritual balance. The impudent youth fled the scene without uttering a word, while poor Alferov, guided by the relentless laws of physics, comically spun around in the air, culminating in his tailbone colliding directly with the spire of the Ministry of Foreign Affairs building. The spire turned out to be cold and painfully solid.

Secondly, as Alferov's coccyx was already injured from a certain spicy yet not at all shameful incident, the pain from the fatal collision with the spire did not stay on the surface but went deep into Alferov and pierced him to the core, causing him to grab the sore spot with both hands and let out a gasp.

And finally, thirdly, and most terribly, his precious briefcase broke free from the hands of the bewildered Alferov and, with a mocking glimmer of its buckle, fell down. After hitting the sharp and prickly frame of the building a couple of times, the briefcase completely split open, and its contents spilled generously onto the square.

From the spire's height, Alferov watched in horror as the items, which he had acquired with care, became public property. There were a full paper bag of antonovka apples, a scarf gifted by his wife, three large note-pads, today's newspaper, yesterday's newspaper, a set of colorful ballpoint pens, eye drops, extra insoles, an excellent Japanese calculator capable of plotting graphs, a case with reading glasses, an umbrella, and most notably, the Document of Distinct Importance, all now irrevocably lost to the public.

The scattered remains of the briefcase were swarmed by tiny black dots, as if a colony of ants had stumbled upon spilled sugar. Alferov snapped out of his stupor and dove down at full speed, only to confirm that he was hopelessly late.

In the middle of the small open space between the Ministry of Foreign Affairs building and the Ring lay the lifeless body of the once graph-plotting Japanese calculator. A homeless dog with kind, intelligent eyes was feasting on the remains of the apples that were strewn all over the square, dissected, bruised, and wounded, as if after an artillery barrage. Today's newspaper glided like a white swan somewhere at the level of the power lines. Yesterday's newspaper, folded into quarters, fell much faster and met its end under the wheels of cars that escaped the clutches of the traffic jam. The insoles met a similar fate. The ants had taken care of everything else.

The Document was nowhere to be found.

After searching for twenty minutes, which felt like an hour to him, Alferov gave up. Aimlessly pacing the square for another fifteen minutes, he surrendered again, and half an hour later, exhausted, he sat down on a greasy and dirty curbstone. The Document was nowhere to be found, and this fact was indisputable.

Finally, a slight panic gripped Alferov.

He vomited onto the dusty pavement.

* * *

The Grand Management was beside himself.

"How could you, Alferov," he asked in a booming voice, "lose the Document, something as valuable as your life is insignificant and foolish?"

"How dare you lose it," he roared, "and how dare you even imagine losing it? How did the word 'lose' even enter your worthless, cotton-filled head?"

"What kind of spineless and groveling idiot must one be," he raged, "to lose the Document and then have the audacity to come here and announce this outrageous fact just like that, haphazardly?"

"But," Alferov attempted to interject.

"Shut it!" the Grand Management bellowed. "Shut it and answer! How do you even dare to live after what you've done, Alferov?"

"Well," he tried to defend himself.

"Shut it!" the Management thundered, wiping copious sweat from its managemental forehead. "Shut it! Shh! You... You are a hatcher, Alferov! A clucking hen!"

There was no way for Alferov to counter such lethal reasoning. He was a clucking hen. The argument was lost.

"Here's what I'll do, Alferov," the Management said, catching his breath and taking a titanic gulp from the steaming cup. "I will punish you."

They'll cut my salary, Alferov thought with gloom but also with some relief, as he had promised to buy his wife a fur coat last month.

"I will severely punish you," the Management said, "and your punishment will be most severe."

Or maybe they will even demote me, Alferov pondered. After all, the Document was of Distinct Importance.

"As you are such a hen," the Management said in a calmer, more composed tone, "I will revoke your registration. You'll use your legs for a bit."

A division of large goosebumps with cold, bare feet marched across Alferov's broad back.

"But it's impossible," he muttered.

"The impossible is possible," said the Management vindictively and winked. "A new administrative punitive measure. You will be our guinea pig. We will test the equipment on you."

At the mention of 'equipment', Alferov felt even worse. They'll cut something out, he realized. He had been afraid of knives and scalpels since childhood.

"It's not necessary," he said.

"It is, Alferov, it is necessary," the Management replied almost sympathetically, and Alferov understood: indeed, it was necessary. There was nothing he could do.

A chair, similar to a dentist's one but reversed, with the patient lying face down and arched so that their back was exposed to the powerful light of a multi-megawatt lamp, was wheeled into the office. Then the secretary entered, holding Alferov's folder, glancing warily at the chair.

This must be the 'equipment', Alferov thought. *They'll bring the knives now.* Strangely, it wasn't the consequences of losing his registration that frightened Alferov, but the process itself, which he imagined to be extremely painful and unpleasant.

"Lie down, Alferov," the Management said. He was seated behind a large oak desk, flipping through the folder they had brought. There, in that folder, was Alferov's entire life in all its endless monotony: daycare, kindergarten, registration, school, institute, wedding, work, the birth of a child, work, work, work, promotion, work, vacation, work. The loss of the Document. Now, lying in the terrifying chair and staring at the drab pattern on the drab carpet, Alferov thought that, overall, he had lived a meaningless life.

And then, in absolute silence, a familiar screech of a fountain pen on cheap paper gasped through the air—the High Management had crossed something out in Alferov's folder, and a strange burning sensation appeared between his shoulder blades. It felt as if a fiery worm was screwing itself into Alferov's back, not painfully but rather sadly.

Odd, thought Alferov, *they are revoking my registration, yet the worm is burrowing inside. Wrong way.*

The burning sensation ended as abruptly as it began, and the Management sharply slammed down the folder. The sound was like squashing a mosquito against thick wallpaper.

"Walk, Alferov," the Management said.

And Alferov rose up and walked.

There were still many tasks to complete that day, unburdening yet time-consuming tasks, so Alferov finished late, around ten o'clock. He didn't feel any consequences of losing his registration, except that the secretary, when he nervously and timidly left the Management's office, avoided looking him in the eye, and after some time, other colleagues followed her lead.

Blabbed, he thought without malice, *she blabbed to the whole department, silly broad. It's fine; they'll get used to it.*

He was almost the last one to leave the Office, bidding a friendly farewell to the embarrassed guard, who was also avoiding his gaze. He walked on the pavement, stretching his legs, which had become stiff from the uncomfortable writing desk, and stopped. He couldn't take off. He had even forgotten how to do it. Something that had been a reflex since childhood disappeared somewhere.

He tried again.

Nothing.

His feet wouldn't leave the ground. There was no lightness in his body. Only a murky, dragging fatigue, accompanied by melancholy.

So, this is it, Alferov realized. *I'm now one of them now, a churka, a non-local. Perhaps I'll have to buy a car.*

The thought of acquiring that metallic, dirty, and smoke-spewing monster almost brought tears to Alferov's eyes. But he held back.

* * *

The night was cloudless, and the foolish white moon barely illuminated Alferov's path as he walked along the overgrown, barely visible trail in the park, leading from the Office located in its very center. The park was unusually quiet and dark; the streetlamps stood too high, and their yellow light couldn't penetrate the thick crowns of the old trees. Above all that was the moon, casting thin, pale rays in all directions, and the path was occasionally lit up by their gleam.

Alferov walked and felt stupid. Firstly, it was unclear how he would get home. Secondly, it was unclear what he would tell his wife and how the neighbors would react. Would they laugh at him? Would ominous whispers start every time he went out to the staircase to take out the trash? Would they tease his daughter at school? No, perhaps they wouldn't tease her; after all, many people go to school without registration, and they manage somehow—maybe even half the population.

Alferov stumbled over a protruding tree root, pulling a break on his train of thought.

Now he would have to leave for work much earlier, he decided, at least two hours earlier. And a car would be a necessity, as much as he hated the idea. Traffic jams, gasoline, fumes, other cars—all of that did not inspire enthusiasm. He wondered if his wife still had her registration. If need be, could she still fly over to the store or to the housing department? Probably, she could.

Alferov stepped onto a wide road with old, worn-out asphalt and hesitated. Where was he flying to from here? South, then southeast, it seemed. The road led somewhere else, but there were no other options. Alferov sighed and started walking along the highway. He suddenly missed his lost insoles. He would probably have to buy completely different shoes, he thought.

A car zoomed past, honking furiously, and enveloped Alferov in acrid exhaust smoke. Another car flashed by with its headlights on. Then one more. Alferov stepped to the side of the road and raised his hand with a protruding thumb, just as he had seen in a movie once. The next car braked, and Alferov opened the door.

"To Oktyabrskaya Square," he said half-questioningly.

"Nah, buddy, I'm not going that way," the driver replied. He was fat and cheerful.

"At least to the Ring," Alferov said.

"That I can do," the driver said. "I'll take you to Smolenskaya, and then you can walk the rest. It's about twenty minutes, tops. For two hundred."

Alferov did a quick calculation. He had two hundred. But he didn't know the fares, so it was worth negotiating.

"One fifty."

The driver nodded, and Alferov, with some effort, squeezed himself into the narrow, square cabin. Inside, it strongly smelled of cigarettes and was surprisingly cold, noticeably colder than outside. Alferov closed the door, and as the car started moving, he discreetly studied the driver.

The man appeared to be around forty years old, with an open, slightly wind-burned face, red from vodka. Thick, calloused fingers firmly gripped the steering wheel. There was a photo of a family—tired woman hugging two scrawny boys—pinned to the sun visor, and next to it a postcard with some old Russian city, Pskov or maybe Suzdal. The driver lit a cigarette and looked at the passenger with an unspoken question. Alferov shrugged, and the cabin filled with smoke.

They arrived quickly, and although Alferov was initially puzzled about how the driver managed to drive this prehistoric jalopy at such a decent speed without crashing into the identical jalopy driving next to it, he quickly got used to it and even stopped fearing the oncoming traffic.

Probably, learning to drive is not difficult, he thought, observing the calm driver, how he held the wheel with one hand, how he flicked the ash down with the snap of a chubby finger onto the road passing by the window.

"One fifty," the driver said, and Alferov reached into his trouser pocket for his wallet.

After paying, he got out of the car, and an exquisite aroma of juicy, sizzling kebab with onions and maybe even tomatoes hit him in the face. His stomach growled, and Alferov remembered that he hadn't eaten anything at all today because of the ridiculous incident. Of course, his wife was waiting at home with dinner, and it was only a twenty-minute walk, as the driver said, but the smell of grilled meat outweighed all reasonable arguments. Alferov followed the scent and ended up on the Arbat thoroughfare.

The kebab was being grilled right on the street, and there was violin and guitar music playing nearby. Gas lamps burned cozily, and people in garish clothes laughed heartily and danced. Short, ancient buildings seemed to drape Arbat with a richly colorful towel, turning it into an endless corridor filled with music, laughter, and light. Alferov, who had only been here during the day, was enchanted and instantly forgot about going home. In fact, he forgot that he was even going somewhere in the first place. He only remembered that he wanted to buy the kebab from the jolly, mustachioed man in the grubby apron and then stroll along the age-old, life-soaked sidewalks, immortalized in song, perhaps even in more than one.

The meat was exceptionally expensive, tough, undercooked, and tasteless, but Alferov was happy.

Slightly swaying, he walked down the street, absentmindedly wiping his dirty, greasy fingers on his new trousers, humming a melody that seemed to flow from nowhere, and inhaling the unique evening air of Arbat, filling his soul with fire. Alferov hesitated for a second and then walked right into the crowd.

At one point, some people caught him and whirled him into their frenzied dance, and then a bear tore his pants to shreds amid persistent cries and laughter from its owners, and while Alferov was fascinatedly pondering how a bear could even be here, he was spun in a dance again, this time by someone else, and then they led him along, and he couldn't help bursting into laughter, then they poured him kvass and then some other drink, that burned his throat and went straight to his stomach, and as he coughed and wiped the tears from his eyes, someone playfully hit him on the back, and then he ran after someone, stumbled, and ended up with a huge bump on his forehead, though it was unclear how he managed that, and then something cold was applied to the bump, and he drank something cold and laughed, and then he hugged someone, and then he hugged the bear, and it tore his pants again, awkwardly catching them with its long black claw, and finally, drunk, steaming, exhausted, and drowning in the music, he sank to the pavement, and someone sat down next to him.

The person had a mound of coal-black hair, a colorful scarf, and a ringing, boisterous laugh, and that was enough for Alferov to fall madly and irreversibly in love with the girl sitting next to him.

When the fog in Alferov's eyes cleared, and he looked more closely at his neighbor, he noticed that she looked older than him, though she was likely younger. Her laughter revealed a golden tooth, and she laughed constantly, and in fact, the word 'girl' could only be applied to her in the broadest sense. But that didn't change a thing.

The neighbor looked at Alferov with her dark, raven-like eye and kissed him, hungrily, slipping her tongue deep into his mouth. Alferov tasted alcohol, honey, and, strangely, salt. Her lips were soft and strong, her breasts firm, and her fingers cold and nimble. Alferov's breathing quickened, and he blushed instantly when, without any inhibition or fear, she unfastened his belt and slipped her hand into his pants.

She must be a roma, Alferov assumed for some reason, while the neighbor kissed him again and whispered something in his ear. Only a few seconds later, Alferov realized that it was, in fact, the price.

His palms were sweaty, and his fingers struggled to bend as he frantically searched his pocket for his wallet and took out the money. The bills trembled slightly in his outstretched hand, but the Romani woman didn't notice, snatching them and hiding them somewhere in her skirt. Then she pulled Alferov up from the floor and dragged him along.

Looking ahead, Alferov noticed with horror the impenetrable darkness of an arch roof. For a moment, he imagined that this maw was about to swallow him, so he closed his eyes and fearfully opened them again only when the woman kissed him once more, passionately and firmly. They stood in the backyard under the arch, safely hidden from the noisy street by a cloud of all-consuming darkness. Alferov could only make out her silhouette, which suddenly seemed to shrink, as if she were squatting. A second later, Alferov pressed himself against the wall, straining all the muscles in his body to avoid screaming, managing only a quiet, prolonged moan.

Fired up, Alferov pushed her onto the floor and settled down beside her, getting tangled in her colorful dress that appeared gray in the darkness, like all cats at night. His face nestled in her soft breasts, and his hands wandered through the maze of her skirts, trying to reach her naked body. The Romani woman neither helped nor hindered, silently approving of the unfolding scene, breathing heavily in excitement.

In the end, his efforts were successful, and as Alferov reached something warm and slightly damp, a blinding hammer of light hit him in the left flank from the quiet courtyard, almost physically pushing Alferov aside. His eyes immediately teared up, but he managed to see a car with its headlights on and red and blue flashing lights, as well as a couple of human silhouettes. The woman shrieked in a beastly manner, and from all the surprise and fear, Alferov ejaculated into his pants.

He jumped up, trying simultaneously to put on his clothes and to say something, but he was immediately knocked down by a precise blow on the nose with a rubber baton from a flying police officer. Alferov once again hurt his long-suffering tailbone, and then four shadows in service caps, like gigantic gray condors, flashed by him and in an instant dissolved in the Arbat lights. Someone shouted.

The roma, who had been lying like a heap of rags on the dirty, spit-covered asphalt, suddenly jumped to her feet, and crouching, ran into the courtyard towards the police car. A person jumped out and kicked her, then grabbed her by the hair and dragged her out onto the street, past Alferov. The woman's eyes were completely wild, even reddish in the glare of the headlights, her face contorted, and her golden tooth glistened as she turned her head, trying to bite the policeman's hand.

A trickle of blood flowed from Alferov's broken nose, and he watched it as if from a distance, like a spectator, until a rough leather boot struck his open stomach, and he writhed in pain. Then they dragged him towards the bright flickering of Arbat's streetlights.

I'm probably going to die now, Alferov thought calmly and remembered that before death, one's entire life is supposed to flash before their eyes, from birth to the present, but he saw nothing except the Arbat pavement passing beneath him.

As they tossed him into the grease-smelling paddy wagon on top of other bodies, he looked at the street bathed in reddish light and noticed two policemen beating the bear with their feet and their batons, right next to the lamppost.

Losing consciousness, Alferov smiled and thought that he would probably be punished at home for the torn pants.

* * *

The cell reeked of urine, vomit, and cellmates. It was a small cube, several paces each way, and the air was hot from people breathing. The walls were sweating like in a sauna. There were many cellmates, and they looked fierce, as if all of them were a warped variation of one man, dirty, scrawny, sick and very unfriendly.

"Oh, a fresh one," one of them said kindly as soon as they pushed Alferov into the tight, foul-smelling room and the door clicked shut. "Shall we register him? Quickly?"

In response, several approving exclamations sounded, and they threw Alferov to the floor near the far wall, stained with something dark. He didn't know what 'register' meant anymore, but he braced himself for the worst, curling up into a ball and covering his face and stomach with his hands. They hit him on the knee just to see his reaction, and he let out a soft yelp from the sharp, intense pain. Then three or four people started beating Alferov, in a lackluster manner, without much interest, and, if one could put it this way, even gently.

They mostly targeted his legs and arms; only once did a stray boot hit him in the nose, and blood spurted out again. Alferov laid still, momentarily shutting off all sensations, including pain. He simply stared through the gap between his hands at the spit-covered floor under his cellmates' feet and didn't think about anything. Finally, seemingly having had enough, they left him alone and didn't touch him again, like a pack of wolves leaving carrion.

They only rummaged through his pockets, but the policemen had already taken everything, including his wallet and passport. So Alferov focused all his efforts on lying still, calmly and motionlessly, pressing his cheek against the cold, foul-smelling floor, and hoping for a miracle. The first part worked well, but the second, not so much. Alferov even considered praying but remembered only 'Thy Kingdom come, Thy Will be done' and that was only because it rhymed, but what came after 'be done', he couldn't recall or perhaps never knew.

The Management was right, he thought, *I'm a hen, always was, and will remain one forever.*

Who asked why people don't fly like birds? Chekhov? Ostrovsky? Well, that's why they don't, poor fuckers...Others in my place would be thinking about their wife and daughter, worrying that I didn't come home, probably calling hospitals, and here I am lying face down in a holding cell, not thinking about anyone, not even myself, not even about death, just lying here a meaningless piece of human waste, scared of my cellmates, and if I suddenly need to piss, I'll just do it right here on the floor because anything is better than standing up in the middle of a holding cell, in front of everyone, and I'll never fly again, no, and I'll probably have to buy a car, and new shoes, and now pants too, and there's no money for that, no, although maybe my wife will find a job, dear God, what am I even thinking, no, I'm not even thinking about death, I don't want to die, what a hen I am, what a hen I am, and hen is not a bird, no, not a bird... I do want to fly again. I do, yes, I do want to fly again, even if they beat me again, yes, I do, even if...

The door to the cell creaked, thumped, and a drowsy male voice said:

"Alferov. On your feet."

They led Alferov along an endless green corridor, passing a row of identical white doors, and finally pushed him into one of them. There, a friendly captain was sitting.

"Have a seat, Alferov," said the captain, smiling. "What a night, huh?"

"Dark," muttered Alferov, unsure of how to respond in such situations.

"He-he, that's for sure," the captain chuckled. "Alferov, wipe the blood, your nose is dripping. Sidorenko, pass a handkerchief."

A sleepy, tall sergeant with a wart on his cheek offered Alferov a piece of white cloth and then unexpectedly took the initiative to wipe Alferov's nose himself. A red streak remained on the cloth.

"Well, Alferov," said the captain, "Don't hold a grudge against the guys; they didn't know you were registered, and they didn't know where you work, you understand? So, we'll let this one slide. It wouldn't look good, a prominent man, a civil servant, married, and hooking up with some whore in an alley. Couldn't find anyone better, Alferov?"

"No."

"Well, alright then, it's your business, you can fuck a goat, he-he, as far as I'm concerned. But, you understand, not on my watch. In any case, you'll write a statement that, say, three unknown individuals attacked you, beat you up, and took all your cash. You understand. If you want, there's a board with composites; you can study them and include the details in your statement. For credibility, he-he. And then, my good fellow, fly away in any direction, free like a pigeon. You understand."

"Give me your paper. I'll sign."

"Alright then," the captain said, smiling even wider. "You understand then."

Alferov took the handkerchief from the sergeant and wiped his nose again. Then he asked:

"What about the roma?"

"What roma? Oh, your girl? Big deal, there she is, in the cell right now. The guys roughed her up, of course, you understand. By the way, why do you call her a roma? She's not a roma, she's Russian, from Pskov. Came here to make some money for the registration. Maybe find herself a nice plump registered husband, he-he, Alferov? We'll send her back there, of course."

"Can I see her?"

"Oh fuck, Alferov, what do you think this is, a museum? Fine, Sidorenko, take our friend and show him his Romani on the way out, since, you understand, he's asking so nicely."

When Alferov signed the last form, and the captain wished him, you understand, a safe journey and many happy returns, he-he, the sergeant led him through the green corridor to a little window. There they gave Alferov his confiscated belongings, including his wallet, which was missing nearly a thousand rubles, probably for credibility, he-he, and a photo of his daughter for some unknown reason. Alferov wanted to protest but didn't bother.

Then Sidorenko showed him the woman from the alley. She was sitting on the floor of another dirty cell, spreading her thin legs in torn skirts wide apart and constantly howling. Instead of the gold tooth, a bloody clot could be seen in her mouth.

"Let's get out of here," Alferov whispered.

The sergeant escorted him to the dispatch and lazily gestured towards the exit.

"Thank you," said Alferov, but received no response.

Outside, a cold, almost wintry wind was blowing, and out of habit, Alferov wiped his no longer bleeding but swollen nose with the once-white handkerchief. His bruised kidneys and tailbone were painfully throbbing, bruises on his arms and legs itched, and his stomach was growling, but he felt strangely good.

But why, thought Alferov, *did they take my daughter's photo?* Then he thought a little more and flew back home.

Alice Underground

by K. D. Paige

I can hear them talking. They don't know that I know they're here. Spread out beneath us, paid barely a thought, they surround us. Sooner or later it will be too late.

I think these things to myself while lying on a fallen log, watching the patterns the sun makes across my closed eyelids. It's warmth tracing a path across my skin. The forest is alive all around me. Chipmunks, squirrels, and all numbers of critters monotonous in their existence. I wonder if they are spared? Not likely, the underground is unforgiving and undiscerning. No one believes me when I tell them what I hear. Little whispers all around, plotting and scheming—they love to plot and scheme. All day long they chatter. What do they talk about? I couldn't say. It's endless, though, and once you notice it, it's hard to tune out. Like that one particular bird whose song caught your ear and won't let go.

I heave a sigh, reaching my arms above my head. My fingers brush against some moss and I feel a flick on my finger. My eyes snap open and I'm momentarily blinded by the light. The chatter stops, holds its collective breath. Waits.

I wonder if they will creep closer if they think I'm unaware. If I'm just like the others who have no idea what's happening all around them. I sit up, glancing around to confirm my suspicions. Their sacrificial scouts are frozen, peeking at me in their creep across the forest floor. In all shapes and sizes, their scouts keep watch; some tricking the most unfortunate into an untimely death. Camouflaged as one another, only the most in sync able to distinguish the difference between them.

I move to sit on the ground, my back pressed against the log, waiting to witness their slow progression. I let my eyes fall closed, a small grin sneaking its way across my face. They cannot get me, I know they are here and everyone knows you can't catch the prey that knows you're coming. In the distance I can hear waves crashing along the shore. I let the rhythmic thrum silence my whirling thoughts.

* * *

Ten years ago I found myself in these very woods. My sister and I ran through the trees while our parents lazed on the beach, watching for the emergence of migrating whales. It was getting late in the day, the golden light of the sun was sinking its way through the trees.

"One more game!" my sister squealed.

I relented, "Fine! But I'm only counting to fifty this time!".

I turned to face the nearest tree and started counting, loudly at first, but then more quietly so I could hear the direction she'd gone. Caught up in the fun, she made no attempt to silence her footsteps. Instead, she crashed her way through the brush, laughing and causing the animals to scatter in her wake.

"Forty eight, forty nine, fifty!" I yelled. Moving my way across the forest floor I set out in pursuit. Muffling my footsteps on decaying leaves, ducking out of the way of branches so as to not give away my location, I closed in. She thought she was being clever, hiding behind the tree she chose. But she kept peeking too often and with the sun setting behind her, I could see the golden halo of my sister's hair, the sun setting it aflame.

She was looking around the tree in the opposite direction when it happened. I was about to jump out at her but something white and spindly shot out of the ground at her feet, wrapping itself around her ankle. She looked down, confusion creasing her brows and settling across her face. It's likely she thought she just got it caught on her leg when she was running but while I watched her reach down to brush away the invasion, more sprouted on her other side.

Within seconds, my sister was covered in these white, rooty fingers and I watched her struggle. Getting pulled to the ground, she was scratching her skin raw. Bloody rivers running down her arms and legs, down her face. Not even in my worst nightmare could I imagine what was about to happen. It wasn't like in the movies. The ground didn't open up and swallow her whole, it was more like she was absorbed, sucked down into the dirt. I couldn't scream. I couldn't move. I have no idea how long it took, but eventually I tore my eyes away from the spot where she disappeared. Throwing down my coat to mark the spot, I sprinted to the beach where our parents were waiting.

"The ground!" heave, gasp, choke. "The ground opened!" I shouted, my legs moving as fast as they could over the rocky beach. My parents stood up from the picnic blanket, eyes wandering the treeline for my sister.

"What are you talking about, honey? The ground opened?" my dad asked, kneeling so he was at eye level with me.

"Where is your sister?" my mom called over her shoulder, making her way towards the trees.

"MOM, NO!" The scream tore from my throat. "You can't go in there, it will get you too!"

Talk about the wrong thing to say. My parents took off. My dad scooped me up and ran into the woods, both of them screaming my sister's name. They searched for what felt like hours, eventually going back to the beach to call for help. While we were waiting for the police and search teams, I tried to find my jacket and that place again, but it was gone.

* * *

They've started to crawl again. I keep peeking from beneath my lashes, monitoring their encroachment. I feel a tickle on my ankle, like an ant crawling up my pants leg, but I know better. One by one they wrap themselves around me. Lashing out, I grab at the bunch around my left ankle. I tear and shred them from my skin. Standing up with a fist full of their snare, I start pulling them like a rope.

Hand over hand I pull and they come up from the ground. Behind me I hear a rumble and I know I don't have much time. I step up onto the log, hoping to give myself another minute or two. There is a wave-like crest building in the soil around me. I glance over my shoulder and stop in my tracks.

My jacket is laying on the ground, still as pink as the day I threw it down. I guess they had me in their sights all along.

Everything pauses. No bird takes flight, no mosquito buzzes around my ear. I step down off the log and bend to pick up my coat. There is tension, like the ground doesn't want to let go. I grunt, pulling it further and further out of the dirt until, like a cap exploding off a soda bottle, my jacket comes free and with it, a creature that could almost be my sister. A collection of the white substance given form, the creature reaches towards me, arms lengthening as more tendrils join its form. From its almost-mouth leaks a smoke, weaving its way toward me.

I hold my breath as I try to get away, backing up to keep the creature in my sights. In my haste, I trip over a rock, the air whooshing from my lungs. The smoke fills my nostrils and I melt. The tension leaves my body, my muscles turn to Jell-O, and the creature guides me to the forest floor before breaking apart. I feel myself being wrapped up and as soon as it starts, just as before, I am absorbed into the dirt. Sinking beneath the surface, I am cocooned in their web, painless decay taking parts of me to feed their expansive network. One of many in an endless cycle, I am fodder, as were those who came before me and who will come after. Beware the woods, beware the network.

Old Bones

by Benjamin Bagenski

I had to work fast and strike true if the horseshoe would get atop the chapel by Hallow's Eve. Something big coming, that year. No top yet to horseshoe. Barely any walls to top, mind. I blamed the tardy build on my seeing to the town's pow-wowin'. I hammered quick, but not so quick I bust my fingers. I found a rhythm: pinch the nail, tap light, tap tap harder. I was building my chapel by sound.

By sound, the bugs told the time. By sound, the loon told the weather. I didn't hear the cat, but I never do. I told Cotton anyhow I be heading to town.

Among all the black, I seen a shimmer, over yon hill. The bog ladies were out. So I detoured off High Road, by Old Hanging Court. At the hanging tree I spit once, twice, throw salt to the roots. I saw no ghosts, but they be sneak-like.

Little ones gathered near town, little people-folk that is, watching Old Bones rattle along. They'd kick my knot-stick out if I let them. Sometimes they go and taunt atop the old wood bridge that cross 'bove-head the footpath into town. When I felt the sting of pebbles, I raised my Book and threatened them a hex. Tell them they best say their prayers. Oh, I can hear them all right, with their damn rhyme:

In the night the child is sleeping,
Far too dark to cut the firewood,
In the daylight one still creeping,
Here comes Old Bones! For your eyes!

Never trust no kinder-folk nor their games. Thankful, when Old Bones' face stopped putting them afright, the Book still did.

Townwards, I stopped at the crossroads to dig me a marble. Coast clear, I sunk the catseye into the dirt with my knot-stick and kick it over. Next pow-wowin' to do were the sunweeds. Every spring I spit the sunseeds, so harvest come and sunweeds grow where seedspit fall. Holy spit, if you drink the right water. They think I'm a strange man strange-gardening, but it keeps the puckwudgies at bay. Ingrates.

* * *

I always stopped at Goodie Waxwick's shop for tea. She'd say "Morning, Ol' Boney" and took me by the shoulder to a seat. I let her, though I knew the way. She put down a cup, and I smelled the leafsteam, heard plop the salt-and-pepper butterlump melt. Goodie Waxwick maybe looked away as this pow-wower adds some spirits.

Still my favorite joke.

Old Man Gunswallow sat nearby. Sour sweat, sour heart. He sat with Old Man Millerson, Old Man Jamesbroke. The oldest Old Mans in town are tots to Old Bones. Put us in a tiny red house, I'm their schoolmarm.

Gunswallow craws: "What're ye buildin' Old Bones?"

Probably Jamesbroke: "I hear hammerin', you buildin' a wall t'be keepin' the boggarts out this year?" Oh, they all laughed, they did.

"Somebody got to," I say, never mind no boggart been seen coastwards in a generation. "Not one week past! From the corner of my nothing, I seen it—a snowflake of purple hue, an unholy June-fly felled to the ground like Satan hisself done fall a-pit. Something big coming, this year."

Oh, they laugh. But unlike the childrens, I know I'll outlive these

Old Mans. I put my coin to the table, and shuffled off for the blacksmith.

I heard the hammer, felt the forge. On goes I to hit my knot-stick on the door. The smith's a clodhobber, but honest. I smell the honest work upon his brow as he stuck his head out the door.

"One horse shoe," I tell him.

"Your horse appreciate you always buying one shoe at a time?"

I fist up a coin. I shout, "Either sell me a shoe, or you'll get mine swift!"

He chuckled: "Alright, old man. I'll get your iron." Well he got me that horse shoe right quick. I can haggle.

* * *

By rope I pulled a cart of loose tins and woods, paid for in copper and pleasant-tides. No water to squeeze from the stones, but I felt sweat sap from my bones. The path to camp is all wet cobble. I know how slow to go by how loud the brook babbles. Sometimes I see a little turtle-man there, head full of water like a teacup. He never bothers me none, nor me him. I could see the shimmering off bogwards yonder, and if anything makes my goose heckles stand, it be the bog ladies' song.

My road was the sound of leaves and gravel 'neath my boots. My feet felt for road dust, my knot-stick felt for brookmud, scouting the path at my Old Boney pace. The wheels of the cart would go stuck, and I'd give it a big rope-pull. So I wandered, boots and mind. Who to do the pow-wowin' when I'm gone and dead? Who to dig the marbles, plant the sunweeds? How much holy pocus until the dead quiet down?

I recalled my boyhood sight, wondered if the world weren't still half color-filled as I recall. I hummed a tune until I forgot it. Daydreamed about my cat's schemes.

I heard feet a-tumbling from the woods, townwards. Thoughts broken, I held my Long Lost Friend high to scare them. Whoever stood ahead of me stood true.

"You're Old Bones," a girl spoke.

I told her: "Old bones, old skin, don't you know."

"Did the devil really take your eyes?"

"Wouldn't you like to know," I said.

"I would, please."

I pocket the book and hold out the cart-rope: "Then help a poor blind old man get this lot over the bridge, and maybe I tell you a thing or two."

* * *

Once past the river where I see the teacup turtlefolk, she set the cart down with a clattering of junk for my project. "Okay, Old Bones."

"Well okay then," said I.

"So did the devil take your eyes?"

A deal is a deal, and so I told it to her straight: "No."

"But!," she started and stopped and started again. "But!"

Oh, I sympathized with the little stranger. Old Bones is what I look like, my skin be cracked and cooked from the sun with a figure thin as my knot-stick. *No eyes to roll nor lids to wink, two windows straight to where I think,* that's what I say to my cats. Said I: "Nobody took them, kiddo, and they are mighty accounted for. Right here, they is."

I pointed to my sockets. "They're just stuck on the other side. So the other side is all I see."

"Then how many fingers am I holding up?"

Children-folk are wickedly clever. "Well suppose if I chopped them off, I would spy their little ghosts wiggling about!" And she laughed at Old Bones!

"It's true," I insisted. "My cat, all I can see is her tiny paw!"

Well! The girl's curiosity smelled like bugs and unstruck lightning. Told me her name was Anny-belle. And it weren't Old Bones, the Ancient Bag of Mysteries she was really curious about after all. It was the cat. Damn cat, following behind, I can never hear the bastard. Told her his name.

"Cotton? But he's not white, he's all—"

"Don't ruin the mystery!" I point again to the hollows where my eyes should be: "How would I know what color Cotton is?"

She ask me where his foot went. I show my lucky catfoot hung 'round my neck. I let Anny-belle play with the catspaw for luck. Now that she stood close, her scent told her story. Charcoal burner. Rubbed dandelion for fragrance. She cooed "How terrible," as she stroked the catspaw. Cotton purred, like he felt the gentle comfort from his offed limb.

I say: "Devils live in the front right paw of any tomcat." Out from her tiny mouth jumped a thousand more questions. Some of them I answer, too.

* * *

That autumn the little ones would singsong up on the town bridge, I step underneath and there goes the warm of the sun, there goes their little chanting. Something rumbling, the evil what sort that wobbles. Maybe a purple or two, from in-between. Something big coming, that year. I murmured a pray and held close the catspaw, something dark behind their little high voices:

> *In the night the child is sleeping,*
> *Far too dark to cut the firewood,*
> *In the daylight one still creeping,*
> *Here comes Old Bones! For your eyes!*
>
> *In the night the child is slumbering,*
> *Far too dark to milk the cows,*
> *In the daylight one still lumbering,*
> *Here comes Old Bones! For your eyes!*
>
> *In the night the child is dreaming,*
> *Far too dark to do chores,*
> *All the while the devil's scheming,*
> *Here comes Old Bones! For your eyes!*

* * *

Anny-belle helped build the chapel and tap my maples. She said it were too small to be a chapel, more a lump of buildedness. I still worked slow, but the girl's working eyes helped. She asked more questions. Questions like: "Old Bones, why are you in such a rush?"

"Our forefathers gone sunk their boats on haunted country, Anny-belle. Hallow's Eve is close. Something big coming, this year," I told her. "Witches lurk the thin border 'tween the living, the dead, the never-was. Land o' the cats, the land o' the gentry. Land o' bog ladies and teacup turtlefolk."

"Bog ladies?"

"Sure thing," says I, nodding. "Raggedy womenfolk in wet gowns, and their sorrowsong will spell your doom!

"Like a banshee? From Ireland?"

I stoked the scruff at the end of my chin, thinking. "I never did hear of any ban-she. And they never did tell me from whence they hail, but they don't seem the traveling type."

"Oh." And that was that. For a moment: "Old Bones, why the tiny chapel anyhow? It's too small for a pew, let alone a pulpit."

Well: "A pow-wower needs to know a trick or two in this wood. Come Hallow's Eve, I say my words and knot my hands, snap each hex and trap I set. Old Bones can look out for Old Bones, but little Cotton needs a place to keep safe. Something big is coming, this year. Speaking of the damn cat," says I, "Leave it be and find Old Bones his hammer."

"If you tell me more about the bog ladies."

I smile a skullytooth grin.

So Anny-belle would come to help and about the pow-wow.

Questions and answers and stories about the cats.

* * *

Anny-belle, she kept up the cat questions all the way through the woods, below the bridge gate, and up to Goodie Waxwick's. I heard Goodie say her 'morning boneses' but she stopped short before arm-walking me to the sit.

"Brought some company, I see" says she half guard half hopeful. Brought a paying customer is what I bring, I told her. Waxwick scoffed some, told Anny-belle, "Let you not that old tightfist pull coin, dearie. And if he sha'nt pay your fare, be it on the house."

Lest spoiled-like she be, I pointed a holy finger heavenward: "Hear that Anny-Belle? You're on the house! Order us two teas, double-like."

"Two teas!" I hear the little one beam. "Double-like!" Waxwick give her lady grumble as I feel us a pair of chairs in the corner. I don't hear no Gunswallow, no Jamesbroke, none of my Old Mans. Anny-belle take to the counter for our teas, and I waits. The window glowed warm, and I maybe start to drift off. Tealeaf and tallow. The plop of butterlumps, one and two.

I hear the rumble of ceramic cups across the rough wood. Goodie Waxwick whispers, tried to whisper below my Old Bone ears. "Helping you be, what with that little hilltop chapel Ol' Boney is raising?"

Anny-belle she practically sang an answer for Goodie Waxwick, about our chapel, about the cats and the learnins. I listen by half and let the sun put her hand on my face. Then perk my ears to devil's gossip:

"Best beware, dearie. The folks who laughs what Old Bones do, they do in ignorance o'his frightful workings. Profit though we did, in ages past, a heavy price was paid. Somebody lost their kind-hearted, green-eyed boy"—now mind, Goodie prattled like a porch cricket, so permit the parable-phrasing—"And now where spy two cavities upon his visage, know a third lay in his heart. Careful, young one, lest—"

I left seat where sat the sun, took two long strides (three counting for my knot-stick), and fisted a coin down hard upon the counter, flinching all the folk. "Goodie Waxwick, you sure do put idle gossip to a hard day's work. We were leaving, Anny-Belle."

"But Old Bones," she cried, "We just got here!"

"And free are the drinks," says Waxwick real quiet. "But a copper penny for my thoughts."

"The drinks are free," says I, "but the gold coin is for the cups!" I tuck my knot-stick under an arm and take our drinks for the road. "And! A meat pie." We waited inside, sulking silent, a good quarter-hour. The tea went cold. Never did come back—good riddance, says I, but do miss my corner-seat.

We march back campwards, cold teas and hot pie, and spots I a fistfull of purple fuzz, drifting across the black. Something big were coming, that year.

After chapel work, we split the meat pie three ways. Anny-belle, Old Bones, and Cotton. Having someone to talk at and be talked at is a nice thing. We discussed iron and pow-wow. Days go. Over porridge, I tell her of marbles, sunweeds, and hexhands. Days go. By the cooking fire, I felt a chill and lean fireward. More purple floating about as dandelion seedlings do. Time was running scant, but there were time to answer all her questions.

"Turtlefolk, kiddin' you not." I poke the fire with my knot-stick, stir the soup. Give the soup a tad of hickory, and the hickory a tad of soup.

"But Old Bones, why are their heads teacups?"

"No idea," says I. "Can't make out a word they say. But I be damned, they careful-dance lest they spill a drop."

"Not like you, running out of Goodie Waxwicks!" I imagined she phantom-mimed shaking two anger-fists, so I smile my skullytooth grin and made the happy sounds.

* * *

Now, eruditing be a beast elusive. It live might close to wordspeak, but build her nest in a wood of what-ifs. Anny-Belle, she were native to the what-if wood herself. The realness were getting thin by then, but still there were time for a lesson or three.

I brought her to town, so I can show her how we sink the marble at the crossroads. She pointed out for me the little things what missed my sight. What sort of flowers flowered by the brook. The painted sign Goodie Waxwick done, of a little boy wedging his finger in the dam. I pointed out what I could see, the teacup turtlefolk and the little floating purple tongues that tells the veil was thinning.

I spat the sunweed, right beneath the bridge what wend its way over the path to town. Show her, holy spit, and she spit too.

"In the night the child is fleeing..."

There it was again, that horrible tune. Children atop the town bridge, I knew their voices. Grown folk, too. Again under the teasing, I hear that deep timbre of something wrong.

"As our Master claims his prize..."

I were still blind to the folk above the gate, you mind, but I could catch them moving-like, bits in the corner where there shouldn't be none. I raised my book and took to hollerin'.

"Walk among things not for seeing..."

Anny-belle was hollerin' at them too, maybe hollerin' at me. It weren't quite the village folk singing, but something out the inbetweens. Where the folks should be I see pinprickles, like will-o-wisps atop of matchsticks. Folk-not-folks between the others, purple waltzing from their lips.

"Here comes New Bones with her eyes!"

Well Anny-belle needn't be hearing such language, so I put my knot-stick to the earth. I'd been saving the sunseeds for Hallow's Eve—the something big coming that year and all—but I gagged the words and twisted the knot-stick and tremored the earth. That hushed'em up real tight!

Out the ground grew the sunweed. I could hear the crackling of their vines, great leaves brushing across the village bridge. Great round gourds, each plopping to the earth like a giant's egg. The bridge twisted and shuddered as the greenery knotted to my hexhand, though my strength waned quicker than candleburn.

Evil hate the sunweeds, and those things in between shrunk back across the veil. It feared the townfolk real good, too.

"You alright, Anny-belle?" I asked. "No wit to fear, little one."

But the girl had gone, frightened off with the rest. My knot-stick was lost in the tangle of growth and twisted wood beams before the village, lost to my blasted sight. I crawl back to camp, real slow-like. The road made for treacherous travel, the day ever black save for those godawful little purple fleckles coming down like snow.

* * *

The camp was quiet without her questions.

I say to nobody, maybe Cotton: "It goes this way. Better this way." Work to do. I slept real long and good, and came back to my chapel. I had to work fast and strike true if the horseshoe would get atop the chapel by midnight.

Hammering is tough when your eyes are on the other side, no matter how well you can see the things that count. My ladder was lashed from trees the twig-folk shun. Green, strong, and light. I leaned it against my shed, iron shoe in hand. A copper nail between my teeth.

From the ladder, I took my first Old Man fall. For the first time I feel how old my bones were. Noonday sun glowed my face, matched by the warm hurt in my back. Who will feed Cotton? In all the dark, I see the ghost of his brother, Increase. I ask him, where you taking me, heaven or hell?

I felt needles in my legs, but they refused a budge. My fingers raked the dirt, trying to make my bony limbs do something. All sudden, my catspook Increase hisses, hair all a'hackle, and fades out smoky. Then I hear it.

Wailing. Awful dirgesong. The bog ladies were coming for me, sense my imposition.

For all the pow-wow and lecturizing, Hallow's Eve clean snuck up on me. I looked bogward, and I saw three greenly-bright figures getting brighter. Screaming in harmony. I plug my ears, hoping to buy a moment to say a lucky prayer before they take me. I wished I had my Book, even if I cannot read the damn thing.

Something landed light on my chest, kneading it like dough. He always played cute around the girl.

"Old Bones?" I heard.

The diregesong faded back to the bog.

* * *

Anny-belle dragged me to my cot. "Old Bones, why your legs gone limp?"

I asked her why she come back, as I tried to slap feeling back to my legs. "I'd never seen magic," she said.

"Magic!" I laughed. "There's no such thing as magic, child! 'Twas but a simple hexin'."

"You poked your stick to the ground, Old Bones, and pumpkins grew."

"Sunweeds," I corrected. "Stirs a great fear in the heart o' evil—evil what started to grip the townsfolk. Something big coming—"

"—Something is here, Old Bones. What about your horseshoe?"

I hand the shoe over to her, groaning through the pain. "I need my apprentice pow-wower to put it up there."

So she put it up there, while I just lay there below, lounging lazy as Cotton. I feel her on the roof, tap light, tap-tap harder. She worked fast and struck true, and the wet lightning funk drift down from on high and I know the charm sunk good. The purple thawed right off. Anny-Belle sat up there awhile, after the hammering stopped.

I could hear her down the ladder, stirring in my tent and rummaging bric-a-brac into sacks. I call out to her, and she squats defiant in my lump of buildedness. Don't ask Old Bones how he know, the squat were defiant.

"Where you going, little one?"

And she said: "Your knot-stick is at the town gate and the sun is going down, Old Bones. I'll say your words and knot my hands, snap each hex and trap you set. I'll tap the marbles, ring the bells, read your Book, grow the pumpkins, carve the faces and light the candles, knock the doors, trick the imps and offer sweets to the puckwudgies, make the teacup turtlefolk bow and hum opposite the bog ladies, and step backwards to the walking wolves."

I run figures in my Old Brain, and it all did seem solid. My whiskers quivered from pride. "Sunweeds," I rightened her. "They be sunweeds. Give me but a moment, for my legs to catch a breathe."

79

"Rest tonight, Old Bones." Cold fingers checked my forehead, and sounds left out the door, leaving the smell of dandelion and charcoal. My blasted legs made partners with my cursed eyes.

"You come back now, Anny-Belle. No chance you ready—get back here! Anny-Belle!" I howled Bones In The Wind. I sat in the chapel, hands on my head, and howled. When I finished, I wiped my eyes, and kept still. No sound. I climbed from the bench, feeling for the cold holy in the dirt. I sat here alone in the little sanctuary, and waited.

I spit the sunseed, I dig the marble, but each year I spit slower, dig slower. I'd wait up all night for Anabelle if I had to. She knew not all the rules, and the forest hungers.

Cotton sat on my lap. The autumn air whistled, and the crickets told me how late it were. I pulled on my arms to the doorway to the dark outside, never leaving the hum.

I watched Hallow's Eve descend, the little purple fizbits coalesce to new shapes, streaming in a blizzard from a rift in the sky. My vision opened from black-and-purple to a mosaic of color lit by the countless beasts living, dead, and never-was come out for Hallow's Eve. Something big was here.

* * *

In the night, the child is sleeping...

At some hour, I fell asleep curled up with Cotton, holy spit pooled below. The cat began his kneading my ribs.

"Good morning, Cotton. Morning, Old Bones."

I smelled a hot cup of Goodie Waxwick's tea, and I knew the townfolk survived the night. I murmured my own morning wishes and heard Anny-Belle put the food out for Cotton. So she says: "One last question, Old Bones."

"Last question," back says I.

"That's no pow-wow. Is it?" She placed the cup on the ground beside me, leafsteam and butter.

I met her eyes. Amid all the dark, I beheld them, bright and blue.

"Never were, kiddo."

Pine Blight

by Nico Harlakenden

> *The tree dreamt first, then the village.*
> *Only the thief awoke rich.*
> — Lapuden folk saying

On Lapuden's notice board, the winter laws still hung:

CURFEW,

FUEL RATIONS,

and the old favorite—

GOETY TO REGISTER GIFTS
OR PAY DOUBLE TITHES.

Someone had nailed a sprig of dead heather through GOETY.

Lue'lin Goety read it on her way to the Drift and kept walking. On the path, she paused to right a toppled bird-snare and cut the loop, freeing the captive.

"Eat worms, little jay," she said to the cold. A copper for the trapper, and the quiet knowledge she'd pay for the kindness again later.

The pines at the Drift called out to her about a fever. She found the source of their worry in a lichenous hollow and knew it at once.

But this one used to dream... Lue was certain of the fact, stopping at a gnarled pine.

The others rustled like sleepers. The trees hadn't said the words —not in a way a person would recognize—but they'd made it clear to her:

*Something's wrong with **that** one.*

And so Lue kneeled at the foot of the half-buried pine, cold patches seeping into her thick trousers as she rested on the knoll in the Marchwood.

This same worrisome tree had once warned her of the tuber famine last sowing season. Lue could feel the outline of that memory clinging to its roots like frost—faint and fading. A last sigh, preserved in bark and rain.

Its bark was leached of color. When Lue pressed one hand-sewn glove to the trunk, it exuded a curious dampness—as if the wood itself were sweating. She leaned closer, and to her dismay, discovered that it was runoff.

Sap.

But not the warm golden kind. It was a silver-gray and gave off a smell not unlike spent lye or wet brass. This was pure noetic metal, direct from the leyspring the grove.

"Well," Lue muttered. "You're not meant to be doing that."

The tree made no reply.

"Dross and dreamrot," she muttered, echoing the phrase her friend Corly used last week. "If it's not one, it's the other." She made a face and scraped her glove clean on a patch of stone. Corly and Lue had just recently argued for an hour by firelight over whether sap could sour.

Lue made a note of this in the margin of her working journal:

Pinus ???
SE end of the Drift.
No dreams. Bird- and squirrel-less.
Sap discolored. Lichen drained of color.
Possibly prophetic rot? Key features absent...

She sat back on her heels and frowned at it, which had historically proven effective with stubborn specimens. After several moments of deliberation, she retrieved a brass handled knife from her satchel—despite being pawned and repawned, she kept the blade sharp. She nicked the edge of the sap-streaked bark, and caught a small sample in a corked glass vial. The sap clung to the glass predictably.

*NB: recheck Vellor's notes re: sapsuckers & scrying disorders in conifers.

Gran's rule: what the ley gives, the body keeps in trace—enough to answer when called by name.

Lue rubbed her temple in thought—another migraine, right behind the eyes. She pinched her nose, racking her brain for any possibility but the pain settled in the way old women say children do—quiet at first, then rearranging furniture.

All leys provided magic. But the pines in the Drift sat over a prophetic leyspring. It had been acting strange since the smoke rose from the west, near Orven Vale. News came days later: The village had been razed by scouts of the Pompos Army. Realm-walkers, they said. With brass rings at their belts and booming voices stolen from the gods. Able to wield every type of magic in the world.

Lue hadn't told anyone, but her spells had begun to stutter since.

*NB: ley pulse irregular since smoke from Orven Vale.

A phrase surfaced in her mind—sharp, unexpected:

Death moving against death.

Lue's ink nib ripped through her notebook page and she froze. The dying pine's sisters reached out, sending first a message then an image:

Two young men in black cloaks walking across a

frozen lake; Dark shadows circling from beneath
the ice; A single, resonant CRACK—

The vision didn't release her. Beneath her glove a thorn she hadn't felt slid into the pad of her thumb. When she pulled away, the prick bled silver first, then red. The Drift had tasted her and filed her name. Somewhere behind Lue, a twig snapped in the underbrush.

A gust of wind disturbed the branches above as if the trees had collectively drawn a breath. Needles fell to the frost around her as a pair of jays startled and vanished into the deeper thickets.

She remained very still, hoping it was a hare—and not a Pompos mage soldier from her worst imaginings. Though her heart beat harder, she forced herself to breathe through her nostrils, cold air stiffening the soft tissue inside painfully.

When enough time passed that she was satisfied whatever intruder had skirted her knoll, she stood, brushing the frost from her knees. Trembling slightly, she held the vial to the light.

The sap shimmered as it pooled at the base of the vial. For a heartbeat, Lue'lin Goety saw her own face.

But then the eyes blinked.

And they weren't hers.

* * *

Vellor Ott'heling kept a scholar's cottage the way a magistrate keeps a gallows: orderly, inevitable, and never for his own neck. Moss obediently rimmed its roofline. Ivy was permitted to climb no higher than the lintel. The hedgerow was kept trimmed by a species of overbred hare which Vellor refused to name, on the grounds that naming things encouraged sentiment, which in turn encouraged mistakes.

Lue arrived ahead of twilight, sap-smeared and pink-nosed. She slammed the door open in her hurry and was greeted by the pleasant aroma of scorched nettle broth and disappointment.

"You're late," Vellor observed, without turning from the workbench. "I was beginning to think you'd been eaten by something philosophical."

"No such luck," Lue replied, removing her boots with the urgency required when entering Vellor's house. "A pine at the Drift is sick!"

"Sick?" Vellor repeated, turning from his work to meet the cyclone of frenetic energy. "Or merely out of sorts?"

"She's leaking silver, Vellor," Lue set the vial on the table between them like a chalice at an altar. Vellor slid a ledger toward her with two fingers.

RECEIVED: 4 coppers.
DEDUCTIONS: lateness, breakage,
Goety surcharge.

There was always a surcharge.

Existing costs extra when you're born wrong.

"And I heard—well. I *saw* something in it." She hesitated before continuing. There had been more—the strange dream-message, the frozen lake, the shadows beneath the ice circling like wolves. Two figures she thought she recognized—

Vellor turned, spectacles already slipping down his long nose. He regarded the vial as one might a spoonful of questionable soup.

"Sap discoloration can result from any number of soil deficiencies. Iron oversaturation. Tannin inversion. You recall the Copper-Bark Epizootic of '47?"

Something in Vellor's tone clipped her instinct to share the vision. Would he catalog it? Mistranslate it? Maybe worse. She'd only meant to warn someone. But she wasn't sure Vellor could see danger unless a decree of it arrived with a Guild seal, delivered on a platter by muscle and breastplate.

"I do. It did not involve a copse of trees sitting on a leyspring, that bled like saints and whispered in dead languages."

"You're romanticizing again, young lady," he dismissed. "A hazard of your particular, shall we say, temperament."

He meant, of course, mantics' temperament. He never said it directly. Too coarse. But Lue recognized it well and blushed.

Before the Lucentum led by Verifactors, before alchemists' elixirs, mage wars, and magic realm-keys for travel—and before a band of kings who called themselves the Guild—a gift like Lue's was a blessing in any village pressed up against the wild. Firekeepers, healers, dreamers, and crafters. Not yet threats to order.

But when the tides turned in the name of progress, the mantics were stripped of their possessions, marched to the edges of the map, and given the same name—Goety—as if to file them all under a single sentence.

Lue had carried that name her whole life. Like a crusted brand, shared by all and owned by none.

She folded her arms to console herself near the crackling fire nestled in the stove. "You know, there are other kinds of knowing besides categorization and boiling things until they surrender."

"*Sir,*" Vellor replied automatically and ignored the barb. He removed the cork from the vial and wafted the scent toward his nose like a courtier assessing a rare cask. He frowned.

"Brass and sulphur," he muttered. "This isn't pine sap."

"No," Lue rolled her eyes and shook the red wisps of curls from her eyes. "It's noetic runoff."

Vellor looked up sharply. Something flickered in his expression—annoyance, maybe. Or fear.

"That's a dangerous conclusion," he said, evenly. "The Guild frowns on spreading that kind of... speculation. Especially in public. If you suspect it is runoff from the ley, I must report it, and you know they'll come to quarantine the Drift."

The trees have never called me or my conclusions dangerous. Not even when I take samples. Lue folded her arms.

"The ley isn't dangerous," she said. "My grandmother said the land gave us a drop of its breath when we were born. That's why we're bound to the ley. Why it—"

Vellor's mouth tightened. "Old folklore. And here I thought you cared for the pines. Noetic runoff is a ticking timebomb."

"Maybe," Lue allowed. "But no one ever says what it actually is. Just what it can become. Potions! Weapons! Realm-keys!" She stared him down. "And I *do* care for the pines." *More than you.*

He pressed the cork back into the vial a little too quickly. "Romanticizing again," he muttered. "Listening to every addlepated whisper is how one becomes infected with nonsense."

"Or the truth," Lue narrowed her eyes.

There was a silence between them. Outside, the wind picked up again. It rattled the louvered shutters like crowbones at a crop field.

"The merchant last week said his brother saw a band of Pompos mages moving northeast from Seulesbourg," Lue arched her eyebrow, after a time. "They passed through Fendeine last week. Two necrem bound at the rear, hands wrapped in copper filament."

"Then I suggest you get back to collecting your ingredients, and keep your mouth shut, Goety. You're cheap, which is better than irreplaceable."

Lue left the cottage with four more coins than she came with, a ceramic cup of broth balanced in both hands, and another chide for good measure. Outside, the cold bit her flesh without the early Spring sun. It was the sort of damp night that clung to the bones and whispered of rheumatism to come if one wasn't careful.

The message from the trees—it felt urgent. At first, she'd thought about Anwel and Tersh: The necrem who worked the unsettled dead and their signature black cloaks. She should check on them in the morning.

A mist had curled low over the tree line. She wondered if the trees were still listening, if they'd whisper back tonight, when no one else would.

Lue sipped. Her breath left in soft puffs, blending with the rising fog. Somewhere in the woods, a whippoorwill gave a short, confused cry.

* * *

By morning, an alchemist had arrived from one of the great coastal cities—even her horses were clean-shod and citified, bearing the unmistakable scent of progress.

She was precisely the sort of emissary from the heart of empire the villagers imagined: polished, perfumed, and used to talking to audiences of slower listeners.

Her name was Maestra Embry.

Lue got caught in the crowd gathered to listen to the visitor. She glanced to the edges of those gathered, wondering if the twins had come to listen. But of course not. They were too smart for public places.

"I've come to study the natural wonders of your region, and teach to you the scientific wonders of ours in Caer Dolwythe," she announced at the square. "There are fluctuations in ley patterns in the pineways: symptoms of environmental stress. Most unnatural—and most correctable."

The villagers were polite, of course. One must be, when someone arrives with a wagon marked in Guild etching, no fewer than three degrees from the Academy, and a recommendation from the Western Exchequer.

"How can you tell?" asked a cantankerous old man beside Lue, pointing the end of his oak cane at the visitor like a weather-worn wand.

Maestra Embry smiled and unfastened a padded case. The villagers leaned in.

Inside, cushioned like a newborn, lay six glass ampoules, each filled with a liquid that shimmered faintly between crimson and gold.

"This," she said, "is khreus."

A hush fell.

Khreus. No one here had seen it in person. There had been stories—of course—but only in the way one speaks of distant plagues.

It was said to be alchemy perfected: heavily refined noetic metal, blended with sacramental reagents, then sealed and blessed. Said to enhance magic, extend life, rewire the rules of all Daedalos.

It looks, Lue thought as she scrunched up her nose and squinted, *like something bled from a god and left to ferment.* Her mind wandered—to the trees at the Drift and the vial she'd tried showing Vellor.

Lue's fingers brushed the vial inside her satchel. She thought briefly of Anwel and Tersh—wherever they'd gone. Even if they didn't know what this was, it was a message for them. She hadn't seen them in days, but they were never far from whatever magic went awry.

She'd only met the twins a few times. Twins from the coast, quiet, strange folk with too-bright eyes and voices that always seemed to echo. No one ever really got close. Even she hadn't dared ask what they kept in the lacquered vials tucked into their belts, or why the air grew sweet and metallic when they sang.

She stepped forward instead of away.

"And what exactly is it made from?" she asked, lightly. The crowd gave her substantial space and watched for any reaction from the alchemist. The midwife rolled her eyes and groaned.

"Oh, the forest girl, *again*."

Embry glanced up anyway, already smiling. "Noetic metal."

"Extracted how? From what?"

"From any number of magical sources," Embry said.

"Like leys?"

"Sure—"

"And it's being distributed as... medicine?"

"As preventative tincture," Embry corrected. "In the presence of ley instability, even modest supplementation can stabilize minor gifts of manteia: fire-sense, dreamflight, the like. Your own senses, even.

"Eventually," Embry added with a bright tone, "the Guild hopes to offer collection sites—the perfect answer to those blasted Pompos mages and their loathsome, greedy desires."

Most of the crowd nodded, not comprehending. An old farmer spat to the side and his wife clutched a medallion at her neck.

Lue blanched at their compliance. She tried another tactic.

"So you're saying the ley is unstable?"

"Yes," said Embry. "Very. All because Pompos mages treat the ley like a feast—gorge and leave rot behind. The Guild treats it respectfully, like a covenant."

Lue smiled then—a small, dry thing—and reached into her satchel. "Then you may be interested in this."

She lifted the corked glass vial into the light. She held her breath.

The villagers leaned closer.

Inside, the sap shimmered—silver, slow-moving, faintly luminous.

"From a pine at the Drift," she said. "It bled when I touched it. The forest has gone quiet!" She let that hang.

"Sounds like the kind of thing those necrem twins would pull," someone muttered behind Lue. "Poison trees to make us afraid."

Embry did not move. But her smile sharpened.

"That is deeply troubling," she said, turning to the villagers with just the right shade of concern. "Then our timeline advances," Embry's voice was precise enough to cut paper. "Stage one leybleed confirmed at the Drift. Origin vectors are plural—anthropic, martial, and archaic. You're lucky we're early." She turned the crowd as if it were on a spit. "Stabilization begins today. Registration prevents rationing. Refuse, and we triage without you."

And sell the rest by weight.

She turned back to Lue—soft, gracious.

"Thank you, Treeguard Goety, for your vigilance. I'll be sure to mention your contribution in my report."

Lue stood in the square, the vial still glowing in her hand. She had tried to light a signal fire. Instead, she'd handed her a proclamation.

The crowd dispersed slowly. Some paused to admire Embry's instruments again, others whispered about registration. Khreus ampoules were already being compared, commented on—*Like spices in a market.*

Lue turned to go.

"Treeguard."

She stopped.

Embry stood a few paces behind her, her expression unreadable.

"A word," she said.

Lue waited, chin lifted.

Embry stepped closer. She didn't lower her voice—but somehow, no one was listening.

"That sample of yours," she purred, "is exactly the kind of early detection that makes field assignments like mine worthwhile."

"I didn't give it to you."

"No," Embry said. "But you gave it to the assembly. And really—wasn't that the point?" The alchemist tapped her quill to her parchment and returned to the crowd.

Lue didn't answer. A fishmonger's wife tugged her toddler behind her skirt as they passed Lue. That quiet, practiced motion taught in bad winters: don't touch the Goety if you want all your fingers in spring.

Behind her, a familiar voice spoke—soft, local, kind.

"Well. Least they caught it early, right?" said Old Darnic, nodding sagely. "Good on you for bringing her the sample. That was smart."

Lue turned her head slowly.

"But I didn't mean to bring it to her."

"Sure, sure," he said, waving a hand. "But you got her what she needed. That's what counts."

He smiled and walked on.

She stood there, the vial a little heavier in her hand than it had been before. All that time in the Drift, listening to the sap whisper back. And now it would be boiled down, sold off, praised as a breakthrough. Used in the war. Progress wore a friendly face and clean hands. The easy minds of Lapuden had always trusted clean hands in their distraction with survival—hands that never split wood, never dug graves, never came away green from the pines. Clean hands pass the laws; stained hands bear the fines.

Lue had to get out of the square. She was about to slip past the last of the milling villagers when someone touched her sleeve.

A shock of buttermilk hair over tanned, soot-smudged skin told her at once it was Corly Pell, the cooper's younger son—though no one called him that anymore.

A mantic in his own right, Corly had burned his first spell into the side of a barn wall when he was twelve, and spent the next six months banned from open flame and public gatherings. These days he was known simply as "the katai"—in the slightly wary tone one might use to speak of changing weather or foxes in the henhouse.

He was tall and a little too angular, all elbows and bright nerves. Unlike Lue, he had not been required to adopt the mantic surname Goety. He'd been permitted to keep Pell, along with a degree of local forgiveness for the accidents that tended to follow him—thanks largely to his family's municipal standing.

"She's not measuring soil disruption," Corly said under his breath, nodding toward the alchemist's wagon. "She's mapping ley fractures. The old kind." He didn't touch her, wouldn't in public, but he angled his body so any thrown stone would meet his ribs first. He slid his palm along his own ribs once, a quiet oath: 'mine to break before yours.'

"To track the bleed in the Drift?" Lue asked quietly.

He gave a short, grim nod.

"Or to find the ones that haven't started bleeding yet."

Lue's throat tightened. Her trees in the Drift sat over a smaller ley spring. There were countless others across the continent.

"She's not just collecting then," she said. "She's prospecting for a greater harvest."

"They've made the Pompos into boogeymen," Corly glanced behind him, "so they can get to the ley first and act as saviors. The Guild doesn't want the magic the Pompos mages are using to stop—they just want to be the ones to own it."

"That khreus is just one bottle they'll pour it into," Lue muttered. She looked up at him—at the flicker of leylight still echoing behind his eyes.

"When you said 'the old kind'," she asked softly, "did you mean a god ley?"

"Maybe," Corly said. "I think some of them might even remember when gods learned to speak."

Lue leaned in, turning an ear, knowing there was more. She didn't break eye contact. Corly flushed and unfolded his arms.

"I... may have felt one. Near the hollow east of Bramble's Watch. There's a Crackle there now. It wasn't there last week. I had nothing to do with it," he added quickly.

Lue narrowed her eyes. The moment for level-headedness had passed. His eyes shimmered like leylight on shallow water. Something in him was vibrating too close to the surface. She didn't know what it meant yet, only that the forest would have noticed.

"*The* Crackle?"

He gave a nervous shrug. "I didn't go in. Just got near it. Just far enough to feel my thoughts go sideways."

That stopped her cold.

Crackles weren't just disturbances—they were tears in the skein of the world. Places where the ley frayed, and other realms brushed close enough to breathe on you. Most only heard about them in folktales, whispered rumors, or warnings etched into rusted boundary signs. Only katai mantics—like Corly—could conjure one. And even then, almost never by accident.

She stared at him. "You're sure?"

He nodded. "The air smelled wrong. Like heat after lightning, but inside your head. And time got... lagged. Like I was walking behind myself."

Despite everything—the fear, the blight, the quieting trees—Lue felt it: the spark of something old and wild catching behind her ribs. Years ago Corly had stood between her and three drunk millers and said, very politely, "Gentlemen, I make worse mistakes than you on purpose." They'd laughed and stopped harassing her. That bravery returned.

"We have to see it," she said.

Corly blinked. "You—you want to go in?"

"I want to know what's trying to get out," she whispered. Her voice had gone a little breathless. "If it's a Crackle, that means something's bleeding through over that strong ley you felt."

He hesitated, then gave a lopsided smile. "Before sunrise?"

She nodded. "If it's still there, we're going through it."

Corly looked both terrified and thrilled.

"Do you... want some tea for the Drift? I brought some."

She smiled despite herself. She showed him the canteen on her hip.

"Already tipped by Vellor. But thank you. I need to find Anwel and Tersh before I head out."

"I haven't seen them in a couple of days, but the western trails felt like some kind of necrem magic had been performed. Like a bell'd been struck beneath the soil and leaves. I bet they're not far."

They parted ways near the square. On her way back toward the woods, Lue passed a pair of village boys crouched near the baker's cart, whispering with wide eyes and crooked grins.

"—dragged off," one boy finished.

"Did you see the copper on their hands? Like bird traps."

"Mantics, ya'know. Always poking into things."

"Necrem don't poke. The go below and drag back the dead."

The first boy made a warding gesture. "My mum says they smear poison in their eyes and dance till they see shadows."

"That's when they speak to 'em. The dead, I mean."

"They say they needed to take'em for defense. To keep the ley from splittin'."

"Gran says necrem swap your husband's soul for a demon's." The boy grinned, brave in daylight.

Lies travel farther than rites. Lue ran to the western trails.

* * *

Memories popped one by one into her memory as she ran.

Odd, but kind.

Dressed always in black.

Anwel had laughed at her jokes during a harvest fire once—short, self-conscious, delighted by its own awkwardness. It had made her feel briefly luminous.

The elders swore they'd seen two black-cloaked figures night fishing on the winter lake last week—ice groaning beneath them rousing busybodies from troubled sleep. The vision had to be about them. Only Lue found no trace of them in the western trails other than the vibration in the soil Corly mentioned.

Copper on their hands... Lue couldn't help but picture the two in their black cloaks being dragged away by a wagon, *But which one?* There were many overlapping tracks on the well-traveled trail. There was nothing she could do.

She thought of Anwel's haunting laugh while working the Drift.

Thought of it while collecting sap from three more trees—each showing signs of the blight.

Thought of it while kneeling in moss that no longer pulsed beneath her touch.

The trees had no further message for her.

By nightfall, she had cried her tears freely among her dying charges and had nothing left but silence. When the cold got to be too much, Lue went inside and lined her boots under the door-latch. She removed her brass knife from her satchel and placed it in the rafters where a hand couldn't find it by polite accident. Small survival tricks, like counting exits as opposed to suitors.

She sat alone in her small thatched hut with its clay-dug floor, a ceramic cup going cold beside her. She thought about the arrival of the alchemist. *Too clean, coordinated.* And now—her friends being rounded up like misbehaving livestock.

Lue was supposed to guard the trees. The village trusted her with their blight and not their bread. Behind her, in the center of the village, the Maestra's caravan glowed with soft golden lamps and inaudible incantations. Ahead, the forest waited.

* * *

It was Corly who showed her the way.

They went before dawn, when the world was liminal and fewer things objected to being crossed—streams, snowbanks, hopefully the Crackle. Marchwood was brittle with frost, and their breath came in long threads that hung in the air, reluctant to vanish.

Corly walked a little ahead and kept turning back, as if he wasn't entirely sure she'd follow.

"You can feel it before you see it," he said. "Like your thoughts are, I dunno, humming the wrong key."

And she could. The closer they got, the more her senses strained—not in fear, but like a limb trying to reach for a missing digit.

Corly helped her down to the roots. "Easy," he said again. "Just breathe."

Lue blinked. The air was wrong now. The forest—different.

"The twins," she murmured. "Anwel and Tersh... they weren't on the western trails."

Corly went still.

"I checked their camp yesterday after chores," he said, voice low. "Everything still there."

Lue closed her eyes. The trees had tried to warn her. She hadn't understood in time.

They crested the hill above Bramble's Watch and found the Crackle.

It looked like a fiery hoop hung in the air—a shimmer, a warp, a glass lens laid over the forest that made all the trees beyond it lean too sharply and flicker at their edges.

Lue stood in awe as the distortion before them sizzled and snapped. She had read once—in one of Vellor's banned compendia—that a kataigem's Crackle was more than a spell. It was a fingerprint. A gate with a soul.

Corly's soul, here, had burned a hole in the world. But she thought twice before saying as much to her friend. Kataigem were said to tear reality open—once, maybe twice, in a lifetime. That Corly had done it without trying made her stomach twist.

The ley beneath their feet pulsed once, as if acknowledging her presence—or warning her away.

Corly hesitated.

"I didn't go in last time."

"That's fine," said Lue. "We'll go in together." She took his hand. Crossing the boundary, they stepped into the shimmering mirror finish and discovered it had a warmer temperature.

The air inside the Crackle was scorched and thin, and everything flickered at a fraction of a second with each movement. The sky was a churning saffron-gray, shot through with specks like watching a blizzard swirl through a small cottage window. The fire of the Crackle did not burn inside at least. It touched and connected—everything.

Corly and Lue exchanged glances, squinting against the air. Corly reached toward the Crackle's edge and the fire bent away from his fingers. Beneath their feet, the earth was pocked with craters. The trees were charred but standing, transfigured. A mantics' grove, gone to bone. The unseen rivers of the ley lines moving beneath them sang in a frequency too high to endure. Lue seized her own ears with her thick gloves in an attempt to drown out the noise.

In the center of the field stood a figure bound in copper lattice. A black-fingered necrem.

Tersh!

His face was streaked purple with some vile tincture. His hands twisted in ritual motion. The air around him was thick with stuttering ghosts—warriors pulled from death like fish from poisoned water. They screamed, but not in human tongues. Their bodies flickered. Their weapons bent when brandished.

"He's summoning the spirits buried in the grove!" Corly hissed, lifting one of her gloves from her ear as the sizzle of leyfire and undead shrieks rose around them. Lue could only stare.

Behind the necrem stood another figure.

A man.

He was tall. Unnaturally still.

The kind of man who looked as though he belonged in a Guild oil painting—hand on the hilt of something wicked, sunlight catching on his cheekbones, nation burning just out of frame. His face was handsome. Strong-jawed, finely carved, with silver just beginning to thread his dark hair. The kind of face that could sell salvation. Or empire. *Or any other flavor of your own demise.*

His voice was velveted brass as he yelled a command to the necrem and turned slowly to face Lue and Corly. He smiled. A slow, deliberate expression, smooth, persuasive—the kind meant to overturn convictions. But it was the tongue behind the smile that unsettled her.

It was too pale. Too fluid. Not clumsy or even monstrous—just expert. It moved with the elegance of a borrowed habit, like it had learned a hundred ways to kiss and convince before it ever belonged to him. Like it had whispered prophecy in a holier mouth, once. Lue's own mouth dried.

Lue's manteia twisted beneath her ribs, like a thread being yanked the wrong way. It was like someone reaching inside her chest, gripping her gift like a disobedient animal, and twisting. She did not see what was wrong. But her magic remembered it.

Her nose started to run, her stomach churned. But worse—her manteia wouldn't stop stuttering in her body. Like it had inhaled something wrong. Something was dimming inside her.

In one gloved hand he held something brass and glimmering. Small diamonds and metal spires fanned out from a suspended bauble—the size of an eye, the color of regret—glowing faintly blue.

A realm-key, Lue recognized the weapon immediately. The shape of invasion, and the signature of Pompos. The last passing merchant had described them in tones of greed and envy, burning the schematics in her brain. But this one seemed different.

In place of the swirling liquid metal that powered these magic baubles:

Flesh.

It twitched inside the glass.

And Lue understood, in the way one understands a wildfire too late to run, that this man had taken something divine and made it useful.

Stolen, she corrected herself.

A reliquary. Though still alive. He raised the key as if to toast her. And then the world—the Crackle itself—screamed.

Corly yanked Lue out and the Crackle shuddered before quickly closing. One moment she was watching a dream made of horror, the next she was back in Marchwood, vomiting bile streaked with silver onto the roots of a tree. Corly steadied her.

The twins. The message. The shadows beneath the lake.

He had taken them. Because she hadn't warned them in time.

"Easy," he said, holding her upright. "You were... bleeding. From the nose. Just a bit."

Her head rang. Her stomach twisted. Her soul felt threadbare.

"I saw him," she said. "I saw what's coming. And it isn't just for us."

"Who was that?"

She didn't answer. Couldn't.

The words were still crawling inside her—words shaped by a ghostly tongue and some unknown magic.

It's like it was pulling something out of me... She looked at the frost-covered forest and for the first time, she did not feel welcome there.

* * *

Lue returned to the village just past midday. She had no recollection of the walk back.

The trees had gone completely still. That was the first thing she noticed. Their presence was still there—vast, old, unblinking—but it no longer touched her back. She reached out with her mind the way she always had, like extending a hand through mist. But their thoughts were gone. Her gift, once a tide that cradled her, now felt like rot beneath the gumline. Her manteia, once a soft tide beneath her ribs, had thinned to a whisper.

The square was crowded with polite chaos. The alchemist Maestra Embry stood beneath a canopy, discussing dosage ratios of khreus with a small group.

One of the elders who'd once banned necrem rites during the new year fast held up his sample thimble with trembling pride.

"Sin is what poor folk call advancement before it hires them," the elder mocked, lifting his thimble.

A week ago that elder had called Lue 'a curse on Lapuden' to her face. Now he stood nodding, as if ladling alchemy down children's throats was an act of stewardship. She imagined knocking the sample from his hand. Instead she smiled, a mean little private thing she hated as soon as she donned it.

"Better an alchemist's vial than a necrem's trick," someone announced to general nodding. "At least the vial's pure."

Samples were being handed out in small, wax-sealed thimbles, marked with symbols in warning as though they were simply another tincture. Lue spotted a child sipping khreus-steeped tea from a painted cup. Her eyes glowed faintly at the edges.

Maestra Embry beamed.

"It's only experimental, of course," she said, loud enough for the crowd to hear. "Part of the Guild's new initiative—Ethical Access Protocols. Full transparency, of course."

The crowd muttered in consideration for its approval.

Lue stood at the edge, stunned. No one looked afraid. They were grateful. Deep in Embry's eyes was an echo of the Man with the Key—the same hunger, just different faces.

Someone bumped Lue's elbow—a well-meaning uncle, one of Vellor's patients.

"You alright, dear?" he said. "You look a little pale. You should try the blend. My back hasn't screamed once since morning."

She fled before she let slip a scream. Voices murmured their disapproval behind her. Someone spat near her heel. Never at her, they were too good for that sordid behavior—only at the ground she'd touched. *Neat little theology: hate the footprint, praise the boot.*

Vellor was waiting at the homestead, pruning dried seedpods into glass jars.

"You've been gone half the day," he accused.

"I crossed into the Crackle," Lue huffed without preamble. "There's a siphoning site near Bramble's Watch. They had Tersh *chained* there! Summoning ghosts like puppets up out of the ground! And a heinous Pompos mage was there—he had a godpiece hanging from his waistcoat!"

Vellor froze mid-prune.

"That's a very serious accusation," he said slowly, rising to his feet. He examined her head to toe.

"It's not an *accusation*, it happened!"

"It's not the priority, Goety. Guild proceedings are underway. What they *really* sent Maestra Embry here for is to negotiate with the Pompos delegation on official grounds. No more backroom dealings—they're forming an accord—"

Her breath caught. "A what?"

"A trade agreement," he said. "In exchange for limited noetic access, the Pompos have agreed to restrict their operations to select ley springs. They've even committed to refining their goods off-site."

"Goods?" Lue shook her head, tears forming. "You're giving them permission to bleed the village dry! To make what I saw—normal?"

Vellor's expression hardened. "That's the problem with mantics like you. You take your gifts personally. The ley doesn't belong to anyone! It's a resource, not a religion. That's why the Guild never approved your advancement..." He clicked his tongue. The words struck harder than they should have. Maybe because she'd still hoped—deep down—that he was on her side.

"It's true!" she insisted. "You're siding with the Guild and the Pompos mages because it's convenient for *you*."

"No," he said, very quietly. "I'm siding with the future."

And that was when she realized—he didn't disbelieve her. He simply no longer cared. That was the secret, wasn't it? They didn't need to convince you it was right. Just that it was inevitable.

"Of course you are," she said. "The future was tailor made for you." She looked at the man she'd once called mentor and saw the future he meant—quiet, sanitized, dead on the inside.

"Close the door on your way out, Goety," he said, as if the word were a broom.

* * *

Lue found him at dusk, crouched near the roots of an ash tree outside her hut. He didn't look up when she approached—just kept tracing a rune into the dirt with the blunt end of a charred stick. It glowed faintly, fire held tight and low, trying not to burn.

"You're back," he shifted to let her sit.

"I shouldn't be," she sniffled, quickly drying her eyes. "Said I take my gifts too personally. That the ley isn't sacred—'it's a resource'. He said it like conventional wisdom." Corly knew who she meant. They passed a flask back and forth. Tea, or maybe something stronger.

"Anyone believe you?" He took her hand, removing her glove.

"No." She didn't resist.

Corly nodded. "I still do." He fished a strip of linen from his pocket, replacing the old bandage on her palm where the Drift had cut her yesterday morning. She gave his hand a squeeze.

"Poor Tersh. The Man with the Key, did you see the tongues?" she met his eyes at last. "In the Crackle. The one in his mouth *and* in one of the realm-keys, all magic. Blue. Still twitching."

He didn't flinch.

"Each a godpiece," he said softly. "For power."

She nodded. "He sealed something sacred—something that used to speak prophecy—into a tool..."

"And now it opens doors for him, to anywhere he wishes," Corly's mouth twisted at the injustice. "I'm not sure how to stop power like that."

They watched the grove sway. Or rather—not sway. The wind moved, but the trees barely answered. It was grief, she realized. Not fear of death, but grief.

"They're quieter," he shifted. "The trees."

"They're sick." Lue used a second stick to uncover emerging fiddleheads from the humus by their log.

"I think they're being made sick."

She looked up at him sharply.

"I think," he continued, "if you wanted permission to drain the ley, you'd first need proof it was already failing. Something to 'remediate.'"

"You think they're poisoning it—" Lue stopped. "Gods, I helped them!" The memory of her arguing in the village square with Maestra Embry returned like a wallop.

"Or maybe they're bleeding it just enough to justify real drainage. Like the alchemists do with the khreus vials—tap, spin, blame the patient for the bruise."

Lue looked down at her palms before wrapping them around her own ribcage. "I can barely reach my manteia anymore. It's like it's pulled back into the marrow."

He tilted his head. "You think it's just you?"

She pursed her lips. Corly was twisting the stick in his fingers.

"What if they're not just targeting the ley? What if they've figured out how to get to the... the somatic metal."

Lue furrowed her brow. "What's that?"

Corly hesitated. "It's in us," he said, quietly. "A trace of noetic metal from the ley, but in the body." Lue was near enough she could feel his shoulder grow warmer and smell the sting on his breath from the flask. "It's what anchors manteia to the body. Our bodies. It's how we touch the ley—and how it touches back. Without it, we're... blanks."

"I've never heard of it." Her voice was small from the creeping sense that she should have.

"You wouldn't," he said, gently. "It's not in the field guides. Just old Guild texts. Weapon forgers know. Alchemists, obviously. My tutor said it was too dangerous to discuss outside closed studies."

She sat back, stunned. "And you didn't think to tell me?"

"I didn't think they'd start harvesting it."

She didn't respond. The words felt like glass in her mouth. "They wouldn't—"

"Maybe they already have. Just not from us. Yet."

A crow passed overhead. It did not caw.

"They dosed a child," she added softly, eyes still watching the branches above them. "With khreus."

He went very still.

"I think we need to leave," he said. "Or at least—not stay quiet."

"I want to find Anwel."

He didn't hesitate.

"Then I'll walk with you." He stared at the grove a moment longer.

"I used to think I'd be the one to fix something," he said. "But maybe this time it's about surviving it."

* * *

The next day they took off west, in the direction of Orven Vale. They packed light but intended never to return to Lapuden.

They stopped near the wreckage of a wagon scorched at the edges, half-buried in ash and fern. Someone had tried to torch it recently. The ground was kicked up with boot marks, too many to count. Certainly not animal prints. Not quite military either.

Trade cart, likely. Lue spotted cracked clay tags that once marked captured goods. One still read serviceable, smeared with soot.

"He escaped," Corly said, voice low. "You think it was Anwel?"

"Maybe. Or someone like him." Lue crouched, brushing ash from a spatter of broken vials and uncovered a twist of copper wires. "Trader must've tried to sell a necrem to the Pompos—"

"And he set the thing on fire." Corly kicked a wheel rim. "Good."

They stepped into the treeline beyond the wreck, following the faint suggestion of movement—not tracks so much as feeling. The air thinned, grew cooler. Lue paused by a grove of young iron-pines—thin, green-streaked bark still glossy from new growth. She touched one.

Still nothing.

She stepped back. "Try," she encouraged, nodding to Corly.

He looked unsure. Embarrassed. "I don't... know how to do anything with it."

"You don't have to do anything. Just let it notice you."

He hesitated, then placed his hand flat against the bark. The reaction was immediate. The pine darkened beneath his palm—just slightly—and a low hum resonated in the soil, like a sigh rippling up through ancient sleep. The ley responded. Not eagerly, but it made it clear that it knew him.

Lue inhaled sharply. Her own manteia stuttered in her chest, a hollow ache throbbed behind her eyes at the seat of her weakened power.

"It listens to you," she said with respect.

"It scares me," he whispered. "Bit me once, when I was little."

"The ley bit you?" Lue tried to suppress a laugh.

He nodded, finally smiling. "I touched a warded grove. Circle I wasn't supposed to go near." He rolled up his sleeve, revealing a faint spiral scar above his wrist.

Lue leaned in, touching the mark. The ley beneath their feet pulsed again—sharper, quicker. Like it recognized both of them now.

Corly flinched. "It burns when you do that."

"I didn't mean to—"

"No," he cut her off. "Do it again."

She touched the scar again. The wind moved. His lips parted. The leyline hummed—but something deeper rose beneath it. Something she recognized from the Crackle. A buzz like a broken filament behind the veil.

"Lue," he said, breath tight, "I think if you keep holding on, I might—" But she'd already stepped away.

"Not here," she said. "Not for practice." He exhaled slowly and obeyed. "I didn't want to hurt you."

"You didn't," he whispered, catching his breath. She stared at his scar. Then at her own tingling fingertips.

"In the Crackle," Corly rubbed the back of his head, "when your nose bled—it wasn't just blood."

Her breath hitched. "What do you mean?"

He watched her eyes. "It was crimson-gold. Like khreus." She went still.

"Was it...?"

Corly dipped his chin. "I think that's what somatic metal looks like."

"Somatic metal," she tried the new word out. She couldn't help but touch her fingers to the bridge of her nose.

"I think... I think that's why alchemists and weapons forgers know about it," he looked at his hands. "Why it's kept so secret. I think they use the metal to ply their trades." Lue finally realized what Corly was saying. They stood in silence for several breaths.

"The Man with the Key, he called to my manteia with his own magic. And I—" Her voice broke. "I answered."

"Not with all of it," Corly insisted. "Just a few drops."

"But how do we know how much we have?" Lue's eyes pleaded with him, clapping a hand to his arm.

Corly didn't know.

The ley shifted beneath them, listening.

* * *

They found the necrem kneeling beside a body.

It lay cradled in the roots of a pine—freshly dead, still warm, too whole for the forest to reclaim. A woman in her thirties, maybe older. No decay, no contusions. Just the slack quiet of a life unstitched too soon.

Anwel didn't flinch as they approached. His face was hollowed with fatigue, eyes ringed dark.

"I didn't steal her," he said.

"We didn't accuse you," Corly said gently.

"But most would." His voice was hoarse.

He turned back to the body. His hands moved with practiced reverence—blackened fingertips not quite touching, tracing above her skin as though reading the heat still held beneath.

"What are you doing?" Lue asked, softly now.

"Listening," Anwel murmured. "Sometimes the manteia hums a little longer. If the pneuma hasn't split apart, and the body agrees—just agrees—I can return the breath. But only for a little while."

"It's not permanent?" Corly asked.

Anwel shook his head. "Not unless you force it. And I won't." His eyes flicked up to meet theirs. "We're not meant to steal from death. Only borrow. Long enough to say goodbye. Or to stop something worse."

What the ley gives, the body keeps in trace—enough to answer when called by name, Lue remembered.

"We borrow, or we become thieves," Anwel pressed his palm to the woman's sternum. For a moment, nothing.

Then her chest rose—shuddered, once. A tremor passed through her limbs. A gasp. Her eyes fluttered open. They weren't empty. But they weren't entirely bright either.

"Mareth," Anwel whispered. "Just a moment. Hear me."

Her gaze found his—then Lue's, then Corly's. She smiled, a brief happiness before the weeping overtook her.

Lue turned away, throat tight, as Mareth embraced the necrem. The sight of the softness and ache was too much.

The breath left Mareth moments later, a sigh at the end of a song. Anwel cradled her back into stillness. Her face, now, was peaceful. Like she'd remembered something worth dying with. Like death could be kind.

Anwel sat back on his heels.

"There's always a cost," he said. "I gave her some of my metal to bridge the current. She gave me the last of her wishes."

He opened his hand.

A bead of gold glimmered in his rough palm—small as a tear, flickering faintly. Already fading.

"You can do that?" Lue whispered.

Anwel didn't answer right away.

"Only if you still believe in leaving with less than you came with," he said at last. "And most don't."

* * *

The attic smelled of old flour and drying herbs.

Lue sat cross-legged beside Corly under the sloped eaves, knees brushing. Both of them listened for village sounds below. Anwel slept in a far corner finally, relinquishing his mourning and the tight grip to memories of his younger brother Tersh.

Lue whispered, "What he did back there..."

"I've never seen someone give part of themselves like that," Corly replied.

She nodded. "It shimmered in his palm. Like it wanted to move, to go. Like it knew Mareth…"

"He said you never come back the same. From death." A long pause.

"He didn't flinch. He gave a piece of himself to bring her back a moment of peace. I don't know if I could do that…"

"You already did," Corly's eyebrows knit together. "At the Drift. When you bled in the Crackle."

"That wasn't a choice," she muttered, rubbing her arms. "That was my body betraying me."

Outside, the bells of second watch chimed faintly. The sound carried like memory over the clay roofs and dark fields.

"We should sleep," she said. "We leave before the third bell."

Corly settled in on his side next to her, brow furrowed in thought. "You think he'll make it?"

Lue didn't answer at first. Her eyes found the low flicker of lantern light spilling up from the stairwell, tracing patterns over the rafters above Anwel's borrowed cot.

"I think," she said finally, "if we don't help him—we won't make it either."

* * *

The birch lane out of town lay gray-blue in the pre-dawn hush.

Anwel walked between them, silent but steady. His coat was patched at the elbows, loaned boots from the miller mismatched, but he walked like someone with nothing left to fear.

"Once we clear Splitrock Ridge," Lue murmured, "we'll be beyond their patrols."

Corly nodded. "The miller has food and a water pouch stashed in the mossy hollow. We'll get to the border trail."

They turned a corner near the grain store and froze.

A figure blocked the path. Oilcloth cloak, polished boots. A minor brass key gleamed at his belt.

The Pompos scout tilted his head like a curious dog. "Leaving early?"

Anwel jumped back. Lue moved herself between them.

"Morning walk," Corly said. "Lovely time of year."

The scout's grin was all perfectly even teeth when he eyed the copper wire remnants on Anwel's wrists—they hadn't the tools or time to remove them. "This one's not supposed to be walking. He's tagged."

"He's leaving," Lue said evenly. "That's all."

The scout's hand brushed the key at his waist. "You know what we use necrem for, don't you?"

She didn't reply.

"The ley's sick," he went on. "Too many corpses clogging the flow. When the fighting starts for real..." He looked at Anwel. "We'll need handlers, to drive them. We need stirrers."

"That's why you're reanimating the fallen," Lue whispered.

"Oh, not *ours*," the scout said with ease. "Ours are sanctified. We'll use yours."

Corly moved first. A burst of heat and flame lanced out, catching the scout's side. He reeled, snarling, but not before raising the brass key and flaring a red bolt into the sky.

"Go!" Anwel barked. "Now!"

They ran. Off the lane, through damp underbrush, branches lashing their arms. Breath tore at their lungs and behind them, bells began to rise like a sickness catching fire.

Only when the sound of pursuit blurred into the wind did Lue risk speaking.

"I think we just declared something," she panted.

Corly's grin was a grim thing, fierce with knowing.

"Yeah, I think we did."

* * *

They reached the fifth village—Naldemere—with snow in their boots and necrem at their heels.

Anwel and seven more refugees to shepherd to the coast and escape across the sea. If rumor was to be believed, there was an outpost to the North in Conwy Rhos, and a band of Necreos priests to the west across the

Emn.

The pass above Naldemere was narrow, ancient, and almost certainly haunted. Which made it perfect. The eight necrem they guided—silent and long-eyed—had chosen it themselves, murmuring ice-prayers to the air between breaths.

Lue and Corly had learned not to ask which dead walked with them.

Lue paused mid-step up a rock ledge. A wave of nausea—too brief to matter, too sharp to ignore—passed through her. She shook it off. Corly's hand lingered a second too long at the curve of her stomach after helping her up. They said nothing.

The mountains were clean and cold. Lue could almost believe they'd done it.

Then the wind changed. Then it stopped, the soundless moment that follows breath and precedes a scream.

And he arrived. He did not step out from the trees or descend from the sky like a message from the gods. He was simply there, where no one had been a heartbeat before.

He wore a high collar and layered robes threaded with a flickering sigil—a Pompos crest. A brass ring of many reliquaries glittered at his side like an ostentatious rosary, each glowing, holding within something twitching like hearts of the unborn.

The last flicker of manteia buckled in Lue's chest. It wasn't just fear. It was recognition. Her somatic metal recoiled behind her eyes, the ley-thread in her bones curling in on itself. Her own name trembled, half-erased by his presence.

"Travelers," he said, with unearned warmth. "Isn't the air *clear* up here?" His tongue, pale blue and slightly too large for his mouth, pulsed like a second heart. A small, terrified jolt pressed upward under Lue's ribs—private, undeniable.

Corly moved protectively between her and the mage. "Who are you?"

The man placed a large hand against his own chest. "A formal question. I approve." He smiled, broad and terrible. "I am called Bluetongue. You may have heard of me. Though not by name, I suspect."

Lue stared at him. "You're the one taking them. The necrem."

"Yes."

"Why?"

Bluetongue's face lit with sincere surprise. "Because I need them." He gestured lazily toward the necrem. "Each one's a conduit. A bridge. A ritual vector with one foot in death, and one in breath. The ley remembers them. The dead listen. What kind of fool wouldn't reap the benefits of that?" He wiggled his fingers circling them, playful as a well-fed cat.

"They're people." Lue's voice was hoarse.

"So are you," he said. "Just be satisfied I'm not harvesting you. Yet." He let that settle. "You mantics are at the bottom of the food chain," he continued. "When you die, pneuma is fresh—newly loosed—it's wild. Volatile! But we Pompos mages?" He tapped his chest. "We bind it, call it, channel it. And *I*... make it useful."

"Into what?" Corly asked. Bluetongue smiled wider.

"Keys." He trailed his long fingers through the baubles at his belt.

Lue recoiled. "We're not even at war!"

"You *are*," Bluetongue sang. "You just haven't read the declaration." He pulled a key from his ring. Shining and polished, studded with sapphire.

"The sea carries vaults," he said. "Minds too old to call gods, too proud to drown. Keys persuade them to open." He lifted a blackened key; inside, a sliver of a smaller, paler tongue twitched once, listening. "The somatic metal required for prophecy is prodigious. It was simply under-utilized."

Lue stepped forward. "You *stole* it?!"

"The oracle offered only passing sight. But who wants to risk mistranslation of one's fortune? Instead, I offered the power real employ. What's the difference?" Bluetongue winked. "Stealing is just taking what someone else won't use properly." Then, as if a thought occurred to him, his gaze slid back to Lue. Studying and pinning her.

"And you," he murmured, clicking his tongue. He took a step closer. "Busy girl. Warning others. Whispering truth where fear would serve better."

"They deserve to know—"

"You still want this to be a parable," his amusement was apparent.

"It's procurement. Flesh, voices, futures. I requisition; you relinquish, little Goety," he said, brushing her hair back from her cheek. "Because you're naïve, you think this is about good or evil. A *ro-mantic* notion." He laughed then—low and confident—and let his gaze drift, slow as venom, to her belly. He took a deliberate step forward. Lue's throat closed.

She hadn't told anyone. Not even Corly, not out loud. But the ley knew, and now Bluetongue did too.

"I'm merciful," he said softly, tilting his head. "Go home. Have your little mantic babe. Raise a happy, humble family... Replenish the stock." He smiled again—almost fond. "Or bury another one here on the trail."

Corly stepped forward, between them again—this time not just to protect her body, but her hope. His hand twitched, almost brushing her, before rising into a warding flare.

"You don't touch what kneels to the ley."

Bluetongue tilted his head, delighted. "Ah. Fire-boy speaks."

"How do you know that—"

"I smell it, boy!" Bluetongue straightened up, offended. "I'm the greatest Pompos mage alive. Born to take your *wasted* powers and make them *worth* something." His grin widened. "I am the future." He offered a courtly half-bow, as if the courtesy absolved the threat.

Corly's fists burned. "You've gutted the world and wear its flesh at your belt. When you run out of gods to steal from—what then?"

Bluetongue shrugged. "I'll make new gods. Ones that bleed when I call them."

Corly inhaled and became fire.

It was not the crackling warmth of camp or hearth. It was old fire, born from ley-thread and inner mettle, the kind of blaze that remembers every injustice. His hands flared gold and white, and the air itself bent backward.

He charged.

He struck Bluetongue like lightning at his very core—and was stopped like a toy. The Pompos mage raised one palm, jostled and struggling to catch his breath from the blow but smirking. Corly's body had frozen, suspended by threads of katai heat that were not his own.

"That," Bluetongue said, collecting himself, "was a mistake."

He flicked his wrist.

Corly's flames collapsed inward, sucked into the brass sigils ringing Bluetongue's wrist like a cage of tiny mouths. Corly's body dropped, smoking. Unmoving.

Lue screamed.

"Greedy little gods," Bluetongue whispered, straightening his robes and flicking his hair from his face. "Always hiding great power in people like you."

Then he raised his hand and the mountain split at its throat. The sky fell open. It rained glass—not shards, but sheets of molten green. Singing, burning, etching spiral glyphs into stone and root.

Anwel and the necrem behind them tried to raise wards, but the manteia turned in their hands—flickered and failed. One collapsed with her arms up, another knelt and wept blood. Many tried to run the rest of the distance to the icy summit.

The forest below ignited in a quiet whooshing sound, sending animals scattering. Trees did not crack or fall—they unwound, their fibers scorched into spiral patterns by the descending glassfire. Everything smelled like copper and finality.

Lue crawled to Corly's side. He was still breathing—but barely.

"Run," he rasped. "Warn them."

"I won't leave—"

"You have to. Or he wins!"

She looked up, searching frantically. Bluetongue stood against the onslaught of flaming glass globules, outlined in ruin. A bauble glowed at his belt and his hand was raised at the necrem, who stood frozen in time up the steep trail. They were held in place by his magic. He smiled back at Lue.

"Tell Caer Dolwythe. Tell Ixoras." He raised a second realm-key. "Tell them a real mage is coming."

And behind him, down the mountain, the sea churned—and *something* in it opened an eye.

Bluetongue vanished with the necrem.

* * *

Corly was dying.

Lue could feel it in the way his cracked skin cooled under her frantic hands as she cradled him, trying to cover his face from the hot rain, but the storm didn't stop.

Glassfire fell in shrieking sheets, carving beauty into ruin. And still, he hadn't let go.

"Lue," he rasped, voice laced with static. "Take the key."

She didn't understand at first. Then she saw it—what remained in his hand. Burned fingers, trembling—clutched the charred loupe, half-melted: A realm-key. He had stolen it from the mage in the scuffle. He raised his free hand, concentrating on the space behind her.

She shook her head, trying to lower his forearm. "You can't—"

"I have to." He pressed the hot key into her palm. "Let me get you out." He was already casting—shaking, gasping, eyes too bright. He leaned into the ley and whispered something only it would understand.

The world split open.

A seam of green lightning tore across the air—not up or down, but through. The Crackle burst into being, ragged and real. It buzzed with his fire. Burned with his name. It was his, and it would hold only as long as he did.

"Go," he cried. "I'll close this side once you're through."

She looked at him. "I love you."

His smile cracked like glass. "Run."

So she ran.

Through the green, into the breach. Through the Crackle. It was the world—but not. The trees were the same shapes, but rendered in eerie chlorite glow. The ground pulsed beneath her feet. Time rippled like silk behind her, burning key in hand.

Above, the storm of molten glass became distant—a memory, not a threat. The Crackle held her, carried her. Corly's fire burned into every flicker. She did not stop running until she saw rooftops ahead— moss-covered and still intact. A village untouched.Behind her, the Crackle sealed shut, and the world—at last—would be warned.

Sawdust to Sawdust

by Ryan O'Leary

The sun sets behind the trees,
 Next the bite of a stiff breeze,
 Gives the hint that you should leave,
 Lest your loved ones soon would grieve,

That your fate was so decided,
 Your head and neck thus divided,
 By axe or saw of Donovan Post,
Woodsman, Revenant, Ghost.

Like all the living dead,
 His blood once fresh, once red,
 His axe and saw, relentless gnaw,
 At trees' green hearts they cut and claw.

Determined was Post,
 Not to stop at almost,
 But to drag the forest's soul,
 Below any measure of whole.

At the undoing of his birth,
 His soul was ripped from off the earth,
 Not for his nature was he sentenced,
 But sins against ours—thus descended.

Some claimed a man so coarse, so uncouth,
 Did not deserve such brutal truth,
 That learning life did not mean forgiving,
 Nor made Post any less unforgiving.

Learning now that wooded life had merit,
 He vowed to protect it, not tear it,
 Post solved all problems with the swing of a blade:
 The trees rise to light; woodsmen fall to the shade.

Post was revived to atone from the soil,
 Seeking echoes of his past life's toil,
 If he finds them, another woodsman may find,
 His campaign axed, his soul enshrined.

Should the call of TIMBER! escape your lips,
 They'll find just your axe—and your fingertips.
 Any saps who wish him stopped,
 Post's grim mission sees them chopped.

Do you condemn this once-made man,
 And his grim and broken plan,
 Or is this rotted phantom, axe in hand,
 Someone you fear you might understand?

Bound

by Chelle G. Lowe

Steam curled like a summoning veil around Thea's body, every breath heavy with lavender and iron. The antique tub had always been her haven. Cast-iron, clawfoot, a relic of a quieter era. But tonight it served as an altar and offering. One nick of the blade, deliberate and unflinching, and calm turned to stillness.

Then to silence, to void.

Thea felt no fear as she waited, patient and calm.

Somewhere in that silence, a voice deeper than bone whispered:

"Come to me. Your home awaits."

When her eyes opened again, the world lurched—no longer porcelain and tile, but a twilight expanse without stars, sky, or sound. Wholly liminal and endless elsewhere.

He stood just beyond the veil of sight. He was tall, cloaked in an aura of living shadow. His eyes were obsidian, polished to a gleam, ancient as dark altars of Vorhaxan, the bewitched halls of the vanquished god.

She knew his name before it was spoken, as if it had long waited in the muscle of her tongue.

"Lord Onyx."

The sound of it stirred the air like incense smoke. Shivers danced down her spine as coils of shadow, neither vapor nor cloth, but something older—grazed her shoulder and slid, deliberate, to her hip bone.

"You have no idea how long I've waited for you," he growled low, his voice like a storm wrapped in velvet to soften the shiver. One of the tactile shadows, with a mind of its own, rose to stroke her throat, tilting her gaze to his.

"Waiting for me?" she asked, her voice a reed-thin tremble. Still, she made no move to pull away. Her body was frozen, her gaze transfixed. The fear began to creep in.

"Yes. You are the thirteenth vessel. The final seal. My bride of the Cold Light." A title, not a name. This was her destiny, etched in generational blood. "The daughters before you bore the burden but not the bond. You are the first to come willingly."

The shadows recoiled, only to return, pouncing with hunger. Thea didn't see him cross the space between them, but suddenly he was there, close enough to taste. Soot-black hair curled against his cheekbones. Smoke flickered like a halo.

Ash began to fall around them like rain.

His hands cupped her face, reverent.

"Thea." Her name fell from his lips like an invocation. "Say yes."

Then she was on her back—unsure if she'd been moved or if the world itself had turned beneath her. Shadows unfurled around her like silk ribbons, curling up her legs, coaxing them apart. She gasped as they passed the inner curve of her thigh, teasing the edge of something sacred.

"What... what are you doing?" she whispered, her voice no longer her own.

"Nothing permanent," he said, gaze solemn. "Not until you give me your word. Until you give me *you*." He leaned in, scent of smoke and something floral—night-blooming. "Say yes, and I'll make you mine."

His touch was patient and knowing. A smoky caress drew slow circles against her most tender flesh, lighting fires where only embers had lived. Her breath hitched. Her hands gripped air—then hair. His.

"You feel it," Onyx said. "The pull. You didn't come here by accident. You came because the bond called to you, across planes."

His body hovered over hers like an eclipse, his knee parting her again. His lips traced a path from the curve of her neck to the edge of her jaw, mapping her like conquered land.

"Be mine," he whispered. "Take your place at my side."

She arched when the shadows slipped deeper, when his mouth found the center of her. Her body keened like a lyre string plucked too hard. Every nerve turned into a string of pleasure.

"Gods—" she gasped, every syllable dissolving into moan. "I'm—Lord, I'm—"

"I know," he said darkly, "I can feel you clenching around my shadows, darling."

When she broke apart, it was like unbinding a spell. Her orgasm was less an ending than an unlocking. A vow. A *yes* she hadn't yet spoken aloud.

He kissed his way up her trembling body. "Exquisite," he murmured. "You positively bloom for me."

"I've never... not like that." Her hands roamed his chest, tracing muscle, soot-smudged skin demarcating every touch they shared, each press of flesh-to-flesh in the raining ash. And the ache of something not quite mortal. "I've never felt—"

"You will feel. Again and again."

He positioned himself at her entrance, shadows wrapping his hips like anointed chains.

"Say yes," he murmured his demand, his forehead resting against hers. "Seal it. Let me give you the life your soul remembers."

A memory surged: Joy turned sour, duty twisted into ritual, a girl's life bartered in silence. The knife that pricked her mother's womb. The chant beneath the birthing bed.

And now this.

His mouth claimed hers before the doubt could return. The kiss was not gentle. It was a ritual. She opened to him with a gasp.

"Yes," she breathed into his lips. "Onyx."

And with that, he filled her.

They cried out in unison, not just from pleasure but from power—something electric and older than either of them surging through the bond. His eyes locked on hers as he began to move, slow and commanding.

The shadows around them tightened, cloaking them in black.

Each thrust echoed a vow: claimed, remade, forbidden.

Her body rose to meet his, not out of instinct, but fate. The tether between them tugged, binding soul to soul.

And as they moved, the darkness of the borderland swallowed them whole.

REDACTED

Too Far From the Sun

by Evan Satinsky

I had never met a god before. Have I still? You, like many others, may call us liars bringing doctored evidence, or delusional fools gullible enough to believe the obvious hoax—that is your right, as part of the never-ending herd of human opinion—but if for one moment you find yourself able to suspend that understandable disbelief, I challenge you to find a better word to describe what we witnessed.

Odd, isn't it, that even after all this time, the same words can apply as readily to the murky depths lapping at our feet as to the glittering vastness above into which we are only beginning to delve? Or perhaps, not so odd; the deep darkness of the ocean—with all the fear and mysticism it invokes—must be layered even deeper into our still-terrestrial DNA than the crack of a twig on a moonless night, or the twinkle of stars through the rustling canopy.

It started as just another Poseidon mission (NOAA has started to rival NASA in the grandiosity of their names) and not even one of the better funded ones. We were to, in the simplest of terms, turn left where all others had turned right. I am sure many who are reading this account are following humanity's progress downward closely enough, but for any who prefer different avenues of curiosity, I shall explain.

When humanity first found the Tartarus Rift we began exploring immediately—stopping only long enough to make sure our crewed and automated submersibles could withstand the added pressures of going deeper into the ocean than any had gone before—and each of the first ten Poseidon missions had taken the first and largest of the pathways which were discovered within Tartarus: the path directly downward. It made sense; when finding a previously hidden crack nearly as deep as the ocean floor gets, it was natural for us to keep going down, and hundreds of discoveries followed along that natural path.

Left, however, was much stranger, and that strangeness started early. We passed many curiosities within the first few days which, if we had been better equipped or gifted more time, we would happily have stopped to investigate: The initial tunnel, cramped and dangerous—even with our high-tech instruments—and crossed in places by surprisingly large crystals which, from the few readings we were able to take with our limited instruments, failed to include any of the likely minerals like quartz, calcite, or barite; near the end of that narrow tunnel, the remains of what must have been multiple very long, sinuous worms which had managed to make it from their home near a thermal vent deep enough into Tartarus to become trapped, and which looked in the ghost-light of our lamps like a knotted shoelace floating in the wind; a cavern, as large as any Poseidon vessel had seen within Tartarus, dotted with clouds of nearly microscopic dust which looked suspiciously like they were moving in patterns too predictable for mere dust; a maze of tunnels shooting off of that cavern which all seemed to lead to themselves or to each other, and which turned us around and lost us nearly a day of travel time despite our sonic maps of the area.

Even if we had had the time and the scientific instruments necessary, the makeup and size of our crew was not conducive to exploring these wondrous finds. The majority of our ten person team were unspecialized crew—or as unspecialized as you can get on a deep-sea exploration submersible. Seafaring experts with both military and civilian backgrounds in going deep and going far—nearly five hundred total years of experience exploring the oceans of Earth. Even if our vessel could not run mostly on its own, our crew could have done it in their sleep.

Then, of course, the Captain; of all the old veteran sailors I have ever met, Myra Kalapolous is the oldest, the most veteran, the most sailor.

She has the presence to give an order and know it will be followed, the wisdom to know the order was correct, and the composure to give those orders calmly in the face of any danger, whether imaginable or not. She walks the deck of a sub with more of the saunter of the imagined, mythical sea captain of pirate filled days than anyone I have ever met. It was Myra who made the difficult but necessary decision each time we encountered one of the aforementioned wonders to move on without doing more than taking pictures.

And myself, the taker of those pictures. I am but a humble photographer—yes, I can feel some of you rolling your eyes; a 'humble photographer' with ten years aboard various deep sea missions culminating in a Pulitzer?

As humble as they come.

But on such a mission as this one, no matter how important a photographer you are, no matter how vital to the mission those tens of millions of frames or how many axes and spectra of data they can capture beyond simple visible light, you will always be merely the photographer. I don't mention this to complain, of course; merely to explain why my part in this story was little more than that of an observer.

Our first few off-shifts within Tartarus crackled with excitement, tamped down by discipline. Unlike on many submarines, even the militarily inclined aboard our vessel had a foremost responsibility to observe for posterity—the human experience of a place being as much use to future scientists as any image I could ever capture—so the Captain kept us mostly stationary while many of the crew slept, with only a couple at a time taking on-duty shifts during these 'nights.'

As each off-shift approached, echoey conversations and childish, manic grins interrupted the motions so rote now in each of us to clean up the minimal detritus of a day of work and to dial down the onboard systems for night-mode. Even the sailors who had been aboard other missions into Tartarus had never seen so many things new to human eyes in so short a time! The conversations were stifled, the smiles hidden, during Captain Kolopolous' rounds, but I have a suspicion that she wished she could have shared in those moments. Responsibility can be a lonely thing.

The rash of discoveries, each of which would surely take a

dedicated mission months to truly unpack, was followed by a relative lull. Hauntingly shaped tunnels narrowed almost beyond the capabilities of our ship to navigate, and then opened wide again to allow our beams of light to scatter around roomier caves—but empty, all empty, as the depths of the sea should be, one feels. The walls of some of these caves glowed with eerie blueish light, but upon investigation we found the source to be a known species of algae; otherwise, we were alone.

During these lifeless, nearly featureless days, I could have sworn we were weaving in and out of caves on Mars or Europa, that the water around us was instead the thin, airless atmosphere which crewed NASA rovers were beginning now to wade through in their own, similarly shaped vessels.

I think many oceanic explorers these days feel a sort of rivalry-laced kinship with the astronauts, our more glamorous siblings in science and adventure, fighting for the eyes (and the funding) of the world while so very far away from its sunny, warm shores. Never more does the rivalry of such a relationship fall away, however, than during those quiet moments of solitude, between adventures, between discoveries, when all of us sailors are alone together on a silent sea.

The sea would resume its miracles shortly. Less than a week into our journey—about a week before we were due to turn around and head back—the tunnels stopped suddenly and our little ship was spat out into a cavern so large that it looked as if we were back in the open ocean.

"Still in Tartarus," said the crewman who was watching the maps. "The far wall is...a thousand meters, wow," he added in a reverent whisper. It beat the previous record for largest Tartarus cavity—the one we had found on our first day inside—by an order of magnitude at least. We stood in silence on the bridge, staring out into the murky water beyond the viewport.

"Look alive," Captain Kalapolous said, not unkindly, to shake the shock from her crew. "How far to the bottom?"

"Only a couple hundred meters."

"Any openings?"

Silence paired with a frown at the lines on the screen. "Probably, but...the data isn't clean enough. There's some sort of interference."

"Should be shallow enough to light sufficiently, don't you think?"

the Captain suggested. The crew took her suggestion as the order it was intended to be and moved into action to set up the lights. I did not have to move far from my posted spot on the bridge in order to ready my lenses for the influx of light.

The floodlights snapped on, filling the surrounding section of the cave with light; the far wall was still out of view, but we could see the floor not far below us. In the washed out illumination—regrettable from a photographic perspective but necessary to fill such a large area of water with light—we weren't sure what we were seeing at first. I heard a couple gasps as members of the crew peered out the viewport at the rocky floor below.

The area was dotted with large holes—entrances to further tunnels, perhaps, a trypophobian nightmare an English muffin would envy. At first glance, it looked like huge swaths of the ground in between each hole swam with the kind of static which was apparently common on some old styles of television screen, or which faded in the more you compressed a moving image file—pixels of white and black and blue waving and jumping and dancing across our vision, writhing around and into the holes. Then the true image began to register in our brains, each crew member realizing what they were seeing one by one.

"It's..."

"They're..."

"What the fuck?!"

"Impossible!"

The whispers hissed to match the movement below.

"Put it up on the screen," Captain Kalapolous said, once again the only level head in the room. I was no exception, and took a long moment before remembering that was my job. I pressed a button and the viewport turned into a screen of itself, the image we had been looking at but with higher resolution and a wider angle with zoom capability, allowing us to see clearly what the foggy window had only hinted at. I zoomed in slightly and the image came into even clearer focus.

What writhed across the ground, swam between, around, into and out of the openings in the floor, were thousands, hundreds of thousands of sea creatures. Fish from bright clownfish and parrotfish to the gaunt and blinded anglerfish and lanternfish more typical of the deep sea, ghostlike squid from umbrella to colossal snaking through massive clouds of jellyfish, anemone and kelp waving with the motion of the water, and between them all, more coral than I had seen outside the great reefs, covered in patches with more glowing algae.

I pressed the color-correction button on my screen, and the gasps renewed as we were shown what it would look like if the light from the sun could filter down far enough to illuminate this scene in all its brilliance. I zoomed back out, showing us as much of this impossible life as we could see in one shot, feeling more like a photographer than I had for the entire journey.

It felt like minutes until someone spoke. "Check the oxygen levels. This must be a carbon monoxide hallucination."

It was a measure of our awe that someone actually turned to check. "Normal. This is real."

"It can't be! Maybe the computer..."

I pressed a button again and the screen turned off, showing us once more the unfiltered light which emanated from our ship, which hit thousands of sea creatures no one had ever seen so deep, and which then returned to grace our optic nerves with the images. I flicked the screen back on once again, the same image but sharper and more vivid. That stopped the doubting voices—whatever we were seeing was really there. Whatever explanation lay beneath this mystery was not one of fallible technology.

"We have to check them out. Let's get closer!"

"Get the instruments ready!" The voices of the crew flipped on a dime, from awe and disbelief to a scientific excitement so pure it made us sound like children on the playground.

"Stop," said Myra, our parent there to remind us it's nearly bedtime. She hadn't moved since the lights had been turned on. Those who had already begun jumping over guard rails toward the door stopped, and all faces turned to her. I imagined I could see on her face the battle occurring within her, but in truth, she was too professional to allow that to become visible.

Still, a few more moments of silence passed as our Captain stared at the screen. Then she took a small breath and spoke. "We will direct our course into whichever is the largest of these holes. We will document the phenomena thoroughly as we go." No one spoke. No one moved. "That is an order."

Those words broke the tension, and almost without bothering to stop off at our brains, our nervous systems told our muscles to move. The navigator turned to input the new course, and I to prepare our sensors for a sweeping pass. I programmed a maximal breadth of data axes; further missions could go into more depth, but if just one spectrum of data jumped well beyond normal and allowed us to guess at the source of this miracle...

Those who were not directly involved with the Captain's two orders, after glancing around at each other and at Captain Kalapolous, made their eager way toward me. Six veteran sailors crowded behind me, some standing on their toes to watch my small consoles. I tried my best to ignore them as I typed, setting everything from the extent of the wavelengths of photon to capture and the sensitivity of the barometry, to the good old-fashioned aperture size and shutter speed.

Like most photographers—even the most amateur of whom prefer an analogue device to the modern auto-focusing nightmares—I always insist on having full control over the entire range of data I can capture. By the time we were approaching the largest of the openings in the floor, I had just about wrapped up my lighting fast typing, and my crewmates had tired of the flashing numbers and most had returned to looking at the screen at the front of the bridge.

I had just turned around to report that I was ready for the pass when the movement on the screen changed. The organic, random flickering of thousands of sea creatures flashed in an instant into synchronized lines, like when iron filings are suddenly magnetized from below. The swarms shot across the screen, and I hurried to zoom out, to give us a better view of what was happening. By the time I had found the correct button, they had all stopped. I selected for maximum distance, a combination of lens angle and computer imaging giving us a bird's eye view from behind us of the whole scene.

The animals which had been swarming happily, even as our ship grew close enough that they surely felt its vibrations through the water, had all broken up into perfect circles—squid and shark, tuna and sea slug holding concentric ranks—covering each of the dozens of holes in the sea floor. The holes continued in all directions past where our light and our cameras could reach, but this pattern continued until those dimmed edges.

"Orders?" a fragile sounding voice asked. We were still moving toward the fish.

"Halt," Captain Kalapolous answered. The submarine slowed and we sat motionless, noiseless, staring at the hairy freckles dotting the floor. The arms of the plant life, which should never have survived under this much pressure, continued to wave in the eddies of current in the now-barren expanses of rock between each hole, now seeming almost ominous among their still surroundings.

"Should we withdraw?"

"No." Myra stood with her arms crossed tightly, the only sign of tension as she stared down the screen. Only she knew what she expected to happen, but my admiration for her leapt to new heights as she continued to act as nonchalant as she did when she ordered us to bed.

The fish moved again. They swarmed so fast I thought they surely would have ripped each other to pieces, but when the frenzy died down, there was no blood in the water. The holes were dark and empty once more, but the creatures had not gone back to their casual grazing. They now floated, just as still as before, in odd formations in the spaces between the holes. And even there, even miles below the surface of the ocean, facing the inexplicable, even at the farthest physical and mental stretches our minds can encounter, the human knack for finding patterns prevailed.

"Those are words!" I don't know who was the brave first to say it aloud, only that it wasn't myself or the Captain, but I know that by then we were all thinking it.

"How many languages are there? I see five already!"

"Does anyone see English?"

"Does anyone read Mandarin?"

Once the chorus started up only one thing could stop it. "Please," our Captain said, and for once, I could hear a note of emotion in her voice, although which one, I could not say. We all shut up at her plea. "Can we translate?" she asked. She glanced around the room, but all eyes quickly landed on me. The others were variously skilled in the mechanical and electrical tools necessary to run a submarine, but there were no true scientists on this mission, not technically. The only instruments we had were recording devices, and I was the photographer. I laughed and shook my head.

"We can translate exactly as many languages as this crew can read, Captain. We all know English. NOAA didn't think to equip us with a translator." Every spacecraft NASA sends up to barren planets in our solar system contains a complex linguistic algorithm which, it is hoped, will be of use if we ever find language-level life out there. No one thought to install this on any Poseidon mission.

She nodded, businesslike. "Raise your hand if you know more than one language." Only five hands went up, and it quickly transpired that three of those were high school spanish. A quick count brought our total number up to five: English, Spanish, German, French, and Swahili. Not exactly running the gamut of human language. Belatedly, tentatively, I raised my hand.

Captain Kalapolous raised her eyebrows at me, and I cleared my throat, suddenly self-conscious, as if I had just raised my hand at a middle school book club. "I can only read English, but I took a few linguistics classes in college. At the very least I might be able to help identify language families and similarities in text."

"Good," she said, and I am not ashamed to admit it felt as gratifying as it had in middle school when the teacher approved of my answers. "We'll do this the old fashioned way, then. Everyone, grab a console and start adding to a shared document. Try to avoid duplicates, and please write neatly."

Feeling even more like I was in middle school, I quickly opened the document and sent it off to my crewmates, before filling in the first cell, carefully tracing what I thought must be a word in an Indian language with my finger onto the screen. Fifty minutes and three slow drifts to a new set of words later we had over five hundred cells filled in, and—excitingly—two translated words; 'fermé,' which in French meant 'sealed' or 'shut,' and the English word 'prohibited,' neither of which boded well.

As the others took a break, I sat down to look over the list. I quickly tagged the languages I thought I recognized. This included some, like

Mandarin or Finnish which, given our linguistic touchstones, we had no hope of translating, but others were more promising. The word which I thought might be Romanian was 'fermă,' which I had to assume had the same definition as the french word, and the Latin 'prohibitus' was clear enough as well. A couple more good guesses showed me enough of the pattern to report.

"They're telling us to leave," I said, after trying and failing to think of a more ceremonious way to give my report. None of the 'resting' crew members had left the bridge, and Captain Kalapolous, who had ordered the rest, had not pressed the issue.

"Us?" asked the Captain, and I frowned, thinking about the question.

"The translators at home will have to answer that based on the context of all of the words, Captain. But my guess..." I glanced behind her at the screen where letters large as our submarine were still scrawled in fish. "My guess is every written human language is down there."

She nodded slowly.

"We're not just going to leave, are we?" Someone asked. "They're just fish." All eyes stayed on our Captain, however. This time, she did not turn to look out the window, but continued to stare at me. Although I thought I was not what she was looking at, I wished she would look elsewhere, but I did not break her gaze.

When she moved, however, it was toward me, and I realized she had been looking at me. She joined me at my photographic console. I could feel the other crew members' eyes on us, but I stayed attentive to my captain. When she spoke, it was quiet enough that I doubted anyone else heard.

"How far can we see—in any spectrum of data—into one of these holes without moving any closer?" she asked. I nodded and began to flip through the options.

"Our best bet would be to shine a focused light or a laser into one of them, or perhaps a sonar blast," I said, speaking just as quietly. "This would allow us to read the reflections and tell if anything is inside, and give us the most range and visibility—hundreds of meters, perhaps more. But..." I looked up at the screen, where the words were still written in aquatic flesh and blood.

Myra nodded; we had no idea what was in there, but whatever it was could do this. That was not something to shine a laser at lightly. "Anything less invasive?"

I continued to scroll. Most of the options I had available were worse than useless this deep in the sea. "Ah," I said, stopping my search. "Electromagnetism."

"Sending out a shock? How is that less invasive?"

"No," I said, suddenly finding myself in the odd position of explaining something to my own captain. "Electroreception. Sensing the electromagnetic fields given off by other living beings. We stole it from sharks. If whatever is in there is alive, we might be able to sense it, and if the signals are strong enough we could even image it with that data—and help from the computer of course."

"Do it."

I began to type furiously, aware that the entire bridge was holding its breath, although all they knew was the captain had asked me to run some kind of test. A few moments later, I had the scan running, streaming data into the computer. I had instructed our sensors to point on their narrowest setting into the closest hole, and to delve as deeply as they were able.

The resulting image loaded onto my screen in narrow bands of black and white pixels, top to bottom; I guessed, correctly, that the captain wouldn't want this one the main viewer. My heart beat in time with the loading of the image, seeming to skip beats when it lagged. Finally, the image was complete.

A mess of white dots surrounded a hole of absolute black—the creatures still floating motionless around the hole. In the very center of the hole, however, was a white oval. I pressed a key and the computer turned the image forty-five degrees, extending it into three dimensions, allowing us to see its true shape. The white oval lengthened, gained form and size as we looked at it from within the wall of the hole, a mass of white with gray shadows which, despite the low resolution, formed a very familiar shape.

It was a tentacle. It extended from its tip, a few dozen meters into the hole, to the end of the sensor image. Tiny blobs of white and gray must have been suction cups, and ran the entire length of the tentacle on one side. The image was still, but the tentacle was curved as if it had been moving, a sinuous little wave to the camera.

The captain stared at the image for a few seconds, and then she leaned over and pressed a few buttons, typed on some keys. I tried not to watch too closely as she removed the file from the screen and encrypted it behind her personal firewall and password. She glanced at me, a glance which confirmed a decision I had already made, not to tell anyone about what I had seen; at least until the information was made public. Then she stood straight and turned back to the rest of the crew.

"We're leaving," she said, and her tone brooked no complaints, but she was not done; to leave, it seemed, was the easy part of her decision. She took a deep breath before continuing. "And my official recommendation as the Captain will be for no further human mission to be planned to this cavern, and for all future explorations of this area of Tartarus, either public or private, to end before the previous tunnel." She finally broke my gaze and swept her eyes over the whole crew. "I would like to make this recommendation on behalf of my crew...but I will not do so if there is no consensus."

After another moment's silence, she added, "I will take each of your answers anonymously during our return trip. I will announce the results once we are back above the waves. I will not forbid any of you from spreading this story however you wish—that decision I will leave up to our government...and to each of our own consciences." With those words—words which I believe to be among the bravest and wisest uttered on planet Earth, either on land or beneath its seas—Captain Myra Kalapolous exited the bridge.

* * *

So it is that I write this account in the hopes that it will help to prepare me in one month to stand before The United States Congress to testify, alone with Captain Kalapolous, why this one small section of the Earth's skin should be closed off to humanity forever. I alone of the seven crew members who agreed with her recommendations was willing to say so to the world. I am not confident of our success; humans have never been good at being told 'no.' But whatever was down there resting in its den—whether god or alien, hallucination or magic dream—wants us, for once in our long and noisy existence on this planet, to stay where we belong.

And after seeing what I saw, I am prepared to comply.

Deities in the Dark Matter

by Sophie Mutiara Nova

While she was bathing, Jaka Tarub took the shawl/wings/flight of

The beautiful woman from heaven: Nawang Wulan

So, she might deign to marry him and become his wife

And hid her wings beneath grains of rice so (by her magic) she

served him and bore him a child, a daughter: Nawangsih

But when Nawang Wulan discovered the depth of

His trickery—she took her shawl back

And returned to the skies

Above, not once looking

Back at the man who

Stole everything

From her.

And tore

The wings

From her

Spirit.

(She did *return to care for her child; but that is another story)*

—JAKA TARUB AND THE SEVEN BIDADARI

Present

Grains press their indentations into my palm as they fall out, one by one, into the ice of the rushing river. I'm up to my knees in the rushing floods, but I couldn't care less as my lower half goes numb. Behind me, I hear the baying of men, voices gathered in choral monstrosity. In front of me, the void. But I can catch the incantation of her voice.

Love, run to me.

And my thoughts, afraid, whining back.

If I run any faster, my legs will give out or I'll give out before them.

I peer beneath me. As the rice falls from my palm and hits the water, it expands. The grains morphing, changing into glittering baubles. Shining, priceless gemstones. The grains erupting into life around my calves hurt—the untold riches leaving me with bruises before the punishing water sweeps them downstream.

"The cores! Don't drop the cores!" Hari howls like a dog, scrabbling useless claws against the INT-3 floating past him. His voice, that cursed voice that's followed me all the way here. I turn back to observe him even as I flee. The sword at his hip followed by the communicator on the other side of his belt. Ready to call the rest of his lunar guard should I displease him. "Do you know what you've done throwing them away like this?"

"Do you know what you've done?" My lip curls at his condescension, "or do you assume they still belong to you after the shit you've pulled?"

"I own your entire world." He counters. "I own your sister."

"She chose you. You don't own her." I spit. "Pitiful fucking choice she made though."

He steps forwards. I take another step back. He scowls in displeasure, coaxing me now like I'm some scared little fawn when he should see my teeth are near sharp as his. "Everything has its origins. Its limits."

"Not gods." I reply. He blinks at me, ever the rational lunar guardsman, logical to a fault. Refusing to believe me as I whisper, "not magic."

I should've died many times over already. Nobody walks in the waters, not on this planet. Our skin is not made for it. Whatever makes water into water on Earth is void. Everything beautiful on this planet aims to kill you—in one way or another. Which makes sense—we were not born of this kind of stardust. We're visitors: interlopers on the astral plane. Invaders of the stars.

But the goddess blessed me. As much as Hari *thinks* he owns this planet—the goddess owns me. She owns me body and soul.

I will be the only thing to kill you. She promised me, and I smile like a stupefied lover post-coitus to remember her oath.

Come to me, she urges, *love, run to me.*

Kill me. I plead to her in my thoughts. But in the real world I echo in refrain:

"She is the only one to kill me." I whisper. "Not you, Hari."

He charges the electric baton at his side. "We'll see about that."

He releases the charged weapon all at once. A crackle as the water's matter hungrily sweeps the electricity. The current carries rapidly, rushing over me.

I close my eyes, letting the power flow over me. Feeling *her* power, crawling its way out of my skin to lay claim to my mortality before Hari can end it.

Not yet, sweet.

When our metal spacecraft crossed the galaxy, we left much behind on Earth—but not our gods. Belief doesn't fall into voids or pressure vacuums. Deities do not die from gravity. No—it takes much more than that. Deities do not turn to dust within the dark matter.

Only our human bodies do. And what use are those when presented with such... such...?

The pain from Hari's weapon attempts to obliterate me. But it is nothing in comparison to the blessed end that awaits me at the hands of my goddess.

"Thank you, goddess." I whisper, rising from electrified waters. "Makasih."

Follow me. Follow, my love.

"How the... how the hell did you survive that?" He gasps.

I grin through what must be madness, *amor fou*. "Told you. *Magic*."

That's when Hari pulls the hunting knife, good and old-fashioned killing. His eyes sharpen. His gaze caught between the voice calling me deeper into the forest, the diamonds spinning about at my feet. Seeing as his electric baton trick was worthless, he has three choices here,

1. Annihilate me by slitting my throat properly.

2. Gather the diamonds.

3. Find... *her*.

"INT-3." I whisper, baiting him like the wild animal he is. "Think how happy your daddy would be if you saved some for him."

"Fuck you." He says even as the offer clearly entices him. He stares at the glittering, discarded ore in the water. I take one step back experimentally. Then two.

"Daddy might finally say he loves you." I tease.

"Fuck you, bitch." He spits, even as he falls to his knees at the river edge, adjusting his rubber gloves as he scrabbles uselessly for the cores bobbing flaccidly in the water.

I know my own choice. Easiest one I've ever made.

I gather all my strength to pull myself from the water. Already, my toes go numb from whatever cursed powers protected me from mortem per electrocution. I grit my teeth so tight they chip—exposed to these strange elements without the proper suit like Hari behind me—I won't last long in this wasteland. But I must push on. I *must* find her.

I glance behind me as I push deeper into the forest, both familiar and unfamiliar. So, like the calcified trees I played beneath before we left for this planet—but also completely foreign. Leaves in hues of unnatural violet and silver. Hari's still on his knees, carefully extracting the INT-3 elements from the water with the mining pack on his toolbelt. Their pure cores will be enough to power the spacecraft back home. Selling them to the right mining company will make him a rich man. Make Bethari not regret her choice.

I push forward, ignoring him. My riches are far less tangible, but no less real. Like the space between matter.

Come to me, love.

Like a moth to the fire that ultimately shreds its wings—I obey my goddess.

* * *

Dewi saya...

When I break into the clearing, I avert my eyes on instinct. I feel her warmth even if I can't see her. Like cathode rays exploding. Like a box of INT-cores, at once stable and exploding. An impossible energy.

But when she presses her hand to my cheek—I collapse faster than any galaxy.

"You'll die if you look at me." My goddess whispers.

"Let me die," I beg.

"How about I let you free?" She ripostes.

I look up.

I see my future, my present...

I see...

My Past

We were running low on rations. That was to be expected considering we were the first-gen pioneers to this planet. Rations ever since we landed were scarce. Our crops grown back on ship were not taking off despite being kept in pristine lab conditions and recycling our wastewater for growth. None of the test seeds were growing in this soil despite its 95% match to Earth soil.

Life simply *refused* to find a way here.

Still, the son of the planetary governor, the "prince" of our planetary expedition, Hari, refused to let those dismal statistics dampen his shine. He strutted into the center of our campsite, hands on his armor-plated utility belt, helmet off to reveal a shag of immaculately groomed locks.

Who had time to do hair while fighting gravity fields?

He did, apparently.

A star-shine crest was emblazoned on the front of his suit, deeming him our newest Lunar Captain, courtesy of some gluttonous donation from his father.

I wonder if my sister noticed...

"He's so hot."

There it is.

"Seriously, how lucky we are to be on the same expedition as *the* Hari Inanis. He was promoted to Lunar Captain before he was old enough to drink!"

"It sure helps his daddy's the president of the largest spacecraft fuel company back on Earth, eh? Can't explore the stars or hire a Lunar Captain if daddy doesn't pay for all the reasons the ships fly in the first place."

She ignored my spiteful cynicism. "His face would make the moon blush."

"Bethari. He's just another man."

"Not him. Can you imagine the kind of power he grew up with? I'll bet he never had to eat the moldy food you brought home for our suppers."

I bristled at that, defensive. "I picked off the mold most nights."

My sister Bethari only sighed, her eyes only leaving his face to glance cursorily at me, ensuring I was still with her. I squeezed her hand, noting how she looked a bit queasy still, peaky from interstellar travel sickness. She leaned more of her weight on me. "Still, he's a dream. A whole dream!"

I shrugged. "He's alright. Bit too broad if you're into that."

"I forget sometimes my sister's a notorious heartbreaker."

"I prefer discerning dater." I scoffed. "Besides, our goal's not to fuck the boss. It's to pocket the cash from this expedition, then we return to Earth and leave this star-voyaging behind for good. No time for dalliances."

But Hari startled me out of my daydreams by focusing his gaze entirely on me. "Data analyst, are you with us? Or too busy daydreaming?"

Shit. "Yes, Captain Hari Inanis. I'm data analyst Cahya Surya reporting for duty."

"Good," he grinned, "then let's begin the meeting, shall we?"

"Yes, Captain." Bethari responded for me, saluting him. "Assistant secretary Bethari Surya, also reporting for duty."

"The Surya family is blessed to have two beautiful and talented daughters on a space expedition." He demurred. "Your parents must be proud."

"Yes, our family is so blessed that our parents died when we were young." I retorted, resorting to my usual, face-slapping macabre humor. "With all due respect, Captain."

"She's sorry, sir." Bethari glared daggers my way. "She's blunt before breakfast."

"No, I'm—" I ignored her and wanted to fight back again, but my sister only dug her elbow in my side in retaliation. *Kiss-ass.*

"Ah," he coughed awkwardly. "Well anyways, as I said, let's begin."

He dipped his head, almost like a shy, flirtatious university student instead of a lunar captain. *And what was with that fake compliment? He can't be seeking my approval.*

He finally turned away when I gracelessly turned to stare at his shoes, pasting on a winning PR smile as he shifted from banality to business.

"I know morale's been dropping lately, and I am happy to announce I found some spare supplies in the back of the ship," *he must mean his family's emergency rations,* "and considering the spring season is upon us—I've decided that I and the rest of the lunar guard shall set up preparations for a feast. Superstitious, I know, but who doesn't enjoy a bit of a party, lads?"

I was already mentally planning the stern message I would send to Hari's center afterward suggesting we *not* splurge our scant rations on a party, but then I turned to Bethari. Seeing her face softened my icy heart a little.

Bethari grabbed my hands whilst I had Hari's overconfident smile still emblazoned on the inside of my eyelids. His veneers were blinding. "Isn't that exciting?" She squealed, "we'll celebrate the feast of the goddess of love! There'll be real cakes and drink and... and oh the drama of all the love confessions and notes!"

"Oh yeah, what a *trip*."

"Come on, Cahya. We didn't spend one year in space travel confinement just for you to be a bore!"

"Oh, I am, but I'd rather be boring than delusional." I fought my instinct to squirm away, already calculating how our rations would suffer for the sake of "morale" and a party. *Hari better not screw this up or we'll be sending out comms for a supply ship months ahead of schedule. Which will take away from my and my sister's ultimate pay day for his avarice.*

"I'm in charge of your feast day makeover!" Bethari squealed.

"Wait, what?"

"You'll be so pretty," she nodded happily, and I so hated the thought of ruining her small victories. She had so few lately. "Prettier!" And then, with a mournful promise in her voice. "It's the least I could do, considering all you did for me, lugging me about the stars. Let me pamper you. Please?"

That bit gutted me. "You aren't supposed to be taking care of me. It works vice-versa, baby sister."

"Still..."

I sighed, relenting. "Alright." I grouched, and the brightness of her smile buried my worries so deep that my subconscious did a flip.

A party... Looking at the shadow that crossed Hari's face as soon as he stepped off the platform and had a moment to himself, I couldn't help but feel the situation was more dire than our dear lunar captain was letting on. I wondered if he was giving us one last hurrah before he sent the inevitable missive to his father that we'd failed. And then I'd have to sign myself and my sister up for yet *another* off-homeworld mission, praying it would offer us enough meal tickets on Earth to survive yet another critical food shortage period that only a dying planet could come up with.

The end of this mission can't come fast enough.

Feast Day Comes

While the rest of the expedition ate their fill (and overate according to our ration guides) back at the main camp, I snuck away to find the ship's chapel.

Old habits die hard. Especially ones that are passed down from dead parents. The guilt, like mold beneath rotting floors, it just never goes away.

The further mortals traveled into the solar system, the quicker we seemed to forget the gods. How could there be a cosmic, infinite paradise squirreled away somewhere if we'd traversed every galaxy, ever comet's path or ray of errant starlight?

But I didn't forget the gods, no matter how hard I tried. Call me superstitious—but I'd lived this long. Considering my rash behavior over the years (hoverbike racing, brothel visits, downstreet gambling) that was nothing short of a miracle I owed to some form of deity.

Today's feast day was in honor of the goddess, the one my parents had prayed to as *dewi saya*—the only goddess from the home country to come with us. The goddess of fertility, hearth, home, spring, and... *love*, of all sappy things. The goddess of abundance and blessing, two things I really couldn't go without this time around.

A prayer can't hurt any more than an empty stomach.

My boots, the good ones Bethari forced me to polish twice, pounded heavy against the metallic echo of the interior of the ship. I passed by the grow-labs where our green-fruited or non-bearing crop trees struggled. The sleeping quarters with the cryo-chambers gone empty. The healer's bay with curious, blinking robot nurses manning all manners of cuts, scrapes, and travel sickness. One reveler drunkenly swaggered in and was treated quickly for alcohol poisoning. *That's one way to cut a mission short.*

The ship's chapel was tucked away in the corner, hidden away somewhere with just enough space to meet regulation standards. It was empty, given solemn pews and a holo-shrine that accepted any input of digital donations to worship what you would.

Dewi saya, dewi saya, please.

If you ever listened, listen to me now...

I wasn't particularly religious, but I found myself (like most mortals) the type to cry out for a god or two when I was scared or in distress. While my sister pasted crushed synth glitter over my eyelids and gloss over my lips—I'd been mentally crunching the numbers for our ration reserves. True to my anxious musings—Hari's decision to throw a wild party for the sake of our morale cut devastatingly into our ration banks. We were six months' over in our consumption versus replenishment. We needed a supply ship by next solar ship passing or we'd all be screwed.

When I told Hari, he just laughed at me.

"Oh, Cahya," he guffawed, "have faith."

"Are you throwing this party because you're scared of gods being real, or are you acting out because you're afraid of being hungry for once in your life?"

"Spoilsport." He huffed.

Hari didn't want to be respected; he wanted to be *needed*, which were two very different things in these circumstances. Sure, I'd considered a roll with him back on Earth and flirted back gaily when he tossed a compliment or two my way because I secretly hoped he might pay us better if I put out, but now? Now that I knew was a colossal fool he was—any passion on my part had long grown cold.

So, here I was, on my knees in front of the empty shrine. Flipping a coin into the offer-box and watching the branded image of *dewi saya* flicker to life in the holo-screen. Long black hair down past her knees, brown skin, dark eyes you could drown in. Of course, it was just an artistic rendering. Nobody had looked upon the goddess, really.

Nobody had looked upon her and survived to tell the tale.

The glitter Bethari pasted over my lids gave me double vision, like seeing ghosts on my periphery-- starlight and light refraction. I clasped my hands together, and feeling quite silly, whispered aloud this time...

"Dewi saya."

Nothing but the pounding of my heart. The dim beeps of the lab echoed by the murmurs of drunken revelry outside.

I tried again, closing my eyes and thinking of funerals too young. Of stacks of bills on weathered kitchen tables. Of going to sleep in cheap cryo-chambers with only an 65% certainty I'd wake up on the planet we were venturing to instead of the forever sleep of death.

I tried again, with intention this time.

Please make this our last off-Earth mission. Please make it a success and let me provide Bethari with enough salary stability she can finally rest instead of making herself sick following me around for the second pay stub.

"Dewi saya?"

I felt her before I saw her.

Laughter as someone stepped behind me, footsteps light as a dancer's. She placed two hands over my eyes. I startled, trying to get away, but her grip was firm. My muscles went slack, unable to move beneath her touch. "What the---what the f—?"

"Don't move." She warned as my vitals monitor beeped angrily on my wrist, noting my spike in heart rate from fear. "Haven't you heard the rules? If you look upon me, you'll die."

I croaked out a reply, unable to speak at first. I tried again, steadying my breath, willing my heartrate to go down. "D-did someone plaster my drink?"

She slipped a finger away from one of my eyes, allowing me to stare at the holo-image of her, of the goddess of love herself. "They never get my image quite right." She murmured with a laugh hidden beneath her words.

"You're more beautiful?" I venture.

She laughed for real this time. "I am so dreadfully repugnant that you will perish immediately upon viewing me."

"You said that already, the dying bit. And I embrace the challenge of surviving.."

"Good to know you're listening, if argumentative." Another sigh escaped her lips. Cool cloth like water over my eyes as she slipped a blindfold over my face. I could see nothing but light glowing silver through the threads, the image broken by the weave of fabric. She smelled like night flowers, the kind that bloomed like weeds past iron grates in our home in the city. The kind that killed rats by dawn because of the lead poisoning in the water they drank up. "Why did you call upon me, child?"

"I've lost my mind…" Cool flesh slid against my cheek, too smooth. Impossibly smooth. Inhuman. I shuddered as she removed her touch. "I'm hallucinating."

"I assure you that you are not. Ask me anything." She plied, bored with my shocked state.

"We're out of food," I finally confessed to this hallucination, face aflame, feeling so small now against something that made space travel, galaxies, and lunar guards seem like child's play. Against an entity that existed outside of chemical bonds and elemental tables and logic. "My sister will starve because our leadership can't admit to his father that he failed."

"And you? Can you admit it if you failed?"

"I just crunch the numbers on this trip."

"But you're a part of this team, these humans. And thus, you failed."

"I…" I think of my sister's face, sick from another expedition flight gone too long. *How much more of this could she take?* "I'm not a part of anything. I work alone."

"Humans. Asking all the time and never giving. It's a pattern that never changes no matter what planet you're on." The rumble of her voice-- hearing it, I felt both immeasurable and horribly finite. Swallowing my pride, I rotated slowly, turning to face the unknowable. Trying to find her even without seeing through the blindfold. I lowered myself slowly, until my forehead pressed against the cool grate. Until I lay prostrate before her.

"Please, my goddess, I'll admit I failed." I plead. "But I beg of you-- help me for my sister's sake. She's ill and can no longer accompany me on my travels. I can't fail her again."

"You humble yourself for a goddess you believe to be a hallucination?"

"I'd worship dirt to save my sister."

"Am I dirt?"

"You're far prettier."

Laughter again, ringing, buoyant. A cool hand like a blessing lifted the blindfold a little, peering past it at my face. I kept my eyes dutifully shut despite my instinct to sneak a glance at her. "The glitter over your eyes looks so pretty. Your sister must love you very much. As you clearly love her."

"She did. She *does*. Please, *dewi saya.*"

She murmured in appreciation at my supplication. She pressed a tied bundle into my hand, the bag felt like silk with tiny grains within it. "Take this. Loosen the string and shake the bag's contents into a bowl and it will never empty. But you must *never* try to tear the bag open. Never become greedy for more than you're given."

"Thank you, *dewi saya.*"

"Good feast day, supplicant."

"Cahya, my name is Cahya."

A pause, a sparkle of recognition in her voice. "Cahya like light. How fitting."

With that, her presence left the chapel, and the holo-screen went dark. Shakily, I pulled myself to my feet, clutching the silk bag tight. My body felt strangely buoyant.

I walked quickly back to the feast day. When I passed the laboratory, I thought I felt a presence stalking closely behind me. I turned to see only shadows.

Ignoring the anxious cloud surrounding me, I shook my head and picked up the pace to get that strange echo out of my head. I had to keep a cool head. The last thing I needed was paranoia in a time like this.

I clutched the mysterious silk bag of grains tight.

Forbidden Fruit

I sprinkled rice into the ship's food stores whenever I had a spare moment between balancing books (negative), counting traces of ores for energy transference (dismal), and sneaking Bethari my rations for mealtimes (starving). I closed my eyes, flushing faintly to recall the feeling of the deity standing beside me. The power that radiated off her. The scent like lavender and spice and something untraceable—the endless essence of the universe itself. Deeper, richer even than blood or starlight.

You ever want someone to crawl into your skin because they drive you so wild?

Ha ha, yeah, me neither. I was just testing you.

...just testing.

Regarding her preternatural gift, I followed *dewi saya* and her instructions to a T, never opening the silk bag's strings fully, always trusting that it would pour out enough without looking or testing or prodding it. And, true to her word, every time I left the stores' grain sacks were plumper than when I entered.

The expedition chefs adjusted quickly. Rice porridge, rice cakes, rice flour rolled into rice dumplings and noodles and all manner of processing. But the rice that came from the goddess's gift wasn't just the grain that grew so scantily on Earth. No, it was richer, somehow. Fuller. A statistical impossibility. The expedition doctors, the medical bots, all listed our blood pressure, sugar, and general bodily nutrition levels as sufficient, even *improved* since eating increased rice rations. Our cheeks filled out, our muscles strengthened, and our hunger lessened. The constant ebb of a migraine and aches in my bones subsided the longer I supplemented our stores with the goddess' gift. We grew faster, stronger, and more resilient.

I was happy to see Bethari sigh, content, before she went to sleep. Her belly full and her mind unbothered by the troubles of the day.

"Are you hungry?" I asked her.

As a dream, she just smiled and replied, "I forgot what that feels like."

"Oh, okay. Good night. Selamat malam."

"Malam..."

And I grinned like a fool because, for once, as an elder sister, I hadn't failed her. I hadn't failed my parents' memories.

And as for any suspicion of our good fortune-- I thought I moved enough numbers around to account for the "extra" rice found in the back. I thought I covered my steps carefully enough, looking twice both ways before sneaking off to supplement the grain stores.

But I couldn't avoid every possibility of being discovered.

I clipped the silk bag to my utility belt at my hip, hearing footsteps follow swiftly. What little light I had fell low as the main door closed. Someone new entered. I had to hide my efforts in refilling the grains, to become a shadow once more. I moved fast, shifting old ration bags over the refilled ones. Trying to draw less attention, only to feel the weight lessen at my hip.

Where was the silk string bag from dewi saya?

Like a child scrambling for fallen game tokens, I crashed to the floor in the darkness, splayed fingers scrabbling against the ground for purchase. Nothing. The gift was nowhere to be found.

"Looking for this?" I looked up to see a figure standing over me, triumphantly holding the coveted silk bag by its delicate tassels. Swinging it in front of me like a pendulum, a child's toy instead of the reality bending feat it was.

"Hari." I grumbled.

"Cahya?" He echoed. "What is this precious thing?"

"It's nothing," I lied, "a trinket, really."

"Is it?" He raised an eyebrow at that, dangerously close to opening the tassels and peering inside, breaking the deity's commandment.

"No!" I swung wildly for it, but he only lifted it higher above my head. A bully on the playground. "Don't open it."

"Quite a reaction for a trinket." He lowered it then, pinning the bag to his side. I did some quick mental calculations of the percentage of success of taking him in a fight, particularly if I clawed at his eyes. "I've been watching you. Or rather—the books you've been turning in. Particularly the ration logs. How fortunate of us to have found all those grain bags hidden in the back."

"How fortunate, indeed."

"Fortunate, or…" And here, he leaned in closer, so close I could see the whites of his eyes. "Is there something else afoot? We were trained for this in the Lunar Guard—of the possibility of mutiny from our crew."

"Was that training before or after your dad signed your captain's checks?"

"Funny. I don't recall comedy being a requirement for being the ship's data analyst. But nor do I remember being a liar a prerequisite either."

It's then that I noticed his height, and most damning, the length of the shadow he cast on the floor. My mind's eye goes back to the shadow that followed me from the chapel, the tunnels. His own confession: *I've been watching you.* Hari was my mysterious stalker. Hari had seen me with the goddess.

"Say it," I dared him, "say it, coward, if you're going to accuse me falsely."

He pulled himself to his full height, all bluster and ego. "You found an alien on this planet. Someone with key knowledge of resources here—unearthly knowledge. Unnatural."

An… alien?

I near doubled over laughing, wiping tears from my eyes. His befuddlement only made me laugh harder. "What?" He queried, defensive now at being left out, "what is it?"

"The goddess is no mere *alien.*" I told him. "*Dewi saya* is a miracle. A miracle who helped save us from starvation and ending our mission early.

"Dewi saya? You can't *truly* believe *the* goddess gifted you this?"

"Why not?"

"Because the stories the priests tell us are nice and all. But they're just that. They're stories to keep us company during our long voyages. Comfort to take with us like spiritual teddy bears into the dark of the unknown."

"And an alien informant who materializes and vanishes in thin air makes more sense to you?"

"I had considered the possibility of star sickness causing a hallucinatory state." He sighed. "I didn't want to do this..." He reached for his side. My eyes lingered on the electrified cattle prod he bore. I stumbled back, afraid of pain—my body already tensing in anticipation of it.

But instead of the cattle prod, he showed me a ring. A lunar band with an inscription upon it, carved hastily with a portable laser. And inscribed within it?

$$B + H$$
Bethari and Hari.

My voice was deadpan, all emotion drawn into the anger burning in the pit of my stomach, the acid heaving there. "You didn't seem the marrying type."

"She asked me," he answered coolly, "so, people-pleaser that I am, I said yes."

"Am I supposed to clap my hands and go *yippee*?"

"I was hoping you'd be happy for us and be a bit more compliant in telling me the truth." All mirth and snark drained from his face. I saw, for a moment, what his father must've seen when he promoted him. Someone trying to be a leader. Someone trying to pose to get their picture into the history books—for better or worse. Someone trying, trying, endlessly trying with the constant fear of failure to bolster him otherwise.

He offered me a bit of space, his hands pressed firmly, militantly into the small of his back. "Do you know why I was chosen to lead this expedition?"

"Daddy took away your hoverbike because of a DUI?"

He smiled a bit more at that. "You really are funny." But his words were dry as he continued. "You think me a spoiled brat. That's fine. I don't blame you for doing so—my birth has positioned me with unique advantages. And for many years, I was a spoiled brat."

"Hmm." I mustered in sympathy.

"My mother died young, and my father grew cold to me in response. I acted out, gambling wildly and getting into minor scandals to get his attention. I quit it all when I realized I could only get his attention by becoming the one thing I never wanted to be."

"Celibate?"

"He wanted me to become like him. A leader. A ruthless pioneer in the spacecraft energy business that the government's always tried to get a cut into." He stared deep into my eyes then, uncomfortably so. "My father offered me his business empire should I return successfully from this trip. He sent me here to grow up fast, and I'll admit my reasons for marrying your sister are twofold. Firstly, she's talented. Charming. Generous and beautiful—but you know this. And secondly, she reminds me a bit of how my mom was with my dad. She will make a perfect business and marriage partner. She'll never want for anything."

"Your father will hand you the keys to the kingdom on the condition you return *successfully* from this trip and tote my sister around like a prize horse."

"Not a prize—my equal.

"Tomato, tom-ah-toe."

He swallows hard, brow furrowed at my smarminess. "My father sent me to this godforsaken hellhole to fulfill a Sisyphean task." He pressed his forehead to the back of my palm, a medieval gesture of supplication, of beggary. "He sent me to a barren planet because, secretly, he wanted me to fail. He might be aging, but he doesn't want to give up power. Nobody would." A bitter laugh at that. "But you? With the secret knowledge you possess, you can change that." He pressed the silk bag into my palm, folding my fingers over it. "Ask your alien informant, your *dewi*, to find me resources the same way she found you the grains. If our mining vessel returns with enough ore, I'll be made my father's right hand, and Bethari will be my queen."

"My mom told me the story of the princess who got turned into a pillar of salt because her husband, the king, also wanted to make her his queen. And when she said no—he turned her into the last stone pillar of a temple so he could own her forever."

"I don't believe in fairy tales," Hari blinked, the picture of innocence. "Do you?"

"You followed me to that chapel, Hari, because you want something from me. You think I didn't see your shadow following me there?"

Carefully, and with a frown of displeasure, he replied: "I don't know what you *think* that you see, Cahya. I assure you I'm not a shadow." *Yet you cast a long one when stalking me down corridors, don't you?* But I leave that unsaid because every good gambler knows to hold their cards tight to their chest until dealt a better hand.

Instead, I leaned in closer, watching the glimmer of his media-trained-mask glitch as I focused in on his eyes. The glimmer there—a silkscreen illusion burning away beneath the fire of truth. "If you discard Bethari once we reach Earth, if you turn your back on her in any way," I hold tight onto the silk bag's tassels, "I'll ask *dewi saya* to explode every last ship in your fleet."

"As I said, I don't humor fairy tales."

"Then, you shouldn't be afraid of the goddess, should you be?"

"Hmm." He echoed my nonchalance, further infuriating me, deigning to condescend to me. And still believing my goddess to be a fluke, a mere extraterrestrial with accidental knowledge—a man humoring a girl overplaying her hand and making threats as empty as his promises-- he smiled wide. "*Of course.*"

Sisters and Covenants

I stormed into our rooms on the ship, careful to wait until the soundproof doors had closed behind me before unleashing full fury on Bethari. *How could you be so stupid, so infantile? After everything I've done for you!*

But I stopped, seeing my sister kneeling beside our makeshift shrine, set up beside her sleeping pod. Seeing her holding onto the digi-photo of our mother and father. My mother gorgeous in a wedding kebaya, my father looking quite handsome in his suit and peci. Seeing her eyes, damp as they gazed upon our parents' faces– faces which we'd almost forgotten to time and grief.

Instead of fury, my voice dropped like rain to the floor as I knelt beside her, facing our ancestral shrine so I wouldn't break into tears immediately facing her hopeful gaze. "Bethari, why him?"

She turned to me, her face aglow, brilliant like her starry namesake. "We've been moving constantly ever since our parents died. On transport ships, on cruisers, on any travel job we could get our hands on for a couple gems." She pressed her fingers over mine. "You don't have to worry about me anymore, kakak. I know I've always held you back. Being the sick kid, the promise you kept to our parents. Taking care of me and working twice as hard on shifts because my fatigue keeps me from working a full one with you. But this way, with Hari taking care of me, I won't be a bother to you anymore."

"You were never a bother, Bethari. Why is Hari Inanis so great?"

"Oh, I don't know. He's pretty. He's rich. He's a great... *kisser.*"

"Marriage to some rich boy won't solve all your problems."

"You're right," she replied, brushing my temple. "But it will solve yours."

"Bethari, please..."

She smiled, but it didn't reach her eyes. In some ways, her smile mimicked the disconnect, the dissociation in Hari's face. It proved to me they really had spent significant time together when I wasn't looking.

"I got sick on our last expedition to a mining town on Venus, you remember that? I woke up from a fever one night, and I saw you crying quietly to not wake me up. It broke my heart. I pretended to sleep to give you some privacy, but I didn't sleep a wink because seeing you so vulnerable when you're usually so tough... it broke something in me."

"I tried to keep quiet. I should've been quieter. I didn't know you saw all that." I licked my lips to keep from tearing up at the memory. Coughing, trying to be tough again. The tough guy she needed me to be. "The transpo-doctors told us it was a result of an allergy you had to the cryo-tanks. Stupid things."

"Hm." I hated that, the condescending 'hm'. She'd picked that up from me. "Babe, some people are just meant to keep their feet firmly on the ground. I'm always getting sick. Mom used to say I had a permanent case of constant *masuk angin,* bad wind in my body. You knew me as a kid! A person looked at me wrong, and I'd be sick for weeks."

"Not always..." I tried to protest.

"Let me finish." She held up a hand—no longer the meek little sister I knew her to be. "Not you. You were the kid to fly off the swing set at the park and bounce back up without so much as a scrape, like life was at zero gravity. That was before they melted down all the playgrounds for space travel parts, anyways. But you, Cahya, you didn't run like regular kids ran. You always flew."

"I don't want to run anymore, B." I clasped her hand in mine, eyes gleaming bright in sadness no matter how the anger burns up my throat. "I want to stay planted with you."

"I wish you knew yourself like I knew you. I hope you find someone for you like Hari is to me—someone to answer all your questions, even the ones you didn't ask." And she shook her head with a secret still left unsaid on her quivering lips. "I'm tired, love. I don't want to argue anymore." She pulled herself to her feet, sliding into her sleeping pod and burrowing her head beneath her blanket. "I've made my decision. I'll marry him." She clutched her hand to her, bearing her new wedding ring, "now, you're free."

Thoughts and Prayers, Birds and Bees

I walked quickly to the ship chapel, but *dewi saya* materialized more quickly this time than the last. I'd barely whispered my prayers, given my offering when I felt her beside me.

"Please," the words came out in a rush, a flood even, "we're a mining vessel, and the leader, Hari, requires energy cores to consider our expedition a success. Our payouts will get severely slashed if we fail, and I cannot fail my—."

"He threatened you. Your little lord." Her voice is ice behind me. Eyes shut tight, I cannot see her, but I can feel the chill in her voice, icicles on every vertebra of my spine.

"He...I..." I swallowed, wringing my hands tight. "He wants to steal my sister from me. He *will* steal her away if I fail."

A clatter at my feet, "these baubles are worthless to me. Go on, open your eyes. I'm behind you now. Look forward, never back. Not yet." Her energy, infinite, radiates behind me. When I open my eyes, I see a pile of INT-cores, the purest energy source, wrapped in a box of stained glass, opaque enough I cannot see the inside. "Same rules apply to the glass box as with the silk bag. Shake the contents from them, and endless ore appears. Try to break the glass or peer inside, try to doubt me, and the spell ends."

"W-why?" I squeaked. "T-thank you, my goddess." The temperature had suddenly dropped in the chapel. The temp gauges whined behind me, and I set my teeth gritting tight against each other to keep from chattering further.

"Don't thank me. Your first request was charming. The second, I do because I find myself liking you, mortal." Her teeth pressed ever so gently against my skin, teasing the breaking of flesh. I threw my head back in surprise at the gesture, inhaling tightly through my teeth.

"Why do I deserve the honor of your favor, dewi saya?"

Her eyes shift then, burning into my own. My blood rushes so as she nears me, heating my flesh to feel her so tantalizingly close. "Do you know what it's like when the men mine the INT-cores from me, young

Cahya? What happens when I dredge it from the depths of this planet to gift it to you?"

"...no, I..." I whimper. "I..." I choke on my words in her presence. My faith drives my wits from me. She tears into me without using her teeth.

"What you call INT-3 is what we call our darah, our blood. Humans cannot traverse the stars without it. But we gods were born from the energy between stardust. We have no need for travel when we are the space between all things. As such," she takes one of my hands, pressing my fingertips to something that gives as soft flesh. Her breasts, resting above something that feels like a heartbeat but much warmer. More powerful. A pulse to the universe itself. "INT-3 is the result of the power of my body bleeding into this planet. It is me forcing myself from the freedom of space into a finite, corporeal form. Squeezing my lifeblood into *something* because you humans so despise the concept of *nothing*. I bleed to create what you humans deem INT-3—the engines that power the universe."

"Why do something that hurts you?" I'm distracted by the feel of the flesh/not-flesh. *But oh, how it* feels *like flesh... Focus.* "Why do you suffer for me?"

"Because the sacrifice frees us. In obliteration, like the little death of coitus that you humans imitate in sex and love, we find peace." Her voice rumbled deeper, more haggard. "But the humans on your ship, particularly the men, mine INT-3 as an infinite resource. They bleed me dry without replenishing me in worship. Take, take, but never give."

"Take the gifts back then. Don't let them take anymore from you."

"Oh, naïve little human. With your boxed-in ideas of right and wrong. Justice in a merciless void, how quaint." Her lips were so close to the back of my head that I felt the whisper of her breath against my neck. "I will call a debt from you. Because as much as I hate being *something*, I find it worth my time: being something with you."

"A debt?"

"A favor for my favor." She laughed, but the sound was ice down my spine as much as heat. As much as danger froze me, it also exhilarated and incinerated and more. "You cannot die without my blessing."

"I cannot die without your blessing? Why not?"

"I won't let you." Her thumb and forefinger pressed into the soft of my throat, pushing my lips up to face her as her breath, the energy between stars, ran down my chin. And she commanded me: "You will *not* die without my blessing." She cursed me even as she swore her eternal oath. "This I swear by the bloody, endless stars."

Then the goddess liquefied like the honey in her words and poured down my throat like rice wine-- burning all that was left of my senses. I tried to scream, but instead, I wept, a pilgrim facing a saint in ecstasy.

In my despair/joy, she expanded and collided, atoms in dark matter. I felt her inside me for one brief, tantalizing moment, but then I felt nothing at all. The yawning, desperate void of absence filled me—soothing me for what was lacking in sustenance.

Finally, trembling, I let myself breathe. Still overcome with aftershocks.

My Dewi left me then, but not her promise.

...not her threat to finally end/free me.

Broken Like Promises

Glass shards were littered at my feet. My sister knelt before me, and I knew before she even opened her mouth what had been done.

"I was cooking," Bethari lied, "and I brushed against it and..."

I looked to the shards of the magical box from Dewi that had produced our blood-begotten ore. The shards of a broken covenant lay jagged. Methodically broken until they're almost dust. "He did this, didn't he? Hari?" I asked, trying to keep stoic while the anger pulsated within me.

"It was an accident." She insisted.

"He grew greedy. He wanted more ore than the box could give." I shook my head, knuckles tight as I splintered my nails into my own flesh. "I calculated the results. Our ore findings had a linear increase up until last week. Then it flatlined. Nothing."

"Please, Cahya. Can't you ask for help again? He needs to succeed or his father—!"

"You can leave him." I countered. "We take the loss. You end the relationship, and we'll find another gig."

But the way she worried the ring into the flesh of her left hand. The way she twisted it so protectively, as though it had become a part of her. Like a dog with a bone between its teeth, Bethari would not end the relationship with Hari.

"I'm tired of traveling amongst the stars. I want to set my feet on the ground for the first time in decades." She confessed. "Please, sister. I want to rest."

"Then rest with me." I insisted.

She turned away. "You know I can't do that. We're like two moons orbiting different planets, Cahya. We must separate eventually. I cannot stay in your shadow!"

"Your future husband's success is a lie. He's the only shadow here."

"Isn't everything lies and smoke and mirrors then?" She stepped closer to me then, a glass shard in her hand. I feared she'd stab me. Which was silly. She'd never do that. "Your goddess is a myth."

"Our parents didn't believe so."

"They died, and she didn't save them for their piety, their endless prayers. Why should we curry favor from heartless gods?"

"She isn't heartless. The INT-3 expedition is bleeding her. It hurts her!"

"You humanize a monster." She pressed her fingers to my cheeks, pressing tight, as though to keep me frozen there. "If she really does exist, then use her for all she can give us in retaliation for her letting our parents die, hell, for letting *Earth* die! Don't follow in their footsteps. Don't martyr yourself and worship a fiend."

"You don't know the truth." I backed away, shaking my head. "I must return to her. I must check on her."

"Cahya!" She pleaded, snot and tears running down her face. "Kakak! Big sister!"

I left her amongst the broken shards and covenant.

A favor for my favor.

Numb, I journeyed back to the ship chapel. The grain bag still at my side. I tipped it, experimentally, to the ground. Nothing. Even if I had done everything right, Hari's folly had damned us all. The goddess's blessing had left us.

I had barely fallen to my knees when a radiance, impossibly bright, hit my eyes. I cried out, pressing my forehead to the ground in the illusion of penance just to avoid being blinded by her rays.

"Your prince violates the resources I give him, just like every other man who calls upon the goddess. He demands instead of pleading as he should."

"My father worshipped you until his death, *dewi saya.*" My words were hollow, voice still aching from the clash with my sister. The chapel is dark, but the radiance I feel from the goddess more than makes up for the lack of clarity in these tenebrous halls.

"Your mother was a strong influence on him. A matriarch who knew her worth. Your sister is weak. She is… *earthly.*"

"She is sick, star travel makes her even sicker. We mortals are not as powerful as you. We are mere shadows in your stead. It's why we cannot look upon you. It's why I'm back here, begging of you to grant your forgiveness."

Fingers pressed tight beneath my chin, to the point I felt her nails dig into her favorite spot in the soft hollow of my throat. "Open your eyes." She commanded me.

"I'll die." I swallowed at the swell of silence that was her response. "Do... do you wish me to die now, *dewi saya?* Is that the favor you ask of me?"

"Religion is a matter of belief. Do you believe you will die should you look upon me?"

"You are very powerful."

"But do you *believe* me to be so?"

I opened my eyes, but kept my gaze firmly affixed upon the ground, the radiance reflected off there. "My parents loved each other until their death. In their love, they made me vow to protect my sister as she was all I had left of them. In my love, I come back to worship a goddess who would kill me to prove myself."

Her voice echoed around me, ringing off the metal of the vessel. "Love is suffering, is that it?"

"I'm sure it is lonely, being a deity left in the dark matter. The closer we get to the stars, the more we humans forget our roots. Forget our gods." The words dripped with fury I did not know I would be capable of as I shuddered, my body wracked by the fear of my imminent death. "Do you want me to...to *love* you, *dewi saya?*"

Her palm pressed against my cheek, a lover's caress. Her fingers ready to move my face into position, to ensure my gaze met hers. To ensure I met my death of her will, to bend my will to hers.

"Come to me." She commanded.

... then she released me, leaving nothing, not even the shards at my feet.

My deity had left me there for the rats in the dark. The shadows, the lunar guard behind me led by an infuriated Hari, dragged me away. My boots skidding against the metallic floor, my sacrificial coin abandoned near the ship's shrine.

"This girl is crazy." Hari said. "She needs to be locked up for her own good."

Nox / Night

The ship's detainment center was in the bowels of the vessel. Bars formed of lasers and electro-shock cords binding my hands together. Should I try to shake the bindings, electric punishment would be distributed onto my flesh, starting at mild levels and cutting off just below critical heart failure if I continued to struggle.

My sister visited me, bringing protein wafers since our nourishing grains had given out. They were tasteless against my tongue. My stomach still pinched, but I knew she'd given up her meals for me, just as I had so often done for her.

"When did you grow up, adik?" I asked the figure in the darkness.

She pressed her hand, still with the manacle of Hari's wedding ring, against my cheek. "When I realized where the power was after our parents died." She replied. "When I realized I had to sacrifice myself to save you from killing yourself for me."

"Mother said we are descended from goddesses."

"Again, with that bitch goddess. Mother is dead. Father not long after. And your goddess failed to save them." She shook her head at me, her eyes pleading. "Don't you understand how the real world works, sister? I must stay with Hari to ensure you are treated well back on Earth after all your treachery. It's my turn to take care of you."

"You must believe me. I'm not mad."

"You're not mad," she told me, "but you are lost."

"No, B! Come back, Bethari! BETHARI!"

She left me then, my conscience wracked with guilt. Perhaps her husband-to-be had called her back to the surface while homespun juries on the planet's surface decided what to do with me. Star sickness they said. *Lost and mad.*

They claimed my sabotaging the INT-3 reserves was the result of too little oxygen going to my brain: a faulty pressure system in my space pod. Caused me to hallucinate. To see things that weren't there-- things like goddesses instead of extraterrestrial informants. Like magical covenants instead of extra grain in the back of the ship, a lucky streak of mining ore in places we hadn't looked before.

Hari came down to the cages to update me himself, to mock me and render my ego even more useless than it was before.

"We made enough ore to scrape by with a positive profit." Hari informed me. "If the hospitals release you on Earth in time, we'd love you to attend our wedding. I know Bethari would appreciate seeing you there. You'd have to be under a nurse's supervision, of course. Star sickness is such a damning disease. Never know when you might snap."

"Where are the guards who pulled me away when I last visited the goddess? They can testify I'm not seeing things."

"Regrettably," Hari buffed his nails on his shirt, "the ship chapel had to close because of a poisonous fungus. They succumbed to their injuries in the med-bay."

He engineered the med bots to kill them.

"Why not kill me too?"

"Why would I kill my future sister-in-law when I can keep her safe in a cell?"

"It was never about being loved for you, was it, Hari? It was all about control."

"You want to know a secret? My mother didn't die of natural causes." His face screws up into something indecipherable. Something so full of hatred that I fear looking upon it and losing my own humanity. "My father killed my mother because she threatened to leave him, and the investors would've pulled out of his company if she left him. He would've looked weak. He didn't want to leave me penniless, and my mom would've left us in the dust. He did what he had to do to create a genius innovation. To help humanity conquer the stars."

"I knew you were a bastard." I growled. "Now the whole world will know it too."

"Oh, sweetheart, do you think I don't have an army of good lawyers to get out of all the scandals I so carelessly caused in my youth?" He laughed, the handsome, unlined face of a man who could literally do no wrong if he tried. "Besides, nobody believes a madwoman, Cahya. You're a data analyst—check the data."

I went for the bars, unthinking, and the electric shock drove me back, yelping, in pain. The heat of the lasers burned me. "You know the truth, Hari! You know the goddess is real." I snarled, close to the bars of my enclosure as possible, close enough to see the curvature of Hari's skull illuminated by the lasers. "You know I'm not sick. That I'm the only one who knows you failed, and that I helped you get enough ore to inherit your daddy's company. Without my help, you'd be nothing."

Intrigued, he moved closer. "It's true then? You *can* get me more ore?"

"The goddess is through with us all." I spat back. "Our greed has all but nullified her blessings here. She's forsaken us."

Hari tutted as he spun on his heel. "Star sickness-- what a shame."

He left me then, trembling and near-tears. "*Dewi saya,*" I whispered. Once, twice. Until my breath gave out in the cold. The temperature gauges nonexistent below-deck. "*Dewi saya,* please."

An unbearable screeching sound. I looked up. The laser-gate of my enclosure had opened of its own accord. My electric bindings fell from my wrists—inoperable.

Laughter rang out as I stumbled to my feet and made my escape from the prison, the sound of screaming sirens chasing behind me.

Stargazing

The ship's chapel had been barred off with laser gates and bio-hazard warnings for invasive spores from our host planet. I took a left, a right turn. Occasional dead ends led to me retracing my steps. The protein wafer turned in my stomach, and my heart hammered its way out of my chest in panic. The yelling of guards behind me. The desperation of Hari not wishing to lose his only chance at impressing his father.

Eventually, I escaped into the open. Sprinting past tired miners and lunar guards. Sprinting with the silk bag spilling grains once more at my hip.

A favor for a favor.

Only I can free you.

I left Hari at the river, scampering in the wet for INT-cores to make his daddy proud. I left my sister behind to an unknowable fate, praying she'd leave him because she no longer owed a debt to take care of me. But she was an adult. Her decisions were her own, to break the cycle of obligation. To become her own person without me. I left my parents at their shrine photo back near our beds, smiling on the happiest day of their life, ignorant of the disasters that were fated in their and their daughters' futures.

I knelt before my goddess in the wilderness of this planet, the last expedition I'd ever be on. Her name spilled past my lips, more precious than any star in this entire galaxy. "*Dewi saya.* Tell me what it is you want to fix this. What is your favor?"

"You know what I want."

"To look upon you?"

To end me?

She tapped her fingers just once against my cheek, a gentle: *yes.*

My heart softened at this. It was what we all wanted but were too afraid or egotistical to admit. To be perceived. To be told: *you're not alone.*

"What happens if I look upon you, *dewi saya*? Do I truly die?"

She tapped her finger twice against my cheek. *No.*

A voice in my head, my deepest fears, told me she really meant:*yes*.

My parents sacrificed themselves for my sister and me. I sacrificed my youth for my sister. My sister sacrificed herself for me. I sacrificed myself to Hari to free her. Hari sacrificed himself for his father. I sacrificed myself to the goddess to save them all. To make all that suffering worth it.

"Save me." I pleaded. "Save me from this cycle of burden."

"Save yourself."

"Then tell me what I must do." I cannot keep the whine from my voice. As much as I try to remain brave, I need her.

In reply, she pressed her thumbs to my lids, tracing my lashes with the edges of her long fingernails. "Cahya means light," she whispered, "light is always uninhibited, even amongst the darkness. And to light, you will return."

I opened my eyes to her radiance, to see the glass box and the silk bag whole again at my feet, unbroken. To see my skin glittering all over, as though covered in stardust. To see her bleeding out rivers of stars and the space between stars. To see what made INT-3 in its purest form. To see what allowed humans to traverse galaxies.

Dewi saya... My goddess, my goddess.

Finally.

She pressed her lips to mine, and I tasted the universe—infinity spun in dark matter. Through her, I became everything.

In becoming one with her, I was finally free.

The Forgotten Before

by Jimmy Mack

Another night in the gutter. Another night sleeping under a tattered overhanging leaking all manner of shit, some literal, from the towering sleepers. Another night failing to get out of this shit hole. Fucking wasteland.

Lizae and I had spent three days scrounging the techpiles after the most recent dumps. Three days of digging through such toxic tech waste that the Q-burns will take cycles to heal. And we recovered nothing. Fucking fuck. We had heard the rumors of experimentals coming from Zaxis R&D. Experimentals that would still be high in raw Q and able to be utilized by wasteland pharmaries. Weeks spent planning to get there before any other trapper. Used the last of our up-cred to pay off anyone who might cause us trou-

"Jahz!! Did you hear what I said? Get outta your fucking head and look! We gotta problem."

Pulling out my scope, sweeping past walls of faded resistance symbols bearing the recent marks of Corp Day executions, I immediately saw what Lizae meant. Coming up the street, maybe only a few minutes from being able to see us, was a full up-patrol, armed to the tits and accompanied by sweeper bots.

"Fucking fuck, we need cover Lizae. Where—shit, are we in the—?"

Lizae, rolling her eyes at me, immediately yanked me into a side path. Then, against what I thought was a solid fabwall, shoved me into an old spi-hole. She crashed through behind me and slammed it closed, plunging us into darkness.

"What are they doing down here," I hissed.

She immediately slapped her hand to my mouth, furiously motioning me to silence. Sweeper bots, equipped with vibration sensor clusters, could hear your heart if they got close enough. Feeling around as slowly as possible, we found the hatch leading deeper into the spi-hole. Second by second, we crept into the more protected section, the one designed to beat sweepers. Once the hatch was slowly lowered back down, we both let out a breath. Safe, at least for the moment.

As soft as possible, I asked again, "What are they doing down here? I haven't seen a full up-patrol in years."

"Maybe they found another supply cache? Like the Req City incident last year? Getting pretty rare, but level 5 FOs are still out there. And those two that got caught last week had at least a couple level 4s, to be fast-trialed and on the wall for execution so quickly..."

Not for the first time, I wondered about her FO knowledge. She had this intuition, this other sense. Like she always knew at first glance what FOs we would stumble across. More than once we were saved by her quick thinking, her ability to fast talk us out of patrol questioning.

But there was always this wall whenever I would ask about what she knew or how she knew it. She would get timid, almost like I had caught doing something secret. And she never talked about what her life was like before we met. Never talked about the death of her parents.

Flipping on our torch beams, we looked around the second level of the spi-hole. A few tables and several chairs dominated the floor with little room for anything else.

Footsteps were quiet as we walked across the confined space, sounds muffled by dust on the floor. The low ceiling combined with the tight floor space made maneuvering difficult. Objects on the tables were illuminated as we swept our beams back and forth, briefly flashing in the intense beam and then fading to an after image. The tables seemed to hold mostly debris, but it was difficult to be sure with the dim lighting. One thing was certain, the amount of dust indicated no one had been here in decades. Maybe longer.

"Jahz? You think this...maybe no one's been here since..."

Lizae was thinking the same. She trailed off, terrified to even say the words, though I knew this kind of spi-hole was practically vibration-proof. But even thinking about it brought a level of terror to my core. The CorpWar.

The end of Before.

Growing up anywhere down here you learned early to never mention Before. Even saying it was enough to get you a digital law level 1 violation. And down here in the wasteland, you didn't want to risk getting caught on the wrong side of how Zaxis enforces the digital laws.

I saw it first, on a table propped up against some box with round knobs. It looked at first like a ration container, but as I looked closer the strangeness of the thing became apparent. Some kind of wider top lid over a smaller thickness, with another wider back covering.

Brushing off the dust, the front was heavily faded, with some kind of drawing, and another set of straight marks: Some up and down, others side to side. Pulling the lid away, which was connected on one side without hinges, revealed flimsy-like pieces similar to the stuff we used to patch the leaking ceiling in our shitty sleeper. Each piece had similar markings like the cover, but smaller. Denser.

I turned around to look at Lizae, who wore a growing expression of...was that fear?.

"Fucking fuck, Jahz. This is a problem! We need to destroy that. You know the digital law penalties for any FO".

"Huh? Destroy? I don't...I mean it's junk or maybe an old set of patch sheets."

I continued to examine the strange object as Lizae crept towards me, tension building in her movements.

"I don't know what the markings...maybe looks a little like the resistance symbols—"

"Stop talking Jahz!", whispering and shouting at the same time.

Her eyes were wide and looking more terrified by the second as stared at the object in my hands.

She was even trembling, looking like bots were about to pour into the room any second.

"Jahz, we shouldn't even be looking at this!!"

"Lizae, it's junk, relax! Did you hit some bad zip or something," I said with a little laugh.

Which was the wrong thing to do because then she was staring at me.

Like I wasn't her best friend for the last ten years.

She was watching me like I was a wanted FO trader.

"Wait, you're not actually suggesting....you seriously think this junk is from—"

My sentence stalled as her body answered first.

Almost like seeing this thing was causing her physical pain.

"STOP TALKING! DON'T EVEN THINK OF THAT WORD WITH BOTS UP THERE!"

She lunged for the object and on instinct I jumped back, bumping into another table. She crashed into the table in front of me, toppling over it as I tried to move out of her way. Bouncing back up, she stalked toward me, feral expression twisting her usually soft features.

"Give it to me Jahz, you have no idea how dangerous that is!"

"You're not making any sense! What—"

"It's from Before! It's why the Corporations enacted the digital laws—it's what destroyed everything!"

I was stunned into silence, complete disbelief that she had just uttered Before.

She stood there gasping, like this seemingly random piece of junk was taking all her air. This was not the Lizae I knew. Not the girl that raced me everyday across the sleeper tops of the Req slums. Not the girl who always seemed to hate the Corporations, so brazen in her defiance of anti-trapper laws.

And no one down here knew why the digital laws were created, at least that's what we've always been told.

She had backed me into a tight corner. Stalking towards me like a reaperbot; expression darkening to something I couldn't even comprehend.

"That...that thing—which led to the wars and destruction and everything—that thing is a *book*."

I stared at her, not understanding the word she had used to give it a name.

"A what?"

* * *

All the soldiers' attention shifted as their neural links activated, including mine. Mission data, parameters, possible target locations, and engagement protocols were transferred from Zaxis Command and linked to helmet displays. Individual neural implants were now linked to me for the duration of the mission. I confirmed back to Zaxis that all links were active and the sweep had commenced.

"Listen up", I barked, soldiers snapping to attention. "Zaxis has labeled this a priority GAMMA sweep. Agents have confirmed multiple unknown spi-holes and high likelihood of illegal activity. Begin sweep procedures."

Bots began moving ahead of our formation, conducting initial scans while search and control teams followed behind.

"Why do you think they pulled so many of us for this?"

"Rook, how many times do I need to repeat myself? What's my number one rule? Stop asking questions."

"Right, sorry sir!"

"And cut that sir shit out. I don't do formal in my command. It's Maz."

Fucking fuck, this kid was gonna keep testing my patience all night.

"We're looking for..."

"Forbidden Objects. Pay attention Rook! And make sure you stick to the quarantine protocols if you encounter anything during this sweep."

I quickly scanned through the data streams from the sweeper bots, so far turning up nothing more than illegal sleeper unit occupancy. Way below our orders and down here in the Wasteland, pretty much just another day. Rook stopped next to me, staring wide-eyed at the line of bots hovering along the left side of the street. I gave him a not so subtle push to get moving.

"They're just bots, Rook..."

"So many of th—"

At that moment, two figures burst out of a dark alley on the right, one of them immediately sprinting down the street, while the other halted in front of the sweeper bots.

They were already dead, they just didn't know it.

Immediately a bot within the group broke off, racing into the dark distance. Two heartbeats later, a brief red flash was the only thing visible as the first figure was neutralized.

The second figure was pulling a container from a pack, likely an incendiary device that, even if set off, would do minimal damage.

But it wouldn't get that far. Another bot emerged from the group, hovering in front of the crouched figure. A brief red flash, and the crouched figure was flat on the ground. Second threat: Neutralized, not that they were ever a threat to begin with.

Rook watched, mouth slightly open, as the entire incident was dealt with in less than ten seconds. "Maz, what...why didn't we—"

"Why didn't we what? Take them in for questioning? As far as Zaxis is concerned, the second they run from a patrol they are guilty. They are sympathizers."

The kid seemed to roll the thought around in his head, trying to understand such exacting brutality. This was certainly his first front row view of a Corporation enacting such swift punishment.

"I know that the digital laws leave no room for interpretation, but—"

"Stop talking, Rook. This is the reality. The quicker you accept that fact, the longer you will live—probably. Now go grab that pack so we can see what this Wastelander was carrying."

Rook grabbed the pack and hustled back, struggling to keep his posture from betraying his fear. He moved to hand the pack to me but I shook my head.

"Open the pack and search. You need to get used to this."

He opened the top of the pack, tossing out food rations and wasteland junk. Reaching further in, he pulled out something else and turned to hand it to me. It was shaded in the dark of the street, but as soon as my hand touched it, I knew what it was.

Fucking fuck this was going to complicate my entire night.

"What's this Maz? Doesn't look like anything—"

"Keep your mouth shut Rook, that's an order. I need to think."

This was so fucking bad.

Runners during a sweep brought more than enough scrutiny. But this...a level 5 FO of this significance. Fuck, why did it have to be a book?

Why did the FO traders continue to ignore my warnings and move books this way?

Looking around, the sweeper bots were already back scanning buildings and the rest of the patrol was split off into their appropriate sub-units. Rook and I were the only ones to see the book. And Rook clearly had no idea what he handed to me. Time to see if this kid was worth all the trouble I went through to get him under my command.

"You remember what I said about no questions Rook? Here's your first lesson on why it's my number one rule."

To Be Frank

by J. R. Phillips

The meek did, in fact, inherit the Earth and sought their just desserts revenge humming to the rhythmic beat of tiny wings. Fran sat with her husband Hank huddled in a walk-in closet—their refuge for the last few days. The small dark space reeked with their refuse. Scraps of metal tins scattered among the moth-eaten rags of someone's abandoned wardrobe.

Her stomach growled and roiled as she looked at the dried crust clinging to the soup cans. They needed real food. Anything other than the salt riddled liquid that left their tongues gritty and sore. The sun rose, a scarlet slash through cracks in the doorways. Fran let out a breath of relief. Another night survived.

It was safer to travel during the day, the light banishing the swarms of insects to their nests. Although the sun allowed other threats to roam boldly. Desperation poisoned the minds of the few survivors they had encountered these last months. Fran understood their paranoia. Scavenging had become a deadly endeavor. Brutal brigades had begun to claim the safety of daylight. They fearlessly roamed the waste with a loud fanfare of pounding fists, and heavy steps.

Cult-like thinking was a disease spreading rampantly. Despite the grotesque rituals required, the promise of safety blinded many to its violent cost. People were desperate for the salvation denied to them.

A shiver ran through Fran as she recalled those first few weeks. Hank and her slipping into the shadows watching their neighbors kneel before the creatures garbed in the discarded skins of their victims. The gathering climaxed with cracked cries of agony. Fran would never forget the sickly-sweet smell that followed. It left her gagging and useless as Hank gently guided her away from the thickening haze.

This was their fourth shelter. Despite being here a few short weeks, they had to move again. Fran looked at their dwindling supplies: one more water bottle, two pieces of chewing gum, and a half-eaten bag of chips. The pull between the safety of this shelter and the need to scavenge for sustenance was pushing her closer to madness. Which choice would kill them faster: starvation or exposure?

The image of their starved bodies succumbing to delusion accosted her. A loving embrace devolving into desperate teeth gnashing on bony shoulders. She shuddered to shake the sounds of squelching mouths and snapping tendons. Only the alternative wasn't much different. Without shelter the winged creatures would devour them all the same. The insects would be more ruthless with her than Hank. He loved her. Sacrificed his sips of soup to her. He surely would be gentle with each pull upon her flesh, and gladly carve his own for her.

"What should we do?" Her voice scratched against the shell of silence surrounding them. It was always like this when they first woke, after spending twelve hours holding their breath. She watched Hank crawl to peer through the crack. He set back on his heels, eyes darting around the small space.

"We need to move, Franny," he whispered. "There's no point in staying here with no water and no food." His stomach groaned its agreement. "If we cut through the neighborhood we should make it to the gas station on the corner before the sun sets fully."

"What if *they're* out there?" she croaked.

"We hide. We run. We say a prayer." He shrugged.

She stared at her husband. His clothes slipping off of his gaunt silhouette. She was sure she looked the same these days, more bone than muscle. Not that either of them was ever a gym person. Not puzzle solvers either. Still, they started to prepare for their move. Fran looped two kitchen knives to her waist with the thin twine gathered from an earlier hideout.

"....five, six, seven, eight, nine," Hank counted under his breath, "Nine bullets left."

He loaded the gun, placed it in his waistband, and stuffed the remaining bullets in his back pocket. She fashioned a knapsack from fraying silk scarves and gathered the only essentials they had left. They stared at each other, and giggled. Whether it was from the hysteria gripping them or the sheer absurdity of this new reality, she couldn't tell. He pulled her into him, careful to avoid the blades as dull as they were.

"You know, I dig this Tomb Raider look on you," his eyes dipped appreciatively up and down her bony figure. Hank had the talent to see past the ever-present grime coating her skin. It made her skin heat. That heat had kept her alive these past months. He leaned down to kiss her, their foreheads touching. Fingers lacing. Now their life was consumed by the small moments. The belly laughs warding off delirium. Each quiet second had become heavy-weighted with the promise of a sudden goodbye. After a few long breaths they pulled apart. Smiles replaced by grim determination.

"Let's do this, babe."

They crept through the house, tip-toeing along the wall of the darkened stairs avoiding the rotted wood. Hank slowly pulled aside the plywood covering the windows. Careful to remove just enough for one eye to glimpse the outside world. After a few moments he cracked the screen door that led to the back yard.

Overgrown grass crunched beneath their feet as they crouched within the dry yellow blades. The naked trees left no shadows to cling to. Fran squinted her eyes against the blazing sun. Its red hue an ever-present reminder of just how different things were now.

Hank silently pointed to a shed two long lawns away. She nodded, scanning the expanse of grass. Her ears strained against the silence as she held her breath. Hank's hand rose, three fingers, two, one. They bolted. Their destination was a smudge of dark wood on the crimson horizon. Two thin shadows moved starkly against the flat fields.

They collapsed against the shed's wall. Fran scanned the structure as she waited for her heart to catch up. A small spark of hope lit-a forgotten warmth. The shed wasn't as dilapidated as she was expecting. Wishful thoughts of canned vegetables had her mouth watering. Fran heard Hank creak open the warped door.

All thought of refuge evaporated as a sickly sweet stench leaked from the doorway. The smell of death wasn't new to them anymore. The body lay cowering in the corner. Rotted flesh still clung to the bones. A quick sweep of the small room had her heart sinking even further. Her fragile wish crumbled completely. There were no supplies here. She let out a sigh reaching into her makeshift satchel. She took a small sip from the water bottle and handed it to Hank.

"How much further to the gas station?"

"About a mile," he said after a small swallow.

"We should come back here if we can. The swarms didn't find him. He still has some meat on his bones," Fran said, trying to keep her voice as scientific as she could manage.

"Yeah, that's true. Finger's crossed, baby," he said smirking. He held out his pinkie to her. She smiled as wide as her cracked lips would allow and latched her own finger to his.

"Fingers crossed." she repeated.

* * *

Fran and Hank were making a slow and steady pace. Making sure to keep close to the bank of an old canal. The water had long since dried leaving behind only cracked mud. No animal made a sound. It was just their soft footsteps. Still, Fran felt exposed on the flat stretch of land. As barren as it was, any sign of life would be easy to spot. Easy to catch.

The ground began to rise ahead of them. Soon the striped roof of the gas station came into view. The quiet remained. Fran finally allowed herself to feel a trickle of relief. Before they left all abandonment and ran for the doors they remained crouched on the small hill.

A few long moments later Hank silently pointed to a rusted car abandoned at the pump. Again, he held up his three fingers, two, one, and they sprinted over the crumbling asphalt. Gravelly steps echoed under the metal awning as they slid behind the vehicle. The spark of hope grew with the proximity of the doors. Thoughts of water and beans made her stomach grumble with anticipation.

Fran knew anything fresh would be long since rotted, but the thought of something like a vegetable had her salivating. They paused once again waiting for any sign that they were not alone. Metal from neglected machinery scraped along the concrete as another dry gust ran its hot fingers through her loose strands.

Finally, Hank silently signaled their move. Just as they were about to take their first step, Fran froze.

Drumbeats swelled in the distance. Her body went frigid. It was *them*. She turned her wide eyes to Hank. She knew they had only seconds to decide. Run for the hill, or bolt for the door. Her thoughts staggered. The drums. Close now. Or was that her own rapid pulse? She couldn't move. Couldn't decide. The beat echoed through her. Anchoring her to the spot.

Fran's stomach sank as her body was flung towards the door. Hank ripped it open and shoved her inside. He pushed her into a run down the middle aisle. Cans of food flashed in her peripheral. The plastic rustled and shook from the steady drumming. The world went dark as they ducked into the supply closet. She looked up to see Hank's shaky smile.

Fran and Hank had been lucky up until this point, only witnessing the depravity from afar. The steady thuds from outside had Fran falling back to those first nights of anarchy. The sounds of women being tortured, violated. The cracks of fists flying into bodies. The wet breaths pleading for mercy.

The smell of burning flesh. Her tongue swelling, A silent gag left her body shaking in Hank's steady grip.

The bell above the door let out a rusty ring. Fran held her breath. Hank reached for the gun. Nine bullets, the thought sharp in her mind.

"Looks like no one's been in here yet," a deep voice rumbled.

"Let's look for some kerosene and get out of here-" a nasally voice replied.

"Doesn't look like they've got that stuff." The first voice said.

"Well, they wouldn't keep it by the food, dumbass. Check the closet. I'll check the back shelves."

Fran's heart stopped. Her skin flashed from hot to cold.

She turned to Hank, the gun shaking in his grip. His eyes darted to her knives. Her fingers fumbled to loosen the knot. Once the blade was in her hands, she pushed Hank back to a darkened corner. They stood behind a sparsely stocked shelf. Heavy steps grew closer. Fran closed her eyes. Maybe they'd get lucky and go unnoticed. Just another couple of dirty rags in a forgotten closet.

Hank placed his body in front of hers. His free hand wrapped around her hips. She felt his chapped lips brush her forehead. Instincts had her gripping him. She clung to him like she clung to this last moment of peace. Tears burned her eyes as fear dug deeper into her bones. The steps came to a stop. The door creaked open. Daylight left a bloody trail on the tile floor.

A putrid aura invaded the small space. The massive form ate the doorway. She peered through her slit lids watching him step towards the shelves. His blue eyes were a bright contrast to the dim space. He took a step forward, seeming to suck away the atmosphere. She refused her lungs despite their burning plea for breath. Dots began to invade her vision. She tightly gripped the knife by her side. He moved closer, his nose twitching. He reached for the large white bottles by their feet. She found herself staring into cold blue eyes.

Without a thought, Fran struck. Her knife tore into his neck, and hot liquid sprayed onto her face. Those blue eyes locked onto hers. She watched with relief as the light deadened. His body contorted into a crumpled slab of muscle onto the floor.

Hank looked at her, a mixture of shock and awe in his eyes. He gripped her shaking hands and squeezed. Despite living in this hellscape for the past six months this was their first kill. When the brimstone fell, most of those left behind simply festered in their disbelief. Fran and Hank quietly gathered supplies. Those first few months flew by, safe and secure in their own basement hidden from the carnage. She had easily ignored the chaos that rapped upon their door with clawing cries for help.

Fran wiped the blood from her eyes, still warm and sticky. Bile rose in her throat. As much as she wanted to celebrate her victory she knew this was far from over. She took two soft breaths before the sound of shuffling feet came closer.

"Devon, hurry up! We only have a couple hours 'till sunset."

Fran and Hank stood with their backs pressed to the wall. The silence rang in her ears. How many of them were there? Her mind raced as it tried to place a number on the drums. It would be best for them to kill this one quietly and slip through the back doors. His footsteps grew louder as they slid across the dirty floor. Suddenly they stopped. Fran bit down on her lip and looked up at Hank. His hand steadily held the gun out.

They crept from behind the shelves. She willed her eyes to adjust to the shady store. A shadow spread on the left blocking their escape. She pointed silently and Hank nodded once. There was no hesitation as he stepped into the aisle. The gunshot reverberated off the tile floors slamming into the concrete walls. And just like that they were running. Running towards the sparse trees and their thin shadows. The grass shattering loudly beneath their feet. They had no destination, no safe harbor. They could only run and hope the rest of the men wouldn't bother wasting their energy. Fran dropped her bloody knife into the field feeling the other bounce at her side. They ran for as long as the adrenaline would carry them.

They collapsed behind three small dried bushes. Fran had no idea how long they had run for. Her heart pounded against her ribs. She refused to blink. Her stinging eyes searching the horizon. The sun now hung low in the sky. There were no drums, no sound of angry steps rushing to exact revenge. No shadows loomed or raced. She took a breath and turned towards Hank. She expected to see his signature soothing smile. The one that let her know she was cute when she overreacted.

Her breath caught as terror sliced through her. Hank's eyes were wide as they stared at something behind her. The gun once again shaking in his grip. Fran slowly turned to see two large figures. Her mind blanked from confusion. This wasn't possible. She blinked rapidly trying to clear her vision.

Towering over them were the two men she had watched crash lifelessly to the tile floor. She quickly scanned the brutes. She saw no splash of crimson, only a thick black substance. One man had it dripping like sour sap from his neck, and the other's chest bubbled with the ichor.

She stared at her own hands. They were stained black. The smell of tar singeing her nostrils. Her gaze lifted to the man she had stabbed. Black voided pits met her instead of the piercing blue they once were. Loud pops sliced through her dazed state. From the corner of her eye she saw the gun recoil with each shot. She couldn't move-couldn't comprehend all that was happening. Fran watched the bullets thud uselessly against the steel frame of the scavengers. They smiled down at her. Sharpened teeth promising pain.

Time stopped for Fran at that moment. Maybe it was the lack of oxygen finally taking full effect. Her head felt heavy. As if her neck could no longer control its movements. Hank's hand fell to her knee. Her head turned painfully slow. Her eyes finally found his, crinkled at the edges, full of love. Something settled within her. An unavoidable truth. He had always been her rock. She knew she would not have survived without him. He alone saved her sanity each night they crawled deeper into closets. Trying to hide from the dreadful hum of wings. Caresses to console her shudders at each bump and rattle against window panes. There it was again, the warmth of him sinking into her cold skin. Hope radiating from him like some divine gift.

She squeezed his hand. Raindrops fell. Her brow furrowed at the sensation. They hadn't had rain, not since the sun shone red. She looked up to the smoggy sky, no rain. She looked back at Hank. His smile remained even as his head slipped from his neck. The sound of it hitting the ground broke the spellbound moment. Smug laughter seeped in and Fran heard a faint sucking noise. Her eyes flew up to the two *things* that had hunted them.

"Mmm mmm, mmm, now that *is* tasty," the nasally voice said as he stuck his bloody fingers into his mouth. She didn't have time to grieve. She needed to run. Her brain finally waded through the sludge.

That man didn't have fingers anymore.

His hand was now dipped in tar, tipped with long talons.

She turned on her knees and struggled to take off, but thick fingers grabbed her by the roots. Sharp pricks of pain needled her scalp. She was dragged her up until her toes were pointed to the ground. She let out a scream and she thrashed to escape his grip. Only for another arm to sweep around her middle.

"Shhhh, don't worry honey. We don't want to eat *you*," the deep voice breathed. His rank breath robbed her of her own. She craned her neck to get away from his whispered threat. He sniffed her and rumbled a laugh that left her feeling oily.

"C'mon Devon, we don't have time to play here," the nasally voice reprimanded. He leaned down, setting his inky sights on her. "You'll be a good girl, won't you? We don't *want* to eat you, but we will if you turn out to be more trouble than you're worth." Devon loosened his grip on her hair and shoved her forward.

* * *

Time passed and gradually the sun dipped lower. Shifting from its blinding blaze to a hazy smudge of glow just above the tree branches. She stumbled up the path through the flattened grass as slowly as she could manage.

The gas station came into view. Her heart beat erratically. She longed for the organ to just give up already. She pictured the bliss of death laying its dark hand over her eyes. Washing her consciousness away from this world.

* * *

A year ago, she would have begged her god to relieve her of this fate. A year ago, she and Hank would be volunteering at the church's food drive. She would have their famous tray of 'Frank's Brownies', and Sheryl would bestow one of those backhanded compliments citing the "rich and interesting flavor." That was before this reckoning. Before she and Hank were deemed unworthy to be saved from this wretched existence.

She took a sharp breath and fell, again. She had fallen three times now. Each time the knife on her waist carved a new shallow line into her flesh. She choked out a pained sob, turning her watery eyes up to her captors.

"Please, can I just rest for a minute? I hurt myself earlier, and I just need a minute to catch my breath." She had little hope for any sympathy from the brutes, but it was the only tactic she had to delay her inevitable fate.

"She *has* fallen a few times. We don't want her too damaged for later," Devon said. That damned spark of hope flickered once more. She turned her eyes to the skinnier of the two. He only smirked as he watched her blood drip in small lines down her leg.

"Maybe you should just carry her, Dev," he said coolly, calling her bluff. He shifted the limp form on his back. She grimaced as Hank's broken body slid into an unnatural position.

She feigned a huff of discomfort stretching her neck to the sky. It wasn't hard as the grief threatened to choke her. The sun sat closer to the thin trunks scattered on the horizon. She knelt for a few moments before standing fully, and put a hand to her temple as if caught in a dizzy spell. She took a slow breath in through her nose.. Rough hands snatched her wrist and pulled her painfully towards the gas station. She chewed her lip and cleared her throat.

"Can I at least get some of the beans from there? I haven't eaten in days," adding quickly, "and maybe some water? " She tried to keep her voice steady, despite her heart's new permanent residence in her throat.

"You *are* rather bony, girl," his nasally voice like needles to her ears. His lips spread into an unsettling grin, "Don't worry, soon you will have all you can eat when we get you *home*. We like to keep our girls full of energy." He turned towards the gas station with Hank's headless corpse dragging behind him.

She tugged back on her arm pathetically. She knew she couldn't fight them. She knew they would enjoy breaking her.

"My throat is just so dry, I don't know if I'll make it to...to wherever that is. You might as well just eat me." Her stomach grumbled loudly.

"Fine. I'll go get you some water. Devon, be careful with her, she's the best one we've found in months."

Devon dragged her around the building. There two more towering figures appeared. They leaned on one of the pumps beside a pile of rusted car parts. Fran's stomach dipped. She shook in Devon's rough grip. He chuckled in her ear and rotted breath clouded around her. Bile stung the soft flesh of her throat. The newest members to her torture squad raked their voided gazes up her body. Their tongues darting from their lips. She wondered if they could taste her fear.

"Found a sweet treat, did ya?" one voiced in a sharp tenor.

"Finally! I think I would have rather been on the spit myself than fuck Delores again. She doesn't even make a sound anymore," the other added with his nose wrinkled in disgust.

"Yeah, and Marsha is such a pet these days. Always frothing at the mouth for more attention."

"Oh yeah, Marsha isn't going to like this one." The men all laughed.

Fran didn't dare open her mouth. She had been around enough men like them. The ones that thrived in packs. The ones that leered at her body as if it was at their disposal. When their beady eyes fixated on her she dutifully placed her own towards the ground.

"Aw, don't be broken already, doll. We want to have a bit of fun with you first." One of the men pushed off from the pump and took a gravelly step in her direction. He reached a grease-stained hand towards her. Fran cringed as she retreated only to find a wall of muscle at her back. Before a dirty fingernail could graze her skin, she was lurched back into Devon's chest.

"No touching. Finders keepers." Devon snarled.

Fran peeked towards the darkening horizon as the men continued to argue over who had first dibs. It was almost time. Black and brown clouds swirled together as they invaded the crimson atmosphere.

She couldn't remember the last time she had seen a sunset. Dull dusty stars fought to be seen. She held her breath and thought of Hank. Her eyes remained dry, and she slowly lowered her hands.

The movement allowed Devon more access to her body. His arm tightened around her waist while his other hand moved over her chest and up to her throat.

She squeezed her eyes shut, willing images of Hank to rise in her mind. Hank's soft hands. Hank's lopsided smile. Hank's familiar scent. Hank's fingers shakily pulling that trigger. Hank's head slipping off his shoulders.

Anger blossomed. Wrath demanded her to scream until her captors' ears bled. But the soft wind coaxed patience for it carried a familiar hum.

She slowly undid the string on her second knife.

"Man this guy is heavy for just being a bag of bones," the nasally voice cut through the discourse. Fran stared as Hank's headless corpse bounced on the gravel at her feet. Her heart squeezed painfully. She barely felt the man batting Devon's hand away from her.

"You know the rules man, no fun stuff until we are back behind the walls, and bellies have been filled," Hank's murderer snarled.

"Yeah well, I'd like to know why Devon thinks he's entitled to the first round with our new toy," said the one that had reached for her.

"We should have a competition," the other chimed in.

"I found her first," Devon said, the promise of bloodshed in his voice.

"Well if we are going to get picky, I'm the one that killed the man," quipped the nasally voice, "so by our traditions I would get to play first."

Fran listened to the scavengers, their voices grating, their hands digging into her-pulling her roughly in all directions.   Devon's grip tightened on her. The circle was shrinking. Fran smiled to herself. A chill settled in the breeze. The swarm was almost here. Her salvation. Hank's justice.

She cleared her throat, "Well, we could all play together couldn't we?" Fran stroked Devon's arm that kept her belted to him.

They became instantly silent. An animalistic nature entered their eyes now glued to the hand she slowly slipped into her shirt. Carefully touching the soft skin of her stomach. Devon's arm loosened. Though it sickened her, she willed herself to relax, and forced herself to writhe against him. The demons were slaves to lust. Greedy by nature they stared at the gift of flesh she presented to them. Their egos drinking in each feigned tribute Fran offered.

Fran moved from one man to the next. One hand stroking their chests and dipping slightly lower with each pass. The other hand, dangling the knife. She continued to tease glimpses of bare skin. Her body moving in rhythm to the hum of approaching wings. Her hooded eyes inspecting their amused expressions. She knew she wouldn't be able to deliver a killing blow. They wouldn't allow her death to be so painless.

But still, there was a way. A path that led to Hank's revenge. A destination she plotted towards since she first fell. Since Devon's breath tickled her neck. Since Hank's head hit the dirt. Man. Fiend. Demon. Whatever the evil before her called itself- she had seen it before. Thwarted it her whole life. Leering eyes, and personal space invaders dodged with fawning giggles and quick feet.

"See? We all know how to share, don't we?" she said softly through a forced smile. She brought her arms above her head. Hank's murderer narrowed his eyes on her.

"That blade will do you no good, sweetie," he spoke down to her. A look of pity in his eyes. She was just a poor little plaything to them. The demons couldn't sense them on the wind. The end. Coming for her.

"Don't you like blood?" Their eyes lingered on her raw lips. Entranced by the combination of her movements and the promise of bloodshed. She saw their pupils dilate. Watched the thick drool drip from their mouths.

The air around her thickened. It was now or never.

Fran pictured Hank's three fingers.

Their signal.

Her throat ached as she sucked her sorrow back again, and smiled before dragging the blade down her arm.

The fiends lunged clumsily for her, sluggish from their shifting cravings. She easily danced from their grip. She refused to be feasted on by *anyone* other than Hank. She was *his* sustenance, and he was hers.

There was no mistaking their arrival. The darkness throbbed around them. The buzzing now deafening. Shadows separated into clouds of small pulsating dots. Laughter welled within her. Agonized screams erupted around her.

Fran welcomed the sensation of tiny mouths pulling her apart.

Each one a promise kept to Hank.

Her euphoria grew with each guttural cry the fiends surrounding her let loose. They had turned into such pitiful things, begging to be spared. Cutting laughter escaped as she heard the nasally voice shouting useless commands. Speaking desperately in the ancient tongue of their dark lord.

The bugs knew no master though. Blind justice. Her vengeance sealed within each stinging bite. Chaos rained upon her captors. Their flesh torn and rendered to ash. Devon's hands blistered and stubborn refused to loosen their grip. Panic rose within her. She did not want to die tied to this demon. She thrashed and slammed the knife into his hands. The insects swarmed to her bidding. Tar dripped in heavy globs from Devon's mutilated grip.

She was tossed to the ground free from the swarm for a few moments. Devon collapsed to his knees.

His skin now ashen from soot. His face twisted from pain, cracked. The flesh withered, sloughing from his bones. Fran didn't have time to relish in the others' remains.

She blindly crawled searching for Hank. Her blistered hands reached the prone form and peace washed over her. She finally allowed all of those tears she'd been saving to fall.

Death would find her soon. Its scavengers would complete their mission of reclamation.

She threaded her pinkie through Hank's rigid one.

"Fingers crossed, baby," Fran whispered.

P3nt3kost

by A. P. Murphy

I: Spellboat Willie

A knock at the door. Lost in a reverie of inquisitors and reddened tongs pincering his scrotum, Kiggitz sat back with a start and dropped his can of meat chunks. Sinusoid the cat sprang up and skittered into the bathroom where its litter tray awaited a deposit of its latest fear.

Kiggitz opened the door on its chain and peered. Phyllis from down the hall. His own age, about fifty-ish, but older in the way that such women as her will always age.

"You seen about the thing?" Phyllis asked.

'Toad adjacent,' thought Kiggitz, memories fresh of witches' confessions, croaking things ripped out of them by their inquisitors.

"What thing?"

"That thing on TV. The thing about the head. Shockin' news."

"Uh... Yeah, very innerestin' Phyllis. I'm busy right now. Research. A good evenin' to ya."

Kiggitz could never bring himself to be outright rude, a poor New Yorker indeed, and he didn't slam the door now. Instead he closed it gently as she carried on about this 'shocking thing' and a head, and who-knows-what-all.

Clunk. Back to work. So much extra effort, the painstaking work of compiling exegeses on secret books by medieval sages and renaissance alchemists. So many hours added to his research program. All the more challenging for a medically-retired janitor with no High School diploma.

His studies already took in monetary theory, the history of the World Economic Forum and of Hollywood entertainment, the Bohemian Grove, the Titanic catastrophe and Dealey Plaza, as well as all the latest ramifications in brain chemistry and endocrinology. A complex web of knowing and becoming.

A more indiscreet investigator would have placed a great big corkboard on the wall and tied together all the nodes with red twine or something equally revealing. But Kiggitz was not going to give any prying eyes the satisfaction of knowing what he knew.

So, unschooled as he was, he had mastered basic encryption and posted his findings via TOR to a secure repository on the darkweb. Virtual links in lines of unseen code took the place of red twine in the obscured network he had traced. He felt like he was picked out alone of all men for the privilege to understand it all. And behind the dross of the everyday lay the knowledge of beyond, which he was ready to grasp.

* * *

To say Kiggitz didn't quite fit in with other humans would be an obvious understatement. Though there was nothing too visibly irregular about his person, he had that sense about him that he'd been fitted for a suit of human skin in the wrong size. Just a touch too slack for such a tightly-wound soul.

He'd worked in school janitoring for a while. Toyed with marriage and family but let it pass by. There'd been some shadow of suspicion in regard to certain incidents at a junior high, but it all blew over. Now Kiggitz collected a meager disability check in relation to a work-related spinal condition that pained him nearly as much as the fallen condition of the world.

While convalescing in physical therapy, his interest in the hidden realm had been piqued by a random podcast, and the tentacles of all the world's corruption had spread from that single spoken suggestion of a reptilian prince in London to include all the occult matter of time present and time past. A vast iceberg slab of secret knowing was his to chip away at.

Putting away the grimoire on medieval witchfinding, he checked now on his YouTube subs. A new video had dropped from his favorite esoteric researcher, his delver into occult knowledge from history. This latest one analyzed a nine-minute cartoon made in 1930 by the animator Dave Fleischer for his brother Max's Fleischer Studios, entitled 'Swing You Sinners!'

He sat down to watch, intrigued at the change in theme towards pop culture. Usually his research tackled the Kabbalah or hermetic alchemy. Inter-war animated shorts were new. He picked up his tin of meat chunk stew and his fork and hit play.

The video starts with the cartoon itself, after the most minimal intro from the YouTuber. In the short, a rascally character called Bimbo finds his way into a graveyard where the gate transforms into a wall. Bimbo is now trapped in the kingdom of death. Spirits sing about how Bimbo will be punished in hell for his sinful life.

> *You're wicked and you're depraved,*
> *And you've been mighty misbehaved*

Soon monster trees and the very gravestones assault him, so he runs into a barn. No respite: here farming implements continue the threats, and a scythe sings out:

> *Brothers and sisters,*
> *Come on get hot.*
> *We'll amputate your vo-do-de-o*
> *And tie your bones in a knot.*

At this point, the scat singing intensifies and the barn interior pulsates like a heart. Bimbo is chased by more menacing ghosts, who trombone him and terrorize him with a straight-edged razor. He leaps out of the barn, which transforms into a giant

**quadruped monster with multiple heads. It pursues him through the
night.**

Where you want your body sent?
Body? Huh! Ain't gonna be no body!

**All the hordes of hell are now chasing Bimbo, so he runs into
a cave where various demonic entities manifest and samba
ritualistically, and we see a devil in the form of a toad creature which
scats disturbingly to the now-frenzied jazz swing.**
**The entities sever Bimbo's head with a giant knife and he's
swallowed by a skull.**
The film ends abruptly.

Kiggitz paused the video and sat back open-mouthed, chunk sauce
trailing down one side of his jaw. He'd seen some highly traumatic footage
in his nightly crawl through the gardens of forbidden knowledge, including
some out-of-focus VHS tape purporting to be the extraction of
adrenochrome from the brains of toddlers. But he'd been steeled to face
those traumas, bolstered by slugs of brandy and ready to endure the worst
for his research.

This cartoon was another thing entirely. It had broken into his
mind in an altogether unexpected way. Cartoons aren't meant to evoke
unspoken rituals, hinted at obscurely in the ancient texts.

He wiped his jowls and watched it once more.

* * *

Kiggitz didn't drink too much, but he kept a bottle of brandy on
hand to recreate a hot concoction his mother used to make for 'the ague'.
There was about a half-bottle left and he slugged most of it down right
away. He breathed deeply for a while, then opened a can of food for
Sinusoid. The cat, replete with purloined beef chunks from the floor,
refused the slop. Kiggitz chugged the tail-end of the cognac bottle and went
out of his building to get some more.

It was dusk now and the sky between the buildings showed a deep vermillion marbling, like a salmon-colored T-shirt tie-dyed with aortic blood from a wound under the sternum. The mood on the street was skittish, with a pre- or post-event feel in the air. Kiggitz was a lumpish middle-aged man not given to the jitters, but his hair tingled electric and he trembled expectantly.

In the bodega he bought a quart bottle of brandy. He cracked the bottle and took another hit as he stepped back out the street. On the way back he ran into Phyllis, the snooper-lady from down his hall, scuffling through the trash cans out on the street.

She put her hand on his arm, pressing down on the brown paper bag and the brandy bottle. "Hey, Kiggitz, you heard about the thing? Seen the head?" She'd forgotten that they'd already done all this in the hallway. Kiggitz mumbled a no-yeah and stumbled past. Whatever she was talking about could be looked into later.

Much later.

The jitters had hit him hard by the time he got safely home, despite the warm feeling starting to soak into his limbs from the brandy. He took another sizable slug and stroked Sinusoid. It purred. A day with both food and attention from its owner was a very good day.

It was getting dark in the living room, so Kiggitz switched on the desk lamp. He went back to check YouTube for the follow-up video from the researcher. It had been posted promptly, as promised: Part 2 of 4. More to come.

"Animators Dave and Max Fleischer had an obsessive rivalry with Walt Disney Studios. Dave, who was known to consume large quantities of medicinal laudanum, had become convinced that Walt Disney was using black magic to gain a commercial advantage over rival studios."

A graphic of a macabre Mickey Mouse appeared on screen, probably ginned up with AI, and a caption: SPELLBOAT WILLIE?

"Dave Fleischer began to read up on necromancy, and consulted 'The Wickedest Man in the World', Aleister Crowley, who in turn put him in touch with a star of the earliest surrealist films, Lucien Bataille. The actor was known in the thirties as a practitioner of magic and was rumored also to be a necromancer. Here he is with a head divided to signify his puzzlement:"

A screen grab showed a clip from an old film. A man with an astonishing likeness to the YouTuber with his head vertically split in two.

The YouTuber raised an eyebrow quizzically and gave the faux-pained expression which he commonly used to show a combined exasperation and world-weary amusement. He was famous as a dry wit for just this precise gesture, and a mordant comment was customary at just this point.

"Just in case you're wondering, it wasn't me from nearly a century ago. Or maybe it *was* me..." Eyebrow. "A me from a previous life? We'd have to ask Pythagoras all about that..."

Watching, Kiggitz burned with impatience for this self-important pedant to get off his motherfucking schtick, and just spell out what the cartoon meant. At last, witticisms exhausted for now, the YouTube guy spilled the beans.

There'd been a follow-up to 'Swing You Sinners!' he said. The next year, 1931, a short with the suggestive title of 'Bimbo's Initiation' showed the protagonist's sojourn in hell and his initiation to an infernal secret society.

"I'm now going to play the cartoon in its entirety before entering into my commentary. Those who are unschooled in esoterica will likely see a weird animated short, very possibly created under the influence of narcotics. Those initiated into occult significations might see something quite other than that. To those—let's say *initiates*—I say: prepare yourselves however you may."

Kiggitz took another hard swig of the brandy and his stomach burned. The film began.

Cheekily, Disney's Mickey Mouse appears, a bootleg presence, to consign Bimbo to the afterlife. He throws a padlock on the portal to the inferno and skedaddles. Squirted through an anal sphincter into an antechamber of masked cultists, Bimbo refuses to join their sect, and is tormented with a number of traps and devices. Slapstick, yes, but evil slapstick.

In the next chamber is a pool, but the water is solid like concrete. Betty Boop appears from a door and beckons invitingly:
"Come inside, Big Boy!"
Galvanized now by lust, Bimbo cries out "What a Pippin!"

and tries to follow her through the door.

He runs through a tunnel where jagged jaws try to close on him. He ends up back in the first room, the antechamber, facing one of the masked cultists. Again he refuses to join. His unknown adversary strips off mask and robe.

Surprise! It's Betty Boop! She twerks to the jive and slaps her curvesome behind. Bimbo's getting aroused now, and who could blame him? The walls lift and there are dozens of the masked cultists. They all strip off to reveal—yes, dozens of Betty Boops! As Bimbo slaps Betty's sweet tushie, they gyre erotically and the iris closes in to black.

The end.

Kiggitz did not feel as affected by this cartoon as by the first, or so he thought. But now he realised he had a throbbing erection and a deep-seated desire to slap the behinds of hundreds of Betty Boops as they can-canned around him in an endless dance number.

He felt cheapened somehow, kind of as if his mind had been violated, but he was undoubtedly horny. Betty had cursed him with her eerie sex magick and he had nowhere to hide from her swell ass.

* * *

Next morning he awoke with an unprecedented hangover and a ragged memory of having been decapitated by French jihadists in Betty Boop facemasks. Sinusoid swung its tail around his face and miaowed.

A phrase rang round his head: *We gotta get boots on the ground.* Sickness dwelled in his belly like a jelly demon. His skull felt cracked and stove in, as if previously subjected to a vandal's heedless booting.

In the kitchen the coffeemaker dripped, and each drop threatened Kiggitz with a deluge of pain. He palmed ibuprofens and murmured hushed profanities so as not to wake the cerebral predator that was for now sleeping in his head.

After a time he permitted himself to remember the night before. How could he have let himself get so spooked by a silly cartoon?

Now he also remembered what neighbor Phyllis had said about a head thing. He'd meant to check on that but forgot all about it. Now he switched on the TV.

The local news led with it:

Youth Group Attacked by Child Knife Assailants.

Blurry photos and pixelated footage registered some *something* not to be seen, the anchor's words shocked but indefinite, speaking around the thing, not of it.

Though his hangover threatened a full-on resurgence, he rushed over to the laptop table and began to check those sites he knew wouldn't censor the photos. What he saw reignited the agony in his brain and threatened to explode it utterly.

A small child, a white boy maybe 9 or 10 years old, stands with an expression beyond ecstasy. His nylon puffer jacket, orange and pastel green, is stained with vermillion swirls, clots of blood. It is not his. In his left hand, arm outstretched horizontally, he carries a hunter's knife, enormous in his small fist. In his right hand, a human head. A girl child with flaming red hair. The rictus on her face is like a warm welcoming smile.

Hello, madness. Come on in.

* * *

YouTube. Part 3 of 4. Kiggitz knew he shouldn't go on with this, not until his brain had calmed.

But there's the thirst.

It can't be denied.

Thirst for the knowledge. To know the final thing, that final secret.

"So here's the thing," said the YouTuber. "There are three things that keep pulling me back to this story.

"One: this is part of an ongoing back-and-forth between the Fleischers and Walt Disney. Disney responded, with a film of his own, set in an Egyptian tomb beneath a pyramid. Some say the film prefigures Walt's own desire to be eternally preserved like the pharaohs, and was in fact a coded instruction for his own burial."

He raised an eyebrow and did his *oh-brother-dig-that-craziness* look.

"Others, perhaps the majority, say simply that Disney presents an alternative Disneyfied vision of the afterlife based on *The Egyptian Book of the Dead* and a promised redemption for the soul whose owner would undergo the proper ritual preparation."

Here all the YouTuber's customary flippant amusement fell away. His mood turned solemn and his voice hushed almost to a whisper.

"Two: There is a lost sequence, a missing middle, between the first film, 'Swing You Sinners!' and the later film 'Bimbo's Initiation'. This film, it is rumoured, depicted a number of forbidden procedures described by Aleister Crowley to Dave Fleischer. Namely, rites derived from the Bornless Ritual, with its invocation to the Headless One:

"I summon you Headless One, who created earth and heaven, who created night and day. My name is a heart encircled by a serpent."

The researcher's recitations of ritual phrases were always perfect, his enunciation sonorous and dripping with portent. This one made the hairs on the nape of Kiggitz's neck stand on end.

"This cartoon film was believed destroyed, but was also once reported to exist among the effects of mysterious and transgressive French author Georges Bataille. He was a cousin of the actor Lucien and somehow came into possession of this film. It's said—not confirmed, but rumored—that Bataille showed the film as a part of the rituals of his own secret society, the *Acéphale* or group of The Headless One. Rumors abound of decapitation and a blood sacrifice to ensure victory of the French Resistance over the Nazis."

Onscreen now a strangely beautiful image of a man, perfectly proportioned like the Da Vinci's *Vitruvian Man*. But with his head missing, stars on his nipples, and his guts a squirming mass of serpents. In his left hand he carries a dagger and in his right hand an orb on fire, maybe like one of those old-timey burning-fuse grenades.

"Bataille died in Paris in 1962, and his daughter, descended on his wife's side from Empress Josephine, inherited the writer and occultist's belongings including the film and notes by Crowley. She moved to New York City where she became a wealthy socialite."

"And the last thing. Sensational as the previous revelations may seem, number three for me is the real kicker. Third of all..."

He did the quizzical eyebrow thing and paused theatrically for effect. Kiggitz started to curse the guy for his showboating. *Get on with it, asshole.*

"Third... Well, in fact this video's gotten kinda long. I'll get into it in my next installment. It's quite involved, and deserves its own at-length discussion of the Orphic Mysteries and the praxis of decapitation sacrifices. Tomorrow, I guess, if all goes well. We switch to New York and the circle of Mrs Amelie van Joost, the twelfth marquise of Beauharnais and daughter of Bataille. Thanks a lot for watching. Like, comment and subscribe."

The YouTuber smiled wanly and faded from the screen. Kigglitz roared with frustrated fury, and kept on roaring until the neighbors above started banging on the ceiling. By this time the brandy bottle was empty and his guts were a roiling mass of serpentine rage.

* * *

By the next day the esoteric researcher had disappeared from YouTube. Channel deleted. Zilch on the social media front. His Subreddit boiled with speculation but very little hard info. Something closed in around this moment and this knowledge teetering on the verge of understanding, and Kiggitz felt like he couldn't stay any longer at home.

But the thought of going *outside*, outside where tiny assassins brandished the severed heads of other children was also unbearable right now.

His hangover raged. It had been unwise of him to chug so much brandy. Unwise to watch the unnerving cartoon. Unwise above all to seek out forbidden photos of inexplicable atrocity. It had awakened demons he knew he had lurking and now they roamed about his synapses at will.

* * *

After a nice long bath he felt much stronger. Not well, mind you, but less fragile. He felt he could now begin to pick up the trail.

Names: Dave Fleischer, Max Fleischer. Aleister Crowley, George Battle,
Battay, or something like that. His daughter.

Rites: Orphic Mystery. The Disney Book of the Dead. Rite of the
Bornless. The Praxis of Decapitation.

Time to hit the darkweb, take a pickaxe to the brittle ore of those forbidden strata, and to see what the hidden iceberg depths would yield of itself.

II: Breaking Down The Barricades
in the Streets of the Dead

June 23. Midsummer, St John's Eve, with the shortest night fast approaching. New moon, to be all dark tonight. As sunset played its futile games over the street below, Kiggitz lowered the blinds. The living room in Kiggitz's apartment had been cleared. A chalk circle had been marked on the cracking vinyl floor, then designs traced out from a sixteenth-century codex, valued in millions but bootlegged as a torrented pdf and hand-copied onto a sheet of paper.

Occult research on a shoestring, budget demonology. Tacks, string, chalk, candles, salt, bought from the corner store. Sacrifice. The whole bit.

This was the culmination of Kiggitz's last two months of intensive research based on the clues in the Fleischer cartoons and leads traced through a tangle of occult arcana. Everything had hinged on the contact linking the cartoonist Fleischer Brothers to Aleister Crowley and the family of Georges Bataille.

Now it only remained to discover if Joe Kiggitz's heart was pure, pure as a magus's heart must be if such a bold transition were to be successfully accomplished.

* * *

Back in April, the day after the 'Brooklyn Babyface Beheadings', as they became snappily known, Kiggitz found that there would never be a final part to the video series on the Fleischer/Disney cartoons and the Headless Rite.

YouTube's esoteric expert had disappeared entirely.

Some on Discord and Reddit suggested he'd packed up and left town. The more lurid ones had him found headless in a ditch in Ohio, with markings carved in his back. One guy posted a blurred photo of a Betty Boop tattoo on a pallid arm and said it was the corpse of the researcher. No convincing traces though.

Soon Kiggitz's dark sleuthing had traced the daughter of George Bataille, Hélène de Lisle, née Bataille, eighty-seven, now known as the Marquise de la Haine, to a private residence in Montauk, on Long Island. He felt that he was hitting his stride as an investigator, but the limits of keyboard and search engine were already reached. Time to put boots on the ground.

He took one of those electric scooters that you can pick up on the streets and rode it up to Long Island. It was a fine spring day and he felt his middle-aged bulk teetering precariously on the scooter would become a delightful sight for drivers and onlookers to take in. He gave them this grace willingly.

The scooter nearly made it to Montauk. Its battery gave out on the last mile. Kiggitz walked it to the end of a jetty and threw it in the sea, which accepted it as gratefully as if it were an offering. He walked on to the house, perked up by sea spray and the chutzpah of pure nihilism.

When the old lady answered the door to the beachfront mansion it was as if prearranged, though they'd never seen or spoken to each other before.

She took him in: adipose, balding, bleary-eyed, pasty-skinned. Fiftyish, sloven, lost.

He took her in: elegant, faded, louche, dessicated, moribund. Not perfect, but good enough. Enough to establish a contact that might extend beyond lifetimes.

Pleasantries of introduction. They went in for Russian-style tea in a samovar.

Rules were established: He was to call her Marquise or else Hélène, but never madame or anything vulgar. She was to call him Mr Kiggitz. There would be plenty of opportunity for intimacy in the time to come. The vagabond jazz of Django Reinhardt and Stephane Grapelli played in her boudoir, scented with jasmine and singed hair.

aFlies blundered at the panes of the broad bay window as they watched the Atlantic roll. They talked of the work. Their shared passion for the rite and the next thing after. La Marquise was able to connect the strands between the Osirian, Eleusinian, and Orphic mystery cults, hook them up to Gnostic and Manichean traditions, and unspool that fat cable of connections right through Neoplatonic mysticism to the alchemists and necromancers working around the Kabbalah in the golden age of magical practice. Kiggitz scribbled in his notebook like a madman.

"Syncretic, they say, *ces imbéciles*? Like that's a bad thing? *Bien sûr*, it's syncretic. What valid system could there be of contact with the *sefirot* and control of demonic forces, derived from just one lousy tradition? More tea, Mr Kiggitz?"

"Uh... Thank you, no. I'm... full. I just... uh, wanted to ask you a little about the studies of your father in this field."

"My father? You know something of the great Georges Bataille?"

"I've heard of him through his acquaintance with the Fleischer brothers, the... uh, animation guys. And his contact around that time with Aleister Crowley?"

Her cheerful countenance clouded up like a mortal rainstorm advancing swift and sudden on a dainty garden party.

"*Aleister Crowley*, you say, Monsieur? All due respect to my father, but he was rather, I would say, *duped* by that fellow. As were so many others. Crowley was a great showman with those googly eyes of his and all that..." she waved her hands, "...flim-flam and sex magick glamor and so on, so forth. But his grasp of Hermeticism was patchy at best. Naturally, *his* is the version of occultism practised by all those charlatans today.'

He bowed his head to his notebook. Wrote, *Crowley stuff NO.*

"So you don't hold much store by Crowley's Bornless Ritual and ...uh, the Headless One?"

"The Headless One?" La Marquise turned her head to scrutinize this visitor closely. "You speak just like that other one, that visitor I had." A silence intervened. Then she stood up, levering herself on her cane, moaning softly at the effort.

"Time for some fresh air, Mr Kiggitz. Let us go for a stroll on the beach."

* * *

It was surprising how loud the seagulls were on the beach. Kiggitz never remembered them this loud. Maybe it was that nobody made them loud in the movies, when the characters walked along the seashore. They had the crashing of waves, sure. But the goddamn screeching of gulls? They never put that in.

"Anoph, Orsita, Atnox, Onigeui, Atziniel, Ankanitei..." La Marquise was reciting with a fine, definite voice.

"Excuse me?"

"...Sabaēl, Boaēl, Sparou, Sōrtērkha, Gabēd. The barbarous names. Do you know them?"

"Of course. Everyone who studies the texts sees them all the time..."

"...But you consider them mere garbage. Noise in the signal. All mere scholars do. Words in no known language, a fun sideline activity for the philologically-inclined. But serious scholars pass them by. A mistake."

She hobbled onwards to where the seagulls wheeled shrieking like banshees over the corpse of something washed up on Montauk beach.

"There's power in them, you mean? But transcription errors..."

"Transcription! *Mais, quelle bétise si énorme!* The scribes and scholars who did this work knew well what they were doing, Kiggitz. Those who came later, the Crowleys of this world who were looking for nice clean lines of poetry. They filtered out the messy parts, and got their poetry, but they sucked out all the efficacy, the jagged surging power of the ritual."

She stopped hobbling down the boardwalk and leaned heavily on her cane. Kiggitz saw now she was breathing deeply and beginning to look her age. He overcame his repulsion to touch and took the old woman's elbow. She leaned into Kiggitz, who could feel the weight of the years, caught the sour dry smell of death. He knew then that this woman, for all her energy and defiance of age, was dying. Not right now, not at this moment, but soon enough.

"The summoning of spirits is not a poetic activity, Mr Kiggitz. It is messy and it is dangerous. Raw with possibilities. Remember what the spirit said to John Dee? *I have broken down the barricades in the streets of the dead. I have defied the laws of all times and all generations.* Rebel insurgency in the borderlands of the afterlife, monsieur Kiggitz! After such knowledge, such liberation, what forgiveness?"

* * *

Most of the time Kiggitz spent scribbling in his notebooks till his wrist ached, while the Marquise poured forth a constant torrent of esoterica, speaking impromptu but with great coherence.

Accursed Share.

Death and Sensuality.

Where was all this going? She knew. She looked into his eyes and he saw the desperation there. The need to go on, even when the time had come. To transgress all border treaties that operated on the frontier of death.

For days he stayed at her beachfront house, drinking Russian tea, eating stale baklava. Filling up his notebooks. The sessions went on and on, and though they might doze a little in their armchairs they would always wake and go on.

The Wonder-Working Word.

On the Magic of the Ancients.

Flowers of Evil.

"Sur l'oreiller du mal c'est Satan Trismégiste
Qui berce longuement notre esprit enchanté"

She recited, but he couldn't understand the French. He paused in his scribbling.

"No, monsieur K? You do not know the poems of Baudelaire? He called Satan the Trismegistus, the thrice-great, like the alchemists they called Hermès the first alchemist. Can you think why? He goes on...

"Aux objets répugnants nous trouvons des appas;
Chaque jour vers l'Enfer nous descendons d'un pas,
Sans horreur, à travers des ténèbres qui puent.

"From repugnant things we find our delights, and each day we descend a step into Hell, but without horror, through stinking shadows." She grinned wide, exposing her yellowed teeth. "Without horror. What lesson do we learn from this? That wisdom comes from cleaning up, like Crowley with the texts, cleaning up the mess? That Satan-Hermès wants everything tidy in his rites? *Non!*"

Now she stood up, leaning on her cane. "The final stages of what you seek will involve a certain... repugnance. Put away your fears, act without any horror. Do what you need to have done."

She unbuttoned the top buttons of her blouse, "Monsieur Aleister Crowley, he did recognize one thing. That there must be some exchange of the carnal in order to initiate magick. Look at your teacup, Kiggitz. I put something there for you while you were napping."

Kiggitz looked. Next to the teacup, resting on a saucer, was a pale blue pill with a diamond on it.

"You will perhaps need this for strength in the task ahead," said the Marquise. "A certain... physical vigor will now be required. Know what Baudelaire said about achieving Hell's wisdom?"

Her blouse fell to the floor, the cane with it.

"Ainsi qu'un débauché pauvre qui baise et mange
Le sein martyrisé d'une antique catin...

"Like the poor depraved soul who slurps and chews on the wizened breasts of an ancient whore, we seek our clandestine pleasures... and when we find them we squeeze them, we squeeze them dry like an old orange."

Kiggitz found himself rising, crossing the living room to nuzzle her withered dugs and to grasp inexpertly at the fastenings of her skirt. She lowered herself carefully onto the wide leather armchair and mewed and laughed, soft as a kitten.

* * *

He guessed it of course. He could smell it on her as they coupled. She was dying, the cancer advanced and the agony of it held at bay by her sheer determination and strength. Now the time was approaching, now the magick had been sealed, and she begged him silently with her eyes to end this stage of the transition.

Descend the step. Without horror. He reached for the pillow and slowly stretched it over her face.

Her house was rich with takings. Cash, jewels. She'd wished him to have it all. He took it. Then he went back to the city.

* * *

After all the meticulous preparations, the fasting, the chalk circles and the inscriptions and the scatterings of salt, the actual ritual was a simple thing.

Blood and other fluids were spilled into a goblet, a life was lost, preparatory incantations were recited, and a bond was made in a form of words acceptable to the dwellers in another space. It was a filthy degrading business permeated with chaos, but it was not at all complex once you knew the forms.

Kiggitz felt at once the presence in him.

Interesting. So this is what it's like.

'Don't hurt me.'

Hurt you? You are my vessel. Why would I want to hurt you? We have a bond.

'A bond?'

A bond, a bargain. Don't come over all coy. It was you who invoked me. You who sealed the bond.

'I'm just a bit... a little spooked.'

Ha ha. Good one. Spooked. You are indeed a little spooked, mon cher.

'Will you help me?'

You know I must. That is the nature of our bargain.

'What will you have in return?'

You know that too.

Movies would have a scene where the cat arches its back and hisses at the invasion of its space by such a preternatural thing. In reality, Sinusoid seemed quite pleased with this intrusion and acted quite familiar with its presence. It mewed contentedly.

'What happens when we step beyond the inscribed circle? Will you return?'

To whence I came? No. The circle is more like an aid to concentration than a boundary. The true circle of our containment is all circumference and no centre.

'So it's done? You're here to stay?'

I would never dream of leaving. We are as one, mon amour. Right now is a critical moment in time. It's very exciting.

* * *

The neighbor guys were chugging beer on the stoop when he went out with the trash.

"Hey Kiggitz, whereya goin'?"

"Take out the trash."

"Ya hear 'bout that baby, got abducted? Stole right out from the stroller over there at the corner."

"Nah, I ain't heard nothin'."

"Whatcha got in yer trash bag there?"

"Trash.""Trash, huh?"

"Yeah, there's trash in my trash bag. I'm... you know... I'm takin' out the trash."

"Let's take a look. C'mon, lemme see there."

The other guys gathered round. Phyllis as well, peering out from above, upper body shoved out of her window. Kiggitz opened the bag and showed them: empty cartons, cans, cookie packets.

"Ya know, you should recycle. Like, separate yer trash, ya know? Save tha muthafuckin' planet."

Kiggitz shuffled off toward the trash wheelie on the street in front of the building.

Told you so. Next time they won't bother looking.

* * *

Living with the presence was like being married or something, only with no downtime. No me-time. Always on. It—she—pushed Kiggitz further and further on the path toward *L'Acéphale,* the Headless One.

Thing about mon papa, Bataille, old Georgie-boy. He was a dabbler, a dilettante. Like you. Not that there's anything wrong. There's a certain virtue in being a sincere amateur. Ecclesiastes: Of the many books there is no end; much study is a weariness of the flesh. But mon père Bataille, he knew just two things: the Headless One and the Chaos.

All those tomes and codices and grimoires you've gathered and scanned and stored away in your darkweb dungeon? Forget that. Let the gift of death's insight, which is promised to each, descend on each like a new Pentecost.

All those nuggets of research, the whos, the wheres? Let them go. Embrace the chaos of unknowing. Let the black blossoms fall where they will. And awaken now in the dark clarity of your own void.

The being's sermon was relentless and eloquent. It convinced Kiggitz to get a passport, fast-track, urgent. It convinced Kiggitz to buy a plane ticket. It convinced Kiggitz to let Sinusoid slowly consume what was left over from the ritual while he was away, and not to risk another sortie with the stoop guys.

Kiggitz's savings plus her loot, diamonds converted to cash. Enough for a one-way trip to Paris and a month or two's research. Boots on the ground. Time to burn down the barricades in the streets of the dead.

III: Desert of the Drinker of Blood

I meet a being who makes me laugh because he is headless, made of innocence and crime;
he holds a steel weapon in his left hand, flames like those of a Sacred Heart in his right.
He reunites in the same eruption Birth and Death. He is not a man. He is not a god
either. He is not me, but he is more than me; I discover myself as him, in other words as a
monster.

—*The Sacred Conspiracy*, 'Acéphale', 1937

There were hundreds of tantalizing threads scattered round the Forest of Marly, which spread out on the western outskirts of Paris. It made Kiggitz long for his laptop and a connection to the darkweb, just so as he could log them all, spool through the web of connections and so weave a tapestry. But what was the point? He wasn't doing that kind of research any more.

He'd left his laptop at home, taking with him to his rented cottage on the western fringe of Paris just a few select notes. Wandering through the forest with his companion was all the research he needed. Vagabond scholarship. Doing the footwork.

Georges Bataille had lived with his lover Colette Peignot in St Germain, just next to the forest, in 1937 and 1938, when the Acéphale Secret Society was active.

Papa was a rolling stone, said the voice. *Wherever he laid his head was his home.*

Just inside the forest was the ruined Castle of Retz. Owned by the Retz or Rais family, from which had come the warlord Gilles de Rais. Former comrade of Joan of Arc, necromancer, notorious murderer of children and drinker of their blood.

Mon semblable, mon frère, said his companion. *He is me, and he is my blood-drinking brother aussi.*

Her father Bataille had written a study of Gilles de Rais, dubbing him The Sacred Monster. The Rais family castle, levelled now amid the trees and leaves in the forest, reputedly had a secret tunnel leading to the nearby Désert de Retz.

Désert, which isn't like a desert in English, he'd learned; *désert* defined as 'a place propitious for cultivating dreams and nostalgia.' Owned by Lewis Disney between 1792 and 1827. Disney's secret place, then, a wonderland for cultivating dreams and nostalgia. An ornate garden and a fantastic tower sculpted as a giant broken column. *Look on my works ye mighty and despair.* Synthetic ruin of a gargantuan past that never was. Words and connections.

There was another wandering around this forest. Apart from Kiggitz himself and that Other with him. A man Kiggitz spied sometimes between trees, but who was gone the next instant, dissolved in the drizzle.

A familiar face. Who was he?

Words and connections to make his head spin. Strange not-strange faces. But there was also that solemn adjuration to *let the black blossoms fall as they may.* So he ignored constellations of concurrences, and instead wandered the forest in the wintertime with the ghost gray Temple of Montmartre off to the east.

On those days when there were clear skies, the dome of the Temple shone golden. Paris: radiant city in the pearl light of the morning mists.

Très jolie, cette p'tite poesie. The voice spoke about her father's practices:

In the late 1930s, as war approached, Bataille *père* would issue instructions for his adepts. On nights with a full moon, take the train to Saint-Nom-la-Bretèche, a tiny station in the middle of the forest. Walk the indicated path to a grove.

Adepts were forbidden to speak of the rites, but there are always blabbermouths. 'I only remember that particular evening as pouring with rain. There was a Greek fire at the foot of a tree struck by lightning.'

Kiggitz walked in radian spider web search patterns from the station seeking a tree struck by lightning. Instead he found a stone altar carved like a baroque card table. Granite as old as time, lichen-stained and cracked; curlicues and dainty details of flowery embellishments. A place of sacrifice?

There were rumours of sacrifices, of violations and undefined orgies with people and things, alive and otherwise. Bataille had written: 'I want to have my throat slashed while violating the girl to whom I will have been able to say: you are the night.' It was said that his lover Colette Peignot had been selected for such a role, that either she or Bataille would in this way be given over to a hecatomb of ecstasy and abnegation.

But she died in 1938 of a humdrum cancer—*comme moi!*—and had left him all alone with war clouds gathering to the east. *And then he met my mother, the sad princess. And the war was as bad as he knew it would be, and he stopped none of it.*

Kiggitz was not used to walking so much. His calves ached after kilometres ambling in foreign woodland. It was critical that no path be taken that had been trodden before; each step must be taken anew on a path newly taken.

He slept deeply in his rented bed and far-off screams from home were hardly at all remembered after he woke up. Always he woke with that other one still there.

Just like being married.

Finally, in 1939, Bataille at long last decreed that The *Acéphale* Society must become worthy of its name. The war was coming and with it the end of play at childish games of death's mystery.

Headlessness, erected to counter Hitler's demonic comb-flicked head, must be made real by true sacrifice.

On a night under the full moon, by an oak blasted by lightning, on his knees he begged them to take the large knife from his left hand and to take off his head. To his disappointment, or his relief, nobody would become his executioner.

As he wept like a child, naked on his knees, the knife fell from his hand. The others, embarrassed, or pitying—who could say?—the others, they just walked away.

* * *

Finally, in 2025, Kiggitz at long last came to understand that his wandering excursions in the woods must only be carried out by night. Nothing could be achieved by drifting around like a tourist during the daylight hours.

I told you so, mon amour.

'You did not.'

Let's not bicker and quibble. I feel assured that if we go out tonight with the full moon blessing our labours, our research will finally yield its fruits.

'What are we looking for again?'

What indeed? 'Wheres' and 'hows' are nothing, even 'whats', 'why' only has the power. It may well be that any quest such as ours is doomed from the outset. But what do I know? I'm just a poor French diable. Far from home, or is it you?

It was not possible to look directly at that Other. It always evaded plain sight, slinking like a swift black cat ahead of his gaze. But Kiggitz sometimes caught quick glimpses of it at the periphery of his sight, or in a mirror. Familiar yet unfamiliar. An unfamiliar familiar. *Mon semblable, mon frère!*

Strands of frayed memory like worn cords in unravelled time.

"What is it that you want me to do?" Kiggitz wailed in the rented room. The sound was startling and strange in that empty little space.

Then a knock at the door of the rented apartment.

* * *

"May I come in?" An American, by his accent, wearing a fat muffler, a woollen toque, and thick black sunglasses despite the night.

He took them off now and pulled on a pair of spectacles. Those eyes... so familiar. The voice too, from somewhere...

Kiggitz gestured for him to pass through into the kitchen. The stranger took off the wool cap and the scarf and sat down at the kitchen table. Now Kiggitz knew him.

"I... I'm... a big fan of your work," he stammered.

The visitor, said the Other. *The man who pressed me for details of my father.*

It was the esoteric researcher from YouTube. Haggard, face papery and pallid, beard clean-shaved—but clearly and recognizably him. He gasped out a request for a drink. Kiggitz fetched him a brandy from the duty-free bottle he'd bought at JFK. He'd never met a celebrity and was feeling quite giddy in the presence of this man who'd set a small corner of the internet alight, and who moreover had created so much mystery with his sudden disappearance from the United States.

"I guess you may be wondering why I dropped in on you like this," said the man.

He knows the place, said the Other.

"See, I was looking, and I saw you looking too... and I kind of followed you back here. The thing is..." he took a large swig from the brandy glass.

He knows the place.

"The thing is, I know the place. That is, I *think* I know the place. We could find it together, if you like."

Question him. Get the location out of him. Then take care of him.

Kiggitz went to fetch a map of the forest, a kitchen towel to gag the screams, and the kitchen knife. The AirBnB owner had a set of excellent kitchen knives.

Trust the French.

* * *

The mist was luminous in the shine of the moon's grace. Kiggitz shuffled softly, his nose streaming and breath clouding up. What he'd done to get to this place. Where two paths meet under the moon and where stood an oak tree blasted by lightning. What he'd done to arrive at this crossroad: the deaths he'd cau–

Told you I'd bring you here. The map in your belly is the labyrinth and this is its centre. Get digging.

Scrabbling with the big kitchen knife, Kiggitz dug at the roots of the tree. He scooped up soil and tossed it behind him. After some time he reached some bones, light and fragile, a little skull cracked like an egg. He threw them aside and dug deeper. The borrowed blade slashing into the root system.

He had a quick flash of it dividing the researcher's head like a melon. The vision of the old film made real. Mess and understanding. Who knew the old man had so much blood in him? Now left behind in a rented apartment he'd never return to.

Going great, Kiggitz. Nearly there.

'Why didn't you tell me about this place before?'

Waiting for you to become ready, for the hour to be propitious. Ripeness is all.

He hit something hard, the *thunk* of it shocking into his shoulder. A little medicine chest covered in moulding leather. Solid though. Don't make 'em like that anymore.

He carved a space out from the soil around it and pulled it free. His breath was ragged and fiery on his chest.

* * *

National Film Board:
Note on Film Preservation

Nitrate-based film has certain excellent qualities, but its chemical composition destabilizes radically over time. As it ages, it has a tendency to shrink, to give off gases that destroy the emulsion, and to become highly flammable at relatively low temperatures. It can ignite spontaneously. Large nitrate fires have occurred, most disastrously at Mexico's *Cineteca Nacional* in 1982, and at a warehouse for the *Cinémathèque Française* outside Paris in 1980.

* * *

Officers Etienne and Fátima were just winding up their patrol at 3.47am. The night had gone quietly, a domestic over in Saint Germain and a suspected break-in at Chambourcy that hadn't been anything serious. Now they were on their last swing around the perimeter. They drove down the Route des Princesses to the place where the forest trails diverge, and the barrier blocks the way to cars. Etienne started to turn the car around.

Fátima caught the thing out of the corner of her eye. Flicker of flame through the trees. Down on the path that leads to the *Table de Vénerie*, this weird altar thing in the middle of the forest. She told Etienne to hold up. He stopped the car just next to the barrier and they both gazed down the path.

Sure enough there was a flame like the light of a burning torch, *un flambeau*, moving up the path towards them. They got out of the car and moved side by side through the barrier towards it.

A person, apparently a man, moving arms outstretched at a steady stride. In his right hand he carried a burning circle. In his left hand something metallic. One hundred metres. What was up with that head?

Etienne started to call it in on his radio. "Forêt de Marly, male suspect behaving... uh, possibly armed, backup requested."

By now it was clear that the item in the left hand was a large knife. The flickering light from the flaming object in his right made it hard to see the face. Head obscured by shadow.

Then it stepped into the space where three paths met and Fátima had her flashlight on it. It was walking straight at them with a flaming firebomb and a knife and no head.

She screamed.

Fifty metres.

Protocol had it that they were to call out repeated warnings: *AGENTS DE POLICE ARMÉS, ARRETEZ-VOUS!* But as they fumbled at their holsters they forgot protocol.

Nothing was called out except panicked yells with no words.

Twenty-five metres.

They aimed, as they are trained to do, for center of body mass. One, two, three, four blasts sounded in less than a second. The figure fell back, chest and torso shredded. The round flaming object rolled right, the knife dropped left.

They advanced, guns raised on the fallen thing, covering each other. Fátima's flashlight carried left-hand played over the figure.

Blood all over the caved chest starting to pool on the gravel.

Down, definitely down.

They reassuringly called *"target down"* to each other and into the radio, but far from diminishing, their hysteria started to ramp up and up when they looked down and saw it.

* * *

```
REPORT FROM PREFECTURE DE POLICE, PARIS, INTO
DEATH OF UNIDENTIFIED MALE, PARC FORÊT DE MARLY
```

Presumed cause of death: multiple gunshot wounds
to thorax. But see below.

Recovered at the scene: A kitchen knife with clods
of soil and traces of blood. One reel of
silver-nitrate cinema film, film destroyed by
fire, spool unburnt, hand-labelled clearly in
English.
Obverse: 'Amputate Your Vo-Do-Dee-Oh. May 1931'.
Reverse: 'David Fleischer and Walt Disney. All
Rights Reserved.'

Suspect condition: Neck severed cleanly, four
centimetres above collarbone. No observable blood
flow from severed neck stump. No blood traces
discernible on neck or shoulders. Whereabouts of
head unknown.
Suspect presumed to have died from condition of
being headless, body subsequently brought down by
small arms fire of agents.

For background on post-decapitation perambulatory
state, refer incident to Special Unit Acéphale,
Department 171, Direction centrale de
renseignement intérieur.

Action recommended: Reassign agents to overseas
duty. Attempt to locate head, trace whereabouts of
suspect before death. Consult with Department 171
on demonological countermeasures to be taken.
Destroy this file.

A Punishment Worth Taking

by Landon K. Mar

Wide double doors opened with a thunderous groan. A young girl with choppy black hair and eyes as dark as the deepest oceans stepped inside. The girl, Yara, stormed into the ornate study with extravagant glass windows that allowed moonlight to trickle inside, casting everything it touched with a white light, cursing the dark recesses it could not reach in a cold, black shadow—a clear division as the night ticked on.

Yara's brow furrowed as her gaze cast about the room. She examined the lavish study that displayed a level of wealth and prestige despite the pall of night. **H**igh bookshelves with hefty tomes and mystical artifacts tucked behind spell-protected glass filled this space. It was gorgeous. But Yara just sneered at every single one of them as she charged past, each step chiming out within the chamber.

Tears glistened on Yara's cheeks as the moonlight caressed her face with the tenderness reminiscent of a hug. Sniffling, the young mage grabbed the collar of her charred shirt and rubbed the evidence of her vulnerability away. Yara dropped her hand down to her side, but not before grazing against a worn locket with a faded picture stuffed peculiarly inside.

When Yara reached the back of the room she stood before a framed world map. She carefully tugged the picture off of its throne on the wall, holding her breath as she did. Setting it aside, she could see there was a perfect square carved into the wall that the map had hidden. Yara raised her hands and weaved intricate glyphs and sigils in the air. The ley lines shimmered and made themselves visible across the air as she plucked each piece with careful precision, doing her best to deconstruct the magical alarm system that her mentor had placed upon it. Her dark brows pinched together while sweat dripped down her face. Yara gritted her teeth, feeling time ticking down the longer she was there. Her mentor may be one of the most sought-after practitioners of the craft in the country—

But Yara was better.

She moved a few ley lines around, **d**rew more symbols in the air with her fingers, and flicked them away with a snap of her wrist. She whispered a few familiar phrases until the magical alarm system was incapacitated, leaving the ley lines to flutter away like rotting petals.

With the alarm disarmed, Yara breathed in deeply as she reached inside, procuring an opalite box. It shone with pearlescent colors as she tilted it with something akin to reverence in the moonlight. Making up her mind, Yara snapped open the lid and inside the velvet-lined box was a golden pocket watch with intricate patterns and raised filigree. The face was spotless— glyphs representing the Twelve Great Stars rendered in metal instead of numbers, something any practicing mage was familiar with. The hands of the watch looked ornate and delicate, as though one gentle breeze would snap them into pieces.

Yara wiped her face once more but with the edge of her torn sleeve this time. The simmering rage she had felt bubbling inside her belly, which had fueled her body the last few days, had burned away. All she felt looking at the object of her desire was a numbness she tried to push past. But when she glanced down at the locket and it hit her—tears welled up in her eyes once more as the small metal frame showed a picture of Yara and her family.

This was it.

This illegal mystical artifact was going to stop the Emperor from murdering her family.

Simply because they were rebels who wanted to end his tyranny.

She fiddled with the grooved knob of the pocket watch and spun the hands with desperation between sobs until it rewound to the time before the murder. She sucked in a breath, hands shaking with adrenaline as she was just a click of her thumb away from activating the artifact. Yara exhaled shakily, savoring the moment and—

"I had a feeling you would be here."

The girl jumped as her eyes widened, realizing she wasn't alone.

Her mentor stepped forward—her dark galaxy-blue robes shone and fluttered with each step like dancing daffodils. There was a frown on the woman's face and her deep cobalt blue eyes furrowed with disappointment. Something about that glaze of disapproval lit something inside of Yara. Something uncontrollable.

"You let them die!" Yara snarled, tightening her hold on the pocket watch but careful not to depress the crown of the winding stem. "You could have told the Emperor to stop—convinced him to let them go, that they were innocent!" Her words grew more amplified with each assertion:

"But you didn't! You helped murdered my family!"

Her mentor let the echo of the young mage's words bound off of the bookshelves around them. When the sounds faded, she shook her head with a desperate plea. "Yara...I'm so sorry. But your family was trying to go against the Emperor, I couldn't go against him. You know how powerful he—"

"No!" Yara jabbed the pocket watch in front of her, her thumb hovering close over the crown. Her mentor gasped at the jolt, reaching her hand out toward Yara and the **a**rtifact.

"I know you're upset, but time travel is not the answer! There are consequences—there's a reason why the Emperor outlawed it in the first place, trust me, Yara. Please." The mentor's face was pallor as she frowned deeper at Yara. "You will be forced to carry the burden of your guilt if you time travel. It will haunt you forever."

"So what?" Yara sniffed as fresh burning tears rolled down her flushed cheeks.

"You cannot go against the rules. You cannot mess with time or prevent the dead from staying dead."

That struck a chord inside of the young girl.

The locket that hung around her neck let out a phantom burn as she recalled the screams of her family being slaughtered before her very eyes.

There was a heavy pause as Yara tossed a wry look at her mentor.

"I'm saving my family no matter the cost. And then, I'm going to kill the Emperor." "Yara!—"

The girl pushed down onto the knob on the pocket watch's graceful stem—when she did, a mechanism forged by dead mages deep within the artifact screamed. The noise reverberated throughout its surroundings until a burst of bright, golden light engulfed the chamber, swallowing Yara whole.

What Lies Buried Below

by Amy Leanne Johnston

She threw me down a hole.

Or... a *chute*, I guess, built into the floor. Long, square, utilitarian —something you'd throw laundry into. Or garbage. Maybe that's all it was to her: a chore. Something boring and vaguely distasteful.

Was I an idiot? Years spent sneaking around, breaking into libraries, studying the symbol inked on the shoulders of Sigil Knights, looking for something, anything, proof, a sign... I thought I was being so careful. So clever. Maybe I got cocky.

Or maybe sometimes you just get caught.

Before she threw me in, she tied my arms tightly behind my back and wrapped strips of cloth over my eyes and mouth. With one delicate finger, she tilted my chin up.

"You know the old stories," she said, her voice light as a lullaby. "*To look upon it is to witness your own end. To speak is to grant it your last breath.* I only wish to give you a fighting chance, dearheart. Now..." She gently pulled the gag out of my mouth. "Any last words?"

 Bile rose in my throat. But what could I say to someone like her? What would give justice to those she made suffer? What would force her to see people as more than a means to an end?

There were no words.

But if I couldn't be verbose, I could damn well be bitter.

My lip raised in contempt. "Long live the queen," I spat.

She hummed, amused.

"Thank you, dear," she said. "I plan to."

Queen Iina, sixth of her name, replaced my gag, put her hand flat on my chest, and pushed me into the dark.

* * *

"Did you hear about the prince?"

Aven stared straight ahead, watching the Sigil Knights spar. The metallic cacophony of ringing swords could not quite drown out the whispers of their fellow squires, seated beside them on the benches.

"No," someone said, leaning forward. "What about him?"

"I heard he's *missing*," the first person said.

"What?!"

"I *know*. This morning his bedroom was empty. The queen's got a whole slew of knights looking for him, and the ones at the wall are on high alert."

The wall.

Aven's stomach twisted.

The sprawling city of Cyphon was surrounded by a giant wall of red and green stone. Beyond it, horrors befitting the cruelest of fairy tales waited, teeth bared, for anyone foolish enough to step outside.

A chill crept down Aven's spine. *I hope you know what you're doing, Raine.*

A horn sounded. The knights all relaxed, dropping their swords and shields to the ground where they stood. The squires around Aven abandoned their conversations and sprang up: dozens of thin, waifish bodies scrambling to be the first to pick up the knights' discarded playthings. They were hoping to showcase their good work ethic and can-do attitude. It was a waste of time, and energy. The knights only paid attention to squires when they had demands to make of them.

Teams of two picked up the swords while teams of three handled the shields. Aven scanned the field before joining a man with angry, gray eyes. Younger—he'd been a squire for only a few weeks now, and it showed. The bags under his eyes, the trembling hands, the graying lips. Another nobleman who'd begun to learn the price of hard work.

Currently, he had his fingers under the rim of a shield, attempting to lift it by himself. His face was red from the effort.

"Good way to break your fingers," Aven said, squatting. "Or your spine. But if that's not what you're going for, maybe I better help."

The man glared at them. "I don't need help from a *commoner*."

"Creative insult," Aven said. They waved someone over. "Very scathing. But no one squire is stronger than any other. And as a *commoner*, I happen to know what brittlesnap does to the human body. I've seen folk take a step and hit the ground as their bones crumbled like chalk inside their leg. Watched the light refuse to leave the eyes of a body that had stopped working, until they had no choice but to die."

They gave the man an even stare. " It's not an experience I recommend."

The man's jaw worked in frustration, but he said nothing more. The third squire arrived and took her position. Together, they hefted the shield up and ferried it inside, releasing it with a *thunk* onto the rack.

Aven exhaled, massaging their tender fingers as they turned to head back out—but a senior squire suddenly filled the archway. Her eyes were wide, her chest heaving. She leaned against the frame, fighting for breath.

"It's... the prince!" she gasped. She doubled over, head between her knees.

Aven's heart climbed up their throat and stayed there, trembling.

"Prince Raine," she said, straightening. She looked over the stunned crowd. "They... they're saying... he's *dead!*"

* * *

I must have blacked out, somewhere on the journey between up and down. I remember the sensation of falling, the feeling of leaving my stomach behind as my body dropped, slamming into the stonework of a steep slope. I barely felt it. Could only feel the blood pumping in my ears, the quiver deep in my chest. I was more scared than I have ever been in my entire life.

It was the fear, I think, that saved me the trip down. Fear that soothed my raging heart with the brief respite of unconsciousness. I almost wish I could've stayed there.

Alas—the impact woke me.

Pain and the taste of iron and a dull ringing in my head. I tried to take stock of the damage, expecting all the bones in my body to be dust. But, somehow, I was intact. Just a few bruises, a welt on my head, and a sharp pain in my mouth. I'd bitten my tongue.

Beneath me, the ground crumbled under my searching fingers. Dirt. During the fall I'd left masonry behind and entered the jagged embrace of rock walls. It smelled stale and untouched. The darkness beyond my blindfold was complete.

Then—something shifted in the dark, and I went very still.

You know the old stories, she had said. And I did.

Many have tried to describe the monster lurking under the streets of Cyphon. They give it spider-like limbs, curving ram horns, glowing red eyes—all nonsense. No one can describe the creature, because no one has ever laid eyes on it and lived to tell the tale.

The Unseen.

I've had my doubts about the existence of monsters *outside* the wall for a long time—but the Unseen has records. Historical accounts. Enough specific, tangible evidence that it cannot be discounted.

Especially not when it was headed right for me.

I waited for as long as I dared, then took a deep breath and held it.

Pff, pff, pff…

Its footfalls, surprisingly delicate against the packed earth.

Wow, I thought, somewhat deliriously, *I'm the only living person in the world who knows the Unseen has* feet.

Pff, pff, pff…

Closer and closer, until there was no denying its presence. Most creatures give off a certain amount of heat, but not the Unseen. Instead, it felt like a winter breeze froze in midair to hover over me, waiting. Watching.

Keep going, I begged it. *Please, just keep going.*

My lungs strained against my chest, begging for air. Sweat broke out on my lower back. With all my might, I willed myself not to tremble.

For what felt like hours it stood there, until every tattered scrap of hope I dared to harbor vanished in the dark.

Then it said, "Pull your hands apart."

Its voice was hollow and heavy, like the faraway ringing of a church bell. I breathed out in a burst, but held my tongue. *It's a trick*, I thought. *Don't speak. Don't even move.* I stayed perfectly still. It couldn't hurt me. Not unless I let it.

"I have all the time in the world," it tolled. "You, however, do not. Queen Iina wanted you out of the way, yes? You can either take that lying down..." I felt it lean closer, the wave of cool air biting against the side of my face. "Or you can get. Back. Up."

I shivered.

I didn't know its motivations, but if this thing was trying to help me, I was in no position to refuse. I rolled onto my stomach, my chin digging into the dirt, and strained against the bindings as best I could.

My arms flung to either side as the ropes fell free. I wasted no time getting as far from the Unseen as I could, knocking my head against the wall and groping at it until I'd pulled myself up.

The Unseen said nothing, but I could hear it breathing—even and deep, like the darkness between us.

I couldn't let my guard down. Legends spoke of the Unseen's trickery, its knack for teasing words out of its victims. I kept my lips sealed tight and forced myself to breathe through my nose. Despite everything, I found myself grateful for the gag.

"Now," it said finally, "follow me."

It padded down the tunnel without another word.

* * *

The hardest part about following the Unseen wasn't the pitch-blackness around us or its near-silent footfalls or the constant ache in every part of my body—it was my own spiraling thoughts.

I didn't know how I was going to die.

No one knows what the Unseen does to its victims for the same reason no one knows what it looks like. Hundreds of years ago, before it was banished underground, the Unseen took people silently, in the dead of night. All it had to do was make a noise, get someone to investigate, and that was that. The person either saw the creature, or they called out to it, and vanished without a trace.

Would I be eaten, or turned into a puff of smoke? Maybe torn to shreds and stuffed into individually labeled jars. There was no telling. But that didn't stop me from envisioning stranger and more gruesome deaths with each turn we took.

"Stop," it said. The echo of its voice was different here, like we'd entered a cavern. Something ahead smelled rotten. "Don't move."

It walked forward and I heard the rattling of glass, the thump of wood, the splat of something heavy and wet hitting the ground. It sounded like the Unseen was rummaging through a garbage heap.

As it did so, I realized the darkness was no longer complete. Under my blindfold, through the gap made by my nose, I could just make out the texture of the cave floor, suffused in a dim, greasy light. Survival instinct beat curiosity, however, and I shut my eyes. Light was my enemy here. So long as I could see, I was at double the risk of meeting my end.

The last sound I heard, after a period of silence, was the tearing of paper and the thud of a rock.

"All right," it said.

We wove through more tunnels until we arrived, again, at a cavern.

I pressed against the cave wall and fought the urge to collapse. My legs had a strange ache to them that's hard to describe. My mind immediately went to brittlesnap—but I didn't feel *weak*. I just felt *sore*. I'm still not sure what to make of it.

With a series of thumps, the Unseen placed several things in front of me. Then its cool presence receded.

"There is food," it said, "and a cot. After I leave, count out two minutes before attempting to light the lantern. Douse the flame when you go to sleep. Should you hear anything at all, close your eyes and keep them closed. Nod if you understand."

What?

It... had set me up a *bedroom*?

"Gestures do not count as speaking," it said, misinterpreting my silence. "Do you understand?"

Feeling numb, I nodded.

"Good. Inside the crate are matches, as well as paper and a stick of charcoal. Write down everything that has happened since you came here, in as much detail as you can. This is *important*. Do you understand?"

Not in the slightest, I thought.

I nodded.

"Good," it sighed. "Then I will leave you."

And it did.

I counted out the minutes, fumbled for the lantern and, once it was lit, collapsed onto the cot. My hands shook. My mind buzzed. The weak light cast timid shadows on the uneven cave walls.

"What," I murmured, "the *fuck*."

* * *

Queen Iina stood on a raised platform in front of the castle gates, flanked on both sides by her Sigil Knights. Directly below, the faces of nobles looked up with a mix of concern and morbid fascination. Behind them stood the commoners, called away from work, crowded against each other in the thoroughfare until not a cobblestone could be seen. It was a rare opportunity for most of them—to see the queen in the flesh. To witness the might of the Sigil Knights with their own eyes.

The knights were as impressive as ever—more so, even, in their formal uniforms. Their wide bodies, healthy, glowing skin, and distinct muscles made everyone in the crowd, nobleman and commoner alike, look like a living corpse. Each knight had their right shoulder exposed, drawing the eye to the black symbol that it bore: four connected spirals arranged in a diamond. The symbol of strength. The power of the knight.

But their glory paled to that of the queen.

Despite the grief hunched on her shoulders, she was stunning. Her golden curls fell perfectly across one shoulder. Her blue eyes, clouded in sorrow, were all the more beautiful for it. She wore a gray dress adorned with intricate black lace. The only sign of color on her person were the royal arm bands, which circled each of her upper arms in gold, their red gems glinting in the midday sun.

She raised her chin.

"Generations ago," she began, "my ancestors made the good people of this city a promise. That they need not live in fear. They built that promise with stone and timber, sweat and blood—and it became our wall. The monsters outside could no longer reach us, and the one that remained, the Unseen, was driven underground, where it could harm no one ever again. And I thought—"

Her voice broke and she looked down, fighting back tears. The crowd held its breath.

"I thought we were in this *together*," she managed. "That we all understood that only with a *united* front could we ensure the safety of everyone in Cyphon. But it is with deep... deep regret... that I must inform you that the body of my son, Prince Raine, was found this morning—just beyond the wall."

The crowd erupted into chatter. The rumors were true! The heir to the throne was no more!

Aven, swathed in the shadows of a nearby alley, clenched their thin fingers into fists.

They'd been with him, just yesterday.

They could have stopped this.

They could have tried *harder*.

* * *

A few years before, Aven had figured out that scaling the castle walls took more cunning than it did raw strength, and ever since had been able to visit the prince whenever they pleased by climbing to his balcony and knocking on the doors.

Raine always answered.

Aven would claim the prince's desk chair and Raine would pace around the room, ever restless. They would talk about anything. They would talk about nothing. They would make up stories and schemes and pretend they could change the world.

It had been a long time since Aven believed they could make a difference. But when they were with Raine, anything seemed possible.

That night, he'd been especially riled up.

"I snuck into the library," he said.

Aven smirked. "Again."

"*Again*, yes," the prince conceded. "Every day, actually, for the past couple weeks. I'm still trying to research these supposed *monsters* outside the wall. Monsters that, I'll remind you, *no one* has *ever* seen."

"No one *alive* has ever seen."

"But that's the thing!" Raine waved a finger in Aven's direction, excited. Aven liked seeing him like this. Liked watching the passion swing his body from one side of the room to the other. "Why *not*? We have knights stationed all over the wall, and you're telling me they've never seen anything on the other side? Even in passing? Have never written *anything* down?"

"They're too busy trying to kill each other in training," Aven said dryly. "I don't know if I've *ever* seen a knight sit down and read a book. Maybe the sigil makes them illiterate."

Raine gave them a look. "You're not taking me seriously."

"I am, I am." They raised their hands in surrender. "Sorry. It's just hard for me to worry about what's *outside* the city when we've got enough problems *inside* it. I mean, every day more commonfolk die to brittlesnap while the nobles wave it off as *poor work ethic*." They laughed humorlessly. "Never mind that we're given less food and rest than the nobles. Never mind that most of *them* have never had to work a day in their life."

Raine's brow furrowed. "Are the other squires giving you a hard time again?"

Aven scoffed. "I can handle *them*. I'm just... getting impatient, I guess." They sighed. "I've been a squire for a *decade*, Raine. And I'm no closer to that sigil."

Before Aven met the prince, they'd worked the fields with their parents. Every day was a struggle just to keep their bones from breaking. And in the end, brittlesnap claimed their mother and father—and Aven was left alone.

The *commoners* needed the sigil's strength, not the knights. What use were they anyway, with the wall in place? There hadn't been reports of monster attacks for as long as any of them could remember. If Aven could figure out the magic of the sigils, they could bring it to the people who actually *needed* it. And their best bet was to see the queen bestow the sigil firsthand. Raine knew that was their goal. He'd been the one to insist on Aven's admittance into the Squire's Guild, which had only ever accepted noblemen among its ranks.

Raine sighed and joined them at the desk.

"I understand, Aven," he said. "I do. But..." He tilted his head to look out the window. Aven followed his gaze. Past the royal orchards, the wall cut the sky in half.

"Something about that wall doesn't sit right with me," he said. "And Mother brushes me off every time I ask about it, and the only ones allowed up there are the knights—which I'm forbidden from becoming, and—hell— Why not let us *see* these monsters, if she wants us so badly to be afraid?"

Aven didn't like the look in his eye. "What are you getting at?"

Raine turned to them. He had wide, blue eyes, just like his mother. "Aven, what if there's *nothing* waiting on the other side? What if we cross that wall and all that greets us is the horizon?"

"You're thinking of doing something stupid."

Raine's mouth quirked. "I was thinking of it more as something *brave.*"

Aven stood. "Raine— It doesn't *matter* if there're monsters or not! *Something* happens to people who cross the wall, and if you think you'll be an exception, then you're a *fool.*"

Raine took this in stride, having obviously expected it. "I'm already packed. I've mapped the route. I... leave tonight."

Aven had never known such fury in all their life, stoked ever hotter by the patience on Prince Raine's face. The certainty in his eyes.

"*No,* you don't!"

"Aven—"

"No, *listen.* You can't just—" Aven halted, the words cramming against each other, elbowing for room in their brain. "It's just a *dream,* Raine! You can dream all you like, but it's *my* job to bring you back to reality. And the reality is this: You will die. You'll *die*."

Their voice broke. They looked away.

After a moment, they felt the hesitant brush of Raine's hand against theirs.

"My mind's made up," he whispered.

Aven couldn't look at him.

"What I need *you* to do," he said, "is tell no one where I've gone. I'll see for myself what those walls are hiding, and then I'll return." He took their hand and squeezed. "I won't abandon you, Aven. I promise."

Aven didn't say a word.

* * *

"He is dead," the queen continued, "and we will not *rest* until we find the person responsible."

Aven blinked back to the present.

Wait.

Responsible?

"Someone kidnapped my son and forced him over that wall," the queen said, anger igniting her voice. "We found his body tied up just outside the gate. He was almost unrecognizable after what those... those *things* did to him. And this injustice will not go unpunished. Hear me!" the queen's voice grew louder, more righteous. "Your prince's death will *not go unavenged!*"

The nobles roared approval, the commoners exchanged wary glances. The Sigil Knights began to stomp their feet in rhythm.

"LONG! LIVE! THE QUEEN!" they bellowed.

"LONG! LIVE! THE QUEEN!"

"LONG! LIVE! THE QUEEN!"

Aven stood in the darkness, struck dumb, still and silent as a wooden post.

The queen was... lying.

The queen was *lying*.

And Aven was the only one who knew.

* * *

The Unseen demanded to see my journal this morning. I don't think it even read it; it just wanted proof I'd been writing. I almost don't want to write now, just to spite it, but I have to admit... something about the journal keeps me centered. The lantern light also, dangerous as it is. I have to be alert for any sound so I don't catch a glimpse of the Unseen, but having the chance to look at my own hands, even for a moment, is worth it. Helps remind me that I'm still *me*. Whole. Alive.

I'm still alive.

The Unseen led me deeper into the tunnels today, a little aimlessly, like it was listening for something. I could hear it run its... hand? (Foot?) (Tentacle?) along the cave wall, concentrating. Finally, it stopped.

"Here," it said. "Something is buried. When I leave, light the lantern and start digging. Understand?"

Questions spread over my tongue like a rash. What was buried? Why did it want it? Why couldn't it just dig it up itself?

I pressed my lips together and nodded.

"Good," it said. "Remember—at the slightest noise, close your eyes and douse the light. I will return with food come midday."

As if I was supposed to know when that was.

It left. After two minutes, I removed my blindfold and struggled with the lantern, which illuminated half a shovel leaned against the tunnel wall. Its handle was snapped off a couple feet from the blade, leaving a forest of splinters at the end.

A small X had been drawn in the dirt.

Start digging, it had said.

I could.

Or, I could make a run for it.

It was foolish, but the instinct was there. The tunnels were long and numerous, surely I could keep myself hidden long enough to find a way out. I've snuck into many places in my life. I've learned how to keep quiet and watchful. But... something stopped me.

Some nagging feeling.

Here, beneath the earth, could be the very thing I've been

250

searching for.

Answers.

I don't know enough yet, to run. I have to bide my time. To play the game. So, I took off my blindfold and gag, wrapped one around either hand, and got to work.

* * *

There was little leverage, with half the shovel's handle gone, and progress was slow. Within minutes, I'd built up a sweat. After an hour, I'd made a hole about waist-deep with nothing to show for it but a couple burgeoning blisters and an aching back.

Honestly, I expected to be worse for wear. I'd been pacing myself, not willing to break any bones in service of this *thing*, but I still should've been feeling the stress. Working saps the vitality from you like nothing else. And I *was* tired but... I wasn't broken. It was like there was this well of energy, suddenly, in the pit of my stomach, that I could draw from. It didn't feel like a foreign power, either. It just felt like *me*.

I wasn't taking any chances, though. I took constant breaks, drinking deeply from the canteen the Unseen had given me.

After all, maybe there was nothing to find. Maybe the Unseen just enjoyed toying with its victims while they were stupid enough to think they'd make it out alive. Down here, brittlesnap is the least of my worries.

At some point it brought me lunch: a half-eaten apple, bread hard as the cave wall, and a handful of nuts just on the side of rancid. I'm beginning to think that first cavern *was* a trash heap, because that's where the Unseen seems to get all my meals. After it left, I poured some water on the bread to soften it, ate, and got back to work.

The day was almost over, the hole up to my head, when—*CLANG!*

I hit something metal.

With an unexpected thrill, I stooped down and pulled the ground away, picturing lost treasures or cursed family heirlooms. What I revealed instead was... a dirty copper teapot.

It was unremarkable. I felt strangely disappointed.

Then I lifted it up—and its weight was staggering. It's... hard to describe. I was *able* to lift it, but it didn't feel *right* that I could. Like yanking on a cobblestone and accidently pulling up the entire street.

I ran my hand over the lid's handle, and pulled it open.

> *The widow Jillial Carte*
> *has a way with despicable things.*
> *Watch as the poison tips,*
> *silent,*
> *into the teacup*
> *of Lady Elaine*
> *and rejoice! Rejoice! Rejoice!*

I saw this woman—Jillial Carte—as if she were right in front of me, in her lady's waiting room. I watched her sprinkle white powder into Lady Elaine's teacup and top if off with a spoonful of sugar. She blamed Elaine for her husband's death, and she was right to do so.

I'd never met either woman before, but I could feel Ms. Carte's disdain like it was my own. Could taste her righteous anger, her bitter triumph. The lady had been bedridden for years and would soon rot in the dirt, as was just. And no one would ever suspect the lowly commoner that took such good care of her.

I dropped the teapot and lunged backwards, hitting the wall of the hole and sliding down, my knees pulled up to my chest.

I couldn't breathe, on account of the heart in my throat.

"A secret," said a voice far down the tunnel. I closed my eyes and fumbled for the lantern, blowing it out.

The cool presence of the Unseen looked down on me.

"The tunnels are full of them," it continued. Then sighed. "Makes it very hard to find any particular one. Come. We'll try again tomorrow."

I made no move to get out of the hole. My mouth tasted like tea leaves. I wasn't sure I could move my legs even if I wanted to try.

The Unseen was silent for a long time.

"I should have warned you," it said, its voice quiet. Regretful. "The secrets buried in these tunnels are not always pleasant. But I worry the more I speak to you, the more likely you are to speak back."

An involuntary shiver racked my body. I pressed my fingers into my knees, willing myself still.

What happens? I thought. *What happens if I speak back?*

And why did *it* care?

I placed one hand over my mouth, trained my closed eyes at where the wave of cold was strongest, and waited.

The Unseen hummed, sounding almost amused. "You want an explanation," it said. "Very well. I am looking for a particular secret. But, while I can sense them, I am not... *solid* enough to do the digging. That is why I need you. Whole, and unharmed. I... won't force you. But you are down here for a reason, right? Let me ask you this."

The cool presence closed in around me, like the Unseen was whispering right in my ear. "Where do you think Queen Iina keeps her biggest secret?" it said. "And what do you think would happen... if it ever got out?"

* * *

When their parents died, Aven had had two options: let themself be taken to the workhouse, or run.

Aven had seen the workhouse—a hobbled collection of damp wood under a sagging roof. The children housed there lasted two years, three if they were careful, before the work wore their bodies to rags.

Aven had seen enough of that to last a lifetime.

They ran.

Twelve-years-old, jobless, homeless, hungry, quivering with grief and rage, Aven hopped the wall of the royal orchards under the cover of night with nothing but the clothes on their back and a trowel from the family farm.

Their ankle gave out as they landed.

A pop and a hot flash of pain. They bit back a howl and leaned against the wall to keep from collapsing.

Stupid, stupid, stupid. One slip-up. One bad fall. That was all it took for some.

When their breathing was under control, they tested their foot.

The pain was bearable. They hobbled as quietly as they could into the orchards, looking for a place to dig.

A thin tree near the east edge perched on a raised mound. Aven knelt. The dirt was graciously soft, and after a few hours they had a cave big enough to slip inside.

Their ankle was swollen now, throbbing. They ignored it, curling up among the roots and covering the entrance in handfuls of displaced earth.

Home, sweet home.

Aven could make this work. They had enough apples to last a lifetime, a shelter, and—most importantly—time to figure out what to do next.

Or so they thought.

The next morning, footfalls roused them from sleep. Right outside their little hovel.

Aven held their breath in the darkness.

The dirt in front of them began to shift and light broke through along with a hand, searching. It brushed against Aven's trowel.

"What in the world?" said a voice. A child's.

With a rush of panic, Aven grabbed the hand and pulled.

The invader landed in the dirt with a yelp, squirming in Aven's grip.

Aven tugged. They tugged back. The invader was just a little stronger.

Pulled halfway out of the cave, Aven squinted against the light and released the hand. The invader—a blond-haired boy with one hand over his eyes—stumbled backwards with a gasp.

For a moment, neither said anything. Aven could feel their pulse in their fingertips.

Then they asked, "Why are your eyes closed?"

"Because—Ah!"

The boy slapped a hand over his mouth.

Aven looked from their cave to the boy and back again.

"Do you think... I'm the Unseen? Because I came from underground?"

The boy said nothing. Aven could almost have laughed. They sat up, carefully moving their ankle to a better position.

"Well, I *am*," they said, "so get out of here before I eat you."

The boy hesitated. "But," he said, voice muffled, "I already said something..."

"I, uh, forgive you," Aven said, "Just—"

The boy's hands dropped.

They stared at each other in shock.

"You're the *prince*," Aven said.

"You're hurt," Raine replied.

Which is where it began.

After convincing Aven not to run away, Raine left to get treatment for their ankle. He returned with that, fresh clothes, and the biggest breakfast Aven had ever seen. They talked the whole day, and for many days after. Raine listened to Aven's story. He *cared*. He cared more than anyone Aven had ever met.

"It doesn't make sense," Raine said one day, frustrated. "Why wouldn't Mother give the commoners sigils, if they need them so badly?"

"Nothing you people do makes sense," Aven said, biting into an apple.

"But, it's not *fair!*"

"Nothing you people do is fair," Aven said. They smirked as Raine shot them an annoyed frown.

"I don't like this," he said, crossing his arms. "I don't like not *knowing* things. Mother never tells me anything. I have to figure it all out myself."

He looked at Aven, his eyes blue and fierce. "Will you help me?"

Aven blinked, caught off-guard. "With what?"

"With *learning!*" he said. "With figuring out what's going on, and making it *right*! If we don't do it, who will?"

The prince held out a hand.

Aven hesitated. What could *they*, one scrawny nobody from nowhere, do against the might of an entire castle? Against years of oppression and bitter tradition?

But they thought of their parents, crumbling. Thought of their farm, left empty and forgotten. Of the crooked workhouse full of homeless children, waiting to die.

Prince Raine thought they had a chance. Who was Aven to disagree?

They took his hand, and shook it.

When the Sigil Knights came to Aven's quarters to question them about Prince Raine's murder, they found it empty. Their things packed and gone. Their bed neatly made.

Aven was no fool. If the queen wanted to call Raine's disappearance foul play, there was only one person she'd put in the role of villain. What an easy way to get rid of the stain on the squire name. To send the commoner back into the dirt.

But Aven wasn't going anywhere.

Raine was either dead and in need of vengeance, or alive... and in need of rescue.

* * *

Do I trust the Unseen?

No. Of course not. For all I know it's working *for* you-know-who and the secrets I uncover will be used to hurt the people they belong to.

But there's a *chance* it's telling the truth. A chance that the Unseen's exile underground is genuine, its animosity well-earned. I need proof, and I won't get it anywhere but in these tunnels.

I have to stick it out. I have to get it to tell me more.

Today, I dug up a rag-stuffed bottle of Jacky's Finest, which someone used to start the fire that destroyed the Lower District workhouse a few years back. I won't write anymore names, in case that's what the Unseen wants. Their secret is safe with me.

* * *

The hunt for Aven kicked off that afternoon. Hordes of Sigil Knights flooding the streets, barging into homes, combing every alley.

Oddly enough, no one thought to check the roofs.

The houses of the Lower District were so crammed together, it was easy for Aven to move from one to the other, always staying just out of sight.

The *hardest* part was finding supplies. After sunset, they would climb down a wall and through a window, looking for food. They didn't like stealing from their own people, but it was the safest place to go. They always left behind a fraction of their squire earnings as payment, though the money began to dwindle fast.

This game of survival went on for a week. Climbing up and down walls, sleeping pressed against chimneys or under porches, ever alert, waiting for the worst of it to pass so they could think about what came next.

Until they crept into the kitchen of a small hovel on the north side, and came face-to-face with a little girl in a nightgown.

* * *

The tunnel today was narrow enough that I could press both hands to either side without moving. The digging was, as you can imagine, cramped and miserable. And don't think I've forgiven the blisters yet. Those bastards can go to hell.

Still, I found the secret. For better or worse, I'm getting a knack for it.

It was the toolbox used to build a false wall at the back of someone's house. It hid a small room of goods stolen from the castle, mostly pickled food and bottles of wine.

* * *

The tunnel was too short to stand in today. I spent the first half of the dig on my stomach, scraping at the dirt with both hands on the shovel's blade, trying not to stab myself in the eye with the jagged end of the handle.

What I found, though, was almost worth it. A detailed map of Cyphon's wall—better than any I ever found in the castle libraries—with labeled points of interest. There is one Sigil Knight, at least, that still knows how to read. And is not as blindly loyal as they claim to be.

* * *

I exhumed a loaf of burnt bread today, which crumbled to dust when I tried to bite it. Inside were three gold pieces. Someone in the castle kitchens sneaks money out to the commoners, pilfered from the coat pockets of unsuspecting nobles.

* * *

The dig today was a little easier, but the secret made my want to gag. A noblewoman has been docking her servants' wages for every contrived mistake, and using the extra money to fund a gambling den in the bowels of the castle.

You can have *her* name, Unseen. It's Michellie Portwright. And I hope she

* * *

"Who are you?" the little girl said. She held a limp stuffed animal in one hand. It was missing a button eye.

Aven's body buzzed, their hand resting on the window frame. Was it worse to leave without a word? Run off into the darkness and hope she took them for a dream?

"Are you the fudge-a-tive?" she asked.

Aven stiffened. "Um..."

"You look like the person in the posters."

Of course there were posters. Aven's face would be all over Cyphon by now. They were public enemy number one.

"I'm..." Aven looked at the girl. She wasn't the least bit afraid. "...What if I am?"

"Papa says the knights don't like you."

"They don't."

"But we don't like the knights."

"...Neither do I."

The girl nodded, like that made sense. Then she leaned forward conspiratorially. "Our cellar is empty," she whispered. "We don't have a lock, but it's dry and warm."

Aven stared at her, stunned.

She gave a big wink. "Just so you know."

* * *

Damn oil ran out, what, two days ago? Three? ...I'm not sure. Everything since I wrote the last entry is fuzzy. Indistinct.

I think... *that's* why the Unseen wants me to write. Not for *its* benefit. For my own.

There's a... numbness in these tunnels. This great, cosmic *pause*. Stories aren't supposed to be written here, they're supposed to be *buried*. And if I'm not careful, that's exactly what I'll be.

Is it fucked up to say I miss the sound of my own voice?

Of course, there's someone else's I miss more. But that name stays with me. These tunnels can't have it.

Cyphon feels worlds away now, but at least I can remember it. Hold its people inside my head. Picture the sun rising above the wall. I can't even remember what I ate for dinner yesterday. Or what secrets I uncovered, if any, in the time that's passed.

But I have oil again. For now. I have to make it count.

Today I found the knife that a nobleman used to kill his common lover, when he found out she was pregnant. His name was Trent Longfellow, but he's already dead and buried, so I can't even hope for his head on a pike.

* * *

With each month that Aven evaded capture, their notoriety grew. The nobles raved of their villainy. The commoners praised their rebellion.

Aven found more homes willing to offer them a place to hide, and got good enough at slipping past the knights to raid the castle kitchens instead of relying on the kindhearted for food. They shared what they could with those who needed it more. They grew more sure in their actions. More clever. More ambitious.

They took a page out of Raine's book, and began sneaking into the queen's library.

They read tome after tome on the founding of Cyphon, the creation of the wall, the supposed monsters that lurked beyond it. Their skepticism that such monsters existed grew with each page they turned. Raine had been onto something... but he hadn't looked hard enough.

One day, while skimming through the library's catalog, Aven found a note beside one of the titles.

MOVED TO THE QUEEN'S PRIVATE COLLECTION

The title of the book was *Rituals of Strength.*

The queen's chamber was on the highest floor of the castle, and its door was under constant guard.

Its windows, however, were not.

* * *

Okay.

First thing's first, write it all down. Then I'll decide how doomed I am.

I was digging today, as usual. I hardly break a sweat anymore. My hands have hardened, over the months. My muscles have grown. It's weird, feeling capable. Feeling like a knight. But it's only one of several weird things about these tunnels. Here's another:

Halfway through the dig today, something shifted in the dark.

I closed my eyes, of course, but I wasn't worried. Usually, the Unseen warns me when it's coming, but it's not infallible.

Then, a voice spoke.

A *different* voice.

"*Well.*"

The tone had the same deep resonance of the Unseen's, the base humming through the hairs on the back of my neck, but this was *sharper* somehow. Less like a church bell and more like a dagger coming out of its sheath. "What do we have here?" it said.

I froze. The Unseen had never mentioned anyone else living in these tunnels. Was it another outcast? Someone the queen decided had seen too much? Or...

"Are you lost, dear?" the voice asked. "What's your name?"

I pressed my lips together, and said nothing. I could hear it circling the hole I'd dug, could feel its gaze raking across me. The chill of its presence blew through me like a stiff wind.

"You've been down here a while," it observed. "Me too. It's scary, isn't it? Being alone in the dark. I could lead you out. Would you like that?"

A bead of sweat slipped down the back of my shirt.

"Or maybe you don't want escape," it said. "Maybe you want *answers*. You could ask me, dear. There's not much I don't know."

I summoned my reserve of courage, turned away, and continued to dig.

"PUSTULE!" it snapped—its voice cut through the tunnel like a bolt of lightning, so loud I dropped the shovel and pressed my hands over my ears. "Vermin! Ghoul among the dead and forgotten! Your insistent heartbeat does not *belong* in these tunnels—"

"Enough!"

I never thought I'd be relieved to hear the Unseen's voice.

"This human is under my protection, Acteus. Find something else to occupy your time."

"*You*," it sneered. "Of course. How long have you kept this little *pet*?"

"That's no concern of yours. *Begone.*"

It scoffed. "It will speak eventually," it said. "They always do."

Then it was gone.

* * *

"...I'm sorry," the Unseen said. It sounded shaken. "I didn't want— I wished to spare you the worry. I thought I could keep the rest away, but somehow she got past me."

She.

The *rest.*

My hands shook. I couldn't tell if it was from terror, or rage.

"You are right to be angry," it said. "I was foolish. I should have warned you. I—am glad you're alright."

I wouldn't have responded, even if I could. My mind was stuck, the other Unseen's parting words grinding against each other like ill-fitting gears.

It will speak eventually.

They always do.

How many people had been sent down here, to die to these *things*? Had any ever escaped? Was there anyone that she *wouldn't* send down here? Any line she wouldn't cross? And what hope did I have of ever getting out? The monster who'd been guiding me was, it seemed, *outnumbered*. And against *it*, I was harshly outmatched. I was one person, digging alone in the dark. Why? For the promise of revenge? For a secret I might never unearth?

I missed the sky.

I climbed out of the hole, shook the dirt off my pants, and walked away.

"Wait!" the Unseen called. "I'll lead you back!"

I started to run.

* * *

The queen's tower faced the courtyard on one side and the wall on the other, every angle under constant observation. Aven would have to climb it at night, while the queen was inside, to avoid detection. They would have to be quiet, and they would have to be quick.

They would also have to make sure not to fall and die.

A lump of fear made a home for itself in the pit of Aven's stomach. They would just have to work around it.

It had been almost a year of sneaking through the city, of breaking into libraries to steal information, into kitchens to steal food. What was one more room? They could do this. They *had* to. They were running out of leads.

When the new moon rose, Aven made their way through the castle grounds, and looked up at Her Majesty's tower.

I'm close, Raine, they thought. *I'm hope there's still something left of you to find.*

* * *

It was stupid. I know it was stupid. I'm lucky I didn't slam face-first into the nearest stalagmite and break my skull.

I finally snapped, and the first thing I did was run.

And now... I have no idea where I am.

It's been hours, at least, of feeling my way through tunnel after tunnel. I don't know what I'm looking for. A way out? The cave with my cot? The Unseen? All I've found are a couple old dig sites, and they did nothing to reorient me. My stomach feels like its caving in on itself. No food, but I have water. That's something.

Now that I know there's more of them, I have to be extra careful. I keep squeezing my eyes shut at every noise. Maybe it's stupid to even be writing this. But I don't know what to do.

I better stop. I have to save oil.

Don't know when I'll be getting more.

* * *

Aven pressed flat against the tower's wall for balance, using the castle's old, pocked brickwork to keep themself stable. They were about a third of the way up, now, and already the ground seemed like a distant memory.

They paused in a stretch of shadow to catch their breath. The hardest part was endurance. They had to be quick, yes, but they also had to use their limited energy wisely. If they pushed too hard, they would slip—and even if Aven could catch themself, they would break a few fingers in the process. They couldn't afford to mess up here. They'd need all their wits about them when they got to the queen's window.

They tilted their head up, plotting the next route.

One step at a time.

* * *

DAMN IT.

I'm back at the same fucking hole I started this morning. My shovel's still at the bottom. The Unseen is gone.

WHERE THE FUCK AM I?

I don't know what to do. I'M SUCH AN IDIOT.

I'm exhausted and starving and... sorry.

I'm so sorry.

I wish that—

Gods.

I wish I had someone to talk to.

* * *

Aven swung their foot up onto the lip of the queen's bedroom window and pulled their weight up. Their hands were shaking. There was no helping it. They pressed them into the glass and took a deep breath.

Don't choke now, Aven.

The wind tugged at their heels. They refused to look down.

Aven drew a metal wire from the sleeve of their shirt—something pried out of a corset they'd stolen during one of their trips though the Upper District—and slid it between the doors of the window. With a flick of their wrist, they popped the latch. Slowly, quietly, they pried the doors apart and slipped inside.

The room was dark, but even so Aven could tell it was enormous, the ceilings high and domed, the four poster bed on the far side of the room layered in rich fabrics and...

And...

Unoccupied.

Where was the—

"Hello, Aven."

They spun around.

A match flared to life, and met the wick of a candle. The stark light sharpened Queen Iina's face, made her look like something ancient and full of teeth.

"I'm so glad you got my invitation."

* * *

Holy shit.

My hands are shaking so badly I can barely write.

I started digging again, more to distract myself than anything else, and about a foot further in, the shovel slid so far into the ground that it almost took me with it. When I tugged it back out, and it came up covered in this thick tar. The stench was awful, like something rotten and sour.

I knew it, then. This was different. This was *important*.

I threw the shovel aside and plunged my hands into the liquid. I was up to my elbows before brushing against something soft and warm.

I pulled out a black heart, beating delicately in my cupped hands.

She walled off our city so we would not realize
what was lost.
What we lose
every day,
with every breath we dare to take.
So long as we live under her—
our strength is her nectar
for everlasting life
and everlasting suffering
for all but herself
and those she deems worthy
of the honor of normalcy.
Queen Iina enjoys being better than us,
stronger than us,
wiser and older and more cunning than us.
She wears the superiority like a perfume.
And will do so as long as she lives...

Queen Iina's greatest secret.

I wanted to shout, wanted to call out to the Unseen, to show it my victory.

But I was alone. I had no idea where the Unseen was, and had no way to find it.

Tar dripped slowly down my arms.

I emptied out the sack I use to hold my supplies, and put the heart inside it. I can feel its pulse through the fabric, against my hip.

I've got it—but what do I do with it?

What do you do with a secret that will break the world in half?

* * *

The bands on Queen Iina's upper arms flashed red, and Aven's knees buckled. Their lungs suddenly paper-thin, their limbs heavy and useless.

The queen tutted.

"You *have* been a bit of a problem, haven't you, dearheart?"

Aven could barely lift their head to look up at her.

"*What—?*" they croaked.

"Riling up the commoners," she continued, "sowing discontent. You've made yourself quite the symbol of rebellion. And put me in a pickle. The commoners are bound to hate me if I publicly execute you. And yet I *certainly* can't let you live."

She pulled Aven's arms behind their back and tied them together. Aven had no strength to resist.

"Better they think you abandoned them, don't you agree? We can squash this feeble little rebellion before things get messy."

Why couldn't Aven move? Their heart thundered in their chest, but the wild adrenaline had no outlet. Only their thoughts moved with any speed. They were an idiot. They got cocky.

But they still had to know.

"*Raine…*"

The queen hummed regretfully. "Yes, poor boy. I can feel when someone leaves my… *bubble.* I'm afraid my son didn't get very far on his quest. But don't you worry about him."

The queen pulled Aven off the floor like they weighed nothing, and led them to a corner of the room, next to her bed. She drew back a rug to reveal a wooden hatch.

"I'd worry more about yourself."

Aven tried to wrench themself free. They may as well have been fighting a marble statue. Queen Iina pulled something from the drawer of her bedside table.

"Trust me," she said, "you'll be grateful for the blindfold. And the gag."

* * *

As I left the newly made tar pit, the heart at my hip beat a little faster. I didn't think anything of it until I took a turn, and it slowed. I doubled back, and it sped up again.

I felt a flicker of hope.

The heart was *leading* me. Like some grotesque game of Hot and Cold. And that was either exactly what I needed—or a recipe for disaster. Was the heart on *her* side... or mine?

Is the purpose of a secret to be kept? Or revealed?

I took the chance.

It led me to the same place the Unseen had, my first day in the tunnels. The stinking trash heap where it got my supplies.

The cavern with the impossible light.

It came from a small gap near the top of what must have been some kind of rockslide, years ago.

I can't tell you how relieved I am to have brought the shovel.

I began climbing, the black heart beating violently at my side, to assess how much work I'd have to do, when my foot pressed down on a rock and my leg buckled as it slid out from under me. Cursing, I rubbed my bruised hip and looked down.

A wad of papers, wrapped in a brittle leather strap, poked out from where I'd disturbed the rock. It looked eerily like my own journal, but older. Worn. On impulse, I shoved it in my pocket.

I don't have time to read it, now. Not when I'm so close. But I'll leave *this* journal here, in its stead. If all goes well, I won't be needing it anymore.

Maybe the Unseen will find it, and know some kind of comfort.

* * *

With one delicate finger, Queen Iina tilted Aven's chin up so they had to meet her eyes.

"You know the old stories," she said, her voice light as a lullaby. "*To look upon it is to witness your own end. To speak is to grant it your last breath.* I only wish to give you a fighting chance, dearheart. Now..." She gently pulled the gag out of their mouth. "Any last words?"

Bile rose in their throat. Regret and shame warred with rage in their heart. They raised their lip.

"Long live the queen," they spat.

She hummed, amused.

"Thank you, dear," she said. "I plan to."

And she pushed Aven into the dark.

* * *

A hand shot up out of a storm drain, scrabbling for purchase on the cobblestones. Another curled its fingers around the grate and pushed.

The old, worn metal gave way with a piercing *screech*. A watery gasp echoed in the alley.

Aven pulled themself into the light of day.

The sky was overcast, yet near-blinding. After almost a year in complete darkness, Aven's eyes felt sickly and weak. Their well-earned strength had abandoned them the closer they got to the surface, and to the queen.

The heart in their bag thundered in time with the one in their chest.

They pulled it out. It glistened like an oil slick in the light of day, beautiful and terrible like the woman it belonged to. With each beat, it pumped sickly tar onto the cobblestones.

"Who's there?"

Aven looked up.

An older, balding gentleman in a leather apron poked his head out of a doorway, bushy eyebrows raised.

Aven smiled in recognition. "Hectar Wilpen!"

The man's expression turned suspicious. "You know me?"

Aven scrambled up and stumbled, catching themself on the alley wall. They lurched towards the man, heart still clutched in their hands.

"You have a false wall in the back of your house," they explained, "where you hide stolen food and wine."

The man's eyes widened. "I—"

"Look," Aven demanded, and thrust the heart into his outstretched hands.

Hectar's face went slack for a moment, then he shoved the heart back.

"What—*what is that?*"

"The queen..." Aven fought for breath. "Tell others. Tell everyone. Chloe Riggenbier is a Sigil Knight, but she's trustworthy. She has this map—she'll understand. Jillial Carte has a bone to pick with the nobles. And the head chef in the castle, Tylee Slane, they'll—"

"Now, hold on a moment." Hectar had gone very pale. "How do you *know* all this? Who are you?"

"That's not important," Aven gasped. "You saw. You *saw*. We have to stop her. You have to *help*. Here, I'll—I'll write the names down."

Aven scrambled for the cluster of papers they'd shoved in their pocket. "Do... do you have a pen?"

The man looked shell-shocked. "Uh... inside," he said. "I..." Hectar sighed deeply. "Come in, I'll find one."

Aven stepped just through the doorway, and leaned against the wall. Hectar moved further into the house.

They put the heart on a side table, where it beat its steady rhythm, and uncurled their desperate fingers from around the papers.

I don't know how long I've been down here, they read.

The writing was smudged. Aven held it closer to their face.

For the briefest moment, I saw the world outside—green hills and lush trees and a sea of endless stars—before the knights found me. It was like they'd known exactly where to look.

They threw me in a sack and brought me to Mother's room.

I'd expected her to be angry. Disappointed. I hadn't expected the glint in her eye.

"My dearest," she said, smiling. "I have been waiting for the excuse."

Then she opened a hatch in the floor and threw me down it.

After that...

I don't know.

I don't know anything. This place... it's empty. It's taking something away from me, every day. I forget myself. Forget where I am. Forget what's down here with me.

But these words... they're real. I'm real. I can't give up hope yet. I can't afford to.

I promised I'd come back.

Aven swallowed. Their legs began to shake.

Raine had been thrown into the tunnels, too. The possibility had occurred to Aven, of course, but they'd found no sign of him. No sign of anyone. So they hadn't let themself think about it. Hadn't dared to wonder, even in their journal, for fear of what it might mean.

Now, they wondered.

How long did Raine last, before he spoke to an Unseen? Caught a glimpse of one? And what had happened to him?

Close your eyes and keep them closed.

The Unseen's insistent warnings. Its vendetta against the queen. Its hesitant care in the face of Aven's silence.

I worry the more I speak to you, the more likely you are to speak back.

Aven felt the reality of it crash against them. Their knees threatened to buckle.

Raine wasn't used to ducking his head and keeping silent. Aven was. Raine hadn't had anyone to help him in the tunnels.

Aven had.

They'd had *Prince Raine.*

Hectar returned with a battered quill and a wary expression.

"You all right, kid?"

Aven shook their head, dazed, but tore a blank piece from the papers and wrote every trustworthy name they could remember, handing it back to him. Then they turned to go.

"Now, wait a second!" Hectar called. "You can't just *leave*. I mean—what am I supposed to do with *that*?"

He gestured at the heart. Black ichor dripped from the table, pooling on the wooden floor.

Aven pursed their lips. "Share it," they said, "with everyone and anyone. Work on a way to fight back. Her armbands... get them off her, if you can."

Hectar pursed his lips. "Everything's going to change..." he said. "Isn't it?"

Aven nodded, slowly. "That's the hope."

"But where are *you* going?" Hectar asked.

Aven looked down the alley, at the open storm drain. They smiled.

"To have a word with a friend of mine."

Hope and Prophecy

by Cera Tansy Reid

"Open it," the Captain commanded, barely hidden excitement hidden behind her stern tone. 'It' was a cryopod, the newest version Youngest had ever seen. Even celebrities didn't have access to tech this advanced. Estra nudged her in the shoulder.

"What?" Youngest whispered.

"Open it," the older woman whispered back. "Youngest does—"

"As Eldest says," Youngest sighed. She stepped forward, eyes flickering over the controls. It would be easy to open; there was no section for a code or biometrics. Not that they would have been too much of a problem. Emergency protocols bypassed any security for a reason. The bio monitor was all green, if a little low, so she reached over and pressed the release. All of the standard checks filtered through, each passing easily. A handful she'd never seen before flickered yellow before verifying. The lid to the cryopod rose with the characteristic gust of rapidly-warmed air.

Inside lay a woman. She looked young, perhaps even younger in appearance than Youngest. She was pale, with the distinctive translucent skin of a manip-clone allowing her superior veins and arteries to be clearly visible. Her dark hair had been roughly shorn and had barely begun to grow back. She wore a loose, undyed tunic and pants, and near-skeletal limbs protruded from frayed hems. She did not wake when the pod opened, nor when the Captain stepped past Youngest, satisfied at the lack of danger.

The Captain pulled out her scanner and pressed it to the prone woman's forehead. It beeped cheerfully and displayed a projection of a DNA sequence. Several long sections were highlighted, and as each one was accepted, the Captain's anxious scowl lessened. Before long, she was grinning.

"Is it the right one?" the second mate asked. Tall and thin, they loomed menacingly over most of the crew on a good day. Now, they all but quivered in excitement.

"If it's not, then I'm the Queen of Sheba."

Cheers rang out amongst the crew, but the Youngest's were half-hearted. She watched the Captain wrest the woman from her cryopod by one skinny arm, grip tight as a vice. The woman crumpled to the ground, still unconscious, but the Captain didn't seem to care. She grabbed the pale woman's chin possessively, stroking the woman's cheek with the back of her hand before pulling back and slapping her. Still, she did not wake.

The Captain scoffed in disgust. "Cryosick. Typical over-genetically modified weakling. Youngest, c'mere." As Youngest stepped forward, the Captain shoved the woman at her. "Get her back to our ship and make sure she doesn't die. Everyone else, let's strip this jalopy to the wires."

The Captain stared pointedly at Youngest until she nodded. She scooped the woman into her arms and carried her toward the cargo bay door. True to how thin she looked, she weighed hardly anything. She was light enough that Youngest had to wonder if her creators had altered her bone density on top of everything else.

Estra paced her to the door and hit the release switch. "Rough luck," she murmured. "This ship is bound to have some good stuff. I'll keep an eye out for you, if you want."

"It's fine. Don't piss off the others on my account," Youngest replied softly. Estra snorted.

"Cap's been a hard-ass on you. You've barely picked up anything since we defrosted you. No one will begrudge me grabbing a little extra for you."

Youngest smiled at Estra. "I appreciate it, truly, but I'm fine."

"Okay then. What about it?" Estra challenged.

"What?"

"*It.*" Estra gestured to the woman cradled in Youngest's arms.

"What do you mean?" Youngest asked, confused. "I'll just take her to medbay, right?"

Estra rolled her eyes. "No one stays in medbay unless they're actually dying or quarantined, You can get it checked out, *maybe* stable, but then Cap is going to expect *you* to manage it."

Youngest's shoulders slumped. "If you find some clothes or blankets, then. If you're sure."

Estra laughed. "Good to see your pride is smaller than your sense. I'll do what I can. You go take care of it. We can't risk loosing our next meal ticket, after all."

The Youngest watched her leave, a wry twist to her mouth. Meal ticket, indeed.

* * *

The ship medbay was sparse and ill-fitted, but enough to handle the ails of a fifty-odd crew, outside a major emergency. As much scorn as the Captain had expressed over the woman being cryosick, it was a somewhat common ailment shipside. Youngest settled the woman on one of the berths and started a warming rehydration protocol. There were no chairs in the med bay, so she sat on another berth and watched the protocol run. She thought the woman's color was getting better.

Not too long ago it had been her waking on one of these berths to strange faces. She wondered if the woman would be upset, or if this was merely a new entry in a long list of unfamiliar awakenings. She had heard the rumors of what manip-clones were used for in the Core. The Captain was old, and canny in her knowledge. If she said this woman could lead them to a stockpile that would ensure their planet's power for decades, then Youngest believed her. But that knowledge had to come from somewhere. She hoped the woman hadn't felt the cost of creating that knowledge.

Movement from the berth drew her attention. The woman twitched, a frown creasing her face. Then she startled, bolt upright.

"Hey, it's okay," Youngest said, crossing to the woman's berth. "It's stardate 627, you're on the *Historian*. You were removed from cryo approximately half an hour ago. Can you speak?"

The woman stared up at her, eyes wide. "Who?" she croaked.

Youngest cursed. "Sorry, I'll get you a soother, one moment." She crossed the medbay, reaching the supply cabinet in a handful of seconds. She gathered herself as she grabbed the soother and returned to the woman. "Here," she held out the pouch. The woman didn't take it. "It's just a throat soother," Youngest promised. The woman took the pouch almost reluctantly. She read the front of the pouch and her eyebrows flew up in surprise. Her eyes darted to Youngest's face, searching. Slowly, she tore open the pouch and drank.

"Who are you?" the woman asked when she had finished. She twisted the empty pouch between her hands.

"Call me Youngest," she told her. "We're from Memria."

"The memory cultists?" the woman asked, frowning slightly.

Youngest coughed. "Yes, well. I suppose that's one way to think of us." She gazed at the woman, at a loss for what to do. "Do you know where you were heading?"

The woman shrugged. "No, but I rarely do. Do you know where you want me to take you?" she asked shrewdly.

Youngest shook her head. "The Captain knows. I'm sure she'll be around to... ask."

"Demand," corrected the woman. Youngest nodded, conceding the point.

"What's your name?" Youngest asked.

"I don't have one," the woman said simply. At Youngest's surprised look, she glared. "I'm a manip-clone. We get serial numbers. If we're lucky, we're told what that number is."

"Can I call you by your serial number?" Youngest asked, hesitant.

"I'm not lucky," the woman said bluntly.

* * *

Less than an hour later, the Captain tracked them down in Youngest's quarters. She had gotten the woman checked over, and had brought her to her quarters. Youngest was trying, without much luck, to get the woman's opinion on bedding and clothing. Estra pulled through and brought a heaping armful, but the woman refused to contribute in splitting the haul. Youngest eventually gave up and just sorted the smaller sizes into a pile for her.

"Well isn't this cozy," the Captain said coldly. "Youngest. I expected you in the medbay."

Youngest jumped to her feet. "Captain," she greeted. "She's fully checked over. She's malnourished and a bit dehydrated, but otherwise no further effects from the cryosleep."

"I don't care," the Captain told Youngest irritably. "I'm taking it to get an initial heading. Since you're determined to domesticate it, you can be it's handler. Come." The Captain turned and left, heading for the bridge. Youngest nudged the woman to follow.

Few people were on the bridge, only the core command and the head navigator. Youngest twitched, then stilled. Everyone here had decades of lived experience on her.

"UPS, come here," the Captain ordered. No one moved. She sighed in frustration. "Youngest, bring it here."

"The... UPS?" youngest asked, thoughts racing. She'd never heard of that before.

"Yes, the Universal Positioning System, the thing you're standing next to. The thing this entire mission is based on. *Move.*"

Youngest glanced at the woman next to her. Her face was serene. She gave no indication that she was insulted, or confused. When she noticed Youngest looking, she quirked an eyebrow at her. She plainly wasn't going to move on her own. Youngest gently took her elbow and guided her over to the nav station.

"Moron," the Captain muttered, glaring at Youngest. She shoved the woman at the station. "All right, don't play around. We know you can get to the Origin. You're going to plot us a course that avoids absolutely anything that will be a danger to this ship and crew. If you don't, I'll take it out of your hide," the Captain said dangerously.

The woman's shoulders dropped, barely noticeable. "The Origin is banned from access by all planetary systems," she said flatly. "Many of their armies guard key access points. I cannot guarantee a safe flight."

"You'll make it as safe as possible, because every time we're fired at, blocked, or delayed in general, we're going to have a discussion that you won't walk away from," the Captain growled. "Understood?"

The woman stared at the Captain for a moment, then inclined her head. She turned and began tapping at the nav station. "The first leg of the journey is fairly straightforward," she said, tapping coordinates. "The most significant problem will be avoiding enough patrols and checkpoints to prevent them from flagging this ship's ID. However, I can only safely bring you so far without additional research. I will need access to a secure terminal and time to plot the next leg." She stared pointedly at the Captain.

The Captain snorted, but seemed pleased with the planned course. "Youngest, do you have a secure terminal in your quarters?" The question was rhetorical; only three personnel quarters on the ship contained a secure terminal. The Captain's, the first mate's, and the second mate's.

"No, Captain," she said.

"I suppose you'll have to move in to your mother's quarter's for the journey, then. You're dismissed. Go move, and take the UPS with you," she said maliciously. "Oh, and Youngest?"

"Yes Captain?"

"You are to guard it every second. If it does something odd on the terminal, I want to know. If it tries to go somewhere, if it tries to contact anyone, you are to restrain it and report to me. If anything at all goes wrong," the Captain said menacingly, "you will be held responsible for it."

"...Yes, Captain."

* * *

Given Youngest's few possessions, the move to her mother's quarters went quickly. The room was bare of furnishings, having been cleared of all but the built-in furniture when her mother last disembarked. She set her pile of blankets and clothing on the table and gestured for the woman to do the same. Youngest raked a hand through her short-cropped hair. "Do you want to start your research, or do you want to get some sleep first?" she asked the woman. The woman gave her a startled look.

"I'll start researching, if that's all right," she said slowly. "I need to set up some processes to run that will take a few hours. Then I'll sleep for a while." She seemed slightly bewildered when Youngest just nodded and began sorting things. "Aren't you going to watch my every move?" she asked, as Youngest made no move towards the terminal.

"I have very little experience with navigation," Youngest said bluntly. "Go ahead, I'll just finish up putting these away."

The woman shook her head, then turned towards the terminal. Despite the veiled threat, every time Youngest glanced over, she was rapidly paging through databases, or stitching together lines of code. By the time Youngest was done, so was the woman. A query box showed on the top right corner, compiling information.

"Are you done then?" Youngest asked.

"For now," the woman answered. "Once it's run for a while, I'll have a better idea of what governments are watching where."

"How long?"

"About six hours."

"Okay," Youngest said. "Why don't we get some sleep then." She moved to the bed, pulling back the blankets she had draped over it. The woman didn't move. Youngest glanced over, puzzled. "Come on, it's big enough for two," she said, gesturing her over. The woman tentatively crossed to the bed and hesitated before climbing into it. She laid down, stiff as a board. Youngest frowned at her, then realized.

"Oh! Oh. I'm sorry. I'll just sleep on the floor." She went to swing her legs off of the bed when the woman touched her arm fleetingly.

"It's fine. The bed is big enough," she said.

"But you thought –" Youngest started to protest.

"It's fine. Go to sleep," the woman said firmly. She turned away from Youngest, tugging a blanket over her shoulders.

Youngest lay awake for a while longer. She had forgotten that, bad as her people treated manip-clones, there were those who did far worse. Well, she hadn't really known in the first place, had she. She only knew about it through her memories. She needed to be better.

* * *

The woman was in the middle of scrolling through government databases when the Captain walked in the next day. "Captain," Youngest greeted, looking up from the screen. The woman had been flicking through far faster than Youngest could read, but every now and again she would pause, and look over something again. Trying to come up with theories about what warranted deeper scrutiny occupied Youngest since they both awoke at the alert signaling the program's end.

Captain grunted and said, "Well? What progress?"

The woman did not so much as look at the Captain. "I am mostly certain of the next leg of the route. I just need to check in on Acastar, and then I will be able to chart the next course."

"Good. Youngest, with me." The Captain pulled her to the side of the room. "Anything strange?"

"Not that I could determine, sir." Youngest stayed carefully blank.

"Good, good." The Captain glanced over at the woman. "When it's done, escort it to the bridge. The head navigator is to check over the route once it's input it, so don't take off right after. Then I expect the both of you to continue."

"Captain, neither of us have eaten in at least a cycle," Youngest mentioned. "She can't run forever on nothing."

The Captain scoffed. "It damn well can run on as much or as little as I say. It's not here to look pretty, no matter what fancy you might be taking to it." Youngest ducked her head. The captain sighed. "But I suppose it can eat when you do. Ancestors know you're useless as it is, much less passing out from not eating. I want the next route put in before you eat, but after, fine."

"Thank you, Captain."

The Captain scoffed and left. Youngest crossed back to the terminal, but what mild enjoyment she had found in the rapidly shifting information was gone. She stared blankly until the screen stopped changing, and a hand tapped her shoulder. Her head snapped toward the woman. She was staring solemnly at her, but once Youngest looked at her again, a mild smile stretched across her face.

"I'm ready for the next route."

"Okay. Let's go then."

Inputting the route, getting it checked, and getting food all went so smoothly that Youngest hardly noticed it happening. Soon, they were back in her mother's quarters, the woman tapping again at the terminal. It only took her a few minutes to set up whatever she was doing, before she left the program to run and moved to sit on the bed. She stared at Youngest, an odd look on her face.

"What is it?" Youngest asked.

"What is your position? You seem too unsure of yourself to be highly ranked, yet your Captain has placed you in charge of me. At the same time, she appears to expect you to fail to control me, even though physically, I would have no chance against you."

Youngest sighed. "What do you know about 'memory cultists'?" she asked, a wry twist to her mouth.

"Not much," the woman admitted. "Memria is a mostly isolationist planet, with a people who claim to be able to pass down memories. There was something I once read about you worshiping knowledge?"

"In the broadest of strokes, that's mostly correct," Youngest told her. "We don't let anyone on planet who hasn't been thoroughly vetted to integrate well into Memria, and those who do enter into our society are often looked down on. It's because we do pass down memories, from generation to generation, each compiling all their knowledge for the next. The oldest families claim to have memories starting on Origin, but for the most part those are accepted to be polite fabrications. Anyone new only has their own memories. Their children, grandchildren, and so on are usually a bit better off, but frankly, anyone without at least ten generations of memory is treated essentially like a child."

"Is that why the Captain treats you like that?" the woman asked, frowning.

Youngest laughed. "Oh, no. I've the opposite problem. You see, at a certain point, it gets difficult to incorporate centuries of memories into a human brain. So, we use cryology to manage aging while the memories incorporate." Youngest smiled crookedly. "How old would you say I am?"

The woman looked at her carefully. "Perhaps twenty-five, maybe twenty-seven," she said, head cocked curiously. "Why?"

"I'm actually fifty-three," Youngest admitted. "But I've only been aware and outside of cryo systems for six months or so, maybe a year total if I include the days I was out as a child for monitoring my physical advancements. So, I have around a millennia's worth of my ancestor's memories, but only a few months of my own."

The woman's eyes flew open when she heard Youngest's age. She sat there for a moment, then shook her head. "How does that work, then? If you appear this age, but are actually twice as old? Do you live longer? How does that impact passing on your own memories?" Her questions came rapid-fire, one train of thought dancing to the next.

Youngest laughed. "If we keep up with the treatments, we can live much longer, yes. My mother appears to be in her seventies, but she's actually over two hundred years old. There's a sweet spot, where your own memories add enough to be worth passing on to a child, but not add too much to the integration. Particularly accomplished people are encouraged to have children again at later ages, but most of the population has at least one child before they have acquired five years of their own memories. That is, for the portion of us who have a lot of memories to get through. Anyone with less than ten generations is required to have at least twenty years of their own memories, in order to help build up their bloodlines quicker."

The woman shook her head again. "Doesn't it get very confusing, with all those memories?" she asked. "How can you tell if it's really you making a decision, and not the weight of a hundred ancestors?"

"It's hard to describe," Youngest said. "They're my memories, even though they're not. Each new member of a bloodline does interpret things differently, although I suppose there are often core similarities, or tendencies. I don't think about it much," she admitted. "It's just how things are, for me."

"I suppose it's hard for me to imagine not being a clone," the woman offered.

"How does that work, by the way. The navigation?" Youngest asked.

The woman thought for a moment. "It's like a pull, in my gut.

Most of the time, it's not directed anywhere in particular, but when I'm looking for something, I'm pulled in it's direction. One of the scientists who made me said they'd based it off of some extinct Origin species, a bird or something."

"A homing pigeon."

"I think that's it. I was... distracted, at the time," she paused, a haunted expression crossing her face. "Anyway, it's not the most useful thing for everyday, I'm told. There are maps and computers that can get people most places. It's the hidden places, the forbidden ones. Those are what I'm created for. But," the woman cautions, "A straight shot to those places often puts those trying to get there in a lot of danger. So I was trained to take in, retain, and use all sorts of information to find routes that are safer. That's what I'm doing now."

"Can you get us to Origin without anyone knowing?" Youngest asked.

"I'm certainly going to try," the woman said, grimly humorous. "Because if I don't, it's going to hurt more for me than it is you."

* * *

The next few cycles were quick and repetitive. The woman researched, alternately running programs to compile new information and reading through it faster than anyone Youngest had ever seen. Periodically, they would input a new route and start the process over again. They were getting closer, Youngest knew, even though the woman had not marked where exactly Origin lay on a starmap. Each time, the route input grew shorter, and required more research. While this made sense to Youngest, the Captain grew frustrated with the reduced amount of progress.

"We barely flew for half a cycle before your route ended the last time!" she shouted at the woman. "What the hell are you doing, holed up in there?"

"We're reaching a crucial part in the journey. There are more people watching in this area, with a perimeter to turn back people who have no business going to Origin. I'm doing my best to keep under the radar, but that means I have to check more information with a shorter payout in travel distance," she said levelly. "Once we're past the next two systems, I'll be able to create longer routes."

"Fine," the Captain growled. "But I want a route that's at least two cycles long tomorrow. We can't keep doing these tiny little legs and then sit around and wait for you to give us a new heading. And if it's not long enough," she growled menacingly, "I'm perfectly willing to... persuade you."

"I'm sure that won't be necessary," Youngest interjected, stepping just slightly in front of the woman, who had gone pale at the threat.

"It better not be!" The Captain snapped, turning away. Youngest ushered the woman off of the bridge, heart pounding. The Captain's temper had worn razor-thin. It was liable to snap at any moment.

"If you can get the route ready by early tomorrow, we can go before the Captain will be awake. It might be safer to stay out of sight, out of mind for now," she said as they headed back to her mother's quarters.

"I don't know if I can," the woman murmured. Her voice was thin. She hadn't slept in over a cycle, and only picked at the food Youngest brought back to the room. She looked even thinner than when Youngest first saw her, and the bruises brought about by the Captain's rough handling bloomed in a sickening bouquet over her skin. They reached the room and Youngest steered her towards the bed.

"Here's what we'll do. You are going to nap, just for a little bit. While you do, I'll get you something to eat, and then you can start on the next route," Youngest said firmly, gently pushing her to lie down.

"No, I can work. I've managed with less before," the woman said, trying to get up. Youngest gently planted one hand on her shoulder.

"You don't have to. You'll be better for even the shortest of breaks. I swear, I'm trying to help. Let me," she said softly. The woman stopped struggling up and looked at her. She sighed and closed her eyes. One hand fell onto Youngest's, and began stroking it. With a jolt, Youngest realized the woman was tracing veins and arteries; invisible under her own skin, but stark under the woman's. Within moments, the movement stopped, and Youngest gently withdrew her hand. She tiptoed out of the room, then headed for the mess. Preoccupied with the woman's condition, it took her a moment to realize Estra was waving at her. Youngest stopped and headed toward the table she sat at.

"How goes it?" Estra asked cheerfully.

"We're making progress, but there's more eyes on where we're trying to travel right now. It's making it harder to create longer routes that are still safe," Youngest said. She slumped on the table. Even though she couldn't be of much help to the woman, she was still staying up with her. She was in better condition because she had started out healthier, but the long days were wearing on her too.

"Sure," Estra smirked. When Youngest glanced up, confused, Estra shook her head at her. "Everyone knows UPS's make up excuses like that all the time. They'll make progress at first, then it gets 'complicated', then as soon as you lean on them just enough, they can magically get you the rest of the way there. They're cunning little things that way."

"I don't think that's what's going on. I asked her, earlier on, about how it worked, and it makes sense that she'd be having trouble now," Youngest said slowly.

Estra shook her head at her. "It's their game, Youngest. Who knows why they all do it, but they do. This one was good for longer, I'll admit, but it's just how these things are."

Youngest stood from the table. "Maybe you're right, but I do think she's trying her best. She's barely eating or sleeping. She just works at those routes, far past when I would have collapsed from exhaustion. She's trying," she said firmly. She turned towards the line for food.

"It's a game, Youngest. You'll see," Estra said with a shrug. "I'm not trying to be mean," she said, noticing the slightly stricken look Youngest couldn't quite conceal. "Just, be smart. You've enough memories to understand your situation."

Her words lingered with Youngest as she got food, returned to the room, and coaxed the woman into drinking a thin broth. How many people had worn themselves as thin as the woman was, all for others to think it was a sick sort of game? Why did no one look and see what she saw? Everyone else on board called the woman it, like she was a machine. Just wind her up and watch her spin. Cuss and kick her when she fell over, then start all over again. Completely ignoring the curious, intelligent mind that gave them results.

"Hey, I've been thinking," Youngest said, before the woman could go back to the terminal. "In my head, I've mostly been calling you 'the woman'. Would you—that is, would you mind a name?"

The woman's lips quirked up. "I suppose. Did you have something in mind?"

"Pandora," Youngest said quietly, watching her face.

"Pandora. I like it," she said. Pandora grinned. "Thank you."

"What for?" Youngest asked, startled.

"I've never had a name. It means a great deal to me, Youngest." Pandora's eyes were a light, cold blue, but in that moment, Youngest felt warmer than she'd ever been before.

* * *

"Hail Historian, this is outpost KITH. What's your destination and purpose?"

"Worthless Federation busybodies," the Captain gritted out before she returned the hail. "Greetings, outpost KITH. We're headed to Acastar on a research trip."

"Anything to declare?"

"No, just crew and supplies," the Captain's tone was the tale-tell sickly sweet of an impending breakdown.

"Very well. Have a safe voyage." The pilot bot gestured and the restraining field lifted. No one breathed until they were completely clear of the outpost. Then the Captain calmly swiveled on one heel and backhanded Pandora. Her head snapped to the side, nearly toppling her to the ground, but she kept her balance like a reed swaying in a storm.

"What did I tell you, UPS?" the Captain gritted out. "No delays, no checkpoints. I suppose you were trying to get picked up, weren't you. Thought they'd scan us and retrieve you, hmm?"

"No, sir," Pandora said softly, her head tipped toward the ground. Only Youngest noticed her hands tense, then release. "This was the only checkpoint within forty clicks that doesn't have a functional scanner. This sector is full of checkpoints; if we wanted to avoid them entirely, we would add several cycles to the journey, and look suspicious. This was the least risky and most expedient route, I promise."

The Captain sneered. "Fine," she snapped after a long moment. "But you tell me before you decide to take us through any more checkpoints for the fucking useless Federation."

"Yes Captain," Pandora murmured.

"You," the Captain barked at Youngest. "Why didn't you inform me of this bullshit?"

Youngest carefully stared at the Captain's chin. "I'm sorry Captain, I didn't think you would care. It was just a checkpoint."

"Just a checkpoint, she says. Hah! They're the collars the Federation twists 'round the neck of any spacefaring folk, yet another way to control anyone and everyone they can. You're naive, girl," the Captain growled lowly. "Why the hell did the Council saddle me with you."

'Probably because my mother made it a condition for taking the fall for you, because she couldn't bear not to have memories of you in her lineage. And the Council couldn't have their great Captain shamed with the failure of your last reckless ghost hunt, so she went into cryo and you were given a last chance.' Youngest had tried to keep her face blank, but something must have slipped.

The Captain cuffed her about the ear, scowling. "Get out of my sight. I want the next section done before the start of next cycle."

Pandora startled toward them, eyes round. Youngest shook her head slightly at her, ignoring the throb of pain the movement triggered. "Yes sir," she muttered, striding quickly to Pandora. She propelled the other woman out of the bridge by her elbow, thinking about absolutely nothing.

* * *

Pandora barely input ten lines into the terminal before spinning and fixing Youngest with an intense stare. Youngest had been at her elbow still, and stumbled back a step at the sudden movement. Pandora's face softened, and she put a gentle hand on Youngest's arm.

"What was that?" Pandora asked lowly.

"What?"

"You know what. She hit you. I know I've been in here most of the voyage, but she doesn't seem like the type that usually hits her crew. What's her problem with you?"

"Don't you need to-"

"The program's already running. You're not getting out of this," Pandora said implacably.

Youngest groaned, rubbing her face. "Let's lay down then. My head's still ringing, and I'm sure you're not doing much better."

Pandora's free hand fluttered dismissively. "Honestly, this is the healthiest I've ever been so long into a journey. A couple slaps, plenty of food and sleep? Practically a vacation."

Youngest cringed at that. She shook her head as they crawled onto the bed. "I'm sorry."

"You're the only reason I'm doing so well. Usually by this point in a voyage I'm half comatose, and more than half black and blue," Pandora said, mouth twisting wryly.

Youngest groaned, sticking her head into a pillow. "That really doesn't make me feel better."

Pandora sighed. "I'm not—This isn't me looking for pity, Youngest," she said, propping herself up with an elbow. "This is how my life has gone. If I couldn't look past the muck to find the bits of pyrite or moissanite, I'd have gone crazy by now. Well, more crazy than I already am," she prevaricated.

"You don't seem crazy," Youngest frowned up at her.

Pandora laughed. "Honey, all UPS's are a little crazy. If you can't bend your mind a little bit, it breaks."

Youngest grimaced. "Honey?"

"What? You can't expect me to believe that 'Youngest' is your true name. So I'll give you a nickname," Pandora grinned hesitantly.

"Why Honey?"

"Because you're so sweet," Pandora tried. At Youngest's flat stare, she deflated. "But if you don't like it, I'll find something else."

"I'm not, though," Youngest argued. "I'm just –"

"You are. Enough delaying, I know you're trying to distract me. Spill," Pandora said, refocusing.

Youngest sighed. "Fine. So. There's a growing faction on Memria that resents the power the Federation has over us. The Captain is a member of that group, and thought she had 'the perfect weapon' found. She wasted a lot of resources and political sway on the search for that, and embarrassed the Council in the doing. Mother said this was her last chance for a position on the Council."

"Why does she want to join the Council?"

"Well, it's the ruling body of Memria. Only 12 hold a seat at once. But I think it was mostly because..." Youngest lowered her voice. "Council members have near-total power in Memria. Whatever her motivation was before, I think she's desperate for that power now because of my mother. She could pardon her. Otherwise, her sentence is five hundred years in cryo."

"What? That's insane!"

"It was a total embarrassment. We don't have executions on Memria, but you might as well die as far as your loved ones are concerned," Youngest shrugged.

"Then what, you're woken up centuries later, after everyone who knew you is dead?" Pandora asked. "That's almost worse!"

"It is and it isn't. There are good odds someone who knew you passed on their memories. Maybe not clearly, maybe not favorably, but a chance. There is *some* danger in combining genetic lines," she explained, reaching for Pandora's hand. "Too much from each side can take too long to assimilate, or if the memories are too similar, there's a risk of false or merged memories. Reproductive partners are carefully chosen. Sometimes I think that's the only reason new people are allowed on Memria. We can circumvent the genetic risks of inbreeding, but not with memories."

"That's almost poetic, that memory is so fragile," Pandora mused.

Youngest laughed humorlessly. "It is beyond frail. The amount of time our researchers have spent trying to make the system work..." she shook her head. "I know my planet's entire culture centers around memory, but I wonder sometimes where we'd be if we looked forward more than we looked back."

"Maybe you can be the first," Pandora said. She leaned down haltingly and hesitated before brushing a fleeting kiss on Youngest's temple. "I'd follow you into the future."

Blushing fiercely, Youngest brought their joined hands to her lips and equally lightly kissed Pandora's knuckles. "Let's focus on getting to the Origin, first."

'Then, maybe. Maybe...' she mused, not daring to complete the thought.

* * *

In the end, Pandora managed to get the Captain's requested route length by early the next cycle. Unfortunately, this was not the success they had hoped for.

"A goddamn asteroid field!" The Captain screamed, looming over Pandora. "Do you have any idea what could have happened!" Pandora stayed silent, looking straight ahead in the way that Youngest had learned meant she was in another place entirely. As such, Youngest saw the danger when Pandora was not in a position to, but was entirely unable to prevent what happened.

"Are you listening to me, you little bitch!" When Pandora remained silent and motionless, the Captain's razor of a temper snapped. She grabbed Pandora by the throat and threw her across the bridge. Youngest lunged forward, trying to catch her, but fell short. A sickening crack rang out, and Pandora curled up, a bitten off keen the only sound she made. One arm hung limply, the shoulder grotesquely misshapen. When the Captain moved to go after her again, Youngest stepped between them.

"Captain, respectfully, please stop. You've made your point. I'm sure she will not make such a mistake again," Youngest spoke carefully, trying desperately not to set her off further. "Let me go patch her up, then we'll start on the next route."

"It can't get us to Origin if it's dead," the navigator chipped in mildly. His face was uncaring, but Youngest saw a spark of worry in his eyes. He had thanked Pandora for her work, she remembered. Every time they had come to input a route, he had thanked her. A glance around the bridge revealed more hidden thoughts. Youngest thought she knew why. No matter how little they thought of Pandora's humanity, they knew her value. It was written into her genetic code, but the key was her mind. If the

Captain truly lost control and killed her, they had no chance of reaching the Origin.

"Fine," the Captain spat. She had seen the same unrest in the crew. "But it's on thin ice, you hear me? One more stunt like that and I'll rip the coordinates from her DNA. Get out of my sight." As she stomped off, Youngest rushed over to Pandora. She gathered her up in her arms, immensely careful of the shoulder. She didn't run to medbay, but only because it would be suspicious, and probably cause her more pain.

"I told you so," Estra murmured as she passed them in the hall. Youngest ground her teeth.

"I don't want to hear it," she muttered, as Pandora curled into herself even further.

"Tough. You're the one who wasn't firm enough, and now the UPS is paying for it. Remember that, before you go blaming the Captain." Estra continued on, not looking back.

Once they reached medbay, she gently set Pandora down on a berth, and, as lightly as possible, palpitated the shoulder. A sharp intake of breath was the only indication she had that Pandora was awake. "It's broken," Youngest murmured. "Your bird bones break easy."

Pandora huffed a soft laugh. "Wish they were light enough I could fly, if they're going to break like a bird's." She watched as Youngest fetched the bone mender and carefully set it up around her shoulder.

"Youngest, why did you name me Pandora?" She asked quietly.

"Well, it's a bit of a story, but we'll be here a while. Want to hear it?" Youngest asked, carefully sitting on the berth with Pandora.

"Yeah. Take my mind off the pain."

"All right. Back at the Origin, there was a story about a woman. Well, I say a story, singular, but truly, as with many myths of the old world it was stories, plural. Each story always found a catalyst in this woman named Pandora. She was always given a container of some sort. A jar, a box; something along those lines. The person who gave it to her changed; husband, father, god. They always warned her to never open it. She always did. Very rarely out of malice; usually she was tricked, or her curiosity grew too intense. Sometimes, she chose to open the box with full knowledge of what would happen. Inside, all the ills of the world were hidden; pestilence, plague, death, and so on. Once what they were trapped in was opened, all of those terrible things were released upon the world."

"Really shows how you feel about me, that you'd name me after someone like that," Pandora joked weakly.

"I'm not finished. Once all that was cruel and evil was gone, there was one thing left in the container. Hope. But hope couldn't escape on its own, it needed to be set free. So Pandora did. That's why we have hope, even with everything bad that happens. One person choose hope. And hope continues on in the face of everything because people keep choosing it."

Pandora was silent for a long moment, but Youngest didn't push.

"That's a lot," she finally said.

"I know."

"I'm not that special," Pandora said.

"You are to me. I just... existed, before we found you. I wasn't supposed to be here, and the Captain ensured I knew that. I have all these memories, but I've hardly lived." Youngest took Pandora's good hand in hers. "I've never had anyone who existed outside of my memories. I've never been given the chance. So I was coasting, waiting for the inevitable moment of going back into storage. I won't say I fell in love at first sight, because I didn't. But I fell for you, your courage, your dignity. I don't care what we find at the end of this journey, what secrets will be revealed, what knowledge we gain. You gave me hope for a future where I'm not just the next body in my bloodline. I don't know if I can pull it off, but..." Youngest hesitated. "After, will you come away with me? Just the two of us."

A soft sound came from the entrance to the medbay. They glanced up, but the door didn't open. They huddled even closer together, and Pandora shook her head, huffing a laugh.

"I'm not a person to them. How would you convince them to give me up? There are secrets in my genetic code even I don't know about. They'll want to dig through me until there's nothing left hidden," Pandora finished, watching Youngest sadly. She stroked her thumb over their joined hands.

"I'm not planning on asking," Youngest admitted. "They're as likely to let me leave as they are you. The problem with genetic memory is that you have to pass it down, and I haven't yet. My mother's body has lived too long out of cryo to be able to carry another child the term without enormous risk. Without the allowance of a surrogate, I'm the last of her line. They could always clone either of us, but it's taboo. That's part of why you're treated so poorly," she said. "They don't consider clones real people. The memory doesn't pass down well, if at all. It's anathema to exist without the memories. The amount of drama there is about relationships with unequal lengths of genetic memories is insane," Youngest laughed. "If they considered you a person, I would be thought of a cradle robber, even though you've actually lived and experienced decades more than me."

Pandora sighed. "Darling, your birth culture is very odd."

Youngest laughed and kissed their hands. "I think every culture seems strange on the outside, but I'll admit, it's very... restrictive. And Darling?"

"You are darling," Pandora muttered. "But maybe not that. How will you steal us away?"

"I'm still working on that," Youngest admitted. "I can't swear we'd be safe, or provided for, or –"

"Yes."

"Yes?"

Pandora sighed fondly. "Dearest, I don't think you realize what you mean to me. You named me after the woman who brought hope; to me, *you* are the hope-bringer. I was doomed to be shuffled from one ship to another, forever only valued as a UPS. But you don't. You think me brave, dignified; I would call it resigned." Pandora reached for Youngest's cheek, cradling her gently. "I have *never* been a person, never had a choice. You give me choices, constantly, even as your own are limited. I can't express what that means to me. I would rather a day free with you than ten lifetimes without you."

"How sweet," came a drawl at the doorway of the medbay. Youngest and Pandora startled apart, Youngest lurching in front of Pandora to block her from view. The second mate stood at the entrance, arms crossed. They were glaring at Youngest, the angriest she had ever seen them.

"Sorry to break your little dreams apart, but you know what we do with traitors."

"Please, we weren't going to jeopardize –" Youngest tried to protest.

"Grab them," they ordered. A handful of crew filtered through the door. Estra was one of them. Her face filled with devastation as she looked at Youngest, but she said nothing.

"Please, leave Pandora alone, it was my idea. She's not responsible for this," Youngest begged, still shielding Pandora. A fluttering hand touched the middle of her back.

"No, it's not responsible for this madness," The second mate agreed. "You will take accountability for trying to steal knowledge and your bloodline from Memria. I can't imagine Captain will be merciful, but perhaps you can plead mercy. Oh wait. You were trying to steal the *one* manip-clone with knowledge of the *origin*, and the bloodline of her *life partner.*"

Youngest cringed, but tried again. "I wasn't –"

She was cut off by a slap from Estra. "Hold your tongue, traitor," she hissed. With that, the rest of the crew surged forward, hauling Youngest away from Pandora.

"Leave her alone, she's still hurt!" Youngest shouted. The crewmen who had gone to haul Pandora off the berth hesitated and looked at the second mate.

"Cuff it to the berth," ordered the second mate. "The traitor goes to the brig."

Youngest looked back at Pandora as she was dragged out. "I love you," she called, and got a cuff over the head for it. She couldn't hear if Pandora said anything through the ringing in her ears as she was pulled away.

* * *

Youngest sat quietly in the brig, worrying at the cuffs on her wrists as she worried about Pandora. She startled to her feet as the door opened, and the Captain stepped through. Neither spoke.

"I knew you would be a problem," the Captain finally said. "I told the council, 'don't send Youngest on a mission this important. I need her mother, my first mate, because her mother can handle whatever needs to be done.' But they insisted someone had to be held responsible, and she begged for it to be her, and that I bring you. Now look what's happened. You fall in love with the first person-shaped thing you find, want to run away with it. You disgust me."

"She's not a thing," Youngest said quietly, firmly. "She is a person, and no amount of treating her like a useful piece of trash, to be used and discarded, will change that."

"Really. Well, if you're so sure of that, let's make a deal," the Captain said. "I'll release you, the both of you. You just have to retrieve the knowledge for me."

"What's the catch?" Youngest demanded.

"I send you in alone, with a feed, so we can see your progress. I'll be watching *it,*" she sneered, "as you go. If it is a person that loves you, it'll react when you are in danger," Captain said poisonously. "If I believe it's reactions are genuine, and you return successfully, I suppose you aren't a fool. I'll let you run off into the ether. I doubt you'll survive long, but that won't be my problem." The Captain shrugged.

"Let me tell her something of this, please. Her entire life, reactions meant weakness, and she was punished for it. She won't break in front of you." Youngest hesitated. "Please. For the love you hold for my mother. Give us a chance to show you that we –"

The Captain grabbed her face roughly and squeezed her jaw painfully. The look on her face could have melted steel, so great was her fury. "You have relinquished all claim to her. Never speak of her, never so much as *think* of her again. Do you understand me?"

The Youngest tried to nod but couldn't. The Captain shook her. "Yes," she gasped.

"Good. You will not speak. If she can truly care for you, she'll break. If not, you will continue your bloodline and face your punishment. You'll agree to my terms, or I'll kill you now to spare your mother the shame of what you've done." The Captain released her hold on Youngest and stepped back.

"Well?"

"I accept," Youngest whispered, defeated.

"We land in two cycles," the Captain told her. "Prepare yourself."

Once she left, Youngest dropped onto the bench, head in her hands.

* * *

The area where they landed the ship was oddly familiar to Youngest. It was a desert, dry and barren, and the only landmarks were strange, spiky black obelisks. There was no life visible for as far as the eye could see. The crew trickled off of the ship, an uneasy silence filling the air. Youngest thought that their memories were haunting them too.

The Captain stood apart from the crew, one hand wrapped around Pandora's bad arm. Youngest wanted desperately to say something, anything to her, but kept her mouth shut. The Captain nodded towards the obelisks. "It's in there. Should be at the center. Remember our agreement." Youngest nodded, looking only at Pandora. Pandora stared at her too. Youngest could almost see her heart breaking when she said nothing, and she turned away before *she* broke and blurted out everything.

As she drew closer to the obelisks, the feeling of unease grew. The structures weren't terribly tall, perhaps twenty or thirty feet at the highest, but they unsettled her in a way she didn't understand. As she entered the first ring, she saw a plaque with a strange script on it. None of her memories had anything similar to it, but it made her uneasy. The next ring brought a pictogram of some sort, which ominously displayed a skull, among other eerie looking symbols. Each ring of obelisks she passed was also marked with a plaque, often covered in a script she couldn't read, occasionally with the same pictogram as the first.

It was clear that the structure had been there a long time. There were pits in the ground, some lightly disguised by debris. A pillar here and there had collapsed, and others creaked ominously. Picking through the hazards, Youngest leaned lightly on one, and the odd metal caved. She jerked away, barely keeping from falling into the hollow structure. It moaned in warning, and began to fall.

She ran. The obelisk missed her, but crashed into another, setting off a wave of dominoes. The rings grew tighter and tighter, with the obelisks slowly becoming upright instead of the haphazard jumble they had been on the outer edges. Still, they never grew tight enough that she couldn't pass through them. They did grow tight enough that the falling obelisks were held up by their fellows, and she breathed a sigh of relief.

Finally, she came to the center of the obelisks. They surrounded a short, squat building, with one final pictogram on the door. As she touched the handle, she paused. It almost sounded like... she thought she heard a scream.

She shook herself. She was almost halfway there. She opened the door and went inside.

A dull, buzzing light flickered on as she stepped inside. In the center of the room, there was a spiral staircase, descending into the earth. She shook the rail before she set foot on the first step, but it held firm. As she descended, more lights flickered on, an eerie hum emanating from them that set her nerves on edge. Her breathing echoed oddly. She could almost swear that she could hear another person breathing, or ten, or a hundred. After ten minutes or so, she caught sight of the bottom. A small room spread out at the foot of the stairs. In the center, there was a pedestal with a small box. Nothing else was in the room. A feeling of familiarity and dread swamped her. Movement at the corner of her eye caused her to whirl, but there was nothing.

She crossed cautiously to it, and lifted the lid of the box. As she did, a memory rose inside her. This box, this room—The memory shattered before she heard more than *never again*. She shook her head, waving the memory away. She looked inside the box.

Inside lay an old paper letter, like the ones the oldest of her ancestor's memories vaguely remembered. She picked it up and unfolded it. At first, she couldn't understand it, before one of her oldest memories slammed into the forefront of her mind.

THIS IS NOT A PLACE OF HONOR.

'What...' she thought, bewildered, before the meaning seeped into her conscious mind.

She dropped the letter back into the box and ran.

* * *

She made it back to where the crew waited in half the time she took to get to the obelisks. Ghosts of memories fluttered around her as she darted through the crumbling structure, dead and dying bodies obscuring her feet as solemn academics echoed warnings first spoken millennia ago. Her pace startled most of the crew, but not the Captain. A giddy grin spread across the Captain's face, right up until Youngest's fist landed in the center of it. Gasps rang out, but her fury no longer cared what happened.

"Nuclear waste! That's what you wanted to find?" she yelled at the Captain. "Are you insane? This is so far past illegal it loops back around and becomes even more illegal! Did any of you know?" she snapped, rounding on the crew. From the horror on their faces, she knew they didn't. No one would have come, if they'd known. "What was your plan?" she demanded. "What was the point? You're lucky our ancestors did their job well, and buried it too deep for the elements to easily access, otherwise we could have been dead already!"

"But we aren't, and now we know it's *here*!" the Captain exclaimed, still giddy even through a broken nose. "Now we can cleanse the galaxy of all the pests who refuse to listen to the past! Are you ready to live in a new era, my people?" she laughed, rising to her feet. "One where memory is the greatest currency, and we can live forever?" No one spoke. This was insane. They all knew that. They were here, at the Origin, because of an insane woman's suicide mission.

She wanted my mother with her, Youngest thought numbly. She thought my mother would 'do what it took'.

All of them were so sick with horror, compounded by the horror of their ancestral memory, that no one noticed Pandora rise from where she lay crumpled on the ground, fist clenched around something. They did notice when she drove it into the Captain's neck, and her mad laugh transformed into a gurgle. The Captain collapsed to the ground once again, blood spilling hot onto the desert sand, as a slip of a woman, beaten, bruised, but not broken, stood over her. Youngest ran to her, heart in her throat, but skidded to a stop a stride away, a horrible thought rising.

"Why are you just standing over there?" Pandora asked, voice raw from screaming.

"I might be radioactive, I was all the way down to the final warning, what if I infect you?" she said, torn.

"I," Pandora informed her, "do not care." She stepped over the Captain's body, fisted her hands in Youngest's shirt, and pulled her into a kiss. They kissed, ignoring the world, until they had to break for air. Youngest rested her forehead against Pandora's, panting.

"What's your name?" Pandora asked suddenly.

"Youngest," she said, confused.

"No, your true name, not that ridiculous title, not a nickname. I know you have one, what is it?" She insisted, wrapping her good arm around Youngest's neck.

"Oh. It's Cassandra."

The Starlight Lounge

by Lena Starlight

The archive smelled like mildew and lemon oil—official scent of city-funded amnesia. The kind of hole that didn't just misplace the reams of documents they'd hired me to file; it misplaced years.

Whole souls, maybe, the temporary nature of my position at the archive dulled my sense of both responsibility and complicity. *Hard to tell, honestly.*

I was two pots of burnt coffee deep, angling to bust free of this cell of capitalism for the fleeting bread and circus that is the weekend, bleeding from a paper cut shaped like a crescent moon when I found it: the reel.

No label. I turned it over. No date. I checked the plastic sleeve against the schmaltzy yellow bulb in the desk lamp. No return slip. It was just sitting there, next on top of the "unsortables" bin waiting for me.

The unsortables was the pile where records went when they didn't fit into any recognized category. Or when someone gets nervous about filing them under their real name or description.

I'd been instructed to update and archive them all, but every time something like a handwritten complaint about a rumored P.D. black site crossed my desk—replete with street names and badge numbers—or a coffee-stained folder labeled *Urban Renewal* turned up, full of aerial photographs scrawled with *blight clearance* across the bottom of the decades-old polaroids date-stamped a year after the neighborhood was declared uninhabitable (with kids still visible on the swingset)—those files never made it to the week's end register.

My personal favorite: a manila envelope marked "Holiday Potluck Planning". I'm not a huge fan of Thanksgiving, but when my dulled curiosity piqued I may have thumbed inside and found a city water sampling report from 2015. Why was it my favorite? In thick, fat-fingered bureaucratic scribbling across the bottom: "Don't send to Lansing."

Above my paygrade, but I'll throw in a sneer *gratis*.

I should've logged this latest find like I had a dozen times before. I knew the protocol: File a ticket. Call Glasmor for approval.

Instead, I threaded it into the top grommet of the heavy Revere P-90 8mm projector produced some time after the second World War, and leaned in like a pervert sniffing haunted panties.

The screen flickered a couple of *zip-zips* through the howl of the fans cooling the incandescent.

Then ...*music?* My eyebrows couldn't help themselves when I heard the tune.

"Jesus fucking christ," I pulled my hand back from the projector. Produced in 1949, the Revere was built like a tank and outfitted with variable speed for fine control. What it didn't have: sound.

But somehow, some old jazz tune was creeping in past the heat exhaust and the shutter clicks. It wasn't playback either, it was a live recording. Crackly, warbly, but undeniably present. I ran my hand around the metal body feeling for the vibrations. The sound was real in a way most things don't feel anymore. At least to me.

On the wall, the image of a woman stood on stage, dressed in red with a silver mic. The air shimmered behind her from some stage curtain with a jazz band somewhere off-frame. The scene was grainy, like some kind of dream film stock, but she was crystal-clear.

Slack-jawed, I leaned forward on one arm, face too close to the powder coated metal. She turned to face the lens, and for a moment—God help me—I swear she saw me.

Then she sang.

Her voice was low and aching, a heretic's prayer once-believed. She sang about apples. About silence. About a kiss gone bad enough to corrupt. I stopped breathing. I caught a flash of something in the mirror behind her.

It wasn't her reflection.

Something whispered in my ear:

"*Don't forget—*"

"Holy fuck!" I jumped, heart hammering to beat the shutter. I looked around frantically but no one was there. The projector's lamp glowed and post-coital smoke gently rolled off the lighthouse. The scent hit me first: overripe apples and... ozone. Like the onset of a summer sun storm, all thunder and lightning and concrete.

I backed up to a wobbly chair with the taped-over cushion the staffing overlords provided me and landed hard. I was losing my mind. The cleaning agents must be toxic too. *That must be why they hire temps.* I leaned an elbow on my desk and covered my mouth, calculating hours spent in this dungeon. *No wonder they don't care what I see down here.*

I glanced down at the desk in thought. I was sure I was having a stroke—or losing my absolute shit.

A feather. Not fluffy like a backyard-chicken or goose down. This one was sleek and dark. Maybe even sharp enough to write with.

One time, the unsortables yielded an invoice for "research-grade LSD". Hastily stamped with a big red APPROVED letters. Dated to the 60's. *Did I use a different coffee pot this morning?*

I was still staring at the thing on my desk when the door creaked open behind me.

"Finch."

Alan Glasmor's voice. He always sounded like he knew something I didn't, and was a little sad I was too dumb to catch up. Are you picturing a thick mustache? Of course you're right. I sat up straighter and slapped my palm down over the feather.

He stood in the doorway, clipboard in one hand, the other tucked into the pocket of his soul-crushingly well-pressed vest.

"You look like you lost a fight with a file cabinet."

"That's optimistic. The cabinet had backup."

I had two shirts and one pair of pants in rotation that technically met the city's dress code for this gig. All three looked like they'd survived a bar fight but not the coin-op—and smelled like an ashtray.

Knowing my schtick, Glasmor didn't skip a beat. "We've got a misfile in Permit Ledger Seven. Building C-190A shows two owners. Both dead. Your resume from the agency said 'computer background', maybe that includes whatever's left of the old system. Think you can be useful?"

He meant: *Can you use DOS.*

I cleared my throat. My tongue was dry. "Just finishing up here."

His eyes drifted toward the projector. The lamp was still on.

"That isn't city inventory," he said, soles of his wingtips creaking with the shift in his weight.

I tried nudging the unsortables drawer shut with my knee—though it made a dry squeaking wood sound—and slid a half-read manila folder over the feather.

"Unsorted bin," I said. "Nothing flagged."

"Those aren't pleasure reads." He took a step forward deliberately. He was giving me no space to lie. "And the last time you started poking around down here, we lost three hours trying to track down a fire code from 1911 that mysteriously turned up under *your* lunchbox—filled with week-old tuna salad."

Alan Glasmor didn't do sighs. He just exhaled meaningfully through his nose, my temp assignment parole officer.

"Don't waste time on things that aren't real, Finch. This place already has too many ghosts."

"Just trying to clear the backlog," I muttered. "Do a couple solo tonight after hours to make up for it."

"No one asked you to do that." He turned, wingtips clicking like they were spelling out T-I-M-E-S-H-E-E-T in Morse code. "Ten minutes," he called over his shoulder. "Then I want your eyes on the ledgers and the old terminals. Not the fog machine."

I waited until his footsteps dissolved into the dead hum of the hallway lights.

Then I pulled the reel from the projector, still warm, and tucked it into the inner pocket of my coat—careful not to smear my fingers on the film.

* * *

I live on the fourth floor of a building that has never been renovated, and probably never will be. The elevator doesn't work. The narrow hallway lights flicker—usually when you're desperately trying to fumble your key in the lock, possibly pissed, possibly with someone waiting to get in behind you.

Or underneath you.

The only thing new was the scent of someone else's cooking that always manages to smell like my childhood—but never quite enough to name. Funny how a steady diet of fried brown takeout permanently erases the ability to identify a home-cooked meal.

I paused at the lobby mailboxes and flicked open the tarnished door labeled 4C. A slim pile waited: utility bill, a city reminder about voter registration deadlines, a coupon flyer for a restaurant that boarded up last October. And something else.

A big red envelope. *Heavy.* I didn't remember subscribing to anything. I turned it over. No address or stamp. When I peeled it open, the scent of dust and ink hit me—familiar, but older than it should've been.

Inside: an issue of something called *The Curious Post*. I stood in the lobby flipping through it.

The layout was off. Too elegant. Serif headlines, long-form columns. Not a single photo or bylines. A faint watermark of a crescent moon behind the masthead.

The top story read:

THE GIRL IN THE GLASS & THE MAN WHO DISAPPEARED

Below it, a tiny diagram like a music staff with twenty-seven little black dots arranged in an arch. No caption. I told myself it was a printer's flourish. My neck didn't buy it. On page four, a boxed notice, small caps, officious in the way only secret things are:

```
CIRCULAR—FOR INTERNAL DISTRIBUTION
Lead custodians report the Scion of Tyranas (code
name: Starlight) located; seizure imminent.
Observed: persistent affinity for glass
(reflective halls, stage light), heightened
response to sonic cues.
Relay sightings via the usual mark. Enter by
mirrors only; do not speak the sainted name
outside the ring.
Transfer to gatehouse scheduled upon next sound
off. Present coin & eye for passage.
—Office of Glass, Order of the Owl
```

An inside spread carried a column on "municipal disappearances" set too close to the gutter, like the words were trying to fall in. In the outer corner, the press registration marks made a crooked sigil—a circle with a dot and a hooked crescent—as if the color plates had kissed in the wrong place.

Halfway down page seven, a sidebar stuttered around a sentence that didn't scan until it did:

```
…reported by Cyrus Finch in last year's audit…
```

My name.

An Erratum box sat at the bottom of the page, small and pious:

```
ERRATUM: In our previous issue, The Knight
Resplendent was misattributed. The correct name is
Tyranas per chapter guidance.
```

I had never held a baby, but I carried the paper up four flights as I imagine one might. Upstairs, the lights in my apartment were dim, and the radiator coughed like it had bronchitis and no desire to improve.

I dropped the mail on the table, mind reeling. Water boiled on the stove, but I didn't bother with tea.

Instead, I sat and read the entire issue. Cover to back. Twice. I looked at the envelope again. Still no return address. But on the back, faint and embossed in red ink, I could just make out a symbol. A circle and an eye—wide open. *All-seeing.*

I lit a cigarette with a bent match from the coffee tin I keep by the window. Took a drag, letting the smoke hang. The paper sat on the table, accusing me—of what, I wasn't sure. I circled my name three times. It didn't change anything, but it made the feeling worse. The feeling that something had been shifted, changed and I hadn't agreed.

* * *

I dreamt of Marcie's Diner, but not the real one. Every booth held a shape pretending to be a person, heads bent. No mouths but plenty of eyes. The EXIT sign blinked.

Then she walked in, swinging the little chime on the metal-and-glass door. Marilyn, or a version printed on the wrong kind of paper. Platinum hair pin-curled, red mouth stretched into that famous you-already-want-me curve. Switching in a tight pencil skirt, clicking her heels like a hot Miss Piggy.

Can muppets click their heels?

Nobody spoke. You don't talk in churches.

A waitress brought over a giant platter of eggs, sunnyside up. The yolks bobbed and trembled over the whites, jittering, drugged-out eyes. An old man at the counter got up and offered Marilyn his arthritic knuckles with a twisted little bow. She accepted like a queen and stepped up onto one of the stools and then sat, somehow naked but shod, in the center of the platter. She looked at me through her half-lidded Marilyn mask and scrunched her nose.

"Eat," she said. Her lips didn't move. The sound came from all around us: the chrome, from the coffee warmer, from the part of me that still thinks hunger is a kind of proof.

I told myself to back out. I told myself doors in dreams go both ways. My feet didn't care. They squeaked me up to the counter like a kindergartener with an empty tray awaiting the holy grail of dinosaur-shaped foods. She leaned both hands back on the counter. Close up, she smelled like fryer oil, carnations, and dirty pennies. There was heat rolling off her like a hood vent.

"On your knees," she almost whispered. Or maybe that was the sizzle of the grill. The egg whites shuddered beneath her like they'd heard the joke before.

I laughed—short, ugly. A reflex. "I'm not the kneeling type."

"Everyone kneels," she said. Still no lips moving. "Some people call it choosing." A fork rested on the rim of the platter, tines dull, handle worn. I didn't pick it up. My hands hung dumb at my sides.

She lifted a lacquered finger, pressed it to my mouth, hot enough to sting. When she pulled away I licked my lips, tasting her perfume and hospital jello. My knees buckled as I took a single step closer. My throat worked against itself, dry and desperate. I wanted to kneel beside that plate. I wanted to worship. The shapes in the booths leaned forward a fraction, witnesses at an exclusive show.

"Go on," she coaxed. "Be kind to the eggs," a giggle and she smiled wide as I leaned in. Her tongue flicked out then—quick, reptile—just the tip.

The yolks bobbed, gold and obscene. The whites trembled. There was a little blood under the plate. Not much, but enough to make the butcher in me sit up and remember the rules about knives.

Knuckles out, bub.

"You're not her," I said. "You're the billboard."

"That's what billboards are for," she said, and laughed—wet, delighted, close to my ear though she hadn't moved. As she shook her head her hair lengthened. She wore the singer's face now—the one from the film strip. "To make you yearn for the right road."

My hands on either side of the platter, I bent at the elbows anyway. The heat rolled off the plate and climbed my face. My eyes watered. The room leaned in.

"Say please," she murmured.

I didn't. I'm stubborn when it doesn't matter.

Her mouth opened. The tongue showed itself properly this time—split for a breath, then slicked back together, glinting muscle. She brought a hand to my jaw at the lip of the counter and traced my lower lip with a nail, nicking it. A clean little pain, bright and humiliating. The shapes in the booths exhaled as one.

I tasted copper and swallowed hard.

The bell at the door rang again—no bell, just the world trying out a sound. The eggs quivered. I felt something warm and wet gush against my hands on the laminate. Something beneath the plate was actively bleeding.

I woke with my mouth wet and the taste of old coins in my throat. I peeled myself off the grease-reeked sheets. My tongue burned where I'd lapped at liquid cholesterol.

The phone rang.

* * *

It was a landline.

Yes, the *landline*. I can't be trusted with the most plastic of burners and the last girl I'd been casually fucking couldn't take a hint—I wasn't about to tell her outright that her nervous laugh drove me batshit.

What am I? A monster?

As a result my world had become especially quiet and especially small. The thing hadn't rung in six months—unless you count telemarketers looking for some guy named Merrill.

I let it ring once more before picking up just to feel the weight of not answering. "Yeah?"

"Cyrus?" A voice—confident, like it hadn't waited tables in years. "Holy shit. It's Gregor. Greg Valance. From your mother's side."

My brain shuddered. Picnic tables. Warm Kool-Aid. A running joke about blowing up the stereo with a paperclip.

"Greg," I said. "Christ. ...You back in town?"

"Just for the week. Conference. They put me up at the Waldron. Place is crawling with orchids and elevator jazz. It's disgusting. You still at that file crypt?"

"More or less." I didn't want to prolong the torture of the conversation by explaining my life's slow descent into temp assignment servitude. Nor did I think ol' Greg could handle the differentiation between one file crypt and another.

"Shit. I figured you'd have gotten out by now. You were always the one with the stories."

I pinched the bridge of my nose. Smoke curled off my knuckles onto my forehead, blessing me like noxious incense.

"Yeah, well. Stories don't pay."

"Tell me about it," Greg said, without a trace of insight or irony. "Hey, you want to grab a drink? Catch up? There's this spot someone mentioned. Starlight Lounge? Kind of a moody joint."

My spine stiffened.

"You pick it?" I fought to keep the suspicion out of my voice.

"Nah. Some guy at the conference said it was 'vibe-y.' Piano, smoke, mirrors. We can pretend we're not pushing forty."

I stubbed out the cigarette. Behind me, the paper shifted like it had just turned a page.

"Sure," I said. "Why not."

* * *

Starlight Lounge. I repeated it silently on the walk over, *quite the earworm.*

It sounded like a place that had always been about to close—or maybe you could only ever make it quarter to, no matter how hot the person asking you there had been. The kind of joint that didn't advertise but never folded.

I found the 8mm reel still in my coat pocket, fumbling for a match I didn't have. I didn't take it out.

Greg was already there—half-drunk on something amber in a cut-glass tumbler, grinning like he owned the city and forgot to tell it.

"There he is," he said, arms open like I was the prodigal son at a father's second wedding. "What's it been—ten years? Fifteen?"

"Give or take," I muttered, sliding onto the stool next to him.

The place was lacquered, low-lit, and mixed media. Pleather booths, real brass, mirrors that had seen a war or two. The stage at the far end was empty, but the mic was lit like it was waiting for a ghost to clear its throat.

"Nice place," I said.

Greg leaned in, his voice dropping to a friendly mock-conspiratorial hush.

"They say it doesn't show up on GPS. One of the techs at the conference swore his car looped the block three times before the sign lit up." He sipped his drink. I noticed he wasn't wearing a wedding ring.

"So what's the conference?" I asked.

He grinned wider.

"Neurolinguistics. Behavioral optimization. All the buzzwords. I mostly show up to shake hands and not say anything stupid."

I raised an eyebrow.

"And the orchids?"

"Oh, the Waldron has a brand now. Luxury greenhouse vibes." He made a vague spiraling gesture in the air. When he noticed me raise an eyebrow into my drink he added, "My wife thinks it's healthy I go alone. Which works out."

"You seeing someone?" *Cut the shit.*

"More like someone sees me. You know how it is."

I didn't answer. Just palmed the pack of cigarettes I laid on the bar. He chuckled like that was an answer.

Then the lights dimmed. The hush moved through the crowd like a tide pushing in.

The mic caught a breath of static.

And then—she was there.

Lena Starlight.

Like the idea of her had been waiting in the wallpaper. Flesh-and-blood but the spitting image of the woman from the reel. A black dress this time, not red. Hair pinned on one side, curled in at the ends. She held the mic the way a priest holds a rosary, like it might break her or save you, depending on the note.

"Good evening, strangers," she purred. "And those who think they aren't."

Even Greg shut up.

She began to sing. A low, curling melody that tasted like clove and old bourbon and what you wish you'd said. My reflection in the backbar missed a blink and then caught up. I looked away.

Drunker than I thought. I didn't recognize the tune, but I knew I'd hum it later and have trouble realizing why. About halfway through the second number, Greg leaned toward me.

"Gonna make a call," he said, tapping his watch like he had somewhere to be. "Old contact in Chicago. I'll be right back."

I nodded, barely registering it. He slid off toward the hallway phone. A man in a navy suit at the end of the bar glanced at him, then at the door. No drink. Just a coin-and-eye tie tack flashing blue when the light turned.

Lena's song ended. She bowed—brief, ironic—and left the mic with a whisper of feedback.

Then she turned and walked straight to me. She sat on the stool Greg had left behind and glanced at my face. *Maybe I'm a riddle she could solve—*

"You shaved in a rush," she said softly, eyes never quite leaving my shoulder—really, the mirror behind me. She pointed lackadaisically at my neck. "Nick just below the jawline."

My hand rose late to the spot. "I didn't notice."

"That's the worst kind," a small, real smile. "The ones that only show up when someone else is looking." Her gaze dropped to my coat. "You brought a storm in your pocket," she leaned in. Not close enough to touch, but enough to make me wish she had.

Bold.

"Do you believe in angels, Mister...?"

"Cyrus," I said, palm too warm. "Finch. And no."

"Good." A breath she'd been holding. Her glance flicked to the bar mirror again—my reflection lagged a heartbeat, then corrected. She nodded to herself, like a mechanic hearing an engine she knows.

"You blur," she said softly. "That's why." Heat rose stupidly, lower than my pride.

Close, her fingers brushed mine—an accident that felt planned. Something small and smooth slid into my coat pocket.

"Don't strike those in the dark," she said, rising.

"Why not?"

"Because that's when *They're* listening." She stood, weight on her back leg. For a second the mirror threw her back at me a half-beat late—and I watched her watch it like we were in a hall of mirrors. The worry crossed her face. She was brave, not stupid.

"Backstage," she said, barely moving her lips. "Three minutes. If the bells start, don't follow."

"Bells?"

But she was already walking, shoulders squared like a small animal deciding to cross an open yard. Navy Suit peeled a thick ham hock off his stool. The men by the door recrossed their arms in the same breath. Greg was still "on the phone."

"Lena—" I tried out her name, because I'm bad at letting an exit be beautiful.

She looked back once, but it wasn't enough to hold her. Then she was gone, backstage.

I reached into my pocket. A red matchbook, stamped with an owl. One eye open—one closed.

Later I'd call it fate, but it was delay; a different kind of consent.

* * *

If I dreamed, it cleaned up after itself.

By the time I came to, sunlight was pushing through the blinds like it had something to prove. My mouth tasted like acid on an old carburetor, and there was a dull weight behind my right eye that promised to evolve into a full-blown sermon by noon.

My blazer was draped over the back of a kitchen chair—unfolded, unloved, vaguely accusing.

I reached into the inside pocket, patting for cigarettes.

What I found was the matchbook.

Red. Glossy. Owl-stamped.

I turned it over in my hands, thumb brushing the place where her fingers had passed it. A warmth bloomed in my chest.

Then I remembered the reel. That heat. The smell—fruit and ozone—when it burned.

I pulled open the breast pocket, rummaged past lint and an old receipt for yesterday's breakfast at Marcie's Diner with three words scribbled on it: "museum drives agenda", the thought of which made me want to lose the sins of the night prior, and found it—still wrapped in its coil of static. Still slightly warped at the edges: The film.

No projector here. My place wasn't *that* kind of furnished. I'd need to relocate. Maybe it'd give me more clarity. Maybe a different ending. Maybe even Lena whispering something new, something meant just for me. I don't know why I thought that. I couldn't explain it. But I also couldn't shake it. Maybe it was the hangover.

I drank from the tap and started making a list.

* * *

Sunday, empty streets, coffee gone cold—I slipped into the archive through the east service door. Only Glasmor still locked it. He wasn't there. He never was on weekends. Overtime during the week? Sure, a respectable salaried citizen. But not the sacred S-days.

Shows a lack of character, really...

The lights buzzed overhead like they were annoyed at being woken up on the Lord's day.

I didn't bother clocking in. No one would care, and that felt worse. I made a note not to turn on more lights than I had to.

Without the other soulless shills the archive felt like an old ruin that hadn't gotten the memo that it was time for capitalist pursuits and efficiency. The whole place hummed with abandonment—too many offices, mostly vacant now, even during the week. The distinct smell of dust-addled office furniture, once lookers in their heyday. A few smelled like dust mites and something worse. But I could imagine them once preserved lovingly with elbow grease and citrus wax. Preservation without purpose, and still this is where the city kept its memory.

Filed in triplicate.

I walked the rows of shelves past the bullpen like they might close behind me. No plan. Just gravity. Every glass case I passed lagged my reflection a half-beat, then caught up, changing its mind.

I pulled the reel free, careful not to smudge the scorched edge. Someone had marked the leader in faded grease pencil—XXVII—and a tiny circle with a dot and a hooked crescent, a devilish joke.

In my office, I threaded it back into the projector. Same steps as before but slower this time. Maybe a little reverence would change the outcome.

Click. Flick. Hum.

And there she was.

Lena Starlight.

Again.

This time, I wasn't stunned. I watched her like I'd been studying her for years; no jumpscares, but something intrinsic propelling me.

On film she's in red; last night at the lounge she wore black. The mismatch itched. That mic—an altar, a weapon, a confession booth. The shimmer behind her—un-glass, un-water, unreal. The band remained out of frame, and I started to wonder if they'd ever been there at all. Her posture shifted slightly. The same movement, the same beat. But her gaze—this time, she met the camera a second late. A beat off and a breath behind. The frame counter blinked 0027, then reset itself to 0000 like the machine was ashamed of forgetting the next number.

But that difference bloomed in me like a sickness. She wasn't just performing anymore. She was watching.

She turned. Looked into the lens. Into me.

Her voice dropped like a coin in a well. Under it, a mosquito-hum of little bells tried to climb a scale and quit.

That same song—low, lush, aching.

I didn't just hear it this time. I felt it in my throat and gulped, hard. The memory of someone else's goodbye I'd decided to keep for myself.

A grief pervert.

She sang of silence. Of forgetting something sweet.

I paused the reel. The frozen frame wasn't my wall anymore—just for a blink it was stone facing inward and a clear slab set over a black mouth. Then, by the next cell, it wasn't. I took a breath. Rewound to the *click* of the tray resetting. Played it again.

This time, I watched for the moment.

The moment she whispered: "Don't forget me this time." The timing was identical to before. But the tone?

Certain. Like she knew I wouldn't.

I scribbled notes. Replayed. Paused. Looked for cues in the corners of the screen, in the folds of her dress, in the way her gaze tilted just slightly off-center. Nothing changed, but everything felt different. Her dark eyes haunted me, something unfinished.

I leaned back from the screen. Lit a cigarette only to find I was shaking. The leader licked my finger as it spun; when I checked, a little friction burn had risen on the pad.

This wasn't just intrigue or curiosity I was experiencing. It was limerence. And I had it bad. Lena Starlight had performed once, on a reel that shouldn't exist, in a room that couldn't be real. I met her in the flesh to seal the deal and now she lived in me like a song that didn't end.

I started comparing details. Laying them out like case files: The reel. The XXVII mark. The hooked-crescent sigil. The article announcing codename 'Starlight'. The red envelope sealed with wax. The matchbook. The feather.

...Her voice. Her face. Her knowing.

Her body.

I shifted in my seat. My hard-on embarrassed me despite the lack of witness. Not for the woman, for the idea of her. The impossibility.

I hated that. Hated the way her whisper seemed to echo down my spine like a hand that already knew the shape of me. I lit another cigarette and told myself it was just stress. Just curiosity.

But I didn't rewind the reel again.

I didn't know what tied all these things together, only that they *were*. That they weren't random. That they were building toward something. And whatever it was, I was already a part of it.

After my arousal subsided, I stepped outside around dusk. I lit another cigarette, hands trembling slightly from the way my brain kept circling her name. Through the glass of the entry door I caught my own reflection lag and then snap into place, the world had decided to keep up—for now.

That's when I saw him.

Across the street. Trench coat. Newsboy cap. Shifting his weight like he was trying not to be seen, but also trying to be noticed.

Gerald Faraday.

I'd only met him once: *former* layout specialist. The kind of guy who stayed behind the scenes and preferred to be mistaken for furniture.

He wasn't looking at me. But he was definitely not *not* looking.

And then he tipped his head—just slightly. The kind of nod you could pretend didn't happen if someone asked.

Then he turned the corner and walked away.

Didn't say a word.

I didn't believe in angels. But I did believe in good timing.

* * *

The scent of the alley behind the municipal archive would often fluctuate between rotten garbage juice and laundry detergent—today it was sodden cardboard and onions with a little too much give. I flicked my cigarette out of low grade disgust and that's when I heard the cough.

He stepped out from behind the dumpster, blinking fast, collar half-turned like he'd dressed in a hurry and hadn't stopped moving since. Wire-rimmed glasses. Mismatched socks peeking out from shoes that had seen better decades.

"Finch," he said, eyes darting to either end of the alley. "God. Okay. Hi. Uh—sorry. You—you don't remember me, do you?"

I squinted and half-lied. "Should I?"

"Jerry Faraday. We met at a city retention seminar. You sat in the back row and didn't clap."

"That sounds like me."

He laughed once, abrupt. "Yeah. Okay. Okay. Listen. I'm not—this isn't official. I'm not supposed to be here. I'm not really here. I'm doing consulting for a tech group in—doesn't matter."

"You followed me?"

"No! Yes. But not in, like, a... weird way." He rubbed his temple and his gaze dropped to my coat. "Or maybe it is weird. I'm not the best at this part."

"This part?"

"You're carrying weather."

"What?"

He flinched at his own words. "That hum. Reflections lag around you lately, right?" He jerked his chin at the glass of the side entry door of the building. My outline blinked late, then caught up. "You've got a reel in there, don't you."

My stomach clenched. "What reel?"

"Don't lie to someone already terrified," he snorted in an attempt at humor. He fished in his coat and produced a crumpled envelope, passed it with both hands.

Inside: a couple old issues of *The Curious Post*. On top, the same one delivered to my apartment.

"You work for them?" I asked.

"Worked." He watched my coat again. "Typesetter. Nights. Before it merged." His voice thinned. "They didn't shut the Post—but they did annex it. Half paper, half pastoral now."

"Why come to me?"

He finally met my eyes. "Because people who carry around storms either serve the Order or get seen by it. And you don't look like clergy.

"If someone gave you anything," he added quickly, "a phrase, a token—don't ignore it. But don't trust it either."

"Why?"

"Same crusade, new banners. Someone sees the signs. Someone follows the wrong string. Someone gets... abrogated."

I took a step closer. "Enough riddles. What are you saying?"

"I'm saying—" He flinched. "I'm saying you're in the next issue, whether you want to be or not."

* * *

The sign said Marcie's, but the red neon had lost its 'C' sometime around the Bush years, so everyone just called it Marie's and let it ride. I liked that about it—places that knew what they were and didn't apologize.

The moment I pushed through the door I got slapped with the smell of burnt toast, diner grease, and that floral chemical tang of saccharine non-dairy creamer. The place was built like a bunker—low ceilings, booths with more scar tissue than vinyl, and chipped counters that had seen more secrets than the confessional at St. Eustace. Someone had scrawled BE KIND TO THE EGGS in sharpie over the pass window. I felt a pang of shame in my gut.

Faraday chose a corner booth, twitching like a wind-up toy someone had half-forgotten to wind down. I heard him demand a coffee from a passing waitress and slap a pocket notebook beside him, slightly open, a ballpoint pen jammed into the wire spine like a bayonet.

"Thanks for coming," he said, voice low and conspiratorial, like someone might've bugged the syrup bottle.

"This safer than the alley?" I slid in across from him. "You said you had proof."

He blinked hard, nodded once. "Fragments. Echoes. What survives sanctified redaction." He tapped the notebook. "Some keep dream journals. I keep edits. Things I remember one way the record insists were different."

"You trust that?"

"I don't trust me," he said, and jabbed hard at the notebook. "I trust patterns. And when you start seeing them—really seeing them—it's like..."

"Like the Mandela effect," I said, just as a waitress with arms like low-stakes threats thunked a fresh mug of coffee in front of him. Her knuckles left behind a small mound of single-serve creamers like candy on Halloween. I ordered the same.

"You think your Girl in Glass is part of the pattern?" I pointed at the title on the front page he brought.

Faraday looked around, then leaned in. "I think she broke it. And someone's trying to stitch it back."

He turned a page in the notebook with a tremble that said he hadn't slept well since the Carter administration. Another waitress cruised past with something vaguely egg-adjacent on a chipped plate.

"You ever heard of sanctified redaction?" he asked.

I frowned. "Sounds like the Vatican version of ghosting a sequel."

"It's worse. They strike the line and remit the sin. And history obeys."

He fished around in his coat and pulled out a page—thin, yellowed, torn from the back of an old contributor's index.

"From a back issue of *The Curious Post*."

I took it from him. The corner bore the seal of the coin-and-eye in blue and a rubricated note:

```
XXVII—enter by mirrors only.
```

Faraday watched me like I was going to disappear mid-sentence.

"Like the matches." I cleared my throat. "So the Girl is—what? A codename? A mask?"

He started to nod, then froze. "Wait. Why'd you say matches?"

"I didn't." My mouth had moved without permission. "I—she gave me—" I stopped, too late. "A red matchbook," I said, hearing the stupidity. "Said don't strike them in the dark."

His expression changed like a curtain being jerked. "You met her," he breathed. "Not just on film." His eyes flicked to my coat, to where the reel lived. "And she put a key in your pocket."

"A souvenir," I lied, shrugging it off.

He shook his head hard. "No. A countersign. A way to grant a window to Them. She told you that, didn't she?"

I didn't answer. Which was answer enough.

He leaned in, voice gone raw. "Listen to me. The Girl in the Glass is Lena Starlight. They've called her a dozen things—scion, witness, false herald—but she's real. And someone pretty high up in the Order wants her."

"The Order?"

"*Ordo Noctuae*. The Order of the Owl."

I swallowed.

Faraday stared like he was watching a car go off a bridge in slow motion. "Then the headline's more right than wrong," he whispered. "It isn't just the girl in the glass. It's the man who disappeared." He tapped the paper with one finger, then pointed at me. "It's you."

My fingers tightened on the edge of the page. The waitress thunked my coffee down in front of me. The rain outside had picked up—angry and directionless.

"I didn't try to save her," I confessed, hating how true it rang.

"That's how they keep her—on the seconds you don't spend." Faraday shut his eyes once, pained. When he opened them he was all business, old training kicking in. "Then you don't go alone. You hear me? Enter by mirrors only. Bring a witness. And next time the room's timing goes all wrong—when men move in sync, when the blue eye blinks—you move first."

He slid the leaf across the table, the coin-and-eye seal staring up like a dare. "You're already in procession," he said. "Decide who you're marching for."

* * *

I dreamt in her voice.

Not in words—just tone. That hush between velvet and static, thumping light behind my ribs like a moth pinned under glass. I chased her through half-remembered places: a train platform that smelled like citrus where my shoes slipped on wet metal, a piano lounge with no pianist and chairs facing the wrong way, a bedroom where all the clocks pointed downward and ticked in time with my pulse.

At some point in the fog, Faraday's voice broke through like a needle on vinyl.

"There's a fruit that doesn't teach you anything," he said. "It makes you forget you wanted to learn in the first place."

A reversal, he called it. The un-apple.

Sweet. Numbing. Forbidden.

I woke with the taste of old liquor in my mouth and a song I couldn't name stuck behind my craw. Sunlight hit me like an interrogation lamp. My alarm must have gone off hours ago, or I'd pummeled it in my sleep. My socks were in the sink. My keys were under the couch. I was already twenty minutes late.

The archive lobby reeked of varnish and chlorine. I slipped in through the side door from the alley, damp from the shower and carrying a coffee I didn't remember paying for.

Almost made it to my desk before I heard the polished shoes.

"Finch."

Alan Glasmor. Pressed like a court summons. Smiling like a man who kept track of every late file in a ledger marked Petty Grievances.

"Rough morning?"

"Don't they all start with existential dread?" I muttered, slipping past him.

Glasmor didn't laugh. He never did.

"I need the E-42 migration files reviewed before end-of-day. The city's finally sending someone to audit the chapter holdings." The way he said chapter put starch in the air. "Try not to redline them with metaphors this time."

"They're historical anomalies," I stretched, avoiding eye contact. "I treat them with respect."

"You treat them like tall tales."

He handed me a folder and a look that said I'll be watching you, even though he already was. As he walked off, he tossed one last barb over his shoulder: "And wipe whatever that look is off your face. This is city records, not a romance novel."

I didn't answer. I just sat down, my heart still racing like I'd forgotten something vital.

Which, to be fair, I had.

The reel was still in my bag, wedged between a notebook and the pack of cigarettes I'd sworn I wasn't smoking anymore. I hadn't dared look at it since the morning I met Faraday. Since Lena...

Since her voice.

I opened the file folder. The first page was blank. Except for the watermark.

A circle. An eye. Open and watching.

Coin-and-eye. Same as the envelope. Same as the dream.

Same as her.

* * *

By Thursday, my apartment looked like a librarian had a nervous breakdown.

The wall above the radiator had become a full-blown conspiracy board—tacks, string, curling clippings, Post-its with things like 'fruit = memory?' and 'who edits the editor??' scrawled in my worst half-sober handwriting. The matchbook was pinned dead center, like it had committed a religious crime. The 8mm reel sat beside it in its canister, quiet and smug, taunting me every time I passed the coffee table.

I hadn't watched it again. Not since Sunday morning.

I called it caution. It was fear—of what might've changed, of what I might remember... or what would remember me.

But I couldn't stop thinking about her.

Lena.

Her voice, wrapping around syllables like they owed her money. The way she touched my hand—just once, soft, almost reverent. Like I was fragile. Like I might shatter.

Needing answers was half true. Wanting her was the other half.

I wanted her.

The ache was sharp now. It edged every thought. Made the world taste tinny. So I went back. Didn't dress up. Didn't call ahead. Just a coat with the collar turned up and my hands in my pockets like I was waiting for someone who owed me.

The Starlight Lounge glowed like a jar of fireflies hopped up on all of the alphabet drugs. Purple light. Gold fringe. Smoke and perfume from another decade. The piano played, but someone else was singing—wrong voice, wrong key. The room was too crowded to be empty, and too empty to feel right.

Of course she wasn't there.

I waited. Drank half a scotch and let it sweat on the bar. Checked the hallway by the powder room. Nothing. No red dress, no black dress. No apple-blossom perfume. The ache sharpened into static.

Then I saw her. Not Lena. *Her.*

A woman leaning against the frame of the side exit, half-lit, half-shadowed. She looked expensive—in the *cost* way. Like loving her came with interest. Red hair cut short and sharp, lips sharper, suit darker than a shuttered chapel, fallen to war or time. Very petite. A cigarette dangled from her fingers, unlit. In the other hand, a small black envelope.

"Cyrus Finch," she said like she'd just pulled the name from a filing cabinet. "You've seen it, haven't you?"

I didn't answer. Just stared.

She stepped forward, that pink tongue flashing behind her teeth like a warning sign. "The reel. You watched it."

I nodded. Slowly.

She smiled like I'd passed a test. "Good. That means it's working."

"What is it?" I asked, growing louder. "A message? A trap? Some kind of curated psychotic break?"

"You think this is performance?" She tilted her head. "You haven't even hit *actus secundus.*"

And that was when I saw the figure behind her.

Pale. Powdered. All limbs and silence. The kind of face that visits dreams just to laugh when you run out of time. I began to sweat.

"Who are you?" I asked the petite woman taunting me.

She held out the envelope.

One word on the front: *Verity.*

"Watch it again," she said. "This time, notice the parts that make your pulse skip. That's where the real story tries to survive. This might give you answers. One. Maybe two, if you're clever."

I took it from her. Cold paper against my palm.

She leaned in.

"Just don't open it alone," she whispered. "Things like this don't like solitude. Bring a witness. Enter by mirrors."

I looked up.

Her eyes were green—but not just. Flecked with gold. Like old coins in an old marble fountain. Her smile was indulgent. Pitying. Like I'd already lost something.

"What—"

"Shh."

She raised her palm and blew.

A fine gray powder scattered into the air. Shimmering. Almost sweet. I flinched—but too late. It hit me like breath on a windowpane—cool, then warm, then gone.

The ground tilted. The light peeled back like stage curtains. My vision fractured—match-flame memories flaring, burning out, returning again in the wrong order.

"Remember me like this," she whispered from inside my pounding ears. "Before the chapter ends." Behind her, the powdered figure crossed his arms, raising his sleeve to show the head of a tattoo—a vulture.

I blinked.

They were gone.

And I was standing in the alley behind the lounge, one hand clenched around the envelope.

Still aching.

Still wanting.

Still unsure which story I was in.

* * *

I broke into the archives at 3:17 a.m. on a Friday.

Don't ask me how I knew—I'd tossed my watch into the sink sometime around midnight because it wouldn't stop ticking.

It wasn't a break-in exactly. I still had my keycard. Still knew the door with the busted sensor. Still remembered where Glasmor kept the old AV carts tucked behind the microfiche. What I didn't remember was deciding to go.

It was the envelope.

It sat on the kitchen table like a loaded weapon, and after I cracked the wax seal and saw what was inside—a single strip of celluloid, unlabeled—I knew I wasn't sleeping. Not until I watched it again.

I told myself I'd bring it all back. The 8mm projector. The reel. Whatever happened. I said it like a prayer—over and over—while I wheeled the thing three blocks with my coat pulled over my head like a film-noir raccoon.

At my apartment, the shadows had already started moving, bored of bullshit.

I cleared the table. I lit the matches. Caution to the wind I lit three of them. The reel clicked into place. I turned the crank and let light spill onto the wall. The apartment disappeared. It was the same performance. At first.

The Starlight Lounge. Lena in red. The microphone reflection catching on her necklace. Her voice curling like smoke. But this time—

This time she looked at me.

Not the camera. Not the crowd. Me.

And she said my name. *Twice.*

"Cyrus..."

Soft. Like a secret. Like she was afraid someone else might hear.

She leaned down, her brown hair brushing the side of my face, and touched me. She moved my hand with the matches aside and whispered in my ear.

My pulse spiked.

The reel kept turning.

"The mirror—*Cave Ordinem.*"

And then everything broke.

Colors twisted. Her face blurred, not from the film but from something watching through it. I felt the pressure before I saw it—the eyes behind the lens. The cold breath of recognition. I wasn't watching anymore.

I was being seen.

I tried to move. Couldn't. My body was miles away, pinned by light and celluloid. And in the glow of the final frame, I saw it—

Lena, concerned. Reaching for me, hand outstretched. Mouth forming something silent.

"Run."

Then a hand—not hers—slammed across the projector from inside the film.

The reel snapped.

Darkness returned.

I lay on the floor for hours. Or minutes. Time had no loyalty anymore.

When I finally came to, I was back in my body. Throat dry. Hands burned where the matches had licked too high. I barely remembered crawling to the couch, but the black envelope was gone. So was the last few frames of the reel.

All that remained was a smear of soot, a faint scent of apples, and a new hole in my memory that felt like a tooth yanked out by force.

Verity had warned me: don't open it alone.

* * *

I skipped work. Figured I'd already gone off the rails; why pretend there were still tracks?

The Starlight Lounge was a graveyard at noon. Nothing sadder, and maybe nothing safer. Neon, dead. Curtains drawn like eyelids in REM. Daylight remembering you a bit too accurately.

Collar up, pulse stupid, hope clinging like the last moth on a storm porch, I went anyway. She was supposed to meet me here before they took her, last week. I was sure of it. It was the only thread left after the reel unraveled. I was now deluded, converted by Father Faraday.

Speak of the devil.

Pacing near the coat check in the front hallway, hands trembling like he was tuning a radio stuck between stations. He looked worse than usual. Gaunt. Eyes flaring with some internal signal only he could hear.

"They got her," he whispered before I even asked.

I slammed him into the wall hard enough to rattle the hat rack. "How the hell do you know that? Who *are* you, Faraday?"

"I told you! My patterns—I d-dream in sequence! She reached out," he said, choking on the words. My jealousy raged.

"You watched the reel again last night, right? I saw it! The hand, in the final frame? That wasn't a metaphor, Cyrus. They were onto you."

I rubbed my face. My mouth tasted like an ashtray. I dragged him into the bar by the lapel. Needed to see it again. Needed her.

But it wasn't Lena waiting inside. It was Verity.

Perched at the far end of the bar, drink in hand, lips stained the color of bruised cherries. She didn't look at me as she slid something across the counter—an empty matchbook.

"Something came through for you last night, archivist."

One phrase inside, etched in pin-perfect cursive:

S—T isn't done yet.

"Lena was a seasoned occultist, she knew what she was doing," Verity said, cool and smooth. "But she strayed too far into the muck with the Order, and stayed too long on screen with your little matches lit. I told you not to watch alone."

Occultist?

"'Came through'?" I scoffed, picturing Verity in a seance. "Who's S—T?"

"Fuck if I know."

I looked around.

Same lounge. Same smell. Same heavy curtains and sticky floors. But the stage was smaller. The air felt rewound. And when I asked the bartender if Lena was performing tonight, he looked at me like I was crazy. maybe I was.

"Crooner? Nah. We haven't had a singer like that since—hell, maybe the sixties?"

He moved on before I could argue. Like the memory was too heavy to hold.

* * *

I didn't expect the door to be unlocked.

But it was—slightly ajar like someone had been waiting for me or didn't care if I walked in on the wreckage. Inside, the lights were on.

And Glasmor was standing in my goddamn apartment.

Two uniforms boxed up the projector like it was a bomb or a stolen crown jewel. Which, I guess, it kind of was. My conspiracy board still clung to the wall above the radiator, but now it had evidence tags fluttering from the corners like little yellow flags marking a battlefield.

Glasmor didn't say anything right away. Just looked at me with that signature, clean-shaven disdain, arms folded, eyes like scales balancing out my worth.

"You've crossed a line," he finally said. "This isn't some fun, delinquent story anymore, Finch. This is *theft*. Tampering. Unauthorized access to restricted materials. I could've called for a full psychiatric hold."

I just stood there dripping rain and shame, one foot still in the hallway, heart pounding like a warped version of myself, broken into my own life.

"It wasn't for work," I muttered. "It was for her."

He blinked once slowly. The kind of blink that ends friendships, marriages, jobs, whole careers.

"Get your shit together, Finch," he said, low and level. "The city's not paying you to chase ghosts through film grain." He slapped the projector as forensics bagged it. I saw a glimmer of a blue eye in the bag.

The cops left with the evidence. Glasmor lingered. His voice dropped another octave. He waved my copy of the paranoiac's newspaper in front of my face.

"You're not the first *Post*-obsessed loose end to get lost in the redaction," he growled. "But I'll tell you the same thing I told all of them: the stories that go too deep don't come back clean."

He turned to leave, throwing the paper on the coffee table like a tired betting slip.

That's when I saw him.

Faraday, hunched in the hallway shadows like a stain the light couldn't lift. Trenchcoat too big, hat pulled ridiculously low. His hands were jammed in his pockets like a caricature of a detective.

Glasmor stopped when he saw him. Didn't even flinch.

"You again," he sneered. "Still whispering riddles in the cracks of history?"

Faraday didn't answer. Just stared. Glasmor left.

The hallway felt colder once he was gone.

Faraday stepped forward, slicking his hair back from his face beneath his hat, rain still dripping from his coat.

"He used to be one too, you know," he squinted. "Glasmor. Not professed, but close. Back before the *Post* lost its funding and found its leash."

I squinted at him. "What does that mean?"

"It means he knows. Or used to. But he stopped believing in it all."

"Believing in what?"

Faraday reached into his coat, slow and deliberate, and pulled out a weathered little pin: a silver coin with an owl. Stylized. Watchful. Silver inlay dulled by age.

"In the *Ordo Noctuae*, the Order of the Owl," he said.

I stared at it. "Is that a cult or a joke?"

He smiled—but it didn't reach his eyes. "Depends who's telling the story."

"Founded long before *The Curious Post* ever went to print. Probably even before ink hit paper at all, but there's no official timeline. They were archivists. Before it all went digital and dead. They tracked the abrogations—the sanctioned deletions. Sanctified redactions. You've felt it, haven't you? Whisper-networks. Dream transmissions. Stories that weren't supposed to be told."

I didn't take the pin or answer. He read me anyway.

"That ache," he said, stepping closer. "That hollow behind your ribs. It isn't just Lena. It's the part of you that remembers a version of things no one else is allowed to see."

He slipped the pin away, but it was now etched in my brain. Or maybe I just couldn't stop feeling it watching me. There was latin rolling across the top of the owl's head:

In tenebris veritas...

"Let me guess," I said. "Secret society, fancy oaths, weekly robes-and-riddles meetings in someone's wine cellar? Orgies?" I perked an eyebrow. He didn't laugh.

"So what?" I continued, slamming a drawer the forensics techs left wide open. "You want me to join? Swear myself to tell the whole truth, and nothing but the truth, or whatever you think this is?"

"No," he said. "I want you to realize something."

He reached into his pocket again and pulled out another red matchbook.

I turned it over in my hand. It looked like the one Lena gave me. Except—it wasn't empty anymore. Faraday looked me dead in the eye.

"The question is, do you want to find out what part you can earnestly play—or let Them write it for you?"

I didn't answer right away, but my answer had been written the moment I watched her sing.

"Who the fuck is *Them*, Faraday?"

"If the Owls are order, then They are chaos."

* * *

I didn't sleep that night.

I just stared at the ceiling while the city muttered around me—pipes groaning, someone's TV bleeding through the wall, ugliest car on the block's car alarm sounding because of a stray cat.

The matchbook sat on the table, wired practically to my nerve endings. The reel beside it. I poured a finger of something dark into a glass I didn't wash. Lit a match just to watch it burn.

And that's when I remembered what she said. Two utterances:

"The Mirror."

"*Cave Ordinem*"—beware the Order.

Did I want to be in the middle of this mess?

When I glanced toward the window and caught my own reflection in the dark glass. My face—drawn, older than I remembered. But my eyes? They weren't looking out.

They were looking back.

And just behind me, barely visible in the corner of the reflection:

A figure.

Red dress. Eyes like gold coins hidden in moss.

She was gone when I turned around. Of course she was. But that was enough.

I opened the drawer. Took out the matchbook. The nifty back issues of *The Curious Post* I had somehow begun amassing. An old bill.

I hadn't taken it, but a glint of the owl pin Faraday "forgot" on my kitchen counter caught my eye. It was heavier than my brain calculated it should be after a lifetime of arcade and vending machine patronage. Like something coiled inside it was waiting for me to make a choice.

I whipped the landline receiver to my ear, pouring myself another drink with one hand and dialing Faraday with the other. No answer.

I couldn't wait. It had to be now.

I slipped the pin onto my collar. I tore the medicine cabinet mirror off the last fraction of a hinge from the built-in in my tiny bathroom and brought it to rest on my coffee table.

I turned the apartment into a chapel for losers.

Two emergency, dollar store tea lights on overturned chipped mugs. I downed the last of the bottom shelf whiskey and drew the badge from memory on the back of an overdue bill: the owl's wide eye, the beak, the Ainurian circle that says 'you shall not pass'. The lines came out wrong, too sharp in places, too soft in others. My hands shook enough that wax spattered; I liked the sting.

"*In Tenebris Veritas*," I whispered to the dark, and felt stupid immediately. The Latin tasted like someone else's wet cigarette butt. I said it again anyway, because that's how prayer works: you keep saying a thing until *it* becomes true, or *you* do.

The mirror gave me my own face and made sure I didn't like it. I put the match under my jaw to get the light right.

"Lena," I said to the glass. "If you can hear me—if you're listening—"

Nothing. My reflection blinked too much. The crack in the mirror looked like a line on a palm no one wanted to read.

I set my hand flat to the glass.

Cold. Then a thin sting in the meat of my lifeline, clean as a paper cut. I didn't pull away.

"Please." The word fell out before I could dress it. "Tell me where you are."

A candle guttered and clawed back. The air in the room went thin. The mirror's blackness thickened, fortified.

She came in wrong, then right. A double exposure that chose a face and made it Lena.

So close. Closer than stage, closer than film. The mouth I remembered, the eyes I'd dreamt, the heat I'd lied to myself about. Her lips didn't move. Mine did. It still felt like a conversation.

"Come closer," her voice said inside my skull, sweet as a bruise.

I did. The mirror flexed. She looked at the pin on my shirt and raised an eyebrow.

"Not him..."

"Say my name," I begged, and hated how the words sounded.

She smiled like she already had.

"Lena..." The name landed soft.

The flame flickered. My reflection did a slow, bad magic trick—eyes darker, mouth flatter, the room around me pulling longer.

"Angel?" I said, because I wanted to be punished.

"Don't insult me." Cheekbones like buttresses, hair entwined with night, that mouth like a red beacon. She didn't look at the me-in-the-mirror. She looked at *me*.

"Closer," she said.

I knelt without thinking about it, face nearly against the glass. I'm not the kneeling kind. But I'm also a liar.

"Why me?" I asked, because men like me always want to be told we're special right before the guillotine.

She smiled. It changed the temperature of the room. *"You're already hollow. I don't have to make space."*

I should've left.

Instead I leaned in. She opened her mouth. Her tongue touched the glass. Something in my gut tightened. At first it was forked—polite serpent, a sexy little invitation. Then the split sealed and the skin went transparent and I saw them waiting under there: the hooks laid flat like a soldier's secret.

"Please," I said, and that word tasted rich.

"Good boy," she said, and the glass warmed.

She kissed me through the mirror. Which is to say the mirror kissed me—cool first, then warm, then warmer. The first touch was clean. The second found my lip. The third slid past it. The barbs pricked—tiny, bright, pain that makes you grateful. I bled a little and didn't mind. The blood dripped to the overdue bill beneath me, making a sharp *splat, splat* pattering sound.

"Say the name," she murmured, voice varnishing my resolve.

"Tell me what to be," I swallowed, suddenly hot. "What name?" My own blood was dripping down my chin like the juice of ruby fruit.

She glanced from my eyes to my body beneath.

Wishful thinking.

The reflection of the bill beneath me caught my eye. The one eyed owl. And beneath it, formed in dark red, *T-Y-R-A-N-A-S*. Below it, the smear made a little two-horned glyph, a circle with a dot and a crescent hooked to its spine. I told myself it was nothing though my stomach twisted.

"Tyranas?" I guessed, sounding it out.

She leaned in again until her mouth hovered a fraction from mine, separated by nothing but the thickness of a lie. *"Again."*

I did. I said the name like I'd always known it, like I'd been born facing the wrong altar and had finally turned around.

I made a sound I have never made sober.

"Please," I whimpered. "I'll do what you want. Please."

"Ask," she breathed, inside the bone behind my ear.

"Where?" I demanded, emboldened by her urging. "Where are you?"

The candle went out. The room shrank to mirror and a throat of black. The sounds of my building slipped far away. Her eyes changed.

"Cyrus?" Lena breathed as though waking from a dream. "Wait, Cyrus!" Her tone woke my blood. Her breath was racing. For a blink, the space behind her wasn't my apartment. It was a chapel whose walls faced inward, a trap made of stone, a hole nailed over with a slab of glass.

"Find the Order," she hurried, palms forward against the glass or something like it, and the words crawled across the back of my neck. She was frightened. "Go to the glass. Go under it. Through it. The typesetter will know—the one who dreams in sequence!"

Faraday. I don't know if I nodded or if my reflection did it for me.

"Say my name," I said again, because men are embarrassing when they're owned.

"What?" She leaned close, confused. The glass was not a full barrier now, just a temperature.

"Say it," I whispered. "Please."

"Cyrus!" She screamed it, shrill, taut, and needy. It woke something in me. Behind her, something grinned wider than a human mouth. For a flicker, the owl's eyes on the paper beneath me weren't eyes and the beak wasn't a beak.

The fog bloomed into jagged panes—hall mirrors bent into a maze—and for a heartbeat her face multiplied, smiling from a dozen angles on a hill that smelled of apples. TYRANAS brightened on the paper in my apartment. Under it, so faint I might've invented it to justify the ache, a second word ghosted the fog like a palimpsest: letters being spelled out, I couldn't keep in my head when I blinked.

S—A—something. Gone.

"Tell me what to do!" I demanded, adrenaline pumping with confusion, because I wanted to be good at this.

"Don't come alone!" Somewhere inside the glass, small bells of a carillon—too many for St. Eustace down the road—tinkled out a Marian tune. The glass cooled.

"Lena," I said, and it was a plea and a promise and a lie, all three. "I'll find you."

Her mouth shaped something—*Two black spires?*—and it vanished

The mirror released me and I fell back on my ass, graceless, its own kind of sacrament. The room had the aftersmell of struck matches and skin. In the dark, my apartment remembered how to be properly poor. The radiator sighed. The fridge kicked on. I breathed until I trusted my lungs to keep doing it without supervision.

Some magus.

I re-lit the candle with shaking hands, fully sober.

My lip ached. I wiped my mouth with the back of my hand and came away with a barfight's worth of blood

'Not alone.'

I reached for the phone, for the matchbook, for whatever passed as faith. I didn't believe in angels.

I believed in instructions.

Outside, rain started in earnest. I whispered to the mirror, because I'm sentimental when it's pointless.

"Be there," I said. "Please."

Something in the black of the glass caught the candlelight and answered with a pulse I felt in my front teeth.

✳ ΚΟΛΟΦΩΝ ✳

χαραγμένον ἐν χαλκῷ,
πλαστικῷ, σιδήρῳ,
καὶ ψηφιακοῖς ὀργάνοις·

δημιουργηθὲν χερσὶν ἀνθρώπων,
καὶ φαντάσματος ὄψει.

δεδεμένον πνεύματι,
Μαιμακτηριῶνος·

εὐλογίαι δαίμονι,
τοῦ βιβλιογραφείου.

www.ingramcontent.com/pod-product-compliance
Lightning Source LLC
Chambersburg PA
CBHW050920030726
47503CB00007BB/2397